Declan Hu...

Declan Hughes was born in Dublin... and daughters. He has worked as a... co-founded the award-winning Roug... ...eatre Company, where he was artistic director and writer-in-residence. The first in the series of Ed Loy mysteries, *The Wrong Kind of Blood*, won the Shamus Award for best first novel and the third, *The Dying Breed*, was nominated for the prestigious Edgar Allan Poe award for best novel.

Praise for *All the Dead Voices*:

'Muscular writing, a smart line in self-deprecating humour, terrific dialogue and an engrossing portrayal of the sights and sounds of Dublin noir' *The Times*

'Loy is a winning combination of caustic cynicism and romantic idealism . . . [Hughes] works with heavy resonant imagery and gives the reader an ending which confounds the expectations of the genre . . . all the more satisfying' *Irish Times*

'A compelling read' *Sunday Times*

'Hughes is in his element describing the sites and sounds of the places Loy visits . . . an enjoyable and satisfying read' *Sunday Tribune*

'There is a wonderful immediacy to Hughes's depiction of recession-hit Ireland . . . Where Hughes excels, however, is his ability to position the reader at the nexus where crime meets civilised society' *Irish Sunday Independent*

'Unrelentingly violent, tightly structured and filled with unflagging action' *Irish Mail on Sunday*

'Dublin's answer to Ian Rankin . . . Gripping, beautifully written' *London Lite*

'Fast and furious with intriguing characters and dialogue . . . a terrific Irish whodunnit' *Cork Independent*

DECLAN HUGHES

All the Dead Voices

JOHN MURRAY

First published in Great Britain in 2009 by John Murray (Publishers)
An Hachette UK Company

First published in paperback in 2010

1

© Declan Hughes 2009

A CIP catalogue record for this title is available from the British Library

ISBN 978-1-84854-039-2

Typeset in Plantin by Servis Filmsetting Ltd, Stockport, Cheshire

Printed and bound by Clays Ltd, St Ives plc

John Murray policy is to use papers that are natural, renewable and recyclable products
and made from wood grown in sustainable forests. The logging and manufacturing
processes are expected to conform to the environmental regulations of the country of
origin.

John Murray (Publishers)
338 Euston Road
London NW1 3BH

www.johnmurray.co.uk

To Isobel and Heather

The night can sweat with terror as before
We pieced our thoughts into philosophy,
And planned to bring the world under a rule,
Who are but weasels fighting in a hole.

W. B. Yeats, 'Nineteen Hundred and Nineteen'

South Armagh, 9 November 1980

It would have been one thing if they'd had to camp out for days on end not knowing when their mark was approaching: two men jammed fast inside a makeshift hide of fencing bales and felled saplings within a hawthorn copse one hundred metres up the hill from the road. Cramped against the wood and wire with the hard earth cold and damp and the harsh November wind flinging scrub dust and the tang of pine resin into their eyes and deep inside their lungs, on top of which neither volunteer could abide the other so to be huddled together in such close physical proximity would have been hard to bear in any conditions. But of course, the Officer Commanding had ensured that the operation was planned to the last detail, and that the two, whose animosity was legendary and a source of private amusement to their colleagues, would spend as little time together as possible.

In Dublin, there was a volunteer at the Port watching for the judge and his wife as they rolled off the ferry and headed for the M1 north to Belfast. He made the call to a volunteer in Newry who provided the signal the button men needed: he drove along the motorway, pulled off onto the hard shoulder within their sight, rolled down his window, rolled it back up and drove away. This told them the judge's car had embarked on the sixty-mile journey from Dublin. They knew the judge liked to drive fast, so they prepared for his arrival inside the hour, traffic permitting.

They were using a roadside bomb – an Improvised Explosive Device – about the size of a gallon canister. It would traditionally have been placed in a culvert or a drain, but the British Army had sealed up all the more obvious culverts for miles around. Instead a spot had been selected by a thicket of almost bare sycamore and a shallow trench had been dug sufficient to house the bottom third of the IED, which was then concealed with mulch and leaves and fallen branches.

Now they were ready. Red, the man with carrot-coloured hair and intelligent, sceptical brown eyes had had reservations about the op when he heard that the judge's wife was going to be with him. But he was such a good target and this was such a rare opportunity that he decided to suppress any qualms he may have felt. This was a war, and there would always be a sliding scale of victims, and if a judge who presided over the repressive Diplock court system, where evidence was heard, verdict delivered and sentence handed down all by one pillar of the British establishment, if such a figure was not a legitimate target, he didn't know what was. And this was the only time he had slipped his security detail, so he knew the risks for his wife. And she was sixty-seven anyway, good innings and all that shite, so away to fuck.

The latter sentiment is where Ice, the dark-headed man with the cold blue eyes, would have begun, if sentiment had been part of his make-up. As it was, his main regret was that the judge and his wife had been visiting their daughter in Cheshire to see their new grandson, their third grandchild. 'Pity they're not coming here, then we'd have the chance to wipe three generations out, cubs and all, lace the set with blood.' Some of the younger volunteers thought this was just talk of the kind you'd hear in a Republican pub when the beer was flowing, but Red knew it was nothing but a true expression of Ice's hate-filled soul. Red didn't hate anyone. He was fighting a war, and in a war, people on both sides died, and that was just the way it was. Red didn't take pleasure in another man's death, but in a war it was us and them and that was all there was about it. Because they depended on the support of the community, and while the community wanted the soldiers gone, and the worst of the RUC and the bigoted bastards in the UDR taken out, they didn't want people shot in front of their children, didn't want wives and girlfriends blown to fuck or any of that crack. Red had seen Ice cheer after killing an RUC man in his front garden, cheer after his children had all flocked around their daddy's dead body and wailed like lost wee souls. And Ice cheering and whooping in the getaway car like a fucking savage. They wouldn't keep the support of the community long if they saw Ice in action.

Because for every IRA murder, there were so many more people involved than the button men, the volunteers who pulled the trigger or detonated the bomb. There were the bomb-makers of course, the engineers who handled the explosives, the nails and bolts and shrapnel, the fuses and timers. There were the people who concealed the device at the arms dump, and those who moved it and set it in place and primed it, those who worked out a radio signal so that it could be set off at a distance, those who stole the cars so the bombers could make their getaway, those who provided the safe houses where they could hide out until the coast was clear.

Obviously the button men were the true killers: none of the rest of it would have added up to much if they hadn't been prepared to flick a switch or pull a trigger. But it's not as if they were sitting in a car outside a pub at random, or concealed in a ditch on a border road, waiting for a likely-looking target to drive past on the off chance. No, first of all someone had to scout the victim, establish him as a scalp worth taking – a UDR or RUC man, a loyalist paramilitary, a British soldier, a judge. And that someone – in this case, the sister of a legal secretary who worked in the judge's chambers – had to pass the information on to someone in the IRA, information about his daily routine, his haunts, his habits. And information about when he broke those habits. When he decided, despite being in the middle of a major case, and against all protocol, that he needed to see his newborn grandson, and that he was going to and to hell with security, he was going to shake his minders and vanish to Cheshire for the weekend.

3

It was an opportunity they likely wouldn't get again. They had to seize it. And so they waited, Red watching the road with binoculars, Ice with his finger poised on the control. It wouldn't be long now.

I

Spy Wednesday

I

The quality of football played in the League of Ireland is not very high as a rule, and if you're not a committed supporter of one of the teams on the field, in this case Shelbourne and Monaghan United, it can tend towards the boring, to put it mildly, but when the bloke behind me said what we needed was a bit of fucking action, I don't think a guy in a balaclava piling out of the fans' car park with a submachine gun and spraying bullets around Tolka Park was what he had in mind. It was all over in a twinkling. The players hit the deck as soon as they realized what was happening, so it was impossible in the instant to know if any of them had been shot; the gunman scarpered towards Richmond Road with the Guards who had been on match duty in pursuit; before the supporters began their stampede towards the exits, I was over the barrier and making my way across the pitch towards Paul Delaney, the gifted Shelbourne No. 9 and the reason I had been at the game. He was curled in a ball by the goalposts at the riverside end with his arms over his head and a high-pitched, droning sound coming from somewhere inside his shaking torso. His teammates were slowly rising to their feet now and counting heads; the Monaghan players were doing the same.

'Paul, are you all right?' I said. 'The gunman's gone, it's all over.'

Paul lifted his head slowly above the frame of his arms, like a man daring to survey the aftermath of a storm from the supposed safety of his house. His tightly cropped blonde head was drained of colour; his pale blue eyes streaked red with fear. Before he had a chance to speak, Barry Jordan, the Shelbourne captain, was upon us.

'You all right, Paulo?'

'Sound, Jordo, yeah.'

'Who's this? You're not supposed to be on the pitch, Mister,' Jordan said to me. Though he was twenty years my junior, and clearly shaken by what had just occurred, he had a natural authority that made me feel like I was somehow in the wrong, even if the field was rapidly filling with panicking fans trying to get to the exits, or hoping at least to find some carnage worth gaping at.

'It's all right, Jordo, this is Ed Loy. He's a . . . a friend of mine,' Delaney said.

Jordan looked me up and down. I'm six two, and I wear a black suit and a black overcoat. I don't look conspicuous in most settings, but I wasn't exactly dressed for a football match.

'I'm an old friend of Paul's brother,' I said. 'He asked me to keep an eye on him.'

I should have kept my mouth shut. Jordan looked at Paul, glanced toward the car park the gunman had erupted from, then appeared to join a few dots with a shake of his head at me. He turned to Paul with a pointing finger, but something between anger and despair rendered him speechless; he nodded at the turf, as if to tamp down his emotions, then ran back to where the Shelbourne players had linked arms to form a circle in the centre of the park.

'You'd better join them, Paul,' I said, with something short of total conviction.

'Do you think so? After you mentioned my brother. Jordo knows now, or thinks he does. They've all heard the rumours. They probably think those shots were meant for me,' Paul said, his voice plaintive with self-pity and fear.

'And what do you think?'

Paul Delaney's colour had returned to normal. He shrugged, possibly aiming for nonchalant unconcern. All he hit was petty, and sullen, and scared.

'No one has any reason to take a shot at me,' he said.

'Well good,' I said. 'Glad to hear it.'

Delaney made a move toward the huddle of red jerseys, then turned back to me.

'Look, Mr Loy, I appreciate you know me brother and everything, and thanks for the concern, but I don't need any help from you, right? From anyone. Tell Dessie I'm grand. Tell him he probably knows Jack Cullen as well as I do. Tell him if anyone's to blame for all this, Jack is.'

The Shelbourne players were chanting something to each other, their heads close together. Again Delaney moved towards them. Again he faltered, this time wheeling around his teammates and taking off on a run in the direction of the dressing rooms. The club stewards were on the floodlit pitch now, encouraging the ghouls and rubberneckers sniffing for blood to disperse; the PA system was announcing the abandonment of the game and urging everyone to leave in a calm, orderly fashion. I joined the throngs queuing for the exit and replayed as much as I could recall of the incident in my mind. So exciting was the game that my attention had wandered, and I had been staring vacantly in the general direction of the Cash & Carry car park, so I had seen the gunman immediately, drawn to the balaclava masking his head, seen him produce the SMG, seen him start firing without any care as to where his target was. Because he wasn't shooting to kill, he wasn't some maniac – he was firing above everyone's head. I could picture him now, the SMG, looked like an Uzi, held aloft for maximum effect – let as many people as possible see the weapon first – and then a volley fired in the air. It was a warning, or a gesture. Had it been for Paul Delaney's benefit, or at his expense? Or was it nothing to do with Delaney in the first place? Maybe it was some anguished Shelbourne fan making an over-demonstrative protest about the need to return to the top flight in the league.

As I walked down Richmond Road and wheeled right through Ballybough heading for the city centre, I turned it over in my mind. I had run up against Paul's brother Dessie when he was a junkie dealing drugs for Podge Halligan. Despite that, I didn't think Delaney was a bad man, and if at times he had been apt to forget it, he had a tough-minded wife ready to jog his memory, and two kids to shame him into toeing the line. With their help and mine, he kicked his habit, and I persuaded a rich client with a guilty conscience to buy him a stake in an Irish pub called Delaney's that Dessie's brother Liam ran on a Greek island whose name I could never remember. By all accounts the bar was a roaring success; every so often I'd get postcards wishing me well, and photographs of sunburned and heavily refreshed Irish folk I didn't know toasting a beaming Dessie.

Dessie wasn't beaming when he called me a few days ago. His brother Paul was eighteen years old and tipped, if not quite for the Premiership elite – he had already had trials with Arsenal and Liverpool, and hadn't made the grade – certainly for a professional career at English Football League level at the very least. And as Dessie said, that'd be Paul pulling anything from 200k to half a mil a year for fifteen-odd years, and then he's made for life if he's bought the right property and made the right investments and hasn't blown it all on the ponies or some gold-digger or up his nose. Which was where Jack Cullen came in. A couple of doorman-size Dubliners called Ollie and Dave came into Delaney's back at the end of February and Dessie sized them up for players straight away. But they were quiet enough, nervy in fact, looking over their shoulders the whole time. They kept to themselves, drank their pints and ate their moussaka and chips and watched the football on satellite and ducked out whenever anyone started getting too friendly. After a week or so, they relaxed a little, and after another week, once Dessie and Liam saw they weren't up to anything, the Delaneys relaxed too. Turns out the boys were on the run: they'd barred Lamp Comerford, Jack Cullen's minder, from getting into the Viscount, a nightclub on Talbot Street, because Lamp was too drunk, not to mention buzzed on coke and any other pill and powder you were having yourself. Lamp rolled back a couple of hours later and emptied a Glock 17 at Ollie and Dave from point blank range. He missed them both with every shot, in the process proving them right to have forbidden him entry: if you can't hit a target from ten feet with a Glock 17, you'd better go home and sleep it off. Especially if you're the feared enforcer for the biggest drug dealer in the North Inner City. So now the word was the lads had a price on their heads and no shortage of ambitious local young heroes willing to claim it. So they fled to the continent, choosing Greece because, as they said, if they'd gone to Spain, they may as well have sent Lamp and Jack Cullen a map, given the number of Irish gangsters decamping to the Costas for the good of their health and so forth.

At least, that was how they put it at first. But then it emerged that that was only part of the truth, that Ollie and Dave had actually come to Delaney's for another reason. The lads had been involved with junior football at Tolka, playing for the Shelbourne Young Reds from under sevens all the way up, a few years ahead of Paul Delaney. Of course, Paul had always been different class, but Ollie and Dave were proud of the association. They loved his pride, his loyalty, the fact that, until he got a big move to an English club, he'd stay at Shels: he would never move to an Irish side for more money. They felt like they had a stake in him, and they wanted to see him, if not quite at Manchester United, certainly doing it mid-table Premiership. They reckoned he was that good. And after that, a bit of confidence, a lucky break, who knew? But the likelihood of that was fading because of Paulo's association with Jack Cullen. He'd been seen in the Viscount with 'associates' of Cullen's, he'd even been at Cullen's daughter's wedding in Marbella. Dessie and Liam argued that Cullen had always been a major Shels fan, and that it was hard to avoid him if you put in the hours at Tolka, he'd be at an under-nines game as soon as a first team fixture. If you grew up in the same streets as these lads, you couldn't turn around and cold-shoulder them or there'd be war. Ollie and Dave conceded that, and said they hoped that's all it was, but that Paulo was getting the reputation of being the go-to guy in soccer when it came to drugs, a kind of middleman dealer for guys who didn't want some skin-pop skanger in their lives. Barry Jordan had come into the Viscount specifically to ask them about it. They'd told Jordan it was all bullshit, but Jordo was no fool, and if he found out, he'd stop at nothing to put Paulo out of the game. You might survive that kind of scandal when you're well set-up, but just trying to break in? Forget it. No one needs grief like that from a newcomer. Another name on the long list of League of Ireland losers, another might-have-been who never was.

Dessie wanted to fly back and knock some sense into Paul straight away, but he felt that, given his past, he lacked a certain credibility on that front, so he asked me to have a word. I told him I wasn't in the business of mentoring waifs and strays, and Dessie said that was just as well, since he didn't think he could afford my mentoring fees, let alone my investigator's rates, and when was I going to come out to Greece and get a tan on the Delaney brothers?

So there I was walking down Gardiner Street towards the Viscount, calling Paul Delaney on his mobile and leaving a voicemail. He had been happy to meet me last night after training in the Crowne Plaza, a shiny new conference hotel set in a mature woodland park off the Santry Road, where he sat drinking water and glowing with rude health and giving every impression of never having taken or even heard of any drug stronger than aspirin. He talked of his ambitions in the game, of the importance of discipline and fitness and diet for athletes over the course of a short career, of how the appointment of the new Irish national team manager, the veteran Italian Giovanni Trappatoni, was a major step in the development of Irish soccer. He talked like a press agent's dream.

Afterwards, in the car park, I smoked a cigarette and Delaney smiled indulgently at me, as if I were taking snuff, and I took in the car he was driving, a red Mazda MX-5 1.8i that the wages Shelbourne FC paid couldn't have financed.

'Nice car,' I said, although it looked to me like the kind of thing a trophy wife might drive to the beauty parlour.

'I'm lucky to have it,' Paul Delaney said without missing a beat. 'The girlfriend's father has a Mazda dealership. Mad into Shels he is. It's not a gift, but as good as, he lets me drive it as if it's mine.'

He smiled at me, his cornflower blue eyes wide with what looked like boyish excitement. I had run out of strategy; moreover, I wanted him to be on the level.

'I have to ask you, Paul – because Dessie and Liam want me to – what's the deal with you and Jack Cullen? Because there's been a lot of talk—'

Delaney smiled wryly and held his hand up.

'I've heard the talk too, Mr Loy, and do you know something? That's all it is. And I'll tell you where it stems from: one incident in the Viscount nightclub. I'm not a regular, I don't drink, and I don't enjoy keeping company with people who do. But I went in one Friday night, because the lads insisted, it was after we beat Bray Wanderers six one—'

'And you got a hat trick,' I said. Delaney winced slightly, as if it was bad taste, or excessive flattery, on my part to bring it up.

'And I was there, and Jack Cullen had a table with all his . . . his people. I was at school with some of them, or their brothers. And everyone knows he owns the place, or at least, someone owns it on his behalf. And it's all, Jack sends over a drink, and then I have to go over and thank him, and I'm stuck at his table while he talks for about three days about Shelbourne in the eighties, and in the seventies, and what his oul' fella told him about Shelbourne in the sixties and the fifties and tradition and locality and Irish football and all this. And then he has to give me a lift home in the big Merc, drops me off in the street outside my apartment block. And of course, the next day, everyone is talking, and some reporter from the *Daily Star* rings me up asking if I'm . . . what was it . . . Druglord Cullen's Football Front? I mean, come on. What would you have done? Cause he's a heavy guy, and if he wants to talk to you . . . it wasn't as if he was cutting up lines on the table, there was nothing like that, he wasn't even drinking. I mean, I know who he is, we all know who he is, but you can't just *ignore* him . . . but then everyone puts two and two together, now the lads themselves, my own teammates, some of them think I'm sneaking into the opposition's dressing room dealing coke after matches, it's ridiculous. End of.'

Fair enough. It helped that Paul hadn't got angry once, or asked me who I thought I was; before he took off in his little red Mazda, he offered to arrange a ticket for me for the Monaghan United game.

'It won't be pretty,' he said. 'Not one for the connoisseurs. But if you want to come along . . .'

2

I had wanted to come along. And now, instead of the clean bill of health I'd been hoping to phone Dessie with, I was passing the plaque outside 94 Talbot Street where the IRA man Séan Treacy was shot and killed by British soldiers during the War of Independence in 1920 and crossing the road and joining the line waiting to get into the Viscount. Six or seven shiny girls in shorts and halter-tops were giggling and squealing in front of me while the doorman flirted dutifully with them. Once they had finally sailed inside on a cloud of cheap perfume, alcopops and pheromones, he beckoned me to one side.

'You might be happier beyond in the Celt there bud. Man's pub, know I mean? Crowd a little young inside, you might find, and the pint is rubbish, to be honest with you.'

He was round-faced and pale with red blotchy skin and a big beer gut, at maybe six four an inch or so taller than me. His eyes were watery grey and twinkly; his hands were weathered bludgeons of callous and gristle and raw bone.

'Charlie Newbanks, is it? Is Ray Moran around tonight?'

'How'd you know my name bud?'

'Dave and Ollie said to say hello.'

Newbanks looked over his shoulder into the club, then leant into me. I could smell cheese and onion crisps on his stale breath.

'We don't want any trouble here bud. You saw for yourself, it's kids we have in tonight just.'

'No trouble. Just a message for Ray. From Dave and Ollie.

No trouble at all.'

'Are they all right, the same lads?'

'They were yesterday,' I said.

Newbanks weighed this with his head inclined, then gave me what looked like a don't-say-I-didn't-warn you smile and nodded me in.

The Viscount had a faux eighteenth-century thing going on, ruched curtains and elaborate chandeliers and gilt-framed mirrors and cheap prints of Hogarth's *Marriage A-la-Mode* sequence hanging on candy pink and lemon yellow Regency-stripe wallpaper. This was underlaid with an eighties disco bar theme, black lacquer tables and chairs and black floorboards and mirror balls sending broken shards of light across the hot excited faces of girls in short dresses and short shorts who didn't look old enough to be out this late, or wearing make-up at all, let alone drinking and on the prowl. Even if it was only half-eight, and they were all in their twenties, and I was too old, just like Newbanks had said. The few lads who were there looked like Gay Best Friends. However scrubbed-up Dublin had become in the past ten years, Irish men were never going to break their habit of tanking up on booze before braving a den of women; they'd probably start filtering in around ten.

The barman was Chinese. Amid the candy store selection of Alcopops and light beers, vodka looked the safest bet. I ordered a large Stoli on the rocks and asked for Ray. A generously proportioned woman with short plum-coloured hair cut in heavy bangs stood too close to me at the bar. I could feel her eyes on me, smell her musk of hairspray and nicotine and cheap booze. After it became clear that she wasn't going to go away, I turned around. She rolled her heavily made-up eyes as if that wasn't the first mistake I had made this evening.

'Well?' she said.

'Well what?' I said.

'Well, d' you fuck, or wha'?'

'Wha',' I said, without hesitation, no expression on my face. She was five six and maybe five or six stone overweight, and she looked like fighting was the other activity in her repertoire. Her densely plastered orange face moved from umbrage through pique to resignation.

'A fuckin' homo, is it? Place is lousy with fuckin' homos. How's a girl to get her hole and the lads all canin' it round in Farrell's?'

I made my face do a sorry-for-your-trouble thing, and then suggested she might go around to Farrell's herself.

'Nah, 'cause Charlie won't let girls in here when we're locked. The lads he's not bothered, or they can hide it better. It's a whatdoyoucallit? Catch, catch . . . situation.'

'22,' I said.

'I'm twenty-eight, actually, but thanks, even if you are a fuckin' homo. And of course, again they get here, I've had too fuckin' many of these,' she said, brandishing a half-empty bottle of something that looked like lemon bleach. 'So even if I get me hole, I don't get the good of it, know I mean? It's like, I may as well not, yeah?'

'Same again?' I said.

'Ah cheers,' she said.

I ordered from the Chinese barman, but the guy who brought them was tall and well built in a dark blue suit with a long thin face, dark hair slicked back and a black pencil moustache.

'Go on and enjoy yourself, Bernie,' he said.

'In a pub full of homos? You need to bring in a *rule*,' Bernie said, clinking the second bottle against the first and wheeling away from the bar.

'Ed Loy,' I said. 'Are you Ray Moran?'

He nodded and flicked his head towards the door. I followed him up two flights of stairs and into a dingy box room that served as an office. There was a desk with a computer and an old telephone/fax machine, shelves with box and concertina files and a year planner and a soft porn calendar on the ochre walls.

Ray Moran sat by the desk, crossing his long legs; he had polished black wing-tip oxfords, just like I did, and French cuffs fastened by silver links inlaid with small emeralds; his jacket had two buttons and narrow lapels, just like mine; as he twirled an elegant hand aloft to suggest that nothing in this room had anything to do with him, a white gold Patek Philippe flashed beneath his cuff. What he did not look like was a man who relied on a tacky bar and nightclub in Talbot Street to pay the bills.

I sat on a recessed windowsill and watched a double-decker bus roll past, momentarily sucking all the sound out of the room. When I turned back, Moran was studying me through intelligent chestnut eyes.

'Dave and Ollie?' he said.

'It's about Paul Delaney,' I said. 'They told Paul's brother about the rumours. And Paul's brother told me.'

'And you would be Ed Loy, the private detective who exposed F.X. Tyrrell and Dr John Howard, who sent Podge Halligan down and lived to tell the tale,' Moran said.

'I would be Ed Loy. But this is not exactly a case.'

'By which you mean . . . what is it, exactly?'

'By which I mean, Dessie Delaney hasn't hired me, for a start. I'm a working man, and I don't give my living away for nothing, not even as a favour, not even to a friend. I mean, where would that end?'

'So this is a favour to Dessie Delaney?'

I nodded.

'And what, you find out what Paul's up to, you call Dessie up and report, end of story?'

'I might give the lad a talking to,' I said.

Ray Moran shook his head.

'Young people today,' he said. 'You can *try* talking to them . . .'

'Stop,' I said. 'Anyway, that's about as far as I want to take it. I don't know what you've heard about me, but a lot of it's not true, and the rest is exaggerated.'

'I've heard you're trouble, Ed Loy. I've heard you start off exactly like this, finding someone's missing garden furniture or luring an old lady's kitten down from a tree. And you end up there's eight people dead and the Garda Commissioner is setting up a new organized crime unit and everyone in this town is looking over his shoulder wondering if he's next. George Halligan should have finished you off when he had the chance.'

'You're welcome,' I said. 'Glad Dave and Ollie didn't hook me up with someone who was gonna be really hostile. But if it's important for you, or whoever you represent, to keep things low key and discreet, a madman with a submachine gun spraying Tolka Park when Paul Delaney's playing is probably not the way to go about it.'

Ray Moran kept his head very still, but he did something inside his mouth that caused his upper lip to quiver.

'You heard about that,' he said, as if it had happened behind closed doors.

'I was there. But everyone will have heard about it by now. I'd say it'll make the nine o'clock news, wouldn't you?'

'I don't think anyone knows what that was about,' Moran said, his face colouring. 'Some madman, as you say. What has that to do with anything?'

'Indeed,' I said. 'But you could equally say it's the type of thing that happens when there's uncertainty in the ranks.'

'What do you mean by that?'

'I don't know. Ollie and Dave stop Lamp Comerford from making a show of himself in Jack Cullen's club, Comerford comes back and shoots the door up and Ollie and Dave have to go on the run? I mean, what does Lamp Comerford have over Cullen? This place is supposed to be legit, right?'

'It is legit—'

'Of course it is. How could it launder all Jack Cullen's drug money otherwise? So fine, it's not exactly where Bono or Liam Neeson bring their mates when they're out and about in Dublin but it's sound enough, and Jack's old Provo mates apparently have enough clout now to keep him relatively free from low-level Garda hassle. But there's a big difference between Jack popping in once in a while for a friends-and-family drink and Lamp firing on his boss's business. You managed to keep that out of the papers, well done. Still, it's not good for the troops' morale, is it? And there's a limit to what the Guards can turn a blind eye to, isn't there?'

Again Moran's face was a mask; again the only movement came from his moustache, which seemed to have a will of its own.

'What do you want, Mr Loy?'

'I want a report on Paul Delaney. Obviously I'd prefer a clean bill of health, but I'll settle for the truth: is he dealing for Jack, or anyone belonging to Jack, is there anything, ah, improper in their association. I know you take care to avert your eyes from that kind of thing, as befits a man with an accountancy practice on Pembroke Road, but I'm sure you could find out if you put your mind to it. You see, I think you're a bit alarmed at what's going on. And obviously you know more about it than I do—'

'Oh I doubt that very much, Mr Loy, what with the calibre of your Garda contacts—'

'None of whom is speaking to me at the moment. Look, I'm not on a crusade here, I don't care about Jack Cullen and his gang and his drug deals and whatever it is you and he think you're doing. I don't like it, but it's not my job to do anything about it, even if Paul Delaney has been sucked into it. I just want to know.'

'So you can give Delaney a talking to. And when he's ignored that talking to, you'll tell his brothers, and they'll be round here annoying everyone. Didn't Dessie work for Podge Halligan? And Larry Knight before that? Dessie might do well to be cautious about a hometown return.'

I drained the vodka in my glass.

'See what you can do,' I said. 'Because maybe that wasn't a madman tonight, maybe that was a warning. But not to Paul Delaney, who is under Jack Cullen's protection. Maybe it was a warning to Jack Cullen. How well do you know Lamp Comerford?'

I was running on fumes now. I stood up and passed Ray Moran my card and opened the door.

'We could clear this up very easily,' I said. 'And then you could get on with, ah, business.'

Moran stroked his moustache with my card and smiled.

On the street, a group of lads was in line for the Viscount. I wondered if Bernie would be pleased to see them. I wondered if she'd be able to see them. I should have been wondering a bit harder about the two lads in navy and grey sportswear, one with a Burberry check baseball hat and one with a snow white baseball hat, standing in the doorway of the Spar supermarket across the street. As it was, I didn't notice them until it was almost too late. I was on Beresford Place when they sideswiped me into the lane that runs up by the Abbey Theatre. Some cardboard boxes broke my fall and I lay still long enough to see a blade flash in the flickering street light. By the time White Hat was on me, blade in hand, I was on my feet and hoisting the cardboard carton that had broken my fall at his head. He faltered, and waved the blade around in front of him in an attempt to keep his balance, but he had lost his bearings; it was the work of seconds to grab his arm and take the knife off him and toss it down the lane; close in now, I pounded his guts with blows, keeping him between me and Check Hat. When I felt White Hat sagging, I let him flop forward and brought my knee up into his face; this took him out but let Check Hat in. Check Hat fancied himself as a kick boxer, and with good reason: he landed a terrific belt to the side of my head with a trainer-shod foot; had he been wearing shoes, I'd've been finished. I went down with the blow, and as he changed feet to keep his balance, I kicked up as hard as I could between his legs. I was wearing new Church's wing tips, the leather stiff and unstretched. Check Hat doubled over and collapsed on the concrete, a high-pitched plaint that sounded like urgent prayer his only sign of life. I tried to get a name out of Check Hat, but he was incoherent with pain. I wasn't feeling too steady myself.

I crossed the river at Butt Bridge, walked the length of Tara Street, then cut along Pearse and up around Westland Row. The side of my head was smarting and I could feel a ghostly tinnitus chiming in my left ear. There was blood on my shirt, and I saw that it came from a gash on my hand; I must have got it taking the knife from White Hat. Occasionally I staggered, and on Fenian Street I got very hot and sweaty and short of breath and thought of going into the Alexander Hotel to throw up, but held it down and pushed on through Denzille Lane to Holles Street.

My building stood across the road from the National Maternity Hospital; my apartment, on the second floor, also had a partial view of Merrion Square; either way, by the time I'd climbed the stairs, I wasn't much interested in looking out the window. I poured myself a Jameson, added water and swallowed. Seconds later, as if it were the expected outcome, which I suppose it should have been, I was on my hands and knees in the bathroom, bringing back up the whiskey and all that had come before it. When I was done, I splashed cold water on my face, reflecting with some kind of satisfaction that the rest of my head now throbbed as hard as my ear. I couldn't seem to stand up straight, so in something between a crouch and a stagger, I made it onto my bed, and fell into a dreamless sleep.

II

Holy Thursday

3

I awoke at dawn and took a hot shower, then turned the hot water off and held my head under the jets until the cold was like a ragged knot in my skull. Afterwards, I sat on the edge of the bath with a towel over my head until something that felt like blood had begun to spread shoots of warmth through the numb flesh. The left side of my head felt like a graft that hadn't taken properly, and that was probably the wrong fit. And my ear looked and felt like it had been scalded. But dwelling on the pain was never a good idea, and this morning I simply didn't have the time: first I was hungry, having forgotten to eat last night, and then I had work to do. I washed down two Nurofen Plus with orange juice, dressed, put the kettle on and went down to Grand Canal Street to get the papers and some eggs. It was a raw, squally morning, and the grey sky spat jets of sleet onto the gravel-sodden ground, and the wind off the river caught you by the throat and made your eyes smart. By the time I'd come back up the stairs my head was clattering again, so I scarfed another two Nurofen with my first cup of coffee. I softened some red onion in olive oil, scrambled three eggs and ate them with a few slices of smoked salmon, my breakfast of choice when I was feeling a little sorry for myself.

The papers were full of CRAZED GUNMAN STALKS STADIUM – the first time Tolka Park's status had ever been thus elevated – with fervid speculation as to whether a US-STYLE CAMPUS SLAUGHTER might have been in the offing; there was more than a hint of disappointment that no such RAMPAGE had occurred. There were no leads as yet, and none of the usual conjecture about which organized crime figure or gangland feud may have been behind the shooting, or whether it was an EMBITTERED LONER ENACTING HIS REVENGE. I turned on the radio to see if RTE had anything to offer, and discovered that the crime reporters had bigger fish to fry this morning. The bodies of two young men had been found in Beresford Lane, brutally beaten and stabbed, their throats cut. I sat like a stone and listened to the details: the Guards had secured the scene, the young men, clad in sportswear and baseball hats, were 'known to Gardaí', the State Pathologist was expected this morning, the murder weapon had not been found. The murder weapon: a knife with a set of my prints, and a fresh sample of my blood. The gash on my hand smarted suddenly, as if reproving me for underestimating its importance, and a hot trickle of blood slithered across my palm. The Guards had my prints on file, and my blood and DNA if they had a big enough fridge, and my preferred take-away curry order and taste in beer for all I knew, but they had no reason to connect me with the victims – unless they found the knife. Provided that was the knife that their killer had used.

I drank another cup of coffee and thought about who had set the two baseball hats on me, and wondered whether they had been ordered to kill me or to scare me off, and whether they had left the murder weapon at the scene, or held on to it to use against me in the future. The only conclusion I came to was that there was more, much more to come, and that there was nothing I could do about any of it right now.

My client wasn't due for an hour, so I went back downstairs and pulled my coat tight and stepped out into the wind. I thought of walking through Merrion Square, with its great Georgian houses overlooking the park, but this wasn't a morning for the early daffodils and crocuses or the first trees in leaf; spring was here, but not in any way you could savour. I turned down Holles Street, passing a couple of hard-faced new mothers in pink wrappers smoking cigarettes in the wheelchair entrance of the National Maternity Hospital, and hooked left along Sandwith Street through the damp tunnel beneath the railway. Lombard Street brought me onto City Quay, and I left the traffic's thunder behind to step on to the Séan O'Casey pedestrian bridge across the Liffey. I stopped halfway across and looked down the docks towards the sea. My head was wet now, and cold from the sleet; I could feel my nose and lips numb on my face; the tattoo of pain in my left ear had finally abated. I could see the latest addition to the docklands' skyline, the glittering asymmetrical towers of glass and steel on opposite quays, 200 metres high, with the inter-connecting pedestrian bridge, the illuminated Independence Bridge, suspended 100 metres above the river between them. It was an extraordinary sight, dwarfing everything else in the area; they said you could see it from miles away, whether at sea, air or land; it was to be the new gateway to the city. There had been years of protests and planning objections, but the Docklands Development Authority had prevailed; the towers and bridge would be officially opened by the Taoiseach, the Irish prime minister, on Easter Monday, the floating anni-versary of the 1916 revolution that was the first marker for the independent republic that followed. At least, that was the official line, but the papers and pubs had been full of enough dissent and debate and division about what 1916 meant, and what independence meant, and what Ireland meant, not to mention what architectural beauty meant, to make your head spin. All you could say for sure was that the towers and the bridge were on the skyline now, and they'd be the gateway to Dublin for many years to come, and we were all going to have to get used to them, whatever we thought. These things were never simple; the bridge I was standing on was named after a great and notoriously cranky playwright who refused to return to Ireland after the Abbey Theatre rejected his fourth play; I doubted whether his shade was especially sanguine about his commemoration over water, especially since it served primarily as a walkway for workers to get from the DART to the International Financial Services Centre, one of the totemic sites of Ireland's recent economic boom and a building the old Marxist would have execrated. But I had lived too long in America to fret overly about preserving the old and frowning upon the new, and my experience had been that those most passionately opposed to new buildings were often sitting on substantial old piles of their own, and so could hardly be described as disinterested observers; in any case, while Merrion Square was a glowing testament to the glories of the city's past, Docklands needed all the help it could get. And at night, the blaze of light stretched across the heavens was something to behold; I never thought I'd see its monumental, carnival like in hard-bitten, downbeat Dublin, and maybe that was enough in itself to commend it.

I walked back the way I came, still getting used to the fact that I now lived in the city centre. When I came back from Los Angeles to bury my mother, I assumed I would turn around and leave before the earth on her grave had subsided. But as one case followed another, I found myself living in the house I had grown up in. That was unsatisfactory for all kinds of reasons, chiefly because while I stayed there, the ghosts of my past refused to let me be. There's a reckoning you can make with history, a reasonable settlement that makes demands but leaves you with your dignity. And then there's a kind of morbid fascination that borders on obsession, a grave-robbing disorder that fills your every waking moment with memories and echoes and dust. Something like that had gotten a hold of me in the house in Quarry Fields and its surrounding streets.

I'd seen it in other people, a kind of living death, where all possibility of change is weighed in terms of what has gone before, and quickly discounted as an insult to the memory of things past. And when I looked in the mirror, or, having stopped looking, when I caught my reflection in the rearview, I saw the same dead eyes telling me that my race was run, that there was nothing new under the sun except the next job of work, the next faithless woman, the next empty glass.

So I got out. I rented the house to Maria and Anita Kravchenko, two Ukrainian women I had met after they ran into some trouble with Brock Taylor's boy Séan Moon. They had had a hard time back then, but Taylor and Moon wouldn't be bothering them any time soon, and they were tough, optimistic women. My friend in the Guards, Detective Inspector Dave Donnelly, had helped ease their visa troubles, and now Anita was working in a nearby restaurant and Maria had a childcare job in a crèche. They had a couple of friends working as nannies who shared the house with them, and the rent they paid more than covered the small mortgage my mother had taken out before she died, alongside the larger mortgage I was paying on my new apartment. I had tried to charge them less than the going rate, but Maria and Anita insisted on paying full whack, and occasionally delivering me loaves of Paska and Kolach, traditional Ukrainian Christmas and Easter bread that tasted good whatever the season, along with strong Ukrainian beer that tasted even better but tended to turn every season into bleak midwinter somewhere in the middle of the third bottle. Maybe I couldn't drink the way I used to. Maybe I didn't want to.

On the steps of the Maternity Hospital, a skinny smoking mother in a peach wrapper with black hair had been joined by what looked like her own skinny mother, who had dyed black hair and was smoking also; there were infants in a double buggy and small children swarming around their feet and the hospital steps and lobby; the women ignored the children, sucking on their cigarettes and muttering to one another like workmen stealing heat around a brazier. A winter spent watching from my window as women who had just given birth stood in biting wind and rain and frost to smoke a cigarette had convinced me as never before of the folly of my addiction; it hadn't yet imbued in me the firm purpose of amendment needed to shake it, however. I stood on the steps of my building now and exhaled blue smoke, an ephemeral salute to skinny, hard-faced mothers and smoking fools everywhere.

4

The door to my apartment opened onto a hallway that led directly to the small kitchen; the bathroom lay to the left; to the right were the two great rooms with high ceilings that I lived and worked in. My office was to the front; it didn't have a glass door with my name on it, or a roll-top desk, and the whiskey was Irish, and in plain view, not hidden in a filing cabinet, but I had done without an office before, and it had somehow helped to make everyone's problems my problems at a time when I had enough of my own to be going on with; I hoped an office would serve as a kind of clearing house for me, impersonal walls within which the dark secrets and thwarted passions of the cases I worked might disperse, or at least be safely caged. Hope springs infernal. There were three big sash windows and a sofa and two armchairs, in case an entire family wanted to hire me, which had happened a few times, with successful but never happy results. There was a pale oak desk and a dark-stained captain's chair that I sat in, the windows behind me; across the desk there was a Lloyd Loom leather chair with a cane back which women liked to sit in; there was one sitting in it now.

Anne Fogarty was about forty but looked thirty-five, or maybe she was thirty-five and looked her age. It was hard to tell these days, when 21-years-olds were so primped and groomed and orange-faced they often looked like startled 55-year-old millionaires' wives with too much work done. She looked well to my eyes, whatever age she was, in indigo jeans and a tight purple wraparound top that exposed just enough flesh at eleven in the morning to keep my gaze determinedly level on her twinkling brown eyes, which was no hardship. Her lips were full and painted red, and her slightly prominent teeth were crisscrossed with metal braces; her wavy hair was dyed honey blonde with the ghost of dark brown roots showing; it fell in wayward bangs to her lightly freckled neck and brushed against the chain that held a glittering silver crucifix at her throat. She wore several silver and jewelled rings, but her ring finger was bare with a tan line wide enough for a wedding ring; as I was looking at hers, I saw her notice mine. I saw her notice my ear also, and something like pity, or horror, shuddered across her face.

She laid a pale green file on my desk, took the cup of black coffee I offered her, sat back and told me why she was here.

'My father was murdered in 1991. At the time, my parents' marriage was effectively over. They were staying together . . . "for the sake of the children" is, I think, the expression, even if the children were old enough to work out for themselves that all was not well in the land of Mammy and Daddy. I was fifteen when it happened, and my sisters were seventeen and fourteen. But whatever we thought was going on, we didn't know about my mother and . . . I'm sorry, this is such a jumble, I should tell you what happened first. It's all in the file, newspaper clippings, accounts of the trial.'

'I'll read the file later. But it's always good to get it straight from the source. Anyway it occurs to you to tell it is fine,' I said. 'Was your mother having an affair?'

A flush of red rippled across Anne Fogarty's face and sparked in blotches on her chest. She laughed in embarrassment, and almost upset her cup of coffee in her lap.

'I'm sorry, was that too direct?' I said.

'Not at all. It's just strange to hear it spoken out loud. For too long the words have been boxed up in my head. My sisters don't want to know about it any more. And the Guards are happy that they know the truth. But they don't. Which is why I'm here, Mr Loy.'

She smiled at me then, bravely, I guess you'd have to say, and I saw a history of suffering in her eyes, and of strength too, the strength to carry a burden by herself a long way after everyone around her has cast it off and wishes she would too. I smiled back, because I thought it would reassure her, and because I wanted to anyway.

'Yes, my mother was having an affair . . . and while Daddy wasn't exactly happy, he put up with it. He sort of had to. He had been first in the infidelity stakes, casual stuff with secretaries and women he met in the pub, and then Mammy found out and was heartbroken. They were childhood sweethearts, and Ma thought it would be roses all the way, the anniversary waltz in their eighties. And it didn't turn out that way. And after the hurt – she spent about a year of my childhood in bed, I was twelve – we didn't know why, we understood in retrospect – at least, I did. Aisling, my older sister, just gave up on Ma, she had no patience for women who "suffered with their nerves", as it was called back then. And it fell to me to look after Midge, that's what we called Margaret, she was still the baby, and Midge never transferred her affection back to Ma afterwards. I'm not sure Ma tried very hard to win it back either. When she got out of the bed, it was like she'd shed a skin: she was cooler, more distant – she wasn't "Mammy" any more, she'd become . . . her own person. I've understood it better since I've had my own. I don't think it's an unusual situation, the man has a few flings, the woman finds out, and she can never quite put her heart together again the way it was. And then she met Steve Owen, and fell in love with him.'

'But you didn't find out about this until later?'

'Until they arrested Ma and Steve for Daddy's murder.'

'They charged them both?'

'No, they went ahead with Steve. A jury found him guilty. The conviction was later found to have been unsafe. He was released on appeal after five years. The appeal court judges criticized the Garda investigation, and the trial judge.'

'And what did the Guards say?'

'Officially, that the investigation remained open. But they leaked to every journalist in town that they weren't looking for anyone else in relation to the murder of Brian Fogarty.'

'And your mother . . .'

'Ma died in '94, three years after Steve was sent to jail. It was like her heart had been broken one time too many.'

We finished our coffee and sat in silence for a while, as if to mark with due respect the sadness of the story she had just told me. Before I had time to ask her about the circumstances of her father's death, she continued.

'Daddy was a tax inspector. The Revenue Commissioners. Worked there all his life, after a commerce degree in UCD. We lived in a semi-d in Farney Park in Sandymount. It was nothing then, but of course, it'd be a mental price now, even with the market on the slide. The neighbours were teachers and civil servants, shopkeepers and salesmen. The lower middle classes, years before they became paper millionaires. Anyway, Da was working at home one morning – he used to do that sometimes, I think it started because he was worried about Ma when she had her whatever, her breakdown. And then he got into the habit of it, he'd work the morning at home, always gone by the time we got back from school for lunch. Only this day, he wasn't gone. Not entirely.'

Anne Fogarty made that smile people make when grief, however seasoned it is, brims of a sudden and threatens to spill, a smile that's both urgent and painful all at once.

'Did you find the body?' I said.

She shook her head, her smile intensifying until it looked like it had been painted on her face and left to dry.

'Midge. When I got home, she was sitting on the doorstep, covered in blood, crying like a baby. I had to walk past her to see what it was, she couldn't get the words out. He was lying on his face at the end of the hall, just at the kitchen door. The back of his head was all red and black. There was blood on the floor, blood on the walls. He'd been beaten to death. The Guards said he had his back to his killer. They deduced from this that Daddy must have known him. To trust him, to turn his back on him. But it could have equally meant, he was being forced along at gun point, couldn't it?'

'I suppose so. Why would he have been forced along at gunpoint? Who would have pulled a gun on him? Was there money in the house?'

'No, it was . . . it was to do with what Daddy was working on. He used to have a thing about ill-gotten gains, how in Ireland, crime always pays. He'd talk about it at the kitchen table, criminals buying property after bank raids, Provos with holiday homes, heroin dealers coining it, living like kings. This was in the days before the Criminal Assets Bureau, there was no will to do anything about these people. Individual Guards wanted to act against them, and so did legal people within the DPP's office and social welfare inspectors, and some of Daddy's colleagues agreed that targeting criminals' wealth was the way to go. But there was no co-operation between the agencies, no joined-up thinking. Daddy used to compile these – dossiers, he called them – present them to his superiors, and wait for them to take action. But nothing ever happened. He got so frustrated about it. He'd leak stuff to journalists, but they were hampered by the libel laws, they could only refer to the individuals in code. And it wasn't as if everyone didn't know who they were. Finally, he sent letters to three particular individuals setting out what he reckoned they were worth in assets, what that amounted to as income, and what their tax liabilities were.'

'He sent them letters,' I said. 'Signed letters?'

'Yeah.'

'And you knew this back then? The day of his death?'

'Not that he'd actually sent the letters. Mammy only told me that later. But it was like . . . the Guards, as soon as they heard about Steve, that was it, it was him and Ma. They wouldn't consider any other possibility.'

'You say your mother told you the letters had been sent. How did she know? She was having an affair . . . were she and your father even speaking?'

'They were keeping up appearances. They were still great friends, actually, even if the romance had come to a halt. Friends and comrades. They always talked, you know, at dinnertime, big debates about politics, the Irish language, what have you. Rows, you might say. But that's when it all used to come out, who was getting away with what. Mammy told me he had made copies of the material he sent to each individual. She gave these documents to the Guards that day, she knew instantly who the main suspects should be.'

'So what happened?'

'There was no proof that he had ever sent the letters. And obviously, they carried no force, no legal force. The defence tried to use them at the trial, but they were ruled inadmissible. And of course the names never got out. The boyfriend did it, with the connivance at least, if not the active participation, of the wife.'

'Rule of Domestic Murder Number One. What happened at the appeal?'

'Steve was convicted on circumstantial evidence – he was in the area, because that's where he lived and worked, he was a teacher in Marian College down the road, he had the opportunity, he had no alibi.'

'Motive?'

Anne Fogarty shrugged.

'A crime of passion. Ma wouldn't leave Daddy. Allegedly,

Steve was upset. He testified that he hadn't wanted her to walk out, but . . .'

'But what?'

'But they had a letter . . . letters . . . between Steve and Mammy . . . where they'd live when they were together, how happy they'd be . . . how they couldn't wait to be free of Brian Fogarty . . . how nice it would be if he were to disappear . . . how Steve couldn't bear it much longer . . .'

Anne Fogarty's voice cracked then, and she exhaled loudly and looked at the floor. I rounded the desk and rescued her cup, which was rattling in its saucer, and refilled it with hot coffee and brought it back to her. She lifted the cup to her lips and drank and raised her eyes to mine and nodded, and I sat down again.

'It was the way lovers talk. We two against the world. They were looking towards . . . four years or so, when Midge was out of school, when we were all grown up.'

'You sure?'

'There was a day . . . a couple of days . . . when I wasn't sure. When I hated Mammy, and wanted to believe she and Steve had done it. But that passed.'

She held my gaze to assure me that it had. In her dark eyes I could see the embers that still glowed, the smoke of doubt that would never quite disperse.

'So it wasn't as if the Guards had taken a personal set against Steve Owen,' I said. 'There was enough in the letters to give them cause to believe he and your mother conspired together, or at least, had considered it.'

'Only if you ignore the other evidence. That's what the judge said at the appeal, that the nature of Daddy's work, even if unofficial, should have been considered. And it emerged that he had registered the letters he sent the three suspects, that the receipts had been collected as evidence, and that that evidence had mysteriously gone missing for the original trial.'

'The finger pointing where – at the prosecution or at the Guards?'

'The finger wagged back and forth, but left everyone off the hook. "An administrative error" was how it was phrased. I think the Guards on the scene found the receipts on him that day, in his wallet or among his papers, bagged them without appreciating their significance, and when the defence asked if there was any sign of them, they deliberately vanished them.'

'Why would they do that? To protect one of the recipients of the letters?'

'Two of the men to whom the letters were sent were Bobby Doyle and Jack Cullen.'

'Bobby Doyle?' I said. 'The same Bobby Doyle who's behind the Independence Day Bridge?'

'The very same.'

'I know he made a settlement with the CAB in '98,' I said. 'But I thought that was just for unpaid taxes. Crime the conventional way. A house on Clyde Road, a couple of hotels and shopping centres and now, Independence Bridge, the most prestigious building project in the history of the state. He's done well, hasn't he?'

'He's done very well. He started off as a slum landlord on the Northside in the late eighties. That's what the settlement was about, undeclared rental income. Before that he'd been in America. And before that . . . well, he's been talked of as one of the businessmen who's sympathetic to Sinn Féin, and there's no evidence to say he's anything else.'

'But you wonder – what? Before he went to America?'

'He's from the North. Was there throughout the seventies. But there's no record of his family, where he lived, what he did. No one seems to know very much about him.'

'And you think . . . what?'

'I don't know. He was one of the names on the list, is what I think. And Jack Cullen—'

'I know a little about Jack Cullen. I know Jack Cullen was in the IRA. Still is, insofar as it exists in any meaningful way. And I know what he does now. What about the third man?'

'The third man you know well, Ed Loy. It was in the papers, you grew up with them all. You sent his brother to jail. The third man was George Halligan.'

5

I made more coffee. When I brought it into my office, Anne Fogarty was standing at the sash windows, staring down at the street. The procession of smoking mothers had been leavened by two thickset middle-aged men in dark coats. One paced; the other scrutinized a folded newspaper. Proud but bored granddads, perhaps, wondering how long they had to put in before they could go home, or to the pub.

'I was born there,' she said, indicating the National Maternity Hospital.

'Me too,' I said.

'And my Ma was a heavy smoker. I wonder if she stood outside like those ones.'

'I think they let you smoke indoors then,' I said. 'They had a room for it. Maybe you could even smoke on the wards.'

'Of course,' she said, smiling, a real smile this time, warmth and wit flashing in her eyes. 'And all the dads with their cigars.'

Her right hand reached quickly for her left then, index and thumb stroking her bare ring finger, and the smile froze.

'Me too,' I said again.

'I noticed,' she said. 'Women always do. It's rare that a man would. Or that it would make any difference.'

She smiled then in another way, and then quickly pouted to push her lips back over her braces; it seemed like a reflex gesture, one she had been in the habit of to cover the slightly protruding teeth the braces were there to correct; however it had come about, it sent a rush of blood straight down my spine and beaded my brow with sweat; when I spoke, my throat was hot and dry.

'It's just my job,' I said. 'It doesn't mean I'm any more . . .'

'Any more what?' she said, the pale tan skin around her eyes crinkling. 'Sensitive? Caring? Ed Loy, these days, plain observant is good.'

I smiled in spite of myself, smiled and found I was unable to rearrange my face, smiled like the fool I was and always had been when it came to women. I had promised myself never again to fall for a client, and here I was. I could smell her now, mild lemon with a verbena musk, and then she did the thing with her lips again and her hair glowed in the light, and I turned and looked out the window and when frowning didn't take, sank my teeth deep into the inside of my lips.

'How did things end up with your husband?' I said, in as disinterested a voice as I could muster; it sounded like I was shouting from under water. Anne Fogarty didn't react as if there was anything amiss.

'Fine, I suppose,' she said. 'We could still be married, except he couldn't keep his cock in his pocket, and I found out. He said, you know how it is, and I did, and I do know how it is, he went away on a lot of foreign trips, so it was all nicely handled, it wasn't as if I'd caught him with my sister or my best friend, he's a bastard, not a gobshite. And I thought I'd be able to handle it – I had imagined it, you know, after the kids came, when things got a bit dreary in the bedroom, I said to myself, well, if he has to go elsewhere for a while, maybe I wouldn't mind. But I did mind. And he couldn't quite understand that. I said, now you're going to know how it is. He thinks I'm one of those awful modern women who don't know when they're well off. That I should have hung around because of the kids. And he makes so much money so that's all right. But it was because of the kids I couldn't. I was angry with him, and I didn't want them to see it, because it wasn't their fault. And I couldn't put it back together again. I had seen all that with my own parents. I didn't want it handing itself on down the way . . .'

She faltered, and suddenly her eyes were filled with tears. In another gesture that looked habitual, she flipped finger and thumb into her eyes, blinked them dry and continued, as if tears brimming to the surface was as inevitable as the turn of the tide. It made sense to me.

'Anyway. That's enough of that. What happened your ear? Sorry, I've been wanting to ask since I came in. If it's none of my business . . .'

My hand shot up to cup the ear, and I hauled it down like it belonged to someone else.

'I got kicked in the side of the head,' I said. 'And you'd probably be better off not making that side of things your business.'

She looked at me then, Anne Fogarty, with her brown eyes still glistening, and her verbena scent fizzing in my nose, in my lungs, in my brain, looked me straight in the eye and said, 'What if I wanted to, Ed Loy?'

This was the time to flash the red light very clearly. The case she had presented me with was going to be a minefield on any number of levels, and Anne Fogarty was, if not exactly explosive, certainly volatile material herself. Just say no.

'Then I wouldn't want to stop you,' I heard myself say in a stupid big voice I recognized as my own.

I held her gaze until her cheeks flushed, and she looked away. She went back to her chair and dipped into her bag and took a card from her purse and pushed it across the desk. It had her numbers and her address on it, and the additional information that she was an interior designer. She lived around the corner from where she had grown up in Sandymount, but in a considerably more expensive house on the seafront. Just as I was wondering what her husband did to make all this possible, she told me.

'The Irish Pub. He exports them all over the world. I used to do the interiors. I don't do that any more. But I did enough to justify the house. If that's what you were asking.'

'I didn't ask,' I said. But of course, I kind of had, and she had answered like she could read my mind. Another warning sign I took as an invitation.

'There's a few more things I need to know before I can take the case.'

'You're going to take the case?' she said, and her eyes widened in relief, and suddenly she looked so uncertain and vulnerable, and I had a glimpse of the desperate teenager, anxious that her parents get along, and I thought I understood something of the pain her divorce had caused her. I was divorced myself, but I had never expected to be married, and when I was, my parents' volatile match was certainly not the model I looked to. And my marriage had been such a storm of grief and betrayal that I was always reluctant to compare it to anyone else's. But I had found that the damaged recognize one another, for good or ill. And you had to keep hoping it would be for good. I had forgotten that for a long long time, forgotten how important it was to hope.

'Of course I am,' I said. 'First thing: the solicitor who took the appeal?'

'Daniel O'Toole. He died in a car crash a few years ago. I would have asked him to take it up, but . . .'

'Okay. Second, what about Steve Owen? Are you in touch? What's his attitude to all of this?'

'I've put his contact details in the file. He doesn't really want to get involved. He took my calls, and he was very sweet – Steve's lovely. But he just didn't want to get into it. Said he knew nothing about the others anyway. He said there was nothing to be gained by raking it all up again.'

'Even though the obvious implication is, the Guards still think he's guilty? And maybe other folk do as well?'

45

'I made that point. He just shrugged. Said he had friends who knew he was innocent, and he didn't care what anyone else thought. But he'll talk to you. As a favour to me.'

'Last thing for now. There's a new Garda Cold Case Unit. A friend of mine has been assigned there, Dave Donnelly. They're looking into a lot of unsolved cases—'

Anne Fogarty stopped me with a shake of her head. As she spoke, a cold anger I hadn't heard before underscored her words.

'That was the first call I made. I read about it in the papers. I thought, this is exactly the kind of case they would look at. I called several times, and kept getting fobbed off with promises that they'd look into it, that they'd call me back. And then, sure enough, they did call me back. Inspector Dave Donnelly called to tell me they were no longer looking for anyone in connection with that murder. I asked how that could be, in the light of the appeal, but he just kept repeating the same thing over and over: the force was no longer looking for anyone, the case was no longer live. What they said off the record after the appeal is now official policy.'

Anne Fogarty wrote me a cheque. I charge a thousand a day, and she wanted to hire me for a week; I said within three days I'd know whether the case had a future. Then I walked her down to the ground floor. Before I had a chance to open the front door, or tell her I'd call her later on, she turned and reached for me, her palm cool on my right cheek, and kissed me on the mouth for a long while, although not long enough.

'I wanted to do that almost as soon as I saw you,' she said, and turned quickly and left, the door slamming behind her, and I had to stop myself from running out after her. I could hear the sound of the blood in my ears, breathe her scent deep inside me. Stupid, I told myself, stupid, stupid, but I didn't believe me, or I did, but I just didn't care. Worse still, I allowed myself hope.

6

When I got back up to my office, I looked down at the street. A man was holding a newborn baby in a car seat while his partner got into the back of a Volvo Estate. The men in the dark coats had been liberated from their vigil. There was something about them that had stuck in my mind, but I couldn't quite retrieve it yet.

I sat at my desk and picked up the phone. Inspector Dave Donnelly of the newly set-up Serious Crime Review Team, the man who had rejected Anne Fogarty's inquiry so emphatically, was my principal Garda contact, and an old friend. The unit had only been running six months, and Dave had been transferred there from the National Bureau of Criminal Investigation; whether it was a promotion or a career setback, he wasn't sure yet. As a private detective, I had an equally ambivalent attitude towards the unit's foundation: either it meant I'd occasionally have a well-placed contact engaged on the same kind of case I was, or it could put me out of any kind of business apart from insurance fraud and divorce work, which paid the bills, but lined the soul with iron. I had to eat the same as everybody else, but I didn't want that to be my only reason for going to work in the morning. Dave and I had a complicated history, but on balance, I think he'd done well out of me: his promotion from Sergeant and his transfer to the NBCI arose from cases I had worked. He knew that, and I knew it, and the health of our relationship relied on neither of us admitting it. And since I was the one who invariably came looking for a favour, it was easy to forget that the balance of responsibility, if not quite of power, was pretty evenly spread. Added to which, Dave had had some alarums and excursions in his marriage recently, and I had played a reluctant part in restoring order and at least a semblance of harmony. Of course, that kind of good turn, even among the closest of friends, seldom goes unpunished.

'I'm busy, Ed.'

'It's about the Fogarty case. Brian Fogarty, a revenue commissioner, murdered in 1991. Steve Owen, the man who was convicted, was released on appeal. I want to know why the Cold Case unit won't reinvestigate.'

There was a long silence, and then Dave said,

'Merrion Square, by Oscar Wilde. Ten minutes. Bring the sandwiches,' and hung up.

The statue of Oscar Wilde reclining on a rock in the park bounded by the magnificent eighteenth-century Merrion Square (a park that is officially known as Archbishop Ryan Park, although nobody in the history of Dublin has ever called it that or ever will) is probably not quite as horrible as the statue of Phil Lynott in Harry Street, but I wouldn't like to be on the panel of judges who had to come to the final decision. Still, there was a nice contrast between languid, elegant Oscar and the bulky steamroller that was Dave Donnelly as he advanced with heavy tread in a suit and overcoat that were too tight for him now he'd put back all the weight he'd lost when he was worried about his wife and his career, plus a stone and a half extra in beer and full Irish breakfasts. I gave him a chicken and avocado on brown but it didn't annoy him as much as I hoped it would; he grunted a hello and flicked his big cropped head and kept moving and I fell into line with him and we did a turn or two around the park, which was giving as good an account of spring as it could muster, given the weather. The horse chestnut trees were coming into leaf;

the sycamore and ash were still bare. The day had brightened, with veins of watery blue seaming the dirty sky, but a salt east wind blew cold off the bay; no one we passed was walking for pleasure.

I was ready to press Dave about the Fogarty case, but the first thing he said brought me to a juddering halt.

'See our old friend Dessie Delaney's brother Paul got hit.'

'He what? I just saw him last night in Tolka Park. The shooter aimed over their heads.'

'The shooter this morning didn't miss. One in the face through the window of his red Mazda. Another three in the head to make sure, and then off on the back of a waiting motorbike.'

I was facing away from Dave when he told me, and grateful for it; the news took me aback, and it would have shown in my face. Whatever I thought Paul Delaney was into, I hadn't expected this. Whatever he'd done wrong, he didn't deserve to die. Worse still, part of me couldn't help feeling it was my fault.

'Then there's the two lads stabbed in the alley. On top of Delaney, that's got three gangland murders on the one o'clock news. Everyone's jumping up and down, the Minster for Justice, opposition spokesmen, the Garda Commissioner saying we're doing all we can. Just as well my cases all stretch back twenty odd years or so, and I can spend my day jaunting in the park with entrepreneurs the like of you.'

'Fuck sake, Paul Delaney.'

'Did you know him well, Ed?'

'Yeah, sure Dessie called me up a couple of days ago, out of the blue. Said he was worried about Paul, heard he'd fallen in with the wrong crowd, drugs, so on. Asked me to keep an eye on him, see what the story was.'

'End of story now,' Dave said grimly. 'Don't know what this fucking town is coming to. Kids stabbing Polish lads in the head with screwdrivers, young fellas getting knifed to death over fifty euro debts, or worse, over looking sideways at the wrong man. The whole place is falling a-fucking-part, I'm not codding you now.'

'Sure I know,' I said. 'What was the deal with the other two boys, Beresford Place, was it?'

'In the lane there. Yeah. Ah, either they were part of Jack Cullen's set-up, or they weren't, and either way they fell foul of him, or Lamp Comerford, or one of the excuses for human beings he surrounds himself with. Was Paul Delaney caught up with Cullen?'

'I don't know. There was talk he was; he said he wasn't. I'd seen him twice, he was a very plausible lad, a nice left foot, should have done well for himself. But he grew up round it all—'

'You don't have to join in, not everyone does. It's not some pothole people fall into—'

'I'm not saying it is, and I'm not making excuses for him. More an explanation. It's what he said to me: he knew Cullen, he couldn't ignore him, he knew all Cullen's people. Does that make him guilty?'

Dave canted his chin in the way he had, to indicate he was conceding the point while still on some level dissenting from it.

'How's Dessie anyhow?'

'Well, I think he was doing grand out there in Greece. Not any more.'

We walked in silence for a while, Dave working away at his sandwich. I had lost my appetite. I was working through the what-ifs, torturing myself with what I had done, and what I had failed to do. I couldn't have been expected to provide twenty-four-hour surveillance for Paul Delaney, but that didn't make his murder any easier to accept, or me any less determined to find his killer. At one point, Dave lifted his head from his sandwich and stared balefully at me, but he kept his counsel. When we got back to Oscar, Dave stopped and looked at his watch.

'All right, look, the Fogarty case. Stay away, don't get involved. Give her back her money. I assume it's Anne, is it? And by the look in your eyes, I can see she made an impression. You'll never change when it comes to skirt, will you?'

'What is this, Dave, are you warning me off, same as you warned Anne Fogarty off?'

Dave looked over his shoulder, as if Oscar Wilde was eavesdropping, then brought his big pan close to mine.

'One of the suspects Anne Fogarty claims are in the frame for her father's murder was in the IRA. One of them is a very respectable businessman who had a few tax issues. One of them is George Halligan, that CAB has been trying to lay a glove on and failing for twelve years. My team are directed to avoid anything with a whiff of paramilitary involvement. So that rules Jack Cullen out. And in any case, what he did back then, before the ceasefire, there's no come-back now: that's all water under the bridge.'

'What about Bobby Doyle? Has he any history of Republican involvement?'

'Not that I know of. He's a Nordie, and a Sinn Féin donor, but I think he got into that in the States, you know, all that Irish-American shite.'

'I thought there was a cross-border unit that were re-investigating unsolved cases from the Troubles.'

'There is, and maybe they'd take an interest, if you can make the link with Cullen. But they probably have cases a lot higher in priority than a dead tax collector in Sandymount. And anyway, there's enough there, in my opinion, to sustain the position that even if Steve Owen's conviction was found to be unsafe, he still looks favourite. Did Anne Fogarty not tell you I told her that?'

'She said you'd just stonewalled her on the phone, kept repeating that the Guards no longer considered the case to be "live".'

Dave raised his eyebrows and shook his great head, pantomiming surprise.

'Is that what she said? And there was I thinking, for once, Ed had a nice girl to deal with, whatever about the case.'

'What do you mean by that?'

'I mean I met Anne Fogarty, I took her for coffee, I talked through the reasons we wouldn't revisit her father's case. I took her to the Merrion Hotel, Ed.'

'Fuck's sake, Dave. I hope Carmel doesn't find out.'

'Stop. I can hear her now. You never take *me* to the Merrion Hotel. But yeah, I did, and do you know why? Because I felt sorry for the girl. And now she's telling you I'm the bad guy?'

I shrugged, as if a client, or a woman, lying to me wasn't unusual. It wasn't, but I had thought this one would be different.

'Do you actually think Steve Owen is still the killer, or does it just make life easier for you?'

Dave exhaled heavily, his eyes flaring red, as if the considerable trial on his patience and good nature I presented was beginning to tell.

'Have you looked at the case in any detail? The investigating officer is retired now, but he'll talk to you if I ask him to. I've had dealings with him a couple of times since I started in SCR, and I've found him straight as a die. Noel Sweeney is his name. And for what it's worth, he's very clear in his mind that it was a crime of passion, with Owen responsible, and the mother every bit as guilty.'

'But the appeal judge—'

'Ah, fuck away off with the appeal judge, who d'you think you are, some earnest cunt from the *Irish Times*? Appeal judges can be as wrong as cops you know, as pig-headed and tendentious and perverse.'

'What about George Halligan? He never had any Provo connections, did he?'

Dave worked out of Seafield throughout the eighties and nineties, home turf for the Halligan crime family.

'Not that I know of. And I'd've heard. Nah, we were watching a few lads all right, but the Halligans always had . . . other priorities.'

'Do you reckon him for the murder? He was what, in his mid-twenties then?'

'Just getting going in a serious way. And he made money quickly, although nothing like the amounts the other boys had racked up. I don't get why Fogarty targeted George, to be honest, he wasn't in that league. And I don't think the Halligans were into hits that early. They were savages, but they would have threatened Fogarty, or beaten him up, not taken him out. Podge maybe, but Podge wasn't off the leash to that extent back then. And George was always very cautious when it came to anything white collar, respectful almost, sure that was his whole vision of himself, as a legitimate businessman. But listen, if you can find some evidence to pin it on George Halligan, go ahead. You'd want to move fast though.'

'Why is that?'

'I thought you'd have heard. Lung cancer. Nothing can be done, so the story goes. Out there in St Bonaventure's. He's got three months to live.'

~

As soon as I got home I read what little there was to read on the Internet about Paul Delaney's murder. They'd been waiting for him in the car park beneath his apartment block on Parnell Street. Passers-by heard the shots and saw the motorcycle tearing off afterwards. Delaney was described as a promising footballer, who was not 'known to Gardaí'. Quite a professional hit for somebody with no criminal connections.

The Beresford Lane victims had been named as Simon Devlin 20, and Dean Cummins, 18. I listened online to a replay of the RTE *News at One* Dave had mentioned, which covered all three murders and the Tolka Park gunman, and which was full of law and order breaking down and people not being safe on the streets and the scourge of drug crime and how twenty years ago disputes that were solved with fists and boots were now being settled with guns and knives. It was depressing stuff, made all the more so by the fact that the whole thing would have a press life of a week at most, reach a crescendo in the Sunday newspapers and then be swiftly replaced by the next outrage. As I was wondering whether the Guards would have notified Dessie Delaney of his brother's killing by now, or whether that duty fell to me, the phone rang. The north inner city grapevine had been burning up the wires to Greece. Dessie sounded as if he'd passed through shock and grief and had moved into cold rage, which was where he proposed to stay.

'What did you find out, Ed?'

'Very little, Dessie, I only had two days. I'm sorry—'

'Don't very little me, and don't sorry me either: I want to know what you barely know yet, what you're not admitting to yourself, what you wanted more facts to back up but won't get now he's dead. And I'm fucking paying you, all right man, for the days you done and however many more it takes, until we find the cunts who done this. Or do we have to look beyond Cullen?'

Great. Two jobs at the same time. That always works.

'All right then. From what I heard, if Paul was involved in anything dirty, he would have been working *for* Cullen. So this would be a blow against Cullen's authority. I was at Tolka last night when the gunman opened up. That was for show, Dessie, and I don't know what it meant, except that there was no one targeted, the rounds went into the sky and were intended to. Now when Barry Jordan, Shels captain, saw me, and made the connection with you, he looked at Paul like there was something wrong. And after the shots, all the Shelbourne players gathered in a huddle. I told Paul he should join them, and I could see he wanted to, but instead, he ran off to the dressing room on his own. There were very definitely rumours, and his teammates were evidently aware of them.

'I spoke to Ray Moran at the Viscount, pushed him on dissent in the ranks, on what Lamp Comerford was up to, didn't get anywhere. Ten minutes after I left the Viscount, two lads jumped me with a knife. I took them both out but left them breathing. This morning they were found with their throats cut. I don't know yet if that was about Paul, or about me, Dessie. There's a chance my prints are on the knife.

'Paul said he'd been summoned to Jack Cullen's table one night after he'd scored a hat trick, that Cullen had given him a lift home, that that's where all the rumours started.'

'What do you think, Ed?'

'Well, on the other side, eighteen years old he was living in an apartment block on Parnell Street—'

'Me and Liam paid his rent, or most of it anyway.'

'Is that so? All right then. There's also, he was driving a little red Mazda coupe that I don't see how he could afford on what Shels are paying him.'

'What? An MX5 18i? The roadster?' Dessie's voice was incredulous. I'd forgotten he was a total petrolhead. Dessie the Driver. 'The fuck did he get that?'

'He said his girlfriend's father had a Mazda dealership, and he's a major Shels fan, let him drive it for nothing.'

There was a long silence on the phone. I could hear laughter in the background, and the clink of glasses, and strains of the kind of sombre-saccharine ballad you only heard in European holiday resorts. Then Dessie cleared his throat.

'That sounds like shite, Ed, to be honest with you.'

'Do you know the girl in question?'

'The last girlfriend we knew about, they broke up over Christmas. He might have a new one, but if he does, it's a bit soon for her Da to be giving him cars. I don't like the sound of that at all.'

'Well. I can look into it. But there's a limit to what I can do for the time being. It's a Garda investigation now.'

'Yeah, but what chance is there they're gonna come up with anything? I mean, how many of these have they solved? It was a pro hit, sounds like: fucking none of them, know I mean? So whatever you can whittle out man, it's better than waiting for them to come up with fuck all.'

'All right. Thing is though, Dessie, if it *was* a pro hit . . .'

'Yeah. Well. That's where we need a closer look at Jack Cullen's organization and his difficulties, isn't it?'

'Are you coming back, Dessie?'

'Of course I'm coming back, what do you think?'

'I think . . . I'll be blunt with you Dessie, I'm not doing intelligence gathering so that you can pull some gangland madman you used to know out of the fire and launch a hit on Jack Cullen or Lamp Comerford or whoever we might find is connected to Paulo's death. There's a limit to how far I'm prepared to go, and I'm nudging up against it now.'

'Is this a warning, Ed? I mean, these cunts just killed my brother.'

'And I'm very sorry, Dessie, and I want his killers badly: he died on my watch, and even if there was nothing I could have done, I can't have that. But if he was dealing drugs for them, for any of them, he's no longer an innocent bystander. And by that, I don't mean he deserved to die. I mean, I'm not going to play a part in avenging his death, unless it means finding evidence against his killers that can be used in court. Do you understand?'

I heard the ballad music again, with a grand underlay of gloopy strings this time; it punctuated the conversation with a melodramatic emphasis it hardly needed; finally, Dessie spoke up.

'That's sound, Ed. Sorry if I was getting carried away, it's just . . . the day that's in it, know I mean? You'll do what you can, yeah?'

I'd do what I could. And I'd tell Dessie what I found out, in spite of all my grand talk. And if someone died because of it, well, maybe that was just the way it had to be: to avenge his brother, and to expiate my guilt, and to protect my reputation too. I wasn't hired, or even asked, to be Paul Delaney's bodyguard; no one warned me that he was in danger. But like I said to Dessie: he died on my watch, and whether it was my fault or not, it was down to me to make it right.

7

As well as serving as an impersonal space in which to meet clients, another upside of having an office was that I could go there to think. Otherwise, I lived in my car, on the move, depending on momentum to yield results, postponing as long as possible the moment I had to go home. Often that worked. But just as often, I got caught up in events over which I had no control, and the case threatened to explode in my face, and sometimes did. Or at least, that was what I thought as I worked my way through the press cuttings and court transcripts in the Brian Fogarty file Anne had brought me, trying to weigh the likely guilt or otherwise of the three major suspects. From what Dave said, and from what I knew about him, George Halligan didn't seem like a runner, although he could never be ruled out or underestimated. The unexplained assets he had back in '91 amounted to a couple of hundred grand in property – two houses and two apartments dotted around the Southside. Two hundred grand wasn't small change back then but it was comparatively little, certainly if you were going to compare with Jack Cullen, who, in the Dublin expression, would have stabbed you for looking at him, and would have had no qualms about having a pesky tax inspector beaten to death, or about doing the job himself. According to Fogarty's letter, Cullen in 1991 had a villa in Marbella, three town houses in Dundalk and half a dozen three- and four-storey rental properties around the North Inner City, all the while signing on for fifty-two pounds forty a week in unemployment assistance payments.

Fogarty's reckoning of Bobby Doyle's assets was even more impressive: Doyle had fourteen substantial Georgian and Victorian houses on the Northside of Dublin and a large, detached residence on what estate agents could not resist calling tree-lined Clyde Road in Dublin 4, among foreign diplomats and the old rich. Very little was known about Doyle back then; he had subsequently become one of the biggest property developers in the state, with shopping centres and housing estates to his credit. Anne Fogarty had included plenty of clippings from the last ten years, including a full two-page profile from a series about property developers in the *Irish Times*, where he featured alongside the other names likely to be seen gracing the sides of the cranes that still hovered above the city. There may have been talk of economic downturn, and even recession, but the big builders and developers had stored up enough fat to weather whatever the market threw at them and come up trumps. Doyle himself kept a very low profile. He didn't race horses or pilot helicopters or boats or any of the stuff men in his position liked to do; indeed, a recurring theme of all the newspaper profiles was how little was known about how he did spend his time: committed family man was the consensus, with at least three children of school-going age being mentioned. Bobby Doyle's wife was another matter. Deirdre Doyle – Dee Dee, as she was referred to on the back page of the *Sunday Independent*, usually in conjunction with the phrase 'fun-loving' – was one of the standing army of society hostesses happy to support the careers of any number of interior decorators, fashion designers, restaurateurs and luxury hoteliers, and always available to march beneath the standard of whatever charity was in vogue. Autism, muscular dystrophy, cystic fibrosis and breast cancer had all benefited from her patronage, with extravagant balls and gala opera and theatre nights attended by fluting hostesses of indeterminate age and their wealthy husbands. I had been at one myself a few months back, escorting Donna Nugent, Bobby Doyle's PR flack and an ex – well, girlfriend would be overstating it – let's just say when I lived in LA and she worked in San Francisco there was a time when I saw a lot of her, and she of me. Donna was very driven, too driven for intimacy, but she had healthy appetites, and always had two or three guys going at the same time. Back then I used to enjoy being one of them. Now I found I didn't any more. After the ball, which was for third world debt, and the lost weekend that followed the ball, which was on Bobby Doyle's tab in a city centre hotel whose name and location I forget, if I ever knew, it had taken me a week to get my balance back, and longer to move my jaw without it aching. Donna was on the TV the following Monday spinning for the Independence Bridge and looking bright of eye and pink of cheek, like she'd just completed a marathon, which I suppose she had, and like she was ready for another, which was more than could be said for me. I stopped answering her calls, but she hadn't stopped calling, suggesting nights she was free and hotels that would suit, maybe the same hotel. I'm not a saint, and Donna Nugent was thirty-four and very easy on the eye, but unless I bumped into her in a bar and she heaved me over her shoulder, it wasn't going to happen. I still felt a little empty and lost after seeing her, as if there had been a terrible incident in the street and nobody had noticed it but me. But since she was my only connection to Bobby Doyle, I was going to have to call Donna Nugent back.

I was going to come up against Jack Cullen in the course of the fallout from Paul Delaney's murder. So before I tackled Cullen and Doyle, I reckoned I should first eliminate George Halligan from the frame, especially if he was going to die at any moment. And since Steve Owen lived in the same direction, I decided it would be worthwhile paying him a call as well.

8

My father was a mechanic, and he left a racing-green 1965 Volvo 122S, not exactly to me, but in the garage of my house. My friend Tommy Owens knocked the car into shape for me, and helps keep it on the road. It's a big beast of a thing, nicknamed the Amazon, the kind of car a child would draw, and it attracts more attention than is sensible for someone who does the kind of work I do, but I somehow got it into my head that driving it helped pay some filial debt I owed, and although I couldn't tell you exactly what that debt was, I feel the obscure obligation to go on repaying it, and probably always will.

St Bonaventure's Nursing Home was a large neo-Gothic villa complete with conical towers and stained-glass windows set in a quiet square on the west side of Seafield, within sound of the rising tide. The last time I had been here, it was to see a dying man who knew the secrets surrounding my father's death, and although he tried not to give them away he told me more than he intended. I marched briskly past the nun at reception as if I knew where I was going. I remembered the wood panelling, the stained-glass windows depicting the stations of the cross and how they were placed about the floors in no particular order; I climbed the stairs past number four, the meeting with the Virgin, and arrived at number nine, the third fall. Most deaths through illness and old age take place between two and six a.m., and I guess that makes sense, since they're the hours when even the hardiest can feel a little fragile, when life's trivial snags are transformed into thorns of steel. But if I were in a nursing home, I think the deathly afternoon torpor would finish me off: the distant sound of afternoon television, the mutter and hiss of respectful visitors, the sour smell of decay and hopelessness and bleach.

There was a steroid-swollen man with a red face and a ponytail and a large leather jacket that looked like a boat cover standing guard outside George's room. That's how I knew it was George's room.

'George asked to see me,' I said. 'Ed Loy.'

Steroid Man stood dead still and expressionless for a minute, maybe more, until I began to wonder if he was deaf, or if I was. Then he inclined his face toward me.

'What you say, Fred?' he said, in an Eastern European accent.

'Ed. Edward Loy.'

He turned and went into the room and shut the door. I could hear George's familiar bark inside, followed by a salvo of coughing. I suppose it sounded worse now he was dying.

Steroid Man reappeared.

'No George don't ask to see you,' he said.

I nodded, and after a suitable pause, he stood aside.

'Yes George ask to see you.'

I nodded again, and went in before I had to endure another of those silences. George Halligan was sitting up in bed wearing black silk pyjamas with a red stripe and a red cravat with a black stripe watching horse racing on TV with the sound down. He had newspapers and a bottle of Roses' lime cordial on a tray in front of him. He didn't look significantly different to how he had looked before, and I wondered how long he had been ill: his face was the usual clenched fist of clefts and creases; the dark moustache, now flecked with grey like the swept-back hair, overwhelmed the narrow mouth; the black eyes glowed like wet coals.

'The fuck do you want?' he growled.

'Thought I'd come and pay my respects,' I said.

'Don't be such a fucking swish,' he said. 'Whatever you want, you can stay and have a drink. No one is coming to visit me except cunts. I'm only in here so I could get away from them crowding around the house, muttering and wailing. And I don't like to drink on me own. Standards. You keep them or you're fucked. Rinse them glasses like a good man.'

I took two glasses across the room to the sink and rinsed them with liquid soap and hot and then cold water. When I brought them back to George, he pointed to the wooden nightstand by his bed. Inside there was a bottle of Tanqueray gin and a black leather- and chrome-clad casket full of ice.

'No lemons?' I said.

'It'd be limes, you fucking smart aleck. Gibsons. Gin and Roses' lime juice.'

'Gimlets.'

'That's what I said. Are you going to mix them, or stand there like a fucking woman, like a fucking wife, in fact, and let the ice melt?'

I mixed them. But I couldn't let it go.

'You said Gibsons, not Gimlets.'

'The fucking difference? Sláinte.'

'These are Gimlets. Gibsons are martinis with pickled onions instead of olives.'

George's eyes flickered with mockery, and his face congealed into a leer of derision.

'Pickled onions?'

'Americans call them cocktail onions.'

'As if that made them any better. Fuck sake, pickled onions. That's . . . that's disgusting, so it is. What was that about, the *war*, was it?'

'I think it was a banker, some businessman anyway, wanted to treat clients to a three martini lunch and get them good and drunk while remaining sober himself. So he told the waiter to keep the drinks coming, but to put water instead of gin in his glass, and to give him an onion rather an olive so he could pick his drink out. Then when he had them good and oiled, he'd slide in for the kill. You know the drill, George.'

George Halligan had once drugged the orange juice and champagne he was serving me and left me to have my head kicked in by his brother Podge. He smiled now, maybe with nostalgia for better days, maybe with approval of an artfully devised stratagem, probably with a mixture of the two.

'Well. Business is business. If you're not winning, the other cunt is.'

His eyes slid across to the horse race unfolding on the TV screen with a look of mild displeasure, as if watching racing was a duty and a chore and no one should expect him to take any pleasure in it. George owned horses now, and took his place in the parade ring among the cashmere and Barbour and fur. A long way from the poverty of Fagan's Villas or the Somerton Flats.

'So. To what do I owe the pleasure? You're hardly here for the good of me health,' George said.

'I'm sorry to hear you're ill, George,' I said, and found that I meant it. Having led a crime family specializing in drug dealing and extortion, having presided over the savage beatings and murders that go with that particular terrain, largely inflicted by his brother Podge, having made a fortune from a life of crime, George Halligan had now gone legit, or as good as, give or take his still being George. The monies had been laundered without the Criminal Assets Bureau ever managing to bring a claim, Podge was in jail, and George had moved into property and race horses like any respectable Irish businessman. He was still a ruthless Irishman, and had very nearly been the death of me on more than one occasion, and would think nothing of giving the order moments after I left his bedside today if he thought I was a threat to his interests. But we had grown up together, and that counted for something; for all that I despised him, I felt a curious bond with him. Maybe it was history; maybe it was the devil I knew: behind him came a line of feral, coked-up twenty-year-olds who'd stab you for spilling their drink. Whatever it was, I knew I'd regret his passing, just as he would regret mine. The difference being, I wouldn't be the cause of his death, unless his hands were at my throat and it was him or me.

'If you don't have your health,' George said, and flashed me something that looked like more than guts, something that looked like the expression I'd seen on his face after his unfancied horse had swept the field, or his favourite had mysteriously lost and George had bet against him, something that looked suspiciously like glee. Not quite the look I associated with terminal cancer. Maybe his meds were kicking in.

'Now Ed. What can I do you for? Nice to share a drink, but I have races here, obligations,' George said, agitating the newspapers on the tray in front of him and waving a nicotine-stained hand towards the TV screen, then disintegrating spontaneously in an avalanche of coughing that sounded like a brick house collapsing unexpectedly. As his face reddened and his neck corded and pulsed beneath the force of the racking tremors, the yellowed hand shifted its angle and pointed unsteadily but determinedly towards his drink. I brought the glowing green liquid to his mouth and, by sheer force of will it seemed, he stopped coughing long enough to down the Gimlet. He spluttered a little, and then there was silence, punctuated first by George tapping his platinum signet ring against the glass and handing it to me to be refilled, which I did, and then by his voice, the bass notes reedy with strain.

'Show's over. Speak up, or get to fuck,' he said, and swallowed half the fresh drink in one.

'Brian Fogarty,' I said. 'A tax inspector, murdered in his home fifteen-odd years ago. Remember it? They sent the wife's lover down. Steve Owen. Then Owen got off on appeal. Conviction unsafe. But the Guards said they weren't looking for anyone else.'

George's face flexed in the way he had, with all the features disappearing into a mask of crevices and folds, a mask somewhere between 'Don't understand' and 'Don't give a fuck'. It didn't look quite as menacing without the wreath of smoke that used to accompany it, but it was far from inviting.

'This tax inspector had three people in his sights. Ill-gotten gains with no apparent income or tax history. Bit of a pioneer he was, back in those pre-CAB days. Anyway George, one of his targets was you.'

George Halligan's face relaxed into a beam of pleasure, as if this was the most delightful thing I could have said to him.

'What are you now, Dave Donnelly's fucking errand boy, running around doing his cold case business for him? Fuck sake Ed, I thought you had some fucking pride. 1993?'

''91.'

'Same difference. The dawn of fucking time.'

'And this is not Dave's case. They knocked it back, in fact.'

'And I'm supposed to . . . fuck, I barely had a pot to piss in back then, I know the country was still on its uppers, but Revenue would want to have been desperate to think I could do much for them. Who are the others?'

That's right, George, why don't I give you my bank details as well, since we're such good friends.

'Were you in the IRA back then, George?'

'The IRA? What kind of fucking madman are you here? Do bank jobs and then give the money to some other bunch of cunts so they can blow up a load of Nordie cunts we couldn't give a fuck about in the name of Ireland? That IRA? You must be fucking joking. I mean, I love my country same as anyone but fuck off, you know?'

'You'd've come across them over the years. Protection money. Concerned Parents Against Drugs.'

'So what? Is there an IRA connection? Some Provo took out a tax inspector. The mourners reached double figures. Just.'

George ventured a laugh at his own witticism, but it curdled into another hacking cough. He came out of it gasping for breath, his eyes streaming. The door opened and Steroid Man looked in. George shook his head and waved him out, picked up his drink and then put it down again untouched. It looked like I was running out of time. Sometimes you have to give to get back.

'One of the others he was targeting was Jack Cullen,' I said.

A tremor flickered across George Halligan's face at the mention of Jack Cullen's name, whether of simple recognition, or particular memory, I couldn't divine; flickered across his face and was gone like smoke across the face of the sky, leaving not a trace behind.

'Poor old Jack has his troubles, doesn't he?' George said solemnly, in feigned sympathy, like an oul' one savouring a neighbour's illness and imminent demise. 'Everyone's heard about Lamp Comerford. And did Cullen have something to do with the Delaney fella?'

George's eyes narrowed, as if seeing me for the first time.

'That's Dessie's brother, of course. Are you involved in that as well? Think the bould Dessimond will be making a return visit to these shores to view the body?'

Dessie Delaney had run with Podge Halligan for a while, and had been ready to give evidence against Podge for murder during the Dawson case, the first I worked after I came back from LA. Podge had pleaded guilty to manslaughter, after pressure from his brothers, and Dessie's evidence was never heard, but his willingness to give it had not been forgotten or forgiven, as was clear from the expression on George Halligan's face. I looked at the wolf-like smile that didn't reach the cold black eyes and saw instantly the lack of compunction with which he would give the order for a hit on Dessie Delaney, and the relatively mild sense of satisfaction it would give him, and any kind of imagined fellow feeling with George Halligan instantly evaporated.

'I wouldn't know, George. But I can tell you this: if Dessie reappears and he runs into grief from anyone connected to the Halligans, you'll pay for it.'

George smiled.

'Big talk, Ed. Not your style. Must be the gin. Good value, aren't they, the oul' Gimlets? Slap you right up there. Small man in a fast car. To be honest with you, I doubt I'll see Easter, Ed. But it's sound of you not to count me out. Now . . . I'm trying to remember this fucker Fogarty.'

'He lived in Sandymount. And he had the book on you George: details of the apartments there in Blackrock, and the two town houses in Castlehill.'

'From little acorns,' George said, his eyes glittering. 'See we got the golf club site turned over and all the properties sold off the plans before the recent, eh, unpleasantness.'

'The recent unpleasantness' was a long-awaited downturn in Dublin's bloated property market, with prices correcting themselves by ten per cent or melting down by thirty to fifty, depending on which economist you listened to. Before any of that happened, values had been soaring, which was when George extorted the old Castlehill Golf Club site from Dawson Construction and arranged for it to be rezoned for high-density development by bribing local politicians, and murdering one of them. So Irish business as usual then. Apart maybe from the murder, and the extortion. And maybe not. The development had a make-your-mind-up name like Castlehill Grange Manor, and hoardings around the site featured enormous photographs of square-jawed men in sports cars and lingerie-clad women in bedrooms the size of football fields. The crass vulgarity of this 'luxury branding' was the subject of much derision in the serious newspapers, but the whole development was sold before a sod was turned, which just went to prove that a gangster like George Halligan had a better grasp of the new Irish rich than the high minded commentariat of the *Irish Times*.

'But I probably didn't come here to listen to you boast, George,' I said.

'I can't take it with me though, Ed,' George said in an uncertain voice, and looked at me through widened eyes, as if I were some combination of priest and accountant who just might be able to give him advice to the contrary. He stared down at his nicotine stained fingers, clasped together on the tray as if in prayer, and nodded, as if what he was about to say was difficult, but for the best.

'Farney Park?' he said.

'That's right.'

'Yeah. I remember it. A murder stood out back then. Not like today, bowsies and corner boys going around shooting each other over the price of a pint. Back of his head stove in, wasn't it?'

'That's right,' I said. George was staring at his hands the while, so it was hard to know how much he knew and how he knew it. But then it would have been just as hard to know by looking into those coal black eyes.

'Word at the time was that there was some kind of paramilitary thing going on all right,' George said quietly.

'The IRA?'

'The INLA was what I heard. The Irish National Liberation Army. They were the mental ones. They took him out in part as a favour to some Provo he was investigating—'

'Jack Cullen?'

'Don't be putting words in me mouth. In part as a favour to some Provo, but the stated reason was to strike a blow against I don't know what, the INLA were Marxist Leninists as well as being fucking savages, the unjust oppressive forces of state repression as represented by the revenue inspectors, they got that bit right at least.'

'Who are we talking about, George? Anyone in particular? Anyone still around?'

'Well . . . I'm just telling you what I heard, right?'

'Go on then, tell me it.'

'Well, one of the names I heard was Ray Moran.'

'Ray Moran? Jack Cullen's representative on earth?'

'The very same. Moran was a student back then, ran the student union in Trinity there, the Ents Officer they called him, entertainment, running all the gigs and so on, involved in every fucking thing. We used to . . . associates of mine used to supply him with drugs, small stuff, hash and E mostly, little bit of coke but no one could afford coke back then, he'd deal it around the college. And then he got in with the IRSP, what's this that stood for?'

'The Irish Republican Socialist Party.'

'The very ones. The political wing. Funny how they all had four names, like the landed English gents they were up in arms against, Jocelyn Fortesque Ffyffe-Trumpington to you son. The INLA were in the doldrums at the time, on account of how they'd spent the previous five years splitting into factions and shooting the fuck out of each other. In the name of Ireland, or socialism, or some shite. Story was the IRSP were throwing shapes as if they were clamping down on drugs, but were actually getting into dealing, to raise money for the lads in the North so that they could, I don't know, finish each other off for keeps. All in a good cause, you might say, and I wouldn't fucking disagree with you. But then of course, in dipping a toe in the drug trade they drifted out of Trinity and down the Lombard Street flats and over the river and who did they bump into only Jack Cullen and his Provo friends, who wrote the book when it came to that particular mode of organization: intimidate the local dealers and keep in with the locals by organizing Concerned Parents vigilante groups. Then make sure the dealers are kicking a major whack of whatever they're making into your coffers. Finally, take a piece of the action yourself by letting dealers operate with your say-so, and under your protection, because they're basically your lads, although you don't concede that until well after everyone knows anyway, but is too scared to do anything about it.'

'And so what, Ray Moran ends up taking out Brian Fogarty as a favour to Jack Cullen?'

'Well, a bit more than a favour. Moran had trespassed on Cullen's patch. For that alone, he could have ended up in the river.'

'Would the INLA and the IRA not have been rivals? I thought there was major strife between competing paramilitary groups?'

'Maybe to begin with, but not at that stage. They weren't quite proxies, although occasionally the INLA did the IRA's dirty work – out-and-out sectarian murders, you know, plugging the Prods they wanted rid of at a time when the IRA were trying to make out their war had nothing to do with religion or tribe. But the truth was, they were let operate with the permission of the Provos, and of course that permission could be withdrawn at any time.'

'So a favour was an order.'

'Something between that and payback. Take this guy out and we'll overlook you infringing on our turf, and you can trot back across the river and we'll leave you alone. Now we know who you are.'

'And Moran's association with Jack Cullen built from there?'

'That's what I heard. Have to understand, Ed, this was all the word on the street, and a long time ago, and the fellas who told me are probably dead. But yeah, that was how they sealed their deal. Blood brothers, you might say. Whether Moran done it himself I doubt, but he was behind it. And few years later, Raymondo's an accountant, he's suddenly setting up in practice in an entire floor of a house on Pembroke Road and living in the other three storeys, twenty-eight years old, he's done very fucking well for himself, hasn't he? How did that happen?'

'Laundering drug money for Jack Cullen. And for the IRA.'

'Is my question to you.'

George eyeballed me then, twinkling in a knowing kind of way, as if he had presented me with a gift that would prove to be of inestimable value, if only I had the wit to figure it out. He picked up his drink then, the lime and the gin a viscous green ooze, and tipped it down his throat in one long draught. Tears came into his eyes, and his face flushed. I wasn't sure that much gin could be good for you when you were dying of lung cancer. But if it made you feel better, what odds? The odds were against it having made George feel any better, however; having gasped for breath as he surrendered his glass, he was now coughing, his flushed face turning a deeper hue of red, coughing as if he was never going to stop. Steroid Man swung into the room at speed; he was at George's side and pouring a glass of water and helping him drink it in seconds; gradually, mercifully, the coughing abated, like a freak storm that blows over.

I didn't think I'd ever see George Halligan again. I was wrong.

9

Steve Owen lived in an apartment building on the main street in Blackrock. Anne Fogarty had rung to arrange the meeting, and when I announced myself at the front door, he buzzed me in and stood waiting in the corridor for when I got out of the elevator on the third floor. The building looked modest enough on the street, wedged between a pub and a Starbuck's, but when you walked into Owen's apartment the view was spectacular: the rear of the building looked directly out over Blackrock DART station and right across Dublin Bay. The great promontory of Howth lay straight ahead; the candy-striped towers of the Pigeon House marked the southerly approach to Dublin Port; the sea roiled from slate grey to aquamarine as shafts of late afternoon sunlight pierced the dirty sky. I became aware of Owen smiling at me and raised a hand in acknowledgement of the spectacle.

'It's a pleasure that never diminishes,' he said in a crisp, careful voice mildly flavoured with the almost camp accent of old Dublin. Owen was in his fifties, tall and slim, almost gaunt, with lank, graying brown hair swept off his high forehead in a side parting. His cheekbones were sharp, his sallow complexion flecked with red; he had a full moustache above a thin mouth and a weak chin; he wore a brown corduroy shirt, blue jeans and brown clogs; a small wooden cross on a leather cord hung around his neck. The apartment was neat and sparsely furnished. There were posters for musicals on the walls, and framed photographs of a younger Owen in costume for what looked like *Oliver!* and *The King and I*; as I suspected from the moustache, it had once been partnered by a beard, and Owen's hair had fallen to his collar. An acoustic guitar leant in a corner, and orchestral music played at low volume from wall-mounted speakers.

'School musicals. Silly of me to set so much store by them, but at the time they were such big events,' Owen said.

He nodded me towards a cane table and chairs in a sunroom whose glass doors gave onto a small balcony.

'Coffee? Or tea? Or something else? I normally have something else around now,' he said hopefully.

I asked for a gin and tonic, and he smiled his approval. The drink he brought me was very light on tonic; I took a sip and left it down on the table; Owen sank half of his in two eager draughts; his unsteady hands were dry and worn; the knuckles red and raw.

'Anne Fogarty said you didn't really want to talk about her father's murder,' I said.

Owen raised his eyebrows and exhaled quickly, almost laughing, as if surprised that I'd got into it so quickly.

'It's not that I don't *want* to, it's more I don't really think I know anything. I mean, the three suspects, I don't know them, I've never met them, all I know *about* them is what I read in the papers. And of course, what I read in preparation for the appeal. So I don't see how I can help.'

He shrugged, and took a sip of his drink. The music stopped, and an announcer said something I couldn't hear, and then more music started, big band jazz this time.

'Lyric FM. Gets me through the day,' he said.

'Are you retired, Mr Owen?'

'Steve, please. Yes, I went back to teaching after prison, but I couldn't get the hang of it again, really. They were very good to me, made sure I got the full pension. And I had a house bought, not far from here. Sold it and bought this, and made a fair few bob in the process. Back a few years ago, when you could.'

His energy was that of a man twenty-five years his senior, a widower measuring out his days in crossword puzzles and radio programmes and afternoon drinks, a brave, wistful smile on his handsome, weak face; I felt a surge of irritation at what looked to me like passivity and bad character. Then I reminded myself that he had spent five years in jail for a crime he didn't commit, and by the time he got out, the woman he loved was dead, and I felt ashamed at my rush to judge him so harshly.

'Did it ever occur to you that you were set up for the killing?' I said.

'They could have done a better job of it if that's what they were up to,' Owen said. 'I mean, they could have planted evidence, got a coat or a scarf of mine and left it near the body. There was no physical evidence at all. They found traces of my fingerprints throughout the house, but then, why wouldn't they, I was there often enough.'

'You were a guest in the family home,' I said.

Owen laughed.

'There must be a lexicon they give you guys. Phrases no one but a cop would use. I thought you might be different, being private, but no. "A guest in the family home". Yes, I was.'

'Anne said they didn't know about you and her mother until after her father died.'

'We took care that they never knew. But that doesn't mean we didn't take risks. I taught in Marian College, about five minutes walk from Farney Park. There were several days when I'd have an hour or two free during the day. And we were having an affair. So you'd hardly have been human if you didn't duck in and out of the house once the kids were in school, and himself was at work. And of course, there's always going to be scares with that kind of crack, people coming

75

home early, hiding under beds and climbing out onto the garage roof. In the early stages, it sometimes feels like that's what having an affair is all about.'

The memories, and the gin, had warmed Owen up; I could see devilment in his eyes, and considerable charm; back in the day, that must have been very attractive. A weak face looks different on a younger man: it can suggest sensitivity and gentleness and other classically feminine qualities that might appeal to an older woman whose husband had betrayed her.

'Was that what it was all about for you?'

'At first, sure. The girls were at St Mary's in Haddington Road, and one of them, not Anne, the younger one—'

'Margaret.'

'Midge, that's right, she was in the chorus when we did *Oklahoma!*, Marian and St Mary's together. And Irene came along to see it, and that's how we met. She made it clear she wanted to meet me again. Made it clear why, too. She was very direct. I was flattered, to put it mildly. And she was about fifteen years older, so there was a bit of a Mrs Robinson thing going on there. And initially I thought, well if this is what it is, what's wrong with it? Every man's fantasy when he's young. And then it turned into something else. It turned into love.'

Owen's eyes fell then, and he took a hit on his drink and looked out to sea.

'And the running around became a little more desperate, and a little less like fun. Odd, isn't it, we don't see it coming, even though we should. We say, of an affair: it's getting serious. We don't want it to be so serious it hurts. But that's what happens. We bring it on ourselves.'

'Anne said Brian Fogarty knew about the affair.'

'Sure, but he didn't want it thrust in his face, and fair enough. I felt sorry for him in a way. He was the previous generation, where the bloke can play around and get away with it. And then Irene turned the tables on him, like some feminist novel, you know? Or a French film. She told him he'd had his fun, she was going to have hers now, if he didn't like it he could take a hike. I don't think he liked it, but he stuck it out. And fair play, only Anne kept loyal to Irene, but all the girls stood by their Daddy. Because he stuck around. When people were laughing up their sleeves at him. He stuck around for those girls.'

'It sounds like you admired him.'

'I did. Well, not at the time, but later. Now. I never hated him or anything. But back then, he was in the way.'

'There were letters between you and Irene. Letters that explicitly wished he was out of the way.'

'And the prosecution made the most of them. I know, they were . . . well look, they are what they are, if you want to take one thing from them you can, but . . . I think we all say things like that, oh I wish so and so was out of the way, I wish he was dead.'

'But we don't all write them down. And the fact that Irene wouldn't leave her husband, the fact that you were urging her to leave but she refused—'

'We talked about it as well, it wasn't just the letters. I wanted her, I didn't care about the kids, I'm being honest now. The way I saw it, he could look after them. Midge and Aisling were barely civil to her anyway, and even Anne . . .'

Owen held up his hands as if disowning his own defence.

'Look, I admit it, I was selfish, I was a little obsessed, I put Irene under a lot of pressure to walk out. Now, I see that she was right and I was wrong. But that's as far as it went. In truth, his death was the last thing I'd've wanted: it would have left Irene with the girls, who were in full-blown adolescence by then. God, they'd eat you. So it wouldn't have been in my interest.'

'But if you'd just called to have it out with him, say. Tell him to let her go. He doesn't want to know, he tells you where to go, he turns his back on you, you get mad and you attack him. I think we can all, in the grip of passion, of obsession for the woman we loved . . . I can certainly imagine doing something like that myself, carried away in the moment.'

Steve Owen looked at me then through eyes that, if not exactly angry, flared with irritation. Instead of speaking, he drained his drink and went to fix another one. As he was preparing it, slicing limes and pouring gin and breaking ice, he began to speak in a low, terse voice that accumulated considerable force as he went on.

'I'm pretty sure when I spoke to Anne Fogarty she told me I should cooperate with you because you were determined to help her bring the man or men who killed her father to justice. I'm pretty sure she didn't suggest she had any suspicion that I was in fact the guilty man. Indeed, since that's what the Guards apparently still believe, despite my name having been cleared by the appeal court, I'd've have told her that if she did harbour any such suspicions the last thing she should do is hire a private detective to try and prove them, that she would just be wasting her money. They're hardly going to try me again for it, are they? But then she doesn't believe I did it in the first place. The question is, why do you?'

Owen joined me at the table then, his angular face set, his breath hard, his eyes clouded with passion, his spare frame rigid, shaking, as if it might suddenly buckle and break. His gin sat on the table, the tonic fizzing, the ice cracking; he clutched the glass with both hands as if it were a talisman or a holy relic that could bring him protection and comfort.

'I don't believe you did it either,' I said. 'Not now. But I guess I wanted to see for myself what I thought of you. What I thought you were capable of.'

'And have you reached a verdict?'

'I'm a hung jury when it comes to people,' I said. 'I try to defer my verdict indefinitely. But I don't think you murdered Brian Fogarty. I can see why the Guards wanted you to have, though.'

'Because if it isn't the spouse it's the spouse's lover.'

'There's that. But also, if it was some kind of organized crime hit, it was going to be very hard even establishing a suspect, let alone making a case.'

'And better the wrong man than none at all.'

'That's not how I operate. And I'm grateful to you for talking to me. And I'm sorry if I caused you any more pain than I needed to.'

Owen looked at me then, and for a moment I thought I saw rage flare in his eyes; if it had, it quickly damped down; he nodded, gratefully, it seemed, and drank half of his gin, and came up with a bewildered smile that didn't take, and turned his gaze out to sea again.

I stood up, but before I made another move, the door to the apartment opened and a woman came in. She had a full head of dark red corkscrew curls and wore a shiny red raincoat, and carried a brown leather satchel and a transparent plastic tubular case that looked like it contained architect's plans; her legs in black opaque tights were thickly muscled; her yellow bandolier suggested she had been cycling, as did the pinkness of her cheeks.

'You must be Ed Loy. Janet Ames. Stephen said you were coming. Stephen?'

Owen didn't speak, or turn around. Janet Ames walked around in front of him and her expression darkened. She whipped the glass of gin out of his hand and marched back towards the front door, gesturing for me to follow. By the time I caught up to her, she had whipped off her raincoat to reveal a grey business suit. Her face was all business too.

'Did you have to go into it all? The murder, Irene's death, all of it raked up again?' She was hissing at me as if that made her words less audible to Owen, although the reverse was surely the more likely outcome. I raised my palms in the air and turned to look back at Owen, and at Dublin Bay spread out behind him.

'It's to try and put it all to rest,' I said. 'To find out who is guilty.'

Janet Ames looked at me as if I had said something pitifully naive.

'It's the innocent who suffer,' she said. 'I don't know that finding who killed Brian Fogarty will change that.'

'I don't know either,' I said. 'But that's what his daughter has hired me to do. Justice doesn't always bring an end to suffering. But at least it's justice.'

She opened the door and I followed her out. A blast of light from the landing brightened her hair to a shimmering autumn gold; it was the kind of hair a man could fall in love with.

It was clear Janet Ames was very much in love with Steve Owen. Before she shut the door on me she said one last thing.

'Please don't come back. He needs to live in the future now. The past will be the death of him.'

10

Noel Sweeney, the retired Garda officer who led the Brian Fogarty murder investigation, lived in Stillorgan, but I only had a landline number for him, and either he didn't have a machine, or it wasn't switched on. I stopped by his house, which was in a cul de sac tucked in off the dual carriageway that, in rush-hour traffic, took me about half an hour to reach, only to find, inevitably, that he wasn't home. I scribbled a quick note mentioning Dave Donnelly's name, added my card to the envelope and dropped it through his letterbox.

Sitting into the Amazon, I lit a cigarette and checked my phone. Donna Nugent had replied to the message I'd left her by inviting me to dinner that evening. Her text, in full, read:

Cum to din 8 in Shanahan's bd n dd n yanks n me fr dessert yum yum lucky u dxxx

Coy, that was Donna. But if bd was Bobby Doyle, she had come through in a major way. The text I sent her back read:

Look forward to it x

The text message is a mode of communication ideally suited to lies. Donna adored it. She'd text you from the other side of a bar. The only way you got to hear her voice these days was if you stood right beside her. And then she usually thought of something else to do with her mouth.

It was going to be a long night.

I eased the Volvo out onto the N11 and joined the south-bound flow of traffic. As I did, a dark blue saloon, an Avensis or a Passat, I couldn't see it clearly, pulled out after me. I couldn't see it clearly, but I thought I had seen it before: outside the nursing home, perhaps. Perhaps not. Past the Radisson, I took a left down Booterstown Avenue. Was the saloon following me? Was the gin making me paranoid? I'd had two Gimlets with George Halligan, and one very strong gin and tonic with Steve Owen. For some reason, I had got it into my head that I wasn't going to drink like a fool any more. Not that I was giving up, I just wasn't going to drink during the day. Or on my own. I certainly wasn't going to drink and drive. And here I was, in broad daylight, swinging onto the Rock Road and heading for the city, checking my rearview to see if two men in a blue Passat, or Avensis, or Primera, maybe, were still following me, if they were following me at all, with about seven or eight measures of gin sluicing through my frame. Tight ship, Loy. I could have said I wasn't feeling the gin at all, which was true, and that it was working as a natural anaesthetic to take my mind off the pain in the left side of my face, which felt true. But still. I couldn't see the car I'd thought was following me, or I could see more than one unmarked blue saloon in traffic behind me. I gave it up and turned on the radio. The news wasn't good. House starts were down, and house prices were dropping, and mortgage lending was down because mortgage rates were going up because not enough people could afford a mortgage because they were too expensive because the bankers, as usual, didn't give a fuck about anyone but themselves, and the American firms that had bankrolled the boom were cutting back, or worse, pulling out, and the government was attributing it to the 'knock-on effect' of the sub-prime crisis, which was all the fault of other bankers who didn't give a fuck about anyone but themselves, not our own, as if this made anything better. Even economists that could have been trusted a year ago to talk things up had reinvented themselves as prophets of doom, while the stalwart prophets of doom who had spent ten years warning people that the boom would end in tears could barely contain their solemn, puritan glee. I switched channels until I found music that seemed to fit, and finally came across the 'Prelude' to *Parsifal*. The strings were doing their thing, but the horns hadn't crashed in yet. I turned up the volume and let Wagner's stately siren song draw me slowly home through the rush hour traffic. By the time I turned off for Holles Street, the music had filled the car with its apocalyptic chill; it came as a relief to see a young couple gingerly putting their newborn in the car and starting their lives over.

As I showered and shaved and dressed, I listened to what the radio had to say about the murders of Paul Delaney, and Simon Devlin and Dean Cummins. Apart from a superb performance from the Minister for Justice, who managed simultaneously to say that urgent steps would have to be taken but that there would be absolutely no need to take them because the Guards were on top of the situation, there was some speculation about all not being well within the North Inner City gang these men were thought to be involved with. I checked my phone: one text message. It read:

The parting glass 6.30

The Parting Glass was the Cullen gang's local. Charlie Newbanks had left a message for me earlier saying a) that he'd text me a time and place to meet Lamp Comerford and b) that if I had any sense, I shouldn't come.

I wore a back linen suit and a white dress shirt with French cuffs. My cufflinks were silver, each fashioned in the shape of a mace; my shoes were black Church's wing-tips. My ear didn't look quite as scalded as before; my face throbbed with a dull pain, but I didn't want to reach inside the flesh and tear it off like I had this morning. I washed some Nurofen Plus down with a small Tanqueray and bitters. I brushed and flossed my teeth and gargled with Listerine and doused myself with Terre D'Hermès cologne and put my black wool

83

and cashmere overcoat on and let myself out of my apartment and immediately found myself bundled back inside by the two men who had been waiting by the door.

First I felt relief, because the men couldn't have looked more like cops if they'd been in uniform; then I remembered Cummins and Devlin and the knife with my prints on it, and the relief gave way to unease. Looking at the cops, the unease seemed to be mutual; the taller and darker of the two men looked neither at me nor at his balding colleague; instead he stared at the floor. I wasn't sure, but I thought I could smell drink off the shorter man, who was of squat build and had a salt-and-pepper moustache. I couldn't tell whether these were the men who had stood outside the NMH earlier that day, or if they had followed me in an unmarked blue car. We stood in the hall, the silence punctuated only by the sound of the heavier man's breathing. After a while, I cleared my throat.

'All dressed up?' the squat man said.

'I was on my way out, as you saw,' I said. 'Is there something I can help you with, detectives?'

The tall man shook his head and sighed. The squat man held what looked like a warning hand out to his colleague.

'No one is taken in by your shit, Ed Loy,' the squat man said.

'What shit is that in particular?' I said.

'What were you doing at Noel Sweeney's house?'

'I was trying to talk to him,' I said. 'Detective Inspector Dave Donnelly of Serious Crime Review gave me his name in connection with a case I'm working on.'

'Detective Inspector Dave Donnelly,' the squat man said with laboured scorn, as if Dave's name were a punchline. 'For fuck's sake,' he added, in case his meaning escaped any of us.

The taller man made a sound then, a harsh snort or grunt that did not sound to me as if it was intended to support his colleague. I could smell the booze clearly now; it seeped from the squat man's pores; his eyes were bloodshot and watery.

'And what "case" would that be?'

'That would be a private matter between my client and me,' I said.

The squat man bellowed like a bull at this and poked me in the chest with the flat of his hand, sending me rocking back against the coats that hung on a rail on the opposite wall.

'Kevin!' the taller man shouted, and seemed about to say more, his reddening face taut with anger; instead he opened the door and went out. The squat man made to follow him, then turned back and came up close to me. I could smell the whiskey on his breath, I could almost tell what brand he drank.

'You . . . watch your fucking step, Ed Loy. Dave Donnelly can't protect you forever. You'll get what's fucking coming to you. It's only a matter of time,' he said, and shoved me back against the coats again. I could hear his heavy tread on the stairs, and the door slam behind him.

I poured myself another Tanqueray and bitters over ice and drank it steadily, staring out at the night, waiting for my heartbeat to slow. When it didn't, I drained the glass anyway and left the apartment.

I went down into the street. The restaurant was on Stephen's Green, but I had a stop to make first. Hard rain whipped up off the river and bit into my face as I crossed Butt Bridge and cut down Beresford Place. Scraps of blue and white Garda tape lay scattered around the entrance to Beresford Lane, and a few drenched bunches of polythene-wrapped convenience store flowers propped against a wall were all that remained of the crime scene, all that commemorated Simon Devlin, 20, and Dean Cummins, 18.

I was overdressed for the Parting Glass, that's for sure, but that wouldn't have been hard; a pair of jeans and a shirt would have made you look like Cary Grant compared to most of the lads. And it was men only, not on any enforced basis, but in the way men's toilets tended to be men only: men only went in there because they had no place else to go; no woman in her right mind would have crossed the door. The dress code was sportswear: grey and navy and formerly white tracksuits, or shiny football shirts: Manchester United, Liverpool, Glasgow Celtic. Heads were shaved. Cary Grant? In a linen suit and a cashmere overcoat, I must have looked like Fred Astaire. The shabby room, festooned with Celtic and Ireland posters and Irish Republican memorabilia, was packed at half-six, Holy Thursday resembling Christmas Eve in the pub calendar, the only two nights in the year the pub would be closed the day after.

The barman was burly and grim-faced with a red complexion and straw-coloured hair; he wore grey Farah slacks and a fawn sweater over a cream shirt, formal dress for this place; if the pub hadn't been such a den of thieves, I'd've put him down as an off-duty or retired Guard; he might have been yet, maybe forced to retire. He looked at me quizzically, as if not entirely sure what I might be after. Two swollen-faced crop heads at the bar stared at me with undisguised hostility.

'Pint of Guinness, please,' I said, sliding my accent down a grade or three.

The barman didn't move; his face lost any degree of welcome or civility it might have possessed, which hadn't been much.

'I've only a twenty-minute break man,' I said. 'Just started at the Gresham Hotel there. Black it is tonight an' all.'

On hearing this, the swollen crop heads slowly realigned their great heads towards the bar; the barman, although not looking entirely satisfied, grimaced and pulled my pint; when Charlie Newbanks, the Viscount's doorman, approached me, the barman's face recovered something of its severe composure. It wouldn't have, if he had heard what Newbanks had to say.

'It's not too late to reconsider,' Charlie said in my ear.

'Good to see you too, Charlie,' I said, loud enough for the bar to hear.

Charlie glared at me. I smiled back. His eyes flashed towards the door, then darted to the back of the pub.

'The Gresham, yeah? I'd take it up to the Sackville if I were you,' he said, his voice quiet and anxious.

'Ah I'm grand where I am, so I am,' I said.

Charlie shrugged his huge shoulders, and the don't-say-I-didn't-warn-you expression he'd worn last night spread across his face, except this time it seemed leavened less with amusement than with unease.

'Bring your jar down with you so,' he said.

I waited a little while longer for my pint to settle, and a little longer again for the barman to notice and to do something about it. Anticipation. It was a kind of prayer. I paid for my drink and walked down the bar. There was a seated area at the back of the pub, four booths with leatherette-covered banquette seats that had seen better days: foam spilled from gaping holes in the seat covering. Charlie was standing by one of the banquettes waiting for me. His face said plainly: you brought this on yourself, son.

He gestured to the sole occupant of the banquette.

'Lamp Comerford, Ed Loy,' he said.

Lamp Comerford was small and stocky, well built, without an inch of fat. In his mid-forties, his hair was completely grey; he wore it in a flat-top he kept teased and gelled to perfection. He had a black goatee and a black moustache, both neatly trimmed; his colouring was dark like an Italian's; his acne-pitted face would have had a five o'clock shadow at nine in the morning. Lamp Comerford didn't look much like an enforcer, and that was where his power lay, or so they said: while you were underestimating him, he had already taken you apart.

I sat in beside him; he looked up at me and nodded.

'Leo Halligan says you're sound. He says you're not bent, and you're not our friend, but you're sound.'

Lamp had a mild lisp that led him to overemphasize his t's and d's.

'Greetings to Leo,' I said. 'How's he keeping?'

'He does all right. He's into retail. The rag trade. Export import. Shop, where is it?'

'Anne Street,' I said.

'That's right. Leather stuff. Real cowboy boots. Very dear.'

'If there's a market,' I said.

'*Exactly*,' Lamp said, nodding his head and smiling as if he'd been vindicated, as if this is what he'd been saying all along in the face of all the nay-sayers and doubting Thomases. He was drunk, for sure; I just wasn't sure how drunk.

'Even if it is totally legit,' he said sceptically.

'Is it?'

'I *think* so.' He shook his head then, solemnly, as if such a thing could not conceivably be, drained his glass and handed it to Charlie Newbanks with an expansive flourish of the hand that swept across the table and almost toppled my pint.

'Reinforcements,' he said to Charlie, and winked at me. 'Before we're fucked entirely, ha?'

Charlie, with no expression in his face, looked at me. I shook my head and put my hand over my pint.

Lamp said, 'Fucked in the flank,' loudly.

Charlie went to the bar.

Immediately, Lamp Comerford pointed at me, his eyes clear, his face all business, nowhere near as drunk as he'd appeared.

'I don't know what you know or don't know. But someone is a fucking tout. And when we find out who, he's going fucking down. Now I'm telling you this because I'm not worried about who you'll tell. We can get you whenever we like. If we decide, you won't leave here tonight, and no one will've seen you walk in. Nod if you're following me.'

'It's not exactly complicated,' I said. 'Every gouger in town spins the same streel of multi-coloured piss. What were you hoping for, applause? A column in the *Sunday World*?'

Lamp glared at me for a moment, then grinned.

'Leo said you had a mouth on you all right.'

'Fuck Leo. And fuck you too. I don't care about who's a tout and who isn't, it's fuck all to do with me. I had one job, which was to keep an eye on Paul Delaney. Made a great fist of that, didn't I? I want to know who killed him, and why. Allied to that, I want to know who tried to have me killed last night. Was that you, or your boss?'

Lamp was still grinning. Then he shook his head, and put a hand on my shoulder.

'Fair play to you man, you've got balls anyway. No one talks to me like that.'

Maybe it was the gin. Maybe it was the fear in Charlie Newbanks' eyes. Maybe it was Lamp standing for every cheap hood with an ego the size of Napoleon's. It wasn't that I underestimated him, it was more that, in the moment, same as with a bottle, or another man's wife, I simply didn't care. I shrugged his hand off my shoulder, genuinely angry now. Lamp was still grinning when Charlie Newbanks brought back the drinks, including, inevitably, a pint for me. I hadn't wanted it, but my first seemed mysteriously to have evaporated.

'Charlie,' said Lamp briskly. Charlie lingered long enough to treat me to another hangdog look of foreboding, then loped off towards the bar. The television was blaring something about the Beresford Lane murders now, and a relative hush had descended on the place. In sympathy, Lamp brought his voice down to a low crackle.

'You could be useful to me,' he said. I didn't reply.

'Leo said you wouldn't, but I thought, no harm in asking. I need to find this tout. Four shipments have been seized in the last six months. They've come in through Cork, via Amsterdam, straight from Spain, doesn't matter a fuck. Someone is letting Dublin Castle in on it. We can't afford this kind of shite. Suppliers are looking to be paid. And we need the few bob ourselves.'

I drank my pint in silence.

'Ten grand if you find out who it is.'

'Who could it be, other than you or your boss? Who else knows?'

Lamp shook his head.

'Loose lips. No one keeps a secret. And the shower of gobshites we employ, they can barely get out of bed without instructions. If Leo says you know your way around, I'll believe him. Ten grand.'

I looked at him.

'Who killed Paul Delaney?'

Lamp shook his head.

'I don't know.'

'Who tried to have me killed?'

'I don't know, truth be told.'

'That'd be a good idea. How do you think we'll get along with that?'

Lamp gave me that grin again, as if he knew he had to mark the joke without finding it in the slightest bit funny.

'Are you and Jack not seeing eye to eye, Lamp?'

'Not at all. Where'd you get that? Jack and I are solid. Serious, where'd you hear that?'

'Well, if you didn't send those boys after me, who did? Jack?

I thought you were supposed to handle that side of things for him. Come on, they were your boys, weren't they?'

'They weren't, end of. Tell me what you've heard about me and Jack.'

'It's only what everyone's saying. And you can't really blame them. I mean, if I owned a club, even a pretty skanky joint like the Viscount, I'd be a little taken aback if the chap I relied upon for protection went and shot it up. A little taken aback, and then, when I'd gotten over my understandable surprise, a trifle irked. I think.'

'That's . . . and I want you to tell them, Ollie and Dave. That was wrong. It should never have happened. I was out of me box that night, they were right to refuse me.'

'Is that an apology then?'

'It should never have happened.'

I laughed. Whenever the IRA botched an operation and slaughtered civilians, which was more often than not, or when they murdered them intentionally, which was not unusual, part of the Republican movement's strategy was to wheel out someone from Sinn Féin to deliver a brazen non-apology apology. It always took exactly the same form as Lamp's: blowing up that mother and her infant children was wrong. It should never have happened. (Implied was: but it's not our fault, it can't be, we have right on our side.) It was like saying to your wife, 'I'm sorry we had a row'. (Nothing to do with me, bitch.) Stood to reason Lamp had Republican form if he'd been Jack Cullen's right-hand-man all this time.

'No, and they're good to come back. Dessie and Liam too. I expect they'll be coming for the funeral, will they?'

Everyone suddenly seemed very interested in the return of the Delaney brothers: first Ray Moran, then George Halligan, now Lamp.

'I didn't see Jack around the Viscount last night,' I said. 'How would he have known I was there, or what I said? Devlin

91

and Cummins followed me directly. They would have been waiting outside for me the second I came out. No, it must have been Ray Moran. His master's voice.'

'Moran doesn't have that kind of authority,' Lamp said. 'But it's probably fair to say you were being watched. Modern technology, it's amazing how quickly word gets around.'

'So nobody knows who these boys were, but Ray Moran spots them picking me up anyway? And was that you then who had to clean it all up last night in the alley? Because the boys were still breathing when I left.'

Lamp grinned, for real this time it looked like.

'Well, that's what you say. And I believe you. But there's them as wouldn't be so sure. Them who'd be excited if they got a little present in the post, or by special delivery. A knife with Cummins' and Devlin's blood. And your prints on it. A good match too, not a partial.'

He'd led me up to it, but I hadn't seen it coming. I took a long draught of Guinness and nodded.

'Don't be that way, Ed.'

'Don't be what way? When someone is threatening to set me up for murder, what way should I be? I don't remember, Lamp, I got expelled from finishing school before they got to that bit. I can't walk across the room with a book on my head either. Tell me how I should be.'

'Ah here, now, this is exactly why I didn't, because I could have, brought it up in the first place. And others would have. It's, and the ten grand still stands, you can take five with you tonight. In fact . . .'

'In fact. That sounds promising. In fact, unless I take the money. . .'

'Exactly. "Unless." I knew you'd see it immediately.'

'Fuck you. That knife is not going to stand up in court. The chain of evidence has been broken, the Guards wouldn't even try and introduce it.'

Lamp couldn't stop grinning; now he practically chuckled.

'Well. First off, it's a pleasure talking to a man of intelligence for a change, a thoughtful man, instead of the fuckwits and cretins I'm thrown together with in an average day. Second, two things: if that knife were to be found at the scene by DI Pearson, the investigating officer – now, for example – they could claim it had been overlooked, or missed, or – and this is what I'd advise DI Pearson to assert – that he had instituted a second search, just in case.'

'The scene is no longer secured. The knife could have come from anywhere. It's bullshit.'

'Not necessarily. The killer dropped it down a drain nearby. DI Pearson's diligence, his never-say-die spirit led him back for a last look. The killer's DNA is on the weapon. But let's say you're right, Ed. You probably are. You strike me as the type of cunt who usually is. And fair enough, even if there are closed circuit photographs of you at or near the scene at that particular time – and I'm pretty sure there are – maybe that wouldn't be enough without the forensic evidence. So you wouldn't be on trial for murder, or even manslaughter, chances are. Which is good, I think, for you in anyway. What mightn't be so good, for a fellow whose way of life depends on making accommodations with the Guards, is every cop in this town knowing that you were there at the time those lads were killed, that you have scars suggesting you took a bit of a battering, and most important, that there's a knife with their blood and your prints all over it.'

That was when I knew he had me.

'Because of course, the Guards aren't going to string you up themselves, but they're not exactly big-chain-of-evidence merchants, the Guards – not deep down. Not when it comes to what they believe. And I think – and of course, I'm not a Guard, far from it, but I think they'd believe you were guilty. And leading on from that, I think every one of them, including your great mate DI Dave Donnelly, wouldn't hesitate – they'd take every opportunity to harass you, prevent you doing your job, badmouth you around town from high to low – and don't forget, young Simon and Dean had friends who might think seriously about avenging their deaths – I think they'd do everything they could to fuck you. And I think that's what you'd end up, Ed Loy – totally fucked.'

I I

The wheels might have been coming off the economy at a frantic rate, but you wouldn't have known a thing about it if the only place you ate your dinner was Shanahan's on the Green. Mind you, if you could afford to dine in Shanahan's Steakhouse every night, you probably didn't care: you'd stored up enough nuts to get you through however long the winter lasted. No one looked very happy on it, mind. In the cocktail bar downstairs, which was called The Oval Office, and boasted a lot of Irish-American memorabilia on the walls, as well as 'the original J.F.K. Rocking Chair from Air Force One', which had something to do with his lower back pain, or so I was told, expensive looking older men were grimly pouring champagne for hard faced younger women who glowed and purred with feigned enthusiasm. Shapeless men of my age with high complexions and bloated features and tragic hair were there with their wives; their women were polished and buffed and groomed, and looked exhausted and desperate and starved, smiling glassily as the shambles they had married shouted his way through some interminable non-anecdote about rugby or property at his shambles of a friend. What was all the money for, the women's despairing faces seemed to cry, if it couldn't keep you young, or let you live forever?

A very beautiful maitre d' with her wavy hair in barrettes who sounded Spanish came down to tell me my party were already seated above in the dining room and looked forward to my joining them. By then I had ordered a Martini, Tanqueray, straight up, with an olive and a twist of lemon, and I had my heart set on drinking it by myself before I joined the dance, not to mention feeling in serious need of it after my instructive encounter with Lamp Comerford, so I told her to say I was taking care of business and I'd be with them shortly. Donna Nugent was at my side before I'd taken another sip.

'I might have known, skulking at the bar! They *will* let you bring it to the table you know, they're Irish Americans, not Saudi Arabians. But no, Ed Loy always has to act like the designated knacker, doesn't he? Jesus, Mary and Joseph, what happened to your *ear*?'

This said as she kissed me on the mouth, gave my chest a tug and brushed the back of her hand across my crotch.

'Hi Donna,' I said. 'You're looking only gorgeous.'

She was too. Donna Nugent had black hair piled up at the front and falling long at the back in a nineteen-forties style, and her huge dark eyes were ringed with black shadow; her lips were pale and her face was full and unlined; she had something between a dimple and a double chin that she was very aware of and kept trying to hide by lifting her head and tossing her hair around; she looked like a little girl pretending to be a pony when she did this, and it always made me laugh. She was tall, about five ten in chunky forties-style heels, and wore a tight black skirt that fell to mid calf and black stockings and a black basque top, as she always did, and was carrying maybe a stone in weight around her bust and hips, which was not unusual; it made her look incredibly sexy, if you were a man, or fat, if you were a woman. Donna was very much a woman.

'Don't stare at me I know I *know* Diet Day One once we get this fucking *bridge* open and I'm not at the trough every Jasus night with this investor and that one I'll be living on rice cakes and Rooibos tea for a month and then you'll see. Skinny bitch. That'll be me.'

'I think you look great, Donna.'

'Fuck off and drink up, I need this job. Here, c'mere.'

Donna took my drink and sank half of it.

'Oh my God that's very good, that is Martinitastic, that's gone straight there. I have a suite in the Shelbourne, incidentally, and no excuses, understood? I don't care what you're after from Bobby, only don't make a show of me, but I want that up front, so to speak.'

'Whatever you say, Donna.'

She leant in and gave me a kiss then, pushing her tongue at mine, her eyes losing their focus for a moment. My eyes weren't the clearest either. Donna always smelt of musk and spice, and of some overwhelming eighties perfume like Opium.

'Later, dude,' she said.

I followed Donna's swaying behind up the stairs of the Georgian building and in to the main dining room, which had all the ceiling roses and the chandeliers and the floor-to-ceiling sash windows and the period mantelpieces and the great gilt-framed mirrors you'd hope for if you wanted to impress on visiting Americans that Dublin had once been a great eighteenth-century city. You could have gone further by pointing out how, because Ireland sat out the Second World War for reasons that are not always clear even to Irish people and certainly to no one else, but that had something to do with not deeming it possible, or at least, wise, to fight alongside the British having fought against them less than twenty years before, even if the enemy was the greatest menace to world freedom, including Ireland's, ever known, there were few bombs dropped on Dublin, so the architectural fabric of that great Georgian city was still intact up until the nineteen sixties when, flush at last with a bit of inward investment, we decided to haul down as much of the colonial oppressor's heritage as we could manage before anyone objected and lash up as many hideous blocks of our own as we could muster, in the name of modernity, progress and independence. But the money soon ran out, and buildings like this managed to survive long enough for us to realize that they belonged to us after all, and were more than worth preserving. I could see eighteenth-century prints on the walls that may have been Hogarth's *Marriage A-la-Mode* sequence, I couldn't see clearly enough, and I had a quick flash of Jack Cullen's Viscount club the previous night: compare and contrast, write on one side of the paper only.

Before we reached our table, Donna turned to me and said:

'Your job is to keep Dee Dee happy. And how does anyone do that? By crawling up her *hole*.'

Thus it was that Bobby Doyle's first impression of me was of a grinning idiot evidently so delighted to be out and about in a fancy restaurant that he couldn't stop giggling.

'Tall Happy Irish Guy!' announced a perfectly groomed slender blonde woman of about fifty in a slow, braying sing-song American accent, as if she were talking to a table full of pre-school children. This, I was told, was Rory McBride; her husband Martin, a pink, balding fellow of about the same age with a ginger-grey moustache and a genial beam on his round face, was an old colleague of Bobby Doyle's from San Francisco. Bobby Doyle sat opposite me, a gaunt, expressionless man with a perfectly shaved head; quiet authority lay behind his glittering eyes; he lifted his hands to me and looked at me directly, a greeting pitched somewhere between an invitation and a warning: sing for your supper and watch your step.

Dee Dee, his wife, was another perfectly groomed slender blonde in her fifties, but her look was a little more opulent than Rory's: white gold at the neck and left wrist, pearl silk dress a little lower cut, breast enhancement a lot more pronounced.

On top of which, she favoured the burnished orange complexion especially beloved of Irish women of all classes, no matter what their colouring, and enough make-up on top of that to make her glow in the dark. Before I could start crawling, Donna leant into me and, in a stage whisper audible two tables away, but which no one at our table affected to hear, said: 'Fuck sake, "Rory", what is the matter with Americans and names? Yeah, yeah, we love the way you're so innovative and new frontier and who do you want to be today, but Rory is a fucking boy's name, okay? And while we're at it, Kelly is a surname, and Shannon is a fucking river. It's Just Wrong!'

'I'm not going to have to separate you two, am I?' said Bobby Doyle, his accent a very mild Northern Irish, Donegal or Derry maybe. He smiled then, the merest quiver of his lips and a flash of his eyes. Donna clapped a hand over her mouth and pantomimed a vow of silence. Rory and Martin made laughing faces without actually laughing; they clearly knew Donna of old.

Rory said, 'Donna is so funny,' as if it were a genetic disorder that civilized people bred out of themselves.

'Do you know what you want, Mr Loy?' Dee Dee asked me in a solemn, wide-eyed manner. Dee Dee smelt strongly of lavender, and had an affected, fluting, over-elocuted accent through which little barbs of Dublin occasionally protruded, and she gave the impression of always being just a little behind the joke, although there was a shrewdness in her pop eyes that made me suspect this was just what she'd like you to believe, and that you'd do well not to underestimate her.

'Does any of us know what we want, deep down, Dee Dee?' I said. Dee Dee popped her wide eyes even wider and put her hand to her mouth, as if I'd propositioned her, as if, indeed, I'd asked to crawl up her hole. She gave a girlish giggle.

'I'm going to have to keep a close eye on you, I can see,' she said happily.

As I scanned my menu, I saw Donna dealing me a nod of approval. I ordered – there was steak or forget about it, essentially – and the menus, which had no prices on them, were taken away. Two bottles of champagne arrived, and when the wine – Veuve Clicquot – was poured, Martin McBride got to his feet and then, after a nudge from his wife, sat down again, cleared his throat and began to speak.

'Friends, it's always good to be back in Ireland, back in the old country, as we don't say much any more, but perhaps should. Because it is the old country so many of us sprang from, and though we've chosen a new world to continue our onward voyage, we come back to the port we set out from, the harbour of refuge that is Ireland, that is the great and ancient city of Dublin.'

Donna Nugent gave a little whoop here, and Bobby Doyle cracked a smile, and leant across and said something quietly to McBride. Donna meanwhile passed me a place-setting name card, on the reverse of which she had written 'A Hunderd Dallars!' It referred to McBride's accent, which was a classic Irish-American stew of mangled vowel sounds and diction that managed to be staccato and drawling at the same time. The wave of Irish emigrants that left for the USA in the eighties rarely altered their accents; that was considered altogether too Paddyish, an Ancient Order of Hibernians type of thing to do. The rare ones who did quickly became figures of fun; I can remember Donna bumping into an old schoolfriend of hers in a bar in North Beach, and turning to me later to say, in disbelief: 'She's turned into an Irish American.' 'A hunderd dallars' was the expression Donna coined for an Irish arrival who had gone native with indecent haste. I wrote the ritual response, 'Down on deh taybill' on the card and passed it back.

'Now I don't want to hog the floor,' McBride said.

'Oh Martin you do,' his wife said.

'And I know it's a cliché for the returned Yank to start wittering on about history and he's barely out of the airport. But I think I can be forgiven for invoking the term historic on this occasion, as we approach Easter Monday, that moveable anniversary of the 1916 rising, which this year is to be memorable for another reason: the opening of a great construction which exemplifies and celebrates all that is great about Irish independence, the first volleys for which were heard way back in the revolution of 1916: a bridge, friends, a bridge from the past to the present, a bridge in the name of God and the dead generations of Irishmen and Irishwomen, a bridge between those who chose the new world but will not set the old aside and those who have returned to the old world to build it anew. Friends – and I mean friends – it's the vision, the obsession, and finally the life's work of one great Irishman. I give you Bobby Doyle and the Independence Bridge!'

We clapped and drank the toast. Doyle looked neither flattered nor embarrassed. Rory made a half-hearted attempt to get him to respond, but he seemed to dismiss the idea with a small wave of his hand. I was waiting for a look from Donna, an indication that at the very least, she found what we had just sat through a little on the ripe side. But Donna's eyes were set to survey at medium, and her smile was fixed and official. Fair enough. She worked for Doyle. Everyone had to eat. Just when it seemed like the moment had passed, Bobby Doyle began to speak. He used that high status trick of starting in a very low, undemonstrative voice, so that his audience had to lean in fast, in a mounting panic, already fearing they might have missed the best bit, maybe the bit where they're singled out for thanks and praise.

'. . . and I don't make any great claims for what I do. I see myself as a builder – there's no fake humility about that, it's what I've always been, whether it's houses for the local authority or a bridge across a river, I'm a builder first and last. And

I've done it because I was looking after Number One in the first instance. If there wasn't any money in it, I wasn't interested. And it's still the same today. But I've always loved my country. And I've always wanted to do what's right by it. And thanks in large part to my friend here, Martin McBride, who backed me when I – I was going to say, when I couldn't get arrested in this country, but that wouldn't be strictly true—'

This remark was greeted with a lot of knowing laughter. Dee Dee's eyes darted around the company, her glassy smile that of the prude who wants to make it clear that she gets the dirty joke, but dissociates herself from it, her white gold charm bracelet rattling as she fanned herself with her extended left hand.

'Anyway, Martin McBride saw something in me – I don't know what exactly, I've always been afraid to ask him – but let's just say, I hope I didn't let him down. My friend and partner Seán's still beyond in San Fran, the company we built there's thriving and surviving. I've come back here and, with Martin's help, we've built something together that . . . let's put it this way, there's civic receptions and lunches for architects and what have you all over Easter in aid of Independence Bridge. I'm eating for Ireland, I can tell you. This is the smallest gathering I'm having by far, but it's the dearest to me. This is for people I trust – with my life, if I had to. Raise your glasses – to Ireland! Sláinte go léir!'

As we drank, it seemed to me that Bobby Doyle was staring directly, pointedly, in my direction. I returned his gaze, and he nodded and looked towards Donna Nugent; when I turned to Donna, she smiled, but the smile was for Bobby Doyle, not for me.

The starters came, and I got into a long, one-sided conversation with Dee Dee Doyle about charity balls, and which disease attracted what kind of crowd, or 'social profile' as Dee Dee put it, and as a result netted the best yield for the charity concerned. Aids was over, Rory, who did the same kind of thing in San Francisco, chipped in, and Dee Dee agreed; unless you linked it to Africa, and you didn't want to do that unless you could get Bono, or at least Geldof – not that it wasn't worthy, just that it could end up mixing the messages. Nowadays, rare diseases were very big: cystic fibrosis, Guillain-Barré syndrome. But cancer was the big one, Dee Dee and Rory agreed. People had an investment in cancer. Cancer was always going to top the charts. Dee Dee actually said this, and then, looking at me, recognized the absurdity of what she had said, rolled her eyes and burst out laughing. She had a dirty, Dublin laugh, a cackle with banshee grace notes; it was a laugh that evidently embarrassed her, and she popped her hand over her mouth to convey this to me; I warmed to her greatly on the strength of it. A woman's laugh rarely lies, not if it's true; a man has spent half his life bellowing at bullshit with the lads till it gets so laughter is just another loud roar he makes.

I ate the rest of my starter – Jumbo Shrimp Cocktail with a lot of bread for soakage – listening to Bobby Doyle and Martin McBride expounding on the property downturn: the cycle was nearly at the bottom, it was time to buy, and buy big, because there was only one direction values were heading, and that was up, the people who had to sell now, well, that was their bad: step up and get the bargains before someone else did, or the market turned. Business is business: either you're winning or the other cunt is, as George Halligan put it. My champagne glass was empty and I dodged a refill, instead drinking a lot of water; there were bottles of St Émilion on the table that Donna, who had been conferring with the waiter and the sommelier throughout, had ordered; I was looking forward to a glass of that with my steak frîtes. Just before the steaks were served, Donna rose and swapped seats with Bobby Doyle. Doyle poured red wine into my glass and quietly said:

'So you think I might have murdered Brian Fogarty? And you thought it was good manners to put it up to me on a night like this, a night with family and friends, to take advantage of your friend Donna's good nature? Just as well Donna has my best interests at heart, isn't it?'

That shook me, as Dubliners say. I hadn't told Donna about the Fogarty case. She hadn't asked why I was nosing around after her boss. But I might have guessed, given how well she knew me, that she would take whatever precautions were necessary. I caught her eye across the table where she was nodding in emphatic agreement with something Martin McBride was saying, and she gave me a little wave and waggled her tongue at me. You're welcome.

'I wasn't exactly going to "put anything up to you". And I don't think you killed anyone.'

'That's not what Donna heard.'

'Well, Donna didn't hear everything. Donna, as we know, is something more than human, but she's not been granted omniscience, not yet, at any rate. Although I'm sure she's working on it.'

'I don't think she's too far off, too be honest with you.'

'Well, I hope it'll be taken into account in her remuneration package.'

'I pay her more than I do myself as it is.'

The steaks arrived, and we devoted ourselves to them for a while in relative silence. Mine was a 12 oz filet mignon, cooked rare to blue; I noticed Bobby Doyle glance at my plate and wince at the blood; he was eating a well done rib eye on the bone. The wine was very good, but I took it slowly; it had been a long day, and it wasn't over yet.

'I know all about you, Edward Loy,' Doyle said once we'd got to the pushing food about our plates stage. You had to hand it to him, he had a flair for the dramatic conversational opener.

'Is that so? I don't know very much about you at all,' I said.

'I know what you've done here: John Dawson, the Howard case, F.X. Tyrrell and his brother the priest at Leopardstown – live on TV, that was a good one – you're not exactly hiding your light under a bushel, are you? Can't be much of a help in keeping your detective work private.'

'Small country. I get by.'

'I don't doubt that. See, I know about you from before, as well, Ed Loy. I know about you when you were in LA, when you were tailing up and down the coast after our Donna here. I know about the Henderson case.'

The Hendersons lived in Cole Valley, near the Haight, in San Francisco. Brendan Henderson was an attorney at 30 Articles, a law firm specializing in human rights cases, and his wife Amy wrote a cookery column for the *San Francisco Chronicle* and looked after their two small children. When she didn't look after their two small children, fourteen-year-old Suzi Berger, a neighbour's child, babysat. She came on holidays with them. It was like she was a part of the family. She was only fourteen, but she was mature for her age, and her family circumstances weren't great: her father had left, and her mother drank. Suzi practically lived in. It was a great situation both ways. Suzi wanted to be a journalist and Amy had given her a lot of help with her writing. Suzi had real promise. And then a friend of Amy's said she thought she had seen Brendan and Suzi in a car together at Big Sur. It was only a fleeting glimpse, so she couldn't be sure. And Brendan had been at a residential human rights conference 30 Articles had hosted in Berkeley that weekend. And Suzi had never been to Big Sur, but would love to go. And Amy wasn't the kind of woman who got jealous, and my God, the whole thing was such a cliché, but looking back things hadn't been quite right between her and Brendan for a while, and she'd even noticed a kind of reserve, an awkwardness that had developed in Suzi. But she was probably just imagining it.

She wasn't just imagining it. I installed wireless covert pinhole video cameras the size of quarters in every room in their house and connected the receiver to a VCR in Amy Henderson's home office. It didn't take long. Seeing her husband fucking the babysitter in the marital bed was one thing, but watching her blow him on the floor of their ten-year-old daughter's room was probably what finished her. She confronted him, and he broke down, and confessed, and apologized, and begged for forgiveness. She confronted Suzi, and at first Suzi tried to play it like The Other Woman, like some scheming bitch she had seen on a daytime soap. But then she lost it: she started to wail, and knead and nuzzle a soft toy, a pink and purple kangaroo that had seen better days. That was when Amy Henderson decided she was going to the cops.

And that was when I got a call from Donna Nugent. I had run into Donna a few months earlier, down in LA, and we had hit it off. I didn't know it, but she had recommended me to Amy Henderson. I never really got the full picture clear in my head, but from what I understood, a couple of lawyers at 30 Articles had done some work on behalf of a couple of Irish men the British authorities wanted to extradite in connection with IRA terrorist activity, work that kept them in the USA. Brendan Henderson was the most prominent and able of these lawyers. There were many within the Irish American community who felt that, in those days before the peace process in Northern Ireland, they could ill afford to lose such a man. In any case, they said, the babysitter was nearly fifteen, and look at her, any man would have taken her for twenty-five, and any red-blooded man would have taken her, no need to lose the head altogether, even if it was San Francisco. A divorce could be arranged and paid for, and Amy would own the house outright, and this was what Donna Nugent had been sent to say to me. Along with the strong implication that things might not look good for me in terms at very least of my PI licence, if I was unable to persuade Amy Henderson to accept these terms.

And what I said to Donna Nugent boiled down to six words: you didn't see the soft toy.

And Donna Nugent burst into tears.

And Amy Henderson went to the cops, and her husband went to jail, and I went back to LA and never thought much about it again until now.

'You know, that was when I hired Donna, the Henderson case,' Doyle said. 'She was working for a friend of mine at the time. There were a few of us in the room. Donna made her report, and . . . well, let's just say the consensus was for giving you a very strong warning indeed, the kind of warning you'd be keen to pass on to Mrs Henderson.'

I shook my head.

'Wouldn't've worked,' I said.

Doyle looked at my left ear, which I could feel throbbing and burning more and more as the evening progressed, and grinned.

'Not on you, maybe. But the evidence of it might well have persuaded Mrs Henderson. Anyway, that was the consensus, and then Donna said it was wrong to think of the babysitter as older than her years, and she mentioned the wee pink and purple soft toy. A kitten, was it?'

'A kangaroo.'

'That's right. So I said, listen lads – and there was some right bad lads in that room, I can tell you – I said, listen lads, we might be fighting for Irish freedom, but it's no type of freedom to turn a blind eye to the degrading of an innocent child. And that was that.'

'So I've you to thank.'

'I wouldn't look at it that way.'

'I don't intend to. So what were you then, officer commanding of the San Francisco IRA?'

Bobby Doyle grimaced with irritation, and ran a hand over the dome of his glowing head.

'You southerners, you're all the same, it's always black and white with yous: are you now, or have you ever been? Are you in or out? For most people it was never as simple as that. You have to understand, in the seventies, there was soldiers on the streets, a majority that didn't want to share power and didn't see why it should, the loyalists gangs were legal, for, for . . . Pete's sake. It was a different time. Now, I was never, as it happens, a member of the IRA. I never fired a gun, I never planted a bomb, I never even threw a stone. Did I understand why shots were fired and stones were flung? Aye right, I did. Did I look the other way when a mark was singled out in a pub? Did I identify a car that could be stolen for a job? Did I let a fellow change his clothes in my house, even stop over night till he saw how the land lay? I certainly did. But eventually . . . you know, that's as much as I'd say. When you're in the thick of it, it's just the way things are. But when you step back, you understand, people are being slaughtered and nothing is changing. That's when I got out. I can't even remember which straw was the last one, someone's granny shot, someone's kids blown to bits. It was no use. And it stayed no use for a long time.'

'But you were in San Francisco, helping to harbour the people who were making it no use.'

'If you want to exert an influence, you have to get involved. You can sit back and keep your hands clean and your motives pure and achieve fuck all, safe and smug in your judgment of who's right and who's wrong. Or you can get stuck in and try and change people's minds – the kind of people who don't like changing their minds – and of course you're going to get your hands dirty. You're going to go out on a limb for some sectarian sociopath who shot up a bar full of Protestant labourers and is now running guns via Miami into Rosslare harbour, and campaign on his behalf as if he's Nelson Mandela. You know it's shite, and you know three quarters of the people who are campaigning alongside you know it's shite too, only a lot of them would be delighted to see those guns go back up to Belfast and take out the Prods he didn't plug the last time, but you keep the faith. Because Enniskillen happens, and even the mad dogs get a bit sickened at that, and the *Eksund* happens, and we know there's a spy in the ranks, and the penny begins to drop with more than the few of us who've known all along that the war is unsustainable, not just in military, but in human terms.'

On Remembrance Day, 8 November 1987, the IRA detonated a bomb near the Cenotaph in Enniskillen, killing twelve civilians and wounding hundreds. A couple of weeks earlier, the *Eksund*, a ship carrying a deadly cargo of AK-47s, grenades, rocket launchers, SAM-7 ground-to-air missiles, assorted machine guns, 106 millimetre cannons, a million rounds of ammunition and two tons of Semtex was on its way from Tripoli to Ireland. The weapons were intended to launch a 'Tet Offensive', a spectacular and ferocious onslaught that would drive the British out of Ireland once and for all. The steering failed off the coast of Brittany, and the crew evacuated. However, when they went about triggering the timing device to blow the craft up and sink it, they discovered the firing unit had been sabotaged. The *Eksund* was discovered, and the weapons traced, and the IRA's last half-realistic plan for victory had been scuppered.

'So what were you then, an outrider for the peace process?'

'I don't know if I'd go that far.'

'I thought you already had.'

The waitress took our dinner plates away. Dee Dee was

bucking to speak to me, indeed, had started to say something about a Multiple Sclerosis Gala at the National Concert Hall and did I think I might bring someone, but before I could turn, Bobby Doyle flicked a hand in her direction and she faded dutifully away.

'Just remind me,' he said. 'Because I've been busy, and I'm at an age when I'm apt to forget things. Just when was it I was supposed to have killed this Brian Fogarty fellow?'

'I'm looking into Brian Fogarty's killing in 1991. Before his death, he was preparing reports on three individuals whose tax affairs didn't seem in order. You're one of them. That provides you with a motive.'

'Who are the other two?'

'I'll let you find that out yourself. You seem to have better sources than I do anyway.'

Bobby Doyle smiled.

'Is it enough to say I didn't do it?'

'It's a start. Of course, the kind of people you knew, maybe someone did it on your behalf.'

'And never showed up looking for payback? I've never had the good fortune to run into those kind of people, as it happens. Where do they live?'

Rory McBride's cawing voice suddenly soared above the table and pounced on her host.

'Bobby, do we not get a look in here? We've come a long way to see you and what do you do, spend the whole meal with Tall Happy Irish Guy. And see, he's not even happy any more.'

Bobby Doyle rose to his feet, grinning.

'You've come a long way, baby!' he crooned, Sinatra style, as he circled the table and brought Rory to her feet and, much to her apparent delight, waltzed in place with her for a moment.

There was a flurry of puddings and coffees and digestifs, but the evening was dwindling down. I spent ten minutes with

Martin McBride, who was very earnest about Ireland, past, present and future. You would never have guessed from his words about how invaluable the work of Sinn Féin had been that the peace process only became possible when the IRA agreed to stop killing people who didn't agree with them, and that, had they not started killing them in the first place, there might have been something resembling peace all along. But I guess he would have called that my bias, and maybe Bobby Doyle had a point: maybe I was happier being right than I was trying to persuade the people who were wrong to change.

Donna and Bobby Doyle spent five minutes together in close colloquy, Donna with her Blackberry, looking like she was taking instruction. While this was going on, Dee Dee Doyle passed me a business card. It had her mobile and private home numbers, her name and the single word Events printed on it. On the reverse, there was a message written in eyebrow pencil: *Call me. I get so lonely.* I turned to her immediately, reflexively, taken aback by the boldness of this; she seemed fixed on something Rory was telling her about beachfront real estate in Maine, and wouldn't catch my eye.

When Bobby Doyle and Rory McBride started gently lilting 'Raglan Road' Donna Nugent stood bolt upright as if by prearranged signal, nodded at me and bade everyone the extravagant farewells she ritually bestowed on old friends or new conquests alike. We were on the street in seconds. We didn't speak as we walked. I didn't notice any unmarked blue saloon cars following me, or cops in pairs looking on, but that didn't mean they weren't there. I checked my messages on the way: the Delaney brothers would get in late on Good Friday night, with Paul's removal to take place on Holy Saturday. Lamp Comerford wanted me to know Ray Moran would be working in his office on Pembroke Road all through Saturday. And Anne Fogarty hoped I was all right, and said she hadn't been entirely straight with me, and wanted to meet me on Saturday so she could explain. Her voice pricked my conscience, as if we had already started something and I was just about to betray it. Before I could get any further with that train of thought, halted at the Dawson Street crossing, Donna Nugent pulled me hard against her and pushed her tongue into my mouth and bit hard on my lower lip until I could taste blood and ground herself against my cock until I felt the aching weight of it and I couldn't think of anything else except the salt and musk glow of her, and nothing would do me until I had her.

The lights changed, and she pulled back her head and saw the haze of lust in my eyes and laughed, baring her teeth, and ran across the road, her heels clattering on the wet stones, and I ran after her, blind to everything but our destination, lost in the delirium of our heated blood.

III

Good Friday

The Shelbourne Hotel.
   We stayed a second night.
   I don't want to talk about it.

Dublin – M1 to Belfast, 9 November 1980
The Coyle Family

Gerry Coyle

Jesus, the roads here are the pits, I'd forgotten. Potholes and cracks and big wedges of tarmacadam where they laid cable or a water pipe and haven't even bothered rolling it flat. No wonder Unionists think the South is a shambles. Cheek of us, we've a country where it takes a year to get a fucking telephone installed but we think they should see sense at last and decide their future's safe with us. And if mass unemployment, no infrastructure, all-round incompetence and politics in thrall to the Catholic Church doesn't tempt you, surely the IRA blowing seven shades of shite out of you will turn the balance. We're some fucking clowns. Now. That's the kind of rant better in than out, at least where Claire is concerned. Keep it for the pub love, she'd say. And mind which pub it is.

Excellent weekend, all things considered. All right, the match was a disappointment, nil-all to Notts Forest, but what could you expect after mid-week, four nil, Aberdeen totally outclassed, Battle of Britain my hole! The boys looked tired but happy, always good to see them in the flesh, Phil Neal and King Kenny, even Hansen got a goal on Wednesday. Don't know what Paisley says to them, but it's working. Third European Cup in May, just have a feeling. You say that every season, Claire'd say. And then sooner or later I'll be right.

Fair enough, Luke was a bit disappointed, long way to come and his first live match and then no goals. But he's just got to get used to suffering like the rest of us. What does he think football is, entertainment? He could have it a lot worse, he could have inherited Chelsea, or Man United. But we mustn't mock the afflicted.

Claire didn't mind the weekend, I think. She knew it was important for Paul, after Nicky's funeral and everything. Poor little guy, Luke and him were like that. And I think Claire got on with . . . Robbie's wife, shit, why can't I remember the names of my friends' wives, it's not as if they're always trading them in. Alison, Claire got on with Alison. Touch and go there I reckoned on Friday night, Alison's . . . got a mouth on her sure enough. But they seemed to hit it off. Opposites attract. There's enough shopping in the boot anyway, if that's anything to judge. Wouldn't have thought the prices are any different to Belfast. No, they said, with one voice, that gleeful way women have when they know you're wrong and they're right, but the shops are! Jigsaw, was that one of them? Don't remember. Anyway, they were probably in better spirits after the match than we were.

Yeah, Claire had an all right time. Just, I don't understand why we can't stop off in Dublin for an hour or two, catch up with the old crowd. Well, I do understand, I just don't think it's fair, and I'm just working very hard not to bring it up again. Because I'll have three pints instead of the two I've promised because Barney or Darragh or Niall will have a third on the table before the second is half done and everyone's having such great crack and I'll be into the third one before I've noticed or because I've no self-control and it's not fair to expect her to keep on eye on me like she's my mammy and then she'll have to drive and she doesn't like driving this car. A 1967 Jaguar Mark 2 3.8 litre, and she doesn't like driving it. Still. Maybe she's right. Home earlier. Nip out for a quick jar with the papers. Get back, she'll be rested up, round the weekend off with a ride if we're lucky. Too pissed for anything last night, and well grumpy about it she was, so fingers crossed she'll have held that thought. Something to look forward to. Things could be worse.

Claire Coyle

There he is, sulking, I don't even have to open my eyes to hear the ostentatiously heavy breathing that denotes heroic self-restraint on his part. He should know rightly why we're not stopping. There we'd be, having sat through an hour of stories about who has the worse hangover and whose party didn't end until three the following afternoon and who got stranded naked on a bog road after a Rory Gallagher gig and what gas crack it all was and then he'd look over at me with his eyes all droopy, the way he does when he wants something, like a kid, and I'd see another pint in front of him, one of his hilarious mates has slipped it to him, don't tell the little woman, as if driving your family home a hundred miles drunk out of your mind is just another gas story to tell in the pub, he knows this car handles too heavy for me, or at least, does over that distance, I warned him, and he's looking at me like I'm his Mammy, please, can I? God, the sex just drops off him when he does that. Wee bit of self-control, wee bit of no, I'll have a rock shandy, I've responsibilities here and I'd sit for as long as it took, through one interminable drinking story after another, and be ready to hop on him afterwards first chance I got, still fancy the arse off him so I do, even if it's better to keep him guessing on that score. Keep them guessing girls, keep them guessing. But when he gives me that look – will you drive us home? Will you take charge? Will you look after me? Before the kids came, sometimes I thought it was cute, thought it was a bit of a turn-on, him giving me the big soft eyes, like he needed looking after, like a wee boy. But I have a wee boy, I don't want my man carrying on like that. Not any more. It's anything but a turn-on is what it is. Still. Was looking forward to it last night. Strange bed, few drinks, got a nice flimsy little thing or two in Next to surprise him, Alison's idea that was. Come in from the bathroom with them on to be greeted with snores. Gerry the whale. Maybe if we're not too wrecked by the time we get home. Of course, knowing him, he'll think he deserves a few pints for all his arduous driving, and he'll stay out too long and I'll be asleep when he gets home and no one will be satisfied. God, would you listen? Pity about us.

Poor Luke. No, not 'Poor Luke', God, I have to break that habit, we're all tiptoeing around him as if he's an unexploded bomb, oh God forgive me did I just say that? I can't believe I even thought it, an unexploded bomb, Jesus. Have to breeze along as if everything's normal, that's what the psychologist says, be there for him if he wants to talk, or equally if he doesn't. Don't try and push him into it, or keep asking him if he's all right in a tone of voice that sounds as if you think he isn't, and you're just waiting for him to burst into tears. He's an eight-year-old boy, and he's a wee man, and his best friend since high babies was blown to bits, and there's no right or wrong way for him to feel or to show or not show what he feels. The wee soul.

Thank God Yvonne is so strong. Never a peep out of her when Luke was getting all the attention. I think she enjoyed the weekend though, enjoyed Alison's wee one, Lynsey. Lively young one. Maybe on the fast side. Make-up at twelve. Up to Alison. Mind you, Alison's on the fast side also, that story she told about Robbie's friend at the Christmas party . . . it was a good laugh, but still . . . God, sometimes I feel like such a prude, maybe I am a prude . . . anyway, no harm done, sure Yvonne's a bit overprotected as it is, she saw a bit of life I suppose. If she had that on her doorstep every day, it might be another matter. But Belfast's not exactly overflowing with life these days, is it?

Yvonne Coyle

SO amazing. I mean, so amAZING! Like 'Don't Stand So Close To Me'. Except for real. I suppose Lynsey might have been spoofing, but I don't think so. But Lynsey's gorgeous, and she looks at least fourteen, and Belinda Forbes said Emily Parker did it when she was fourteen with a student she met at a Queens' Student Union disco. Students! God! I don't know that Mum took to Lynsey, I could see her eyeing her, that way she has where she's smiling but it looks like she's bitten her tongue. And she was wearing make-up and her hair was dyed blonde. I know what Mum would say if we saw a girl who looked like that in Belfast. A bit common, that's what she'd say. A bit v-u-l-g-a-r. Mind you, Lynsey's Mum. I mean. Not just the make-up, but the hair, the size of the hair. And that laugh. Not really like any of Mum's friends. But then, by the Saturday, Mum was laughing the same way. As if . . . well, as if they were making jokes about You Know What. S-E-X. God! And then in Next, Mum and Lynsey's Mum in the underwear department, laughing away – more of a cackle, really. SO embarrassing. Making a show of themselves, so they were, but the assistants seemed to think it was great crack altogether. I couldn't look! Lynsey just rolled her eyes, like it was too boring. Got to let your hair down every now and then, Mum said to me. I think she was a bit embarrassed. She looked all shiny, the way she does when Dad gets her to have a second glass of wine.

Imagine doing it with a teacher! Not that I want to. So disgusting! Not that I don't want to at all, I just . . . Mum says I'm too young to think about boys. But I do think about them. Not old men though, not teachers. Students! God, students, that's different. Some of the boys Daddy teaches are dreamy. *And if he had a motorbike. A trials bike, that's what Belinda Forbes said, but I don't know what that is. That's cause your Dad's from Dublin, Belinda Forbes said, you don't understand our unique motorcycling culture in the province here. Maybe I don't. But I could learn. I don't think motorbikes are common. And even if they are, who's to judge? Not so sure Mum is any more, if she's going to be Lynsey's Mum's best friend and laugh like that . . .*

'Please don't stand so close to me . . . '

Luke Coyle

Match was really boring. Crowd was good but. 'You'll Never Walk Alone', just like on TV. Swore a lot so they did, really bad swears, every second word was cunt or fuck or arsehole. Dad just grinned, like I was used to it. How would he know? I am used to it. But he doesn't know that.

After the match was good though, MacDonald's, I had two Big Macs! Wonder how they make that sauce. Deadly so it is. Even if you knew, you probably couldn't make it at home, like chipper chips. Then in the pub with Dad and his friend. Call me Robbie, roight? Bought me Shoot *and* Goal *and 2000 AD and three Cokes. Because the match was so boring, or because of Nicky. I heard Dad telling him about Nicky in that voice he uses, very sad but kind of important, as if this is not something that's happened to everyone. Then they were talking on about university stuff. Call Me Robbie teaches the same as Dad except in Liverpool, electrical engineering. Or electronic. Dad explained the difference, but I can't remember it. Call Me Robbie's from Dublin too, sounds the same as Dad. Roight. Take it easy. Excellent. Sound like they're half asleep. Call Me Robbie's wife isn't like Mum though.*

Big tits. Huge tits.

I saw her bra. You couldn't not, it was black under her white blouse, and over it too, at the buttons. You couldn't not see it.

Dad saw me looking, winked at me.

What's that supposed to mean?

Went out for food before we started back. Brunch, that's what Call Me Robbie said it was. Four sausages two fried eggs chips bacon black and white pudding no fried bread or soda farls ketchup liver if you wanted it but I didn't and two sausages Yvonne didn't want because she's on a diet since when I think that was because of Lynsey you could nearly see up Lynsey's skirt it was that short and beans and mushrooms. Not as good as an Ulster Fry, but it wasn't bad.

Heard Mum talking to Lynsey's Mum about Nicky then.

I wish they'd give it up.

I wish I could tell them.

Only thing I'm sad about, he didn't have Adam and Stuart with him, the three of them'd be gone and good riddance.

How did you feel?

Relief. That's what I'm not allowed say.

Wasn't my fault.

Nicky passing notes to me every day in school after I sat with Craig this term. You're DEAD after school.

Tried to shrug it off, but he kept on about it.

So we had a fight, and I floored him.

Then walking home, Adam and Stuart got me by the railway lane, kicked me in the balls and rubbed dog shit in my face and hair. Washed it off without Mum knowing.

Then I was too scared to do anything, because I knew Nicky's brothers would get me.

Every day, the notes. You're dead after. Signed Killer.

I'd pretend I was sick in my stomach.

I used to get sent home because the pains in my stomach were making me cry.

Everyone knew.

No one did anything. They were all scared of Adam and Stuart. Once they made someone who tried to fight back eat his own shite. That story's true. Everyone knew it.

Everyone knew all of it. Except Mum and Dad.

Dad didn't have a clue. Neither did Mum. Worse. She was great friends with Nicky's Mum. Always asking me, why don't we get Nicky over at the weekend. Why don't we bring Nicky to the zoo.

Don't want to. Don't know. Just don't.

Every night I prayed: please make it stop.

And then Nicky went up the shops at big break, against the rules, and he got caught in a car bomb blast.

All the school turned out for the funeral. The wee white coffin. And I was up there with my Mum near the family, because our Mums were such great friends. Because we were such great friends.

No one at school let on. Even Adam and Stuart, they just went along with it. They're not after me any more. I was Nicky's best friend since forever. How must I be feeling about the little guy?

I'm supposed to feel sad. But I don't. He made my life a misery. And now it isn't any more. Now he's not here.

It's not my fault.

I felt relieved.

Almost happy.

Don't be afraid of the dark . . .

Hungry now.

I wonder if we'll stop off for a bite along the way.

Sausages and egg and chips . . .

IV

Holy Saturday

IV

Holy Saturday

12

Dessie Delaney shifted in his seat, but there was only so much shifting you could do when you were sat alongside a fat fuck like his brother. The waves of heat coming off him now, beer sweat and sunburn and worse. Unbelievable Liam ever got laid at all, let alone as often as he did. Course, it helps if you don't give a shite what you're sticking it into. Six hour delay in Athens airport they had, so of course Liam is lorrying back the pints bigtime, crying, actually crying, me little brother Paul, someone's going to pay, all this, desperate maudlin Paddy Irishman shite, Dessie can't listen to another word of it, and suddenly there's this enormous orange one in purple Lycra and black leggings and dyed black hair in a top knot with *pigtails* who was on the island, a regular in the bar, Liam was doing her whenever her husband's back was turned, that is, whenever he was mouldy with the gargle, which was pretty much all the time, he was a Stella-after-breakfast merchant. Dessie turns away to let them say whatever the fuck it is they have to say to each other, the mind boggles, and when he turns back haven't the pair of them have vanished, into a disabled toilet Liam tells Dessie later, plenty of room in there, you'd fucking need it the pair of you, Dessie doesn't say, Jasus. Across the gantry in the mirror behind the optics, Dessie could see the purple one's husband, all red faced and beery, adrift among his bickering children, four or five of them clamoring for his attention, or each other's, or somebody's.

Time was, Dessie would have got upset. He didn't know Liam was such a shagger when he went out first – hadn't seen him for years, had only been a kid when he'd left. And Liam had done him a favour letting him into the business in the first place, Dessie was just out of rehab, true, but he'd been in lousy shape, if it hadn't been for Sharon, she just pitched straight in, cooking, cleaning, serving behind the bar, no one like Sharon for work. Dessie'd been worried Sharon would take against Liam when she saw what he was like – he'd been worried he'd take against him himself. She had told Dessie once if he ever stepped out of line she'd cut it off and film him bleeding to death so she could watch it every Christmas as an after-dinner treat. But Sharon said Liam was different. For a start, Liam had no kids, and then there was the fact that Rita, his wife, was a lazy-arsed wagon who spent all her time flying back to Ireland to take care of her hypochondriac mother who was always on the point of dying but never fucking did, and all her time in bed when she was here, because she 'suffered from her nerves', which Sharon said was an old-style medically-approved way of being a lazy-arsed wagon. Anyhow, in some way Dessie couldn't quite figure but wasn't allowed to resent, Sharon viewed Liam's extra-curriculars with indulgence, amusement even, and would cover for him whenever he'd ducked into the storeroom with another happily married housewife.

Colm Meany, they all said. He's the spit of Colm Meany. Dessie couldn't see it at all. Colm Meany as Pavarotti, more like. Sharon said it was the same as a fat politician you'd see with some gorgeous young one hanging out of him – it was about power. All these Irish women come on holidays and what do their husbands do? They booze morning noon and night, ignore the wives, ignore the kids, sit around with lads the same as themselves shitin' on about football. You'll never beat the Irish! Wives have been looking forward to this all year, here they are, completely ignored, and who pays attention to them? Liam Delaney of Delaney's Irish Pub. The Man Himself. Complimenting their hair, remembering what they drink, dealing out his store of charm and good humour and one liners and who's this you remind me of, Michelle Pfeiffer/Helen Mirren/Glenn Close when she was young. And on the third day, there he is before them, Colm Meany for a holiday romance. Liam started renting the DVDs so he could quote the great man himself, *The Snapper* and *Layer Cake* and all. *Deep Space Nine*, Sharon said, that's the one you need. That's where you should be. Fair play, Liam laughed at that. He didn't take it seriously. I'm a fucking eejit kiddo, just like anyone else, he'd say to Dessie. Only I've found a way to make a go of being a fucking eejit. What's more, I'm a lucky fucking eejit. And that's the trick.

Liam's head fell towards the window and he began to snore. Two thirty a.m. – Dessie hadn't set his phone back yet. Time enough when they landed. He knew Liam would head straight to the funeral home, and then into the pub until the removal if he was let. Dessie didn't drink much any more, but even if he did, he had better things to do than sit around like a cunt, shouting about Jack Cullen or Lamp Comerford when he knew precisely fuck-all squared about it. Liam was full of shite about the old days and what blags he pulled and all this. Liam was a lucky fucking eejit and no mistake. Liam had been a driver like Dessie only not as good, but Liam hit the jackpot first time out. Brock Taylor's regular wheelman broke his leg the day before the Securicor job in Naas and Liam got the nod on account of everyone knew what a petrolhead he was. Brock's gang walked away with three and a half mil, Liam took 450k in the divvy-up. In 1996. He just legged it to Greece pronto, bought the bar, never looked back. That was the extent of Liam's life of crime. He could talk seven shades about who was going to answer to him and what he was going to do to them but he knew and everyone else knew it was all shite. Dessie was different. Dessie hadn't run with the likes of Larry Knight and Podge Halligan for nothing. Dessie knew someone had to pay. Sharon knew it too. She looked at him before he left – she could look a man in the eye, that counted for something, even at his lowest with smack he'd whisper to himself that, even if he couldn't meet her eye now, he'd chosen her because he wanted to, and that meant maybe one day soon, he could again – and if she'd thought he was going to hit the booze, or worse, start using again, she'd have dropped him where he stood, but she knew this was different. Like the time those cunts from Drimnagh threw her brother off the warehouse roof and broke his back and he died soon after. Dessie seen it happen, and he told Sharon he was going to Larry Knight with the names. She knew what Larry would do, sure her brother was dealing for him. Still, she knew it had to be done. She never faltered. Larry's boys done those cunts bigtime, two still haven't even turned up, somewhere at the bottom of the Grand Canal is the story, no one cares enough to search. This was the same: she looked straight at him, and nodded, and all she said was, be careful, and don't be stupid: the kids'll be asking where you are. And I want you to tell them in person.

If that wasn't an incentive, Dessie didn't know what was.

The stewardess came around. Dessie knew you weren't supposed to call them that any more, but fuck it, she looked like one. He passed her Liam's lukewarm beer and asked for another Diet Coke.

Paul. Fuck. Eighteen. Just a kid himself. He had the worst start but the best chances. Half brother he was, just like Dessie and Liam. Ma just couldn't settle. That was the nice way of putting it. Best not to speak ill of the dead, and it was Paul's Da that done for her too, having pimped her out and then accused her of robbing him. He died of Aids a couple of years into a life sentence in the 'Joy. Best thing that could have happened to him really, to be rid of those two, he went into foster care there in Drumcondra. Liam sent money back from the start, Dessie chipped in once he'd cleaned up – he hadn't really seen Paul for a long while before then – and Paul made his way. He'd come out to see them, wanted his own place, bit of distance from the foster parents, who were a little on the Holy Joe side. Liam and Dessie rented the apartment for him, Liam mainly, fair play to him, and of course there was the football, above all there was the football, they were all building towards the football. Towards the future. Towards one Delaney brother doing things the right way.

Not going to happen now. Maybe it never was, if what Ollie and Dave said was true. Dessie'd talk to Ed Loy, see what he'd turned up. Dessie never thought he'd warm to anyone who'd broken his arm. But in fairness, Dessie was holding a knife to Loy's throat at the time. Lot of fuckers wouldn't have let you live after that. Dessie always said he wouldn't have killed Loy. Just self-defence. Didn't know whether that was true or not, he was so strung out all the time back then, he'd've done anything. But he was never violent, not intentionally, and definitely never a killer. That all came later.

No, Loy was sound. Dessie owed him. If it hadn't've been for Loy stepping in, there'd've been no rehab, no Greece, no Sharon. He was a dangerous fucker though. One of those guys, very calm on the surface, very still, and then he just fucking erupts. You'd be waiting for it, taking steps to avoid it. Not mental like Podge, but you'd be a fool if you weren't wary of him. Dessie knew Loy wouldn't go along with what he had in mind. He just had to play Loy as best he could, so he could pick his brains and then use what he learnt. Wouldn't be easy, since Loy was not exactly stupid. But none of it was going to be easy. Apart from the killing itself. Dessie couldn't get over how easy that had been when it came down to it, for him at any rate.

It was in Greece, after everything. They'd been there a year, the kids had picked up the language, little Greeks themselves at the local school, Sharon and him were like teenagers again, almost. It was a whole new life. And then one of Podge Halligan's boys shows up. Nose Ring, his name was, except he didn't have the nose ring any more, and where his head had been shaved, now he had his hair plastered halfway down his forehead in a greasy fringe. Stupid fucking hairstyle, Dessie had it himself once when he lived in navy grey and white sportswear just like Nose Ring still wore. Dessie clocked him the second he walked in. It took Nose Ring longer, on account of a) Dessie having grown his hair to the collar, dressing in jeans and a black T-shirt and no longer looking like a total fucking knacker, and b) Nose Ring being thick as two short ones. But gradually, he pieced it together: the face, the name above the door, the past. That's what Dessie found seated at the bar one night after everyone else had left, with a knowing smirk on its stupid face: The Past. Even if the DPP had ruled against taking a case against Podge based on Dessie's evidence on account of Dessie being a totally unreliable and untrustworthy junkie, even if Podge had eventually pleaded guilty to manslaughter under pressure from his brothers, there was nothing good gonna come from Nose Ring knowing where he was. It was in that instant that Dessie made up his mind: Nose Ring's smirk, his look that said *I know you*, his malevolent *Howya Dessie!* Dessie knew there was no deal he could make that would keep Nose Ring quiet: he was too greedy. The past would return and destroy them. It wasn't fair. And Dessie wasn't gonna let it happen.

Liam had the night off, and he had let the local girls go home, so there was just the two of them in the bar. Nose Ring started in on how he didn't recognize him at first, with the hair and everything. Dessie gestured outside and made a face and said something about the Greek cops and his licence, and why didn't they go in the back there, he had a bottle of Jameson for old friends. He nodded Nose Ring behind the bar and followed him into the dark kitchen and took a heavy steel pan from the stove near the door as he walked and hit Nose Ring hard on the back of the head with it before he had a chance to turn around even, and Nose Ring went down face first with a crack on the tiles. Blood came out his ears and his mouth and brimmed on the hard floor. Dessie brought the pan down on the back of Nose Ring's head twice more. He could feel the skull cracking, feel the fragments giving against the soft sponge of the brain. But the thing was, it was almost as if he wasn't paying attention to what he was doing, or more, that he had done it all before, done it so often he barely took it in. What Dessie remembered was that, as he flipped the pan on its edge to smash it down for a final blow that would split Nose Ring's head in two, he noticed a container of milk on the counter. Better get that milk back in the fridge before it goes off, was what Dessie Delaney was thinking as he made double sure the first man he had ever killed was dead. And having the thought didn't shake him in the slightest; indeed, hard on that thought crowded another: he'd want to get his clothes off to stop them getting spattered with blood. He looked at what remained of Nose Ring, set the pan down, washed his hands, put the milk in the fridge, stripped naked, tossed his clothes in the bathroom and then went about the business of cutting up and disposing of the body without any thought other than how long it was going to take, and how, after he'd had a shower in the staff bathroom, he'd have to clean the bathroom itself and then have a second shower. Cutting up the body didn't bother him either. They kept the knives sharp anyway for jointing the lamb, and a dead body doesn't bleed to any significant degree. Even if it had, he wasn't sure it would have affected him in any way. He cut the limbs off and packed them as one in the heavy disposal sacks they used for animal waste. He removed the hands and the head and stowed them separately, then bagged the torso. Into each bag he added a couple of weights from the old brass steel kitchen scales, the only downside he could see to his plan; that scales was like some kind of family heirloom to the head chef. He did a preliminary clean-up then, making sure the outside lining of the bags was sprayed with disinfectant and wiped until any visible stains were gone. Then he doubled and sealed the bags to secure the body parts. He sealed his blood-stained clothes in a bag of their own. This was when he realized he'd need three showers. He took the first of them and dressed in the shorts, T-shirt and trainers he kept to run on the beach. He went outside to his Kia Sorento and laid the back seat down, making sure none of the children's soft toys or computer games were on the floor. Then he briskly packed the sacks containing the remains of Nose Ring into the back of the Kia and shut the door.

Maybe it was the thought of who'd usually be crowding into the SUV, the sound of his kids, the happy family rough-and-tumble in the back seat, but that was when Dessie had his first pang. Later, he compared it to how you'd feel if you were having an affair: you can't resist it, you're in the swim of it, it's the best thing ever, and then you think of your family and your heart buckles of a sudden. Not that Dessie had the nerves for an affair. But it seemed, apart from that one twinge of regret – and that had nothing to do with the dead man, not really – it seemed as if Dessie had nerves of steel when it came to taking a life. Strange thing to learn about yourself at the age of twenty-eight, like suddenly discovering you were gay, or no, bisexual, Dessie thought later, it's not as if you wanted to be, or went looking for it, but now you discovered it was something you could do, well, it was another string to your bow. And the more Dessie tried to remind himself of what he had felt about killing before, the horror, the pity, all the things he thought were normal, the less able he was to summon them up. This was his new reality, and he wore it lightly.

Once the boot was full, Dessie locked the Kia, went back inside and took another shower. Then he washed the kitchen floor and wiped down all the counter tops and splash backs and did the same in the bathroom. He took a third shower and dressed in the shorts, T-shirt and trainers. Dawn was starting to break as he drove the Kia up into the hills behind the bar. About a mile past the quarry, there was a freshwater lake that had claimed three lives in the past six months, so treacherous were its currents. Dessie pulled the Kia in behind a thicket of pines and took the weighted bag with Nose Ring's head and hands and flung it as far as he could. It disappeared beneath the grey surface with barely a splash, like a stone sinking into wet cement. The limbs and the torso followed.

The thing Dessie remembered most about it all was what happened next. He drove home, and wasn't Sharon waiting up for him, what time do you call this, where were you, ready to eat the face off him. Jealous mind, you'd have to say Sharon had, so much so he sometimes wondered was she up to no good herself. But it wasn't like him, so fair enough. Anyway, Dessie was scared of Sharon at the best of times. But tonight, this morning actually, quarter to six, he just shook his head and passed her the sack with the bloodstained clothes in it and said, these need either washing or burning, you decide, and Sharon looked at the clothes and didn't say a word, and Dessie didn't say a word either, then or later. But things were different after that, between them, and overall. Not that she thought he was a great fellow all of a sudden for having killed someone, not that she was tiptoeing around him or nervous in his company. But he knew she got a bit of a land. Maybe she noticed him a bit more, was *aware* of him a bit more. Maybe it was just, things were different now, and they always would be.

No one ever came calling about Nose Ring. No one seemed to miss him. He'd been on his own, far as Dessie could tell. Suppose they must have missed him off his flight back, marked him down as absent, passed it on to the cops. Drunk Irishman misses flight shock. Even if he went missing, no one looking for him. Over twenty-one. See ya.

He'd need to get some coffee into Liam before they landed. And then they were going to have to have a little talk. Fucker had been drunk since they heard about Paul's death, fair enough, but it was time to step up now. They could go to the funeral home first thing, sure, Dessie wanted that too, wanted to see Paul's body, but then they had work to do.

Dessie was going to lay the situation out for Liam. He'd tried to explain it already, but Liam couldn't take in: it was as if he'd been telling him some bloke in the bar was throwing shapes at him. 'I'll get the fuckers that done this,' Liam said. Well, that was Dessie's plan too. The problem was, if either Jack Cullen or Lamp Comerford were the fuckers that done this, or someone on their behalf, what did Liam think was gonna happen when Paul's brothers rolled into town? Did he think Cullen and Comerford'd just be sitting around in the Parting Glass or the Viscount, waiting for them to pile in and take a pop? Or might they take steps at the very least to guard against the did-you-kill-my-pint/spill-my-brother-tendency? Might it occur to them that when you plug a lad whose brothers were once players themselves, attack might be the best form of defence? If Dessie was in their shoes, he'd have had someone watching the flights from Greece every day, he'd set someone to follow them in from the airport, he'd want to know exactly what they were up to every second of the time they were here. He wouldn't have them killed, or at least, not before the funeral on Monday, because there'd be too much publicity and too much grief. And in any case, maybe Dessie and Liam had been players, but it had been lower division, if not non-league stuff: Liam drove getaway on one blag, a major blag for sure, but just the one; Dessie was a skinpop junkie who done a bunk. Neither would need to be killed. Warned off, at most.

But Cullen and Comerford didn't know about Dessie. They didn't know he had killed a man without scruple, barely noticing what he had done. They didn't know he was prepared to do that again, that he'd been in contact with Larry Knight, who was very sympathetic and would do what he could to help. Jack Cullen had been a thorn in Larry Knight's side for a long time, and while Larry would never move against him – once a Provo, always a Provo, Dessie knew Larry couldn't sustain the heat that would come from a war with Jack Cullen, a war that would only end one way. Larry hadn't clung on from the heroin days of the early eighties, building things up, seeing rivals fall and sending some of them on their way, to go down now. Larry wanted to be Last Man Standing. And if there was a chance to eliminate a rival from a distance, Larry was game ball with it. Dessie was going to see Larry Knight, and Liam was coming with him, and at the very least, they were going to make sure they had what they'd need to protect themselves if it came to it.

The other threat, and you could never discount it, would come from the Halligans. It might have been that they were happier with Podge behind bars, and there'd be no official action, or none sanctioned by George or Leo in anyway. But you couldn't be sure: the principle of touting on a Halligan brother was not to be encouraged, and Dessie's death'd be a sign to anyone thinking of doing likewise. And while both George and Leo were spending less time on the street these days, they'd still have a nobody like Dessie rubbed out without a second thought. And then there was Podge. No doubt about it, Podge'd have his ear to the ground. Even from jail Podge'd know what was going on, probably quicker than George or Leo themselves. Podge'd have no qualms about having Dessie hit: at his brother's funeral, at the graveside, on the altar, the more spectacular, the more obscene, the more grotesque the better. Podge wasn't interested in peace on the streets. Why would he be? Wasn't he safe in the 'Joy? Peace on the streets meant business was booming for everyone but him. Fuck that. And hitting Dessie was personal. Hitting Dessie would make Podge happy.

Wasn't gonna happen.

Not in this life.

Wits about them, eyes wide open, ready for anything.

No fucking bother.

The Delaney Brothers.

13

At around five on Holy Saturday morning, Donna Nugent finally fell asleep. I pulled my clothes on and quietly left the room. I walked from the Shelbourne to Holles Street, where I took a Valium, went to bed and, after a while, slept. I'd set the alarm for ten, and when I woke, I got up with some difficulty and went to the kitchen to fix some coffee. Passing the living room, I had a momentary hallucination that Tommy Owens was sitting in one of my armchairs doing something with his mobile phone. I stayed in the kitchen until the coffee had brewed, and until I had drunk some of it, enough to make me feel at least semi-conscious. Every part of me seemed to ache; blood was seeping from my nose, and I had been grinding my teeth; I felt a profound, indefinable sense of dread. I refilled my mug and brought it through to the living room, where Tommy Owens, in the flesh, was now standing by one of the sash windows looking down into the yard. I toyed briefly with the idea of asking him how he'd got in, but decided against it. Tommy's ability to do this kind of stuff was simultaneously what made him so useful and so annoying.

'Jesus Ed, you look like shit. Someone's been giving you a doing. Who was it? Must have been a woman, Jack Cullen's boys aren't that good.'

It occurred to me to answer, but when I opened my mouth, my jaw ached so much I closed it again at once, like a fish.

'What's for breakfast then? Smoked salmon and scrambled eggs sounds good to me.'

I looked at Tommy for a moment. He had passed through a phase of relative conformity after his mother died and he'd been working as sacristan at the Church of the Immaculate Conception in Bayview, but either the Catholic Church had abandoned its standards altogether or Tommy had leapt over the wall. His hair had returned to the bird's nest thatch that was its natural state; his chin bore the weasel wisps that the charitable might call a goatee; he wore olive green combats and black Caterpillar boots and an Iggy Pop T-shirt and a brown flight jacket; his face radiated his traditional aura of mischief and derision; his tiny eyes flashed merrily, guiltily, about the room, begging to be found out, wondering what to steal. He looked good though: healthy, resilient, cocky, all the things I didn't feel. The coffee had brought me out in a sweat, and had me shaking a little, or shivering in the morning chill, I wasn't sure which. Tommy came up close and peered at me.

'Fuck sake Ed, are you on drugs? Have you been doing coke? You have, you fucking monkey!'

Tommy's incredulous grin was gleeful at first, but it quickly ripened to embrace dismay and then disgust. I held up a hand and did the fish thing with my mouth a couple of times. I didn't know what to say, and even if I had, I couldn't say it. Nothing was working. I felt like hell. I wanted to sleep for a month. There were thirty-seven missed calls on my phone. I had tried, and I had failed, and now I felt like going home. I looked at Tommy and thought that I might cry. His face softened and compassion entered his eyes and I nearly did. Maybe I did, I don't know. I wasn't entirely sure what was happening to me. Tommy took my arm and led me to the bathroom and pushed me in and I had a very long hot shower and then as long as I could bear of a cold one. By the time I came out and got dressed, a mug of fresh coffee and a plate of scrambled eggs and smoked salmon was waiting for me on the table. We ate in silence, until eventually

I recovered basic motor skills like assembling thoughts and forming words, and I formed enough of them to tell him what I thought I'd been doing. Tommy laughed a little, and then a lot. Then he shook his head and sat back in what's-the-world-coming-to mode.

'She always looks like such a nice girl on the television,' Tommy said. 'She was on fucking *Questions and Answers* with the great and the good so she was, giving it this and that about the drug problem.'

'What was her solution?' I said.

'You know. All this about social deprivation.'

'I blame the parents.'

'Well, Donna doesn't. ASBO's the wrong way to go. She blames the lack of facilities. Sports grounds. Youth clubs. That's what would wean nineteen-year-old killers off guns and drugs, apparently, youth clubs. Is she a bit of a Shinner, Ed?'

'I think we'd have to say she's very close to someone who was, and maybe still is. Strange thing is, I don't really know her very well.'

'There's plenty of women I don't know very well, but I don't get to spend Good Friday in bed in a fancy hotel suite with them and a big bag of drugs on their boss's tab,' Tommy said. 'And if I did, I wouldn't be so fucking gloomy about it, I can tell you that for nothing.'

'I'm not gloomy. What can I say? I'm just a simple lad. Don't have the constitutional fortitude for the high life.'

'You're being very brave about it though.'

'Anyway, you'd end up falling in love with them.'

'You usually fall in love with them yourself. What's different about Donna Nugent?'

'Maybe that's why I'm so gloomy.'

'So young, so doomed. Except, not that young really.'

'I'm as young as you are, Tommy. I just don't look it. Today.

Anyway, what's up? If it's just social, you saved my day, or at least, set me up for it. Thank you. If not, spit it out.'

Tommy and I had been friends all our lives. He was the only person from Ireland to visit me when I lived in LA, apart from my mother. When I came back, Tommy was a total shambles, running drugs across borders, a mule for Podge Halligan. But while initially I seemed to spend a lot of my time getting Tommy out of scrapes, lately Tommy had begun to return the favour. I wouldn't say he was indispensable, but when someone saves your life, it's hard to begrudge him letting himself into your apartment when he feels like it, even if you're pretty sure you never gave him a key.

I watched him now as he hauled himself across to the window, his ruined foot the legacy of a stomping George Halligan gave him so Leo wouldn't stab Tommy for stealing his bike. He raised the sash and sat on the sill and lit a cigarette and directed a gust of smoke out into what was for the moment a bright spring morning. When he turned back, his face was suddenly grave. Tommy had an old woman's sense of conversational melodrama: if there was an announcement or a revelation to be made, he liked to set a solemn tone well in advance. I always felt he was just about holding back from saying 'Do you know what I'm going to tell you?' Generally speaking, it was no laughing matter, however; nor was it this morning.

'Charlie Newbanks came to see me last night. He's worried about you. And after what he told me, so am I.'

Before he could get any further, I stood up and signalled to him to follow me through to the office. Tommy rolled his eyes, but I didn't care. Maybe all the blood and the rage, the bitterness and disappointment and loss that clung to every case I worked couldn't be corralled in one room of my apartment, maybe it was destined to seep through the walls and taint the air throughout. It didn't mean I wasn't going to try. Someone once told me acknowledging the difficulty of prayer was itself a prayer, and what's more, the kind of prayer God wanted to hear. I wasn't conscious of carrying around gouts of wisdom to console myself with in the wee small hours, but there are some things that stick with you. There was a long time when I didn't see the point in trying at all, when the death of my daughter and the ruin of my marriage and the death of my mother all folded into one great shroud that I tried to hide beneath, that I hoped might one day smother me; the delirium of murder and betrayal, of abuse and violence and hatred that arose from the cases I worked was a welcome distraction from my own grief, maybe even an objective justification of my entitlement to it. But grief that's too well nurtured curdles into self-pity; sodden with booze, it slides towards self-loathing, self-destruction follows you down; then one day without noticing, you're having trouble seeing your reflection in the mirror; worse, you don't even care any more. I had been living there a long time. Sometimes I felt like that's where I still was, where I'd always be. The only thing was, I didn't want to be. The only thing was, now I thought I had to try.

In the office, Tommy walked to the window and scowled down at the street.

'All those mothers and babies. Do you not find it fucking depressing, Ed? I know I would, every day. All that fucking optimism and energy and let's hear it for the future. Jasus.'

Now it was my turn to laugh.

'I don't mind it, Tommy. And it looks like it's cheering them up. Anyway, there we were, you and Charlie Newbanks. Is there any point in asking how you know him?'

On top of the flair for melodrama, Tommy had an old woman's nose for gossip too; over the course of a lifetime of petty and not so petty crime, it had given him a near-encyclopedic knowledge of and often a personal acquaintance with pretty much every lowlife south of the river; I suppose my perennial surprise at how much further his tentacles extended was a reflection of how little I wanted to know about that side of him. 'Until it's useful to you,' Tommy would sniff with an indignation he wasn't quite able to sustain. I think he had things he'd prefer to keep to himself as well. Don't we all?

Tommy grimaced now at my ignorance, as if I were a lazy student who simply wouldn't pay attention; sometimes he forgot I'd spent the best part of twenty-five years away. Not this time though.

'Charlie Newbanks was at national school with us, Ed. He only came in 6th class, he'd been living in town and his da done a bunk to England, and his ma was left with eight or nine and couldn't cope, and Charlie and his sister were farmed out to their granny, the da's ma stepping up to do her bit. Do you not remember? Ah you probably wouldn't, Charlie went to the Tech then, with all the other corner boys. Not your scene at all.'

Tommy leered happily at this, always happy to maintain that I was some kind of snooty rich kid, when, as he knew, his parents – a civil servant and a teacher – had been more assuredly 'middle class', one of Tommy's favourite epithets, than the motor mechanic and shop-assistant who raised me. But Tommy was drawn to trouble, and trouble followed him; Tommy cultivated the street, and the street rose up to embrace him; in accent and manner and habits, he had almost become what he beheld. Almost, but not quite.

'No, I would have been away at Harrow by then, Tommy. Or maybe I was grouse shooting on our country estate. Charlie Newbanks. At the Tech. And?'

'I was doing nights there when I started at your da's garage. And Charlie and me, we hung around, we did a bit of this and that. Charlie done his apprenticeship as a sparks, kept his hand in throughout the eighties. Rewiring houses, fuseboards, powerpoints, checking each place out as a target, which had valuables or a safe, keeping a note, then maybe six months later, maybe a year, in and out. Paintings, one time, this big house out in Howth. Anyway, it all got a bit too heavy for me, Charlie hooked up with his brother back in Cumberland Street, Portland Row there. They were talking about doing some huge fucking stately home down the country, Laois or Offaly or some fucking place, going in armed, tying the old couple who lived there up, all this.'

'And you drew the line.'

'I fucking did, you know I did, and don't be fucking looking at me as if I had to think about it. So the lads went in and wasn't it a set-up, there was Special Branch and all sorts and a gun fight and Charlie's brother got shot, brown bread, can you believe it, dead on account of some fucking art? Well out of that one. Few years on Charlie's doing a little dealing in his neighbourhood, dope mainly, a little E, I'm doing the same around the colleges, Bolton Street, Kevin Street, Trinity, we bump into each other up in Cathal Brugha Street there, the College of Catering, one of his boys is throwing shapes cause he thinks I'm on his patch, Charlie to the rescue. So we hook up. He's working for Jack Cullen then, or for one of Jack's boys. Now Cullen was one of the big players in the heroin trade throughout the eighties, when the North Inner City was rotten with it. 'Course it was being run for him by other people, mainly by Lamp Comerford, so Jack could be seen supporting the Concerned Parents Against Drugs groups and so forth like the socially concerned Provo he was supposed to be, but that's what was happening. But then smack got so you couldn't give it away, Aids and Hep C and skeletons rattling around with McDonald's cups of methadone, fuck all margin in that. Now it's the nineties and there's talk of an IRA cease-fire and Jack Cullen's boys are getting set up for the future, it's coke and E all the way, drugs for people with a few dinars in their pockets.'

'George Halligan told me some of this already, about how Cullen and Ray Moran met. Were you working for George back then?'

'For Leo mostly. Leo had the notion I'd be right for the students, wouldn't intimidate the little darlings. Anyway, what I'm saying is, Charlie and me go back, all right? Charlie's sound. Cullen brought him in after his brother was killed, because Charlie had built up quite a rep as a blagger; Cullen put him in charge of a fair few jobs to keep the IRA accounts healthy. The Cullen gang were the Southern Command's highest earners: banks, post offices, security vehicles, and that was mainly down to Charlie. Don't think he ever joined the 'RA himself, but I could be wrong. Those days are done now but. He crews for Lamp on the door at the Viscount and a couple of Jack's other spots now, but he's a plain dealer, not a psycho.'

'He must have had to look the other way quite a lot if he's crewing for Lamp.'

'So he looks the other way: that's as much as to say, he lives there, he knows them, what else is he gonna do? Shut the fuck up and stop interrupting me will you? What I was going to tell you was, I used to deal with Ray Moran when he was Ents Officer at Trinity, I gave him freebies so I could deal at the gigs they had in the Buttery and the Exam Hall and at the Trinity Ball and the rest of it. Only doesn't Mister Smartarse Fucking Student get the idea that he could do this himself if he can get a supplier. And he has all these new friends in the IRSP, who have friends in the INLA, who can source dope for him. So I'm getting edged out of the picture, fair enough, Leo knows the score, you don't want to be having skirmishes over turf in Trinity fucking College, bring all sorts of attention down on you. So Moran starts making a few bob, and the INLA get behind him, officially or not, it's hard to know with that mob, couple of lads down from Belfast, anyway, they start clearing the few dinars and that's when they think, fish in a barrel time, let's take the city on, they spill out into the Lombard Street flats and across the river right onto Jack Cullen's patch, not Moran, he'd have had more sense, or else he'd just be too fucking scared to go north of Pearse Street, it's the Nordie boys pushing this now. I get a call from Charlie Newbanks 'cause at first they think it's me, they think it's the Halligans losing the fucking place and Lamp Comerford has boys tooling up to fucking do us. So I explain, no, it's these INLA gobshites, trying to keep Moran out of it cause I feel sorry for the fucker, you know, out of his depth, but Charlie knows straight away who it is and Moran gets hauled in. Lamp Comerford scares the fuck out of Moran and tapes his eyes up and drives him around and so on, then delivers him to Jack Cullen in person.

'Now it's what happened next that's the interesting bit.'

With that, Tommy stopped and looked enigmatic. Or at least, I assumed that was the intention; in fact, he just looked like he'd come to a halt and maybe forgotten what he was talking about.

'All right then, Tommy: what happened next?'

Tommy grinned from ear to ear.

'Nobody knows.'

'What do you mean, nobody knows? What's interesting about that?'

'What's interesting is, whatever happened in there, Ray Moran goes in a scared-as-fuck student who's been doing a bit of small-time dealing, and he comes out with a deal to be Jack Cullen's bagman, his front, his representative on earth. How did that happen? Nobody knows.'

'George says Moran killed Brian Fogarty for Cullen, or had him killed.'

'That's just bullshit, I was talking to Charlie last night about this. How does Moran transform himself overnight into a killer? And even if he was capable of it, why would Jack Cullen depend on him?'

'He wanted Fogarty taken out, but he didn't want it traced to him. And it needn't have been Moran himself: he had those INLA guys, they were always happy to do the IRA's bidding, or at least, they were if they knew what was good for them. And then Moran is tied to Jack Cullen for life.'

Tommy shrugged.

'That's possible, I suppose. Charlie doesn't think it happened that way though. Charlie thinks it was Lamp who done Fogarty. Almost as if he was jealous of Moran. Because the whole thing was, the same time Moran came on the scene, the IRA ceasefire was being talked about in Republican circles, and Cullen had read the runes, he could see what a lot of people couldn't: that sooner or later, there'd be no place for the armed struggle, no place for the Provos. And he was like, we need a new way to operate, we can't keep taking our rivals out, we can't keep doing things the old way. The Lamp Comerford way. Charlie said Lamp was bulling when he heard this, he felt he was being sidelined.'

'Was Lamp in the IRA himself?'

'Yeah, but he didn't want to face the facts: he thought they could just go on bombing and shooting. And the thing was, Cullen wasn't talking about going straight, he had nothing to do with Sinn Féin, he couldn't stand the political side. He had no intention of becoming, like, a councillor and then working up to being a TD. He had his operation, he'd built it up through the years, he wanted to keep it intact. But he saw they'd have to step up a level, and he saw it early: before the Criminal Assets Bureau was even thought of.'

'Except by people the likes of Brian Fogarty.'

'Maybe that's what planted it in Cullen's mind, when he got the letter: this may not have any official weight now, but it's only a matter of time.'

'So what, Lamp thought he was being sidelined? And to prove his worth, he took Fogarty out? Why?'

'Charlie doesn't think there was any great thought process. Lamp just reacted. Like I say, he was jealous, he got emotional. And then Fogarty's dead, and it's like, look at that, will your new boy do that for you? Because Lamp came up with Jack. Lamp was Jack's man, all the way. And then that night, Jack suddenly has someone else, someone who could do what Lamp never could: help to give him security, a certain kind of legitimacy. Of course, Lamp provides what Ray Moran doesn't have: muscle. And that's how it's been ever since, between the three of them. And now things are starting to come apart.'

'Lamp said he thinks there's a tout in the gang. That too many drug shipments are being intercepted by the NDU.'

'And Lamp wants you to sort it out. He's given you money to sort it out. On top of the knife that done those lads in Beresford Lane. And how do you think all that's going to work?'

'I haven't thought much about it at all, to be honest. All I know is, provided Lamp's telling the truth and he has the knife, I'm in as much trouble as he wants me to be in: he can certainly destroy my ability to do my job. He has a good chance of my being charged with manslaughter, maybe even murder.'

'It's a lot worse than that, Ed. Charlie asked me one thing: if it comes to it, are you a killer? Because if you get among Lamp and Jack Cullen and even Ray Moran, what it's going to be about is, who is the last man standing? If Lamp suspects Jack of touting, you can be damn sure Jack has his eye on Lamp.'

'I'm not sure what my options are, Tommy. I mean, if Lamp pulls the plug on me, I'm finished anyway.'

'Charlie said you should leave the country.'

'Leave the country?'

'Go back to the States, yeah. Because if you don't, if you stick around, Charlie says it's only a matter of time before you go down. Forget about the Guards. Forget about your job. No matter what you do, how you seem to help. For getting in the way, for being a threat, or just to be on the safe side, one of them is going to take you out.'

14

I walked Tommy down to the street, but who should we see standing by the stairwell in the main hall only Leo Halligan, as if he were Tommy's personal bodyguard, even if I knew that wasn't the case and saw from Tommy's face that he was as surprised as I was, although it turned out that Tommy was merely surprised by how quickly Leo had got here: Leo in jeans and black biker jacket and dark green cowboy boots and hair slicked up and back in a DA, Leo smelling of lemon cologne and French cigarettes, rail thin and deathly pale and looking for all the world like the villain in a nineteen-sixties French film.

'You've got two Branch men out front watching you, Ed. That can't be good. Unless of course, they're watching *him*.'

Leo Halligan gestured to Tommy with the mixture of affection and contempt that most people who knew him found themselves resorting to sooner or later.

'Special Detective Unit, I think they're called these days.'

'They're the Branch and they always will be. Poking their noses into organized crime now the security of the nation is a done deal. Or so my brother George tells me. I of course wouldn't know these days, being in the high street retail business.'

'To what do I owe the honour, Leo?'

'To this gimpy fuck. He tells me you're in trouble, and together we should all pay a visit.'

'To whom? And with all due respect, what the fuck is it to you?'

Leo winced in a is-this-all-the-thanks-I-get kind of way, and laughed out loud.

'Exactly what I was thinking, and I had to get out of bed an' all. I don't know, is the answer. But since I knew the quare fella back then, and in passing since, it might be rude not to.'

'Which quare fella are we talking about?'

Leo looked at Tommy, a thumb flipped towards me.

'Is Ed awake, Tommy? Only he seems a little slow to me.'

'He's just tired, Leo.'

'Aren't we all? The quare fella who goes by Ray Moran. Is there a back way we can leave?'

I wasn't exactly crazy about my day being ordered by one of the Halligan brothers, but I was curious to see where it would lead, and the overcast blear of my hangover meant my will wasn't as sturdy as it might have been. I led them down one flight of stairs and out into the back yard. There was a stone mews house beyond the parked cars, and the gate to a path that gave onto Denzille Lane and that way we wheeled south towards Merrion Street. It was five minutes' walk the length of Baggot Street to Pembroke Road on an overcast Holy Saturday morning, the pavements damp and the smell of rain in the sharp air. The cafes were filling and the pubs were opening and American and French tourists were wandering about in bright waterproof jackets.

Ray Moran's practice was on the south side of Pembroke Road, a fine three-storey above basement Georgian house with a brass plate on the gleaming black palings. The great bulk of Charlie Newbanks shambled over from a parked car as we approached.

'You're all right for fifteen,' he said, addressing Tommy and Leo. 'No receptionist today, just go straight in on the ground floor, the door's open. I've told his security I'll handle it, sent them up the road for a pint. I'll keep any footfall away. Fifteen mind.'

'Has he a piece?' Leo said.

Charlie shook his head, then looked at me.

'Don't say I didn't warn you about all this.'

I shrugged. What choice did I have? You take the case, you take what goes with it. Don't be a gardener and then complain about the dirt. I suppose I could have thanked Newbanks, but I didn't want to: maybe he was trying to help, but he wasn't on my side: he was still a gangster, no matter how often he looked the other way.

We climbed the stone steps to the great red panelled door and walked past the vacant reception and past the open door of an empty conference room and straight without knocking into Ray Moran's office which had another brass plate on the door and Ray Moran in shirt sleeves and black braces behind a large pale oak desk and before Moran's face had time to register surprise at our entrance or who we were or anything much at all Leo Halligan had leapt onto his desk and kicked him three times around the head and face with the points of his green cowboy boots.

Moran's nose erupted in blood which flowed through the hands he held to his face to protect himself from any further harm. He cried out as Leo leapt on top of him and straddled him and rode his swivel chair back against a wall of framed diplomas and certificates and tapped Moran's head sharply against as many as he could reach, moving right to left along the wall until the chair was crunching through shards of broken glass and Moran was whimpering. Leo sprang off him then and wiped blood off his jacket and brushed glass off his hands. He extended a hand to Tommy and waved it and Tommy, alert to the semaphore, found a bathroom and returned with two wet towels and Leo used one to clean himself up and passed the second to the sobbing Moran, whose face and shirt front were covered in blood.

'Now we don't have to waste time threatening you. 'Cause

you see, that's just hello, you slimy little cunt, hello and how are you and tell us what we need to know and stop the fucking whimpering you little squally baby! Are you a fucking girl? Are you? Are you? Well don't be fucking crying like one then. Are you a squally baby? You bad cunt, clean yourself off and shut the fuck up!'

Then Leo paused from his rant and turned to me and winked. A certain part of me was riven with nausea and despair at the cruelty I was witnessing, but I have to confess, it wasn't hard to set that part aside; Moran was the respectable face of an ugly business that brought death and suffering to thousands, one of many accountants and solicitors that richly deserved a Saturday morning like this, possibly every Saturday. I couldn't condone it, but it was difficult to deny Moran had it coming to him: call it an acceptable level of hypocrisy on my part.

'Hold the nose then, below the bridge, well maybe it is fucking broken, what do you want me to do, here, let me feel it for you . . . no, it's grand, you've just got a fucking nose bleed, be a fucking man about it.'

Moran's cries had subsided, and under Leo's care, he was now sitting up and holding his nose with the blood-drenched towel to stanch the flow. Leo repositioned him behind his desk and made an expansive gesture with his hands to suggest that, the performance having now concluded, the floor was now open for questions. Leo remained at Ray Moran's side. Moran brought the hand that wasn't holding his nose up to shield his face from Leo, or to mask him from his sight. There was a line, and I had probably crossed it, but still. I nodded to Leo to come around my side of the desk, where there were chairs enough for three; Tommy was sitting in one of them, shaking, tapping his feet, his eyes fixed on the floor. Leo didn't want to budge, but after a bout of shrugging and eye rolling, he came around and sat beside me.

'Now,' I said. 'Sorry about that. Didn't know it was going to happen. But everyone has to take one for the team some time, don't they? Even you.'

Moran looked at me through blood-smeared, filmy eyes that blinked insistently.

'Dean Cummins and Simon Devlin,' I said. 'Who were they working for? Jack? Or Lamp?'

Moran shook his head.

'I know you must have seen them, at the very least. And told Lamp about them. Or Jack, who told Lamp. And Lamp must have moved very fast. Unless of course he knew all along what they were doing, because they were his boys. Otherwise, how would Lamp have known where they were going?'

Moran shook his head again, his lips pursed, his jaw clenched tight.

'I'll be over that desk and take the head off your shoulders and shit down the hole if you shake it one more fucking time,' Leo said.

Ray Moran grimaced and, with almost a whoop of pain, pushed his tongue through his lips and spat something onto the desk. It was a tooth. Tears were coursing silently down his bloody cheeks. I got up and found a small office kitchen in the hall, adjacent to the bathroom. I boiled water and found some salt and put it in a cup and when the water boiled I dissolved the salt and added some cold water and brought the cup and a second cup in and gave them to Ray Moran, along with two Nurofen Plus I had in my coat.

'Rinse with the hot and spit into the empty cup,' I said, and he did this a few times, having taken the Nurofen, and Leo looking at me the while as if I had put my arm around Moran and begun to stroke his hair, and none of it made me feel better about anything that had happened in the room, but maybe I wasn't supposed to feel better, maybe that was one of the unspoken perks of my job. Moran rinsed and spat again, then set the cups down on his desk beside the tooth and wiped his mouth and eyes with the sleeve of his shirt. He looked frightened, but that was a measure of his intelligence; anyone with any sense was scared of Leo Halligan.

'Simon Devlin and Dean Cummins were in the INLA,' Moran said.

'They were what?' Leo said.

'They were in the INLA. I had spotted them earlier that evening, I had alerted Jack and Lamp to their presence. We think one of them may have been the masked gunman who shot the volley into the air above in Tolka Park.'

'And what were they doing, just hanging around across the road from the Viscount, unarmed?' I said.

'The INLA?' Leo said again.

Moran looked at Leo with what I can only describe as irritation. Full marks for his spirit.

'The INLA, yes, for the third time. Is there something about that you want to discuss?'

'Don't get fucking narky with me man,' Leo said and rose out of his chair. I stood up and placed myself between Leo and the desk.

'Enough,' I said. 'We're here to learn something. If your blood's up, go and take it out on someone else.'

Leo's eyes flashed at the admonition. He sat down, muttering something which quickly bubbled to the surface.

'I wouldn't have thought even the INLA would mess with Jack Cullen's people. Not after the last time.'

Moran didn't quite smile, but something in his face allowed that there was at least irony in what he was about to say.

'I think this was a kind of softening up exercise. Come onto Jack's territory, throw a few blatant shapes, make it look unsafe, volatile, out of control, and then see what happens.'

'To take advantage of the rift between Lamp and Jack?' I said.

'What rift is that?' Moran said.

I looked at Moran, then at Leo, then back at Moran. I wasn't proud of it, but that's what I did. It seemed to work.

'Certainly the perception that there isn't entire harmony between Jack and Lamp is a factor. And of course, since what concerns you most directly is the fact that you were jumped that night, what seems most likely is that Devlin and Cummins mistook you for me.'

'And they were ready to shank you? Why?'

'Because he's a turncoat,' Tommy said. 'Because he used to be involved with the INLA himself. Because that's where he started out.'

Moran shrugged.

'I can't discount that. But I don't think that's where it's coming from. And I don't think they would have stabbed me, or at least, not to death. I think they saw me as another way of making their presence felt, of sending a message. Maybe it was personal, but that's not what the whole thing's about.'

'Explain the INLA angle to me. I mean, this isn't exactly about liberating the Irish people, is it?'

'The INLA in Dublin is run by a headbanger called Shay Rollins,' Leo said. 'Rollins is based out in Clondalkin and he's been feuding with a drug dealer over in Tallaght for about a year now over territory out there. But I don't see why he'd want to move in on the IRA, or the ex-IRA. Mind you, we always steered clear of the Provos anyway, so I wouldn't know.'

Moran nodded in agreement with the latter.

'The INLA are split in three,' he said. 'Two factions are based in the North, they're on ceasefire, they don't want any return to violence. Apart from shooting rival drug dealers. They're semi-political, semi-criminal, if you like. The Dublin INLA are mainly criminal, and what they're looking at is what they see as a weakened IRA organization on the ground now the ceasefire has bedded in and the war is well and truly over. An example is protection rackets: the IRA ran them, Jack and Lamp ran them, every dealer in their territory had to kick in, and if they didn't, they'd be shot in the legs, and if they still held out, someone would end up dead to encourage the others. Now they can't do that any more. And sadly, it's the only language that's understood down there. So the INLA have been moving in and testing the water, beating the shit out of IRA men who can't retaliate the way they once would have. They see there's an opening. And of course, when this stuff starts happening, everyone gets very excited, and starts making mistakes and blaming each other and looking for touts and sellouts.'

'What about your connection with the INLA? You were tight back in the day. I thought there was only one way out of an organization like that.'

'Once I went to work for Jack, I was given the equivalent of an honorable discharge. Basically, I never heard from them again. And the faction I was involved with was from the North, not from Dublin. So I don't think that is an issue any more. But like I say, it can't be discounted. The truth is, they want to hit Jack Cullen any way they can. If along the way they could characterize me as a turncoat, all the better for them. But they don't need the excuse. No one expects them to be anything other than mental.'

'Doesn't seem like they've gotten very far yet,' I said. 'I mean, all they have is Cummins and Devlin dead. What have they achieved?'

Ray Moran didn't have to answer that. Leo and Tommy had been nodding their heads throughout Ray Moran's last speech, like the audience at a movie when the killer is revealed and they're simultaneously thrilled and furious they didn't see it all along.

'Paulo Delaney,' they said, with one breath.

'The INLA killed Paul Delaney?' I said.

Moran raised his eyebrows.

'We're not sure what it was. For a start, Paul was never dealing, that's all nonsense.'

'Where did the Mazda come from?'

'From Jack. Jack was . . . very fond of Paul, like a father. People have this picture of Jack like he's some kind of mad dog, spitting fury, kill you as soon as look at you. A lot of those guys who were involved in the armed struggle, it suited them to have that kind of image, quite frankly. But he's not like that. He'd seen Paul Delaney play football, seen him grow up. He looked at him like a son.'

'And his own son died in a car crash a few years back. Nineteen,' Leo said.

'Yes, well, there's probably a bit of that as well. He's very upset.'

'And the thinking is, it was the INLA? They targeted him to get at Jack?' I said.

'Who else?'

'What about Lamp Comerford?'

Moran didn't exactly roll his eyes – given his current condition, he'd probably have vomited if he'd tried – but he made no effort to hide his impatience.

'Look, Lamp got stoked one night and fired up the doorway of the Viscount. It's all been forgiven. Sure one night, Jack burnt down his own house because he couldn't get his key to work in the lock. Fun with the insurance company over that one. These are . . . volatile guys. But Lamp and Jack have been together a long time.'

'With you in the middle.'

'That's not where I'm happiest, but if I have to keep the peace sometimes, so be it. There are three of us: we take it in turns.'

'Lamp thinks there's a tout in the gang. He offered me ten grand to find out who it was. Not so much an offer as a kind

159

of blackmail, actually given he has, or he claims to have, the knife that killed Devlin and Cummins – with my prints on it.'

Moran stared at me for a while with no expression on his face. I was pretty sure what I'd said had come as a complete surprise to him. When he spoke, his voice was shaking. If he'd appeared frightened before, that was just a rehearsal: this was the show.

'A tout . . . what did he mean? Did he have anyone in mind? In relation to what? To Paul Delaney?'

'To the shipments the National Drug Unit keep picking up. Lamp thinks they must have someone on the inside. He said it doesn't seem to matter which route they use: it's clear they're getting expert intelligence.'

Moran exhaled with apparent relief and shook his head: no longer agitated, simply bewildered.

'I don't know . . . why would he ask you?'

'Because he thought I could find out.'

Moran nodded emphatically, not so much because he agreed, but because he wanted us to go away, nodded and looked down sorrowfully at his tooth.

15

I was in the habit of withholding information, sometimes going so far as to withhold it from myself; now I sat in my apartment and tried to make serious use of that habit, in the hope that I might bury in some lower depth of the mind what I had just been party to. When that didn't work, I picked up my mobile.

Noel Sweeney, the detective who'd worked the original Fogarty case, had rung a few times and left a message; when I called him back, he answered on the second ring.

'Don't tell me, you're not just a private detective, you're a priest as well, and Good Friday's the busiest day of your year.'

'I'm sorry I didn't get back to you sooner.'

'Ah don't be talking, Father. Sure God moves in mysterious ways, his wonders to perform.'

'I'm sure that's true. Would it be possible to meet up with you at some stage to talk about the Fogarty case?'

'I'll meet you at the scene of the crime, Father, how would that be?'

'I beg your pardon?'

'The old Fogarty house in Farney Park. By a happy coincidence, it's on the market. Douglas Newman Good has an open view there at midday. Don't suppose I'll have any trouble recognizing you, Father – unless you're one of these modern priests, more concerned with the profane than the sacred. Barely priests at all, the same fellas.'

I allowed that that was almost certainly the kind of priest I was and, having arranged to see him outside the house in Sandymount, hung up. Sweeney's humour was laid on with a trowel, but there was an edge to his voice that made me think he played the fool but was far from being one. Or maybe in my intensely hungover condition, I was ready to invest the mildest of remarks with portents of doom. The ominous 'Prelude' from *Parsifal* coiled insistently around my brain, while lurid images from my lost twenty-four hours with Donna Nugent flashed before my eyes like prosecution evidence; I wanted to call Anne Fogarty back, but I felt guilty, as if I had betrayed her, or that she would think I had; counsel for the defence reminded me that she had lied when she told me how unhelpful Dave had been over the matter of reinvestigating her father's murder, that she had neglected to mention the family home was on the market, and that in any case, all there was between us was a kiss and maybe the slim chance of something more; the jury was no help: they stared at me with unforgiving eyes, making it clear that I had had too much fun and now it was time to pay. I involuntarily held my head in my hands, then caught sight of my reflection in the window. Jesus. A grown man bowed in despair at eleven thirty in the morning. Get a grip, Ed Loy. You've so much poison in your system you've no clear idea how you feel about anything. Don't look too long at the mother cradling her newborn outside the maternity hospital there, you might burst into tears at the beauty of it all. Get a grip, Loy. You flew too high, and now you're landing hard: it's not the first time, and knowing you, it won't be the last. So you don't do drugs as a general rule: you did them last night, and nobody forced you. So what if Donna Nugent is the exception to the rule: you could have said no and you didn't, not because you were drunk, but because you didn't want to. Think about that when Anne Fogarty looks at you the way she did and you start mistaking yourself for someone she can trust. She's not the kind of woman a man like you could hope for. You get the wounded and the crazed, the mentally halt and the spiritually lame, the slender, hollow-eyed girls of low self-esteem. At best, you get Donna: the life and soul of the all night party, but with true feelings off limits and ice in the soul. Get a grip, Ed Loy. Get a grip and do the only thing you're good for, the only thing you know how to do: go to work.

On my way out, I called Anne Fogarty. Not surprisingly, but much to my relief, she didn't ask me to account for myself, or charge me with infidelity, or tell me I was fired and she wanted her money back. If anything, she sounded like she was the one with a guilty conscience.

'Oh Ed, I'm so glad you called. I wanted to say . . . well, I suppose you know by now, he's a friend of yours after all . . . I don't know why I said he was unhelpful, maybe I wanted you to think you were my only hope. Sorry, that sounds desperate, in every sense, desperate housewife alert! Sorry.'

'It's okay. I'm actually, I'm on my way out now—'

'Of course, I don't want to get in the way of your work.'

I wondered whether I should mention where I was going, but decided against it: if she knew the house was on the market, I wanted to see her face when I asked her why she hadn't told me. And of course it was entirely possible that she didn't know, that the Fogarty family home coming up for sale at this time was a complete coincidence. I'd believe that myself, if I believed in coincidence when it came to a case. Which I didn't.

'But we could catch up later,' I said. 'I could call around in the afternoon.'

'There's actually something I wanted you to see, at three? It's in a church, but it's not a church service.'

It would have made no difference to me if it had been. Churches were the city's refuges, harbours for the weary and the soul sick of any religion and none, respite from those who

163

only wanted a piece of you. I'd as soon go to a church as anywhere, even when I wasn't hungover. I said I'd love to come,
and Anne named a small church by the banks of the Grand
Canal and I said I'd see her outside beforehand.

~

The estate agent's board was up outside the house in Farney
Park, a quiet street of mostly semi-detached houses built in
the nineteen thirties. A couple of years back, the vendors
could have expected one and a half million for this kind of
family home in Dublin 4, maybe a couple of hundred k more.
Today it was on the market for 1.25, and the anxious look
in the auctioneer's eyes as she stood in the porch, beckoning passers-by in from the street, perhaps told its own story:
whatever the vendors thought, they were going to have to
settle for less. It wasn't really much to do with estate agents
anyway, or with the vendors, for that matter. The banks were
running the downturn, just as they had fuelled the boom: if
this house miraculously went sale agreed at the asking price of
1.25 (and achieving an asking price was a miracle these days),
that would only hold until the bank's valuer bounced along to
value it at 1.1, say; then the buyers would let the sellers know
what the new price was, and there was nothing the sellers
could do except hold out for the kind of buyer who didn't need
to borrow from a bank, and that kind of buyer wasn't generally
to be found paying full price in a fire sale. The bank didn't
really want to lend anyone money, because their borrowing
costs had shot up, so they were working to bring about a kind
of equilibrium, where sellers didn't want to sell so low and
buyers couldn't afford to borrow so high. Equilibrium they
called it: deadlock was more like it, with activity paralyzed
and the tax take down, it was only a matter of time before the
government agreed to give the banks – who were all still in
substantial profit – low interest loans to kick start the market.

The public shouldered the risks and the banks made all the profits: free enterprise, Irish style.

The question of the vendors intruded more insistently when I stepped into the hall. The woodchip wallpaper was tattered and peeling, the stipple ceiling cracked and grimy, the rough sisal carpet worn to a bare sheen. The estate agent, whose name was Lorna, was blonde and young and had the brave, faintly manic face of a hostess giving a party while her marriage is falling apart. She showed me a lot of teeth and chattered about ideal location and massive potential and then, as she saw me take in the pock marks of damp that scarred the ceilings and walls and the prolapsed furniture and decomposing curtains, briskly muttered something about an executor's sale before scuttling off towards a young couple who were trying to get out into the back garden.

An executor's sale was exactly what it looked like, except it was fifteen years too late. There were still books on the shelves in the living room, and a dinner service on a sideboard by the dining room table, and delph and cutlery in the kitchen, but nothing that seemed personal or distinctive. There were four bedrooms upstairs, but again, little trace of the occupants remained: discoloured oblongs on the walls where posters and mirrors had hung; a green snake with yellow eyes that had served as a draught excluder; a broad-toothed hair comb with a handle; a faded cassette inlay card from the Pixies' album *Bossanova!*

I went downstairs and, from the front door, according to what I had been told, retraced the killer's steps; as far as I knew, he had struck from behind as Brian Fogarty was leading him, or being led, towards the kitchen. There was a rug in the hall where I reckoned he would have fallen; I went down on my knees and lifted the rug, but the carpet beneath had been removed and imperfectly replaced; the rug served to conceal the ridges and upturned seams at the join. In its own way, it was as vivid as the bloodstains I hadn't expected to see would have been. I hunkered there for a moment, trying to clear my mind of everything but the ancient legend: This Be The Place. When I looked up, a tall, thin man with a beak of a nose and silvery hair swept back from a high, tanned brow was looking down at me. He wore an off-white cotton overcoat and an olive green cotton suit. He looked like what I thought a European architect might look like, which made it all the more surprising when he spoke.

'If you look at the surrounding wallpaper, you'll notice it has been replaced also, but they did a better job with that. Mind you, I suppose the carpet just looks like a botch job unless you know what it's covering up.'

Without rising, I studied the wallpaper and saw it was slightly brighter and in better condition on either side of the rug than it was further down the hall. Again I had an acute sense of the blood that had flowed; this time it felt even more intense than before, as if the cover-up was worse than the original crime. I stood up and extended my hand.

'Ed Loy,' I said. 'You must be Noel Sweeney.'

'There isn't exactly a queue for the title,' he said. His voice was dry, faintly ironic, with a Dublin drawl I couldn't place exactly; the skittishness he had displayed on the phone wasn't in evidence now. He wore oblong glasses, behind which cold blue eyes held me in their gaze.

'We should get out of here,' he said. 'There's nothing more to see.'

I nodded and found Lorna in the kitchen, where I thanked her and said it was probably a bit big for me. She smiled glassily, not quite impervious to rejection yet, but getting there steadily, another estate agent who woke up one morning and found she had to work for a living. On my way out, I stopped one last time at the spot where Brian Fogarty had fallen, and looked for anything else that might be relevant. The only thing I noticed was that there was a small rectangular bulge in the wall he would have faced at about head height, over which the wallpaper had simply been hung. I worked at the bulge with a key and the paper cracked and tore; beneath was a ceramic wall bracket, the kind you'd hang an old-style can opener on.

Halfway down the drive, I turned to fix in my mind the last impression Anne had given me: of her little sister Margaret sitting in the porch crying, covered in blood, having just discovered her father's body. Noel Sweeney looked at me as I did this, and his mouth curled in something that was as close to a smile as it was to anything else.

'Let's take a walk,' he said. 'We'll cut onto Herbert Road and have a look at the school Owen taught at. Give you the full picture.'

I had already seen down the length of Herbert Road to the new Lansdowne stadium from the pinker of the three Fogarty sisters' bedrooms. I assumed it was Margaret's, since she was the youngest, and since it was also the smallest. It looked out over the back garden, and there was a gate in the fence at the bottom that led directly onto where Herbert and Tritonville Road met. I had wondered whether Steve Owen had used it as a shortcut when he was seeing Irene Fogarty. As we walked around in an elaborate semi-circle to get onto to Herbert Road, I concluded that he must have, and wondered about the sister who might have been watching from her bedroom. What must it have been like growing up in a house where your mother was having an affair with a teacher from the local boys' school? If she was as indiscreet and reckless as Steve Owen claimed, surely the girls must have known, despite what Anne Fogarty claimed. Was that relevant? It was difficult at this stage in a case to distinguish between background and foreground: everything counted or nothing did. You couldn't overemphasize what seemed obvious lest you ignore the tiny detail that was the key to the entire picture.

I sometimes thought it was like one of those paintings whose true meaning lay in the way the subjects are facing or holding their hands, or in the precise configuration of the objects that surround them: what appears clear dissolves into murk at the first close inspection; if you're patient and cunning – and lucky – eventually the clouds disperse, and you see it all with a new clarity, as if for the first time, but also as if it had been apparent all along.

We were at the gates to Marian College at this stage, this detective I had asked to meet and I, with the Dodder river flowing beneath us and the new Lansdowne Stadium under construction a stone's throw away and the red-brick school rising beyond the small playing field at its front, and I realized we'd been walking for ten minutes in total silence. I looked at him and found he was watching me with the same shrewd, semi-amused scrutiny.

'Worked it out yet?' he said. 'Going to tell me where I went wrong?'

'Anne Fogarty said neither she nor her sisters knew about their mother's affair. Do you think that's likely? Teenage girls?'

Sweeney nodded, his mind immediately on the case.

'They claimed not to. My questioning of them wasn't exactly intensive. But they were all that upset over their father, it's hard not to think one of them wouldn't have spoken up if she'd seen anything. What made you wonder? The size of the house? Or maybe the view?'

From where we stood at the entrance to the school, Sweeney pointed down Herbert Road in the direction of Farney Park. I nodded.

'From what Steve Owen told me, there was a certain amount of running around – French farce stuff, climbing in windows, hiding on garage roofs and so forth.'

'The view from the back bedroom,' Sweeney said.

'Margaret's room?' I said.

'No, it was Aisling's, actually. The older sister. But it had been Margaret's, you're half right. When the mother took to her bed, the father commandeered one of the girls' rooms. Anne and Margaret had to share. Aisling claimed Margaret's room for herself. Eldest sister, studying for her exams, so forth.'

I nodded and turned away, momentarily weary of the semi-detached suburban cosiness of it all. Gangsters and blaggers, that was my meat, tough guys and wide boys, wayward women and strong alcohol; I hadn't signed up for which girl gets what bedroom, had I?

'Don't suppose it matters much anyway,' I said.

'I suppose that all depends on whether you think Owen was guilty or not.'

'Dave Donnelly says you're in no doubt he was responsible, with the mother at least consenting, if not actually caught up in it.'

Sweeney smiled his half smile again and shook his head.

'Dave Donnelly,' he said, and not in a good way. 'Tell me this, I gather he's a friend of yours, is the same Dave Donnelly just a time-serving lickspittle or would he actually go out of his way to bury a case because it might prove inconvenient for the Garda powers that be?'

I flushed, and put a hand up to my mouth so I didn't say the first thing that came to me, then I took it away again.

'I don't know anything about Dave that doesn't say he's a good cop. And I know enough about him as a man to know what you've just said is bullshit.'

There was a lot to follow that I didn't say, but I think some scowling and exhaling got the point across. Sweeney held his hands up and laughed.

'All right then. He is a friend of yours. Good to see. Loyalty: if he can command it, he must be worth something.

It's probably not down to him anyway, he's fronting for other people inside in Serious Crime Review, I know they're swamped with cases, need to eliminate as many as possible on whatever pretext they can find.'

'What are you talking about? Dave said . . . are you not convinced Owen was guilty?'

Sweeney looked up the drive towards the school buildings. 'Do you want to take a closer look?'

I shook my head, and we turned back towards Farney Park. I asked him a second time if he didn't think Owen was guilty, and he said tartly that there were a lot of people it suited to think that way. I thought about this for a while: about Cullen's IRA membership and Doyle's Republican connections, and about Ray Moran and the INLA. As we walked, it seemed to me that Sweeney had begun to look edgier; he looked over his shoulder more than once; when I told him I thought I had seen two men watching my apartment from across the road, and following me in an unmarked blue car, and about the cops who visited me and asked why I had called to his house, he tucked me past the iron gates of the detached house we were passing and in behind the high granite wall, an urgent expression in his cold blue eyes. When he spoke, his voice was hoarse and unsteady, as if he had been waiting a long time to say his piece.

'I never saw the copies of the letters Fogarty sent to Cullen, Doyle and Halligan, not during the original investigation. That evidence vanished somewhere inside Garda Headquarters. If I had known about it, it would have changed everything. All we had against Owen was circumstantial. I'm not saying it wasn't strong – those letters went beyond what a normal man would have said in those circumstances. And there was something about that weak-chinned fucker I didn't like, he was a vain boy, an underhand smirker, even at the trial, he always had this air about him, as if it was all unreal and a big mistake, surely no one could possibly want to put away someone as wonderful as him.'

'And if he didn't do it—'

'For sure, if he didn't do it, that all makes sense, he was entitled to feel it was all unreal. Whatever kind of man he was.'

Sweeney turned to me then.

'I want to know. There's a lot of people who don't, and maybe some of those people are manipulating your friend Dave Donnelly. But I was the one who got it wrong all those years ago. The first thing I said after Owen's conviction was ruled unsafe was, let's open it up, let's investigate the three boys. Nobody wanted to know, for a variety of reasons. So anything I can do, I'll do. Because when it comes down to it, a man was murdered eighteen years ago, and justice hasn't been done.'

'And the variety of reasons includes what? Keeping the Peace Process shiny and clean? Not treading on the toes of those who helped bring it about, and who keep it on course? That sounds like the Special Branch, or whatever we call them today, the Special Detective Unit?'

Sweeney's eyes flashed but he said nothing. I continued.

'It was hardly your fault you got it wrong: if evidence was suppressed back in '91, when the IRA were still bombing and shooting, what hope did you have?'

'I'm not looking for excuses. I'm looking to set things right. If you swear to tell no one – especially not your friend Dave Donnelly – I think I can help you. From the best motive in the world, self-interest. Does that sound to you like a deal?'

Sweeney's voice had dropped to a cracked whisper. We stood on soft grass beneath a sprouting sycamore, a boat hiding us out of sight of the stone villa in whose garden we'd sought refuge. There was a garden seat beneath a laurel tree that made me think of a park bench, and that made me think of spies meeting in an espionage novel. It seemed faintly absurd, and yet when I looked in Sweeney's eyes, I knew he was deadly serious. I nodded, and made to leave; he shook his head and led me along the side of the house and through a gateway that gave onto a lane running all the way to the bottom of Newbridge Avenue. Before we got onto the street, Sweeney held me back until he had checked the lay of the land to his satisfaction. When he turned to let me know it was all clear, there must have been a flicker of something less than gravity in my eyes, enough for Sweeney to haul me back up the lane a stretch.

'You may think this is funny, Ed. If so, either you don't care about your safety the way you need to, or you don't understand how serious these people are. I know you're reckless, and you lead with your chin, and maybe that's been fine up to now, although that ear's got to hurt, but these people aren't messing around. And if I'm going to help you, I'm going to be at risk as well. So let me know if you're going to take this seriously, or you can go solo and welcome.'

It was a version of the speech Tommy Owens had given me. Except Tommy had been talking about the criminals. Noel Sweeney was warning me about the cops. I nodded, and followed Sweeney down towards Irishtown and through a warren of alleyways and lanes that backed onto Ringsend Park; finally he knocked on the side door of a pub and we were admitted to a room that felt like an oul' one's tiny parlour: a red formica-topped table, a couple of battered kitchen chairs, the smell of cooking oil and boiled cabbage and stale smoke, an old bakelite radio set on a bocketty occasional table. Presently a very fat man in collar and tie and a red wool waistcoat came in through dirty beaded door curtains carrying a tray laden with toasted sandwiches and pints of Guinness. He had greased-back dyed black hair and port wine jowls and his hands shook, but there was a fire in his tiny black eyes that burned clear. He popped the tray on the table.

'Noel,' he said.

'Seamus.'

'Anyone else?'

'Not unless I've gone to seed utterly.'

Seamus nodded, smiling faintly, as if this unlikely but not impossible fate would come to us all. I wondered how he'd be able to tell when it came to him.

'This is Mister Loy,' Sweeney said. His voice was different when he spoke to Seamus: at once rougher and more musical, it was as if he had put on an Irish accent. Seamus's blotchy red face presented itself to me impassively. He smelt of whiskey and of soap.

'Good man,' he said, and nodded. It was the blandest of salutes, but I felt strangely bolstered by it, as if, already, I had made all the right decisions, and now I had my feet under the top table. A voice in my head entered the reservation that, given the night I'd had, lunchtime pints were probably not the wisest choice. But as ever with me, it was a very small voice.

'How's the Mammy?' Sweeney said, improbably.

Seamus smiled meekly.

'She'll bury us all,' he said.

'And isn't she entitled to?' Sweeney cried, his accent getting broader by the minute.

Seamus gave us a smile in the form of a grimace and retreated. Sweeney's face set back into the tense, watchful configuration it held when I first met him. He winked at me and took a drink of his pint.

'It's safe here. Always has been. Seamus might not look like much, but he can hold the line. A bit old-fashioned, but that's not the worst thing.'

'Is his mother really alive?'

'She's seventy-two. Sure Seamus isn't much more than fifty.'

We ate and drank in the silence that was becoming habitual

between us. For all the caution and unease he had displayed when he learned I might have a tail on me, Sweeney's presence found a natural pitch somewhere between calming and bracing. I found the vibration sympathetic. Once we had eaten and drunk, and follow-up pints, perfectly timed, had arrived – maybe Seamus was watching us on a monitor – Sweeney began to talk.

'Once they found Steve Owen's conviction unsafe, once the evidence emerged that Brian Fogarty had these serious criminals with motives to kill him, I asked to be assigned to the reinvestigation. I was a detective inspector in Irishtown Garda Station up the road there. First I was refused because I had a full list of case pendings. Then it was made known to me that the case was going to be transferred to the National Bureau of Criminal Investigation. I asked a friend in there: no sign of it. Next thing, it was the subject of a turf war between the NBCI and the Branch, some of whom had transferred into the NBCI, some of whom were in the SDU, and some of whom were hanging around Garda Headquarters getting in everyone else's way. Then Veronica Guerin was murdered and the Criminal Assets Bureau was set up. Suddenly this was the new reality: it was too difficult to prosecute gangland figures, not to mention terrorists, for murder. But you could confiscate their assets if they were found to be the proceeds of crime. The mechanism that Brian Fogarty had anticipated was finally in place, with a legal right to seize property and cash if its owners couldn't account for its legitimacy. It wasn't the reopening of the case that I had wanted, but it was something: it would bring some strained justice to the Brian Fogarty case if the criminals he had established cases against were finally punished, in however limited a way. So I waited, and I waited, and finally, and it seemed in retrospect inevitably, nothing happened, and I quickly learned that nothing would. At that stage I had been promoted out to a desk job in the Phoenix Park, head down, all passion spent, pension on its way.'

Sweeney took a long drink of stout and stared grimly into his glass; the life force seemed suddenly to have left him; he looked vulnerable, forlorn, almost broken. He took a second draught and downed the memory with it; when he looked at me again, it was business as usual.

'Bobby Doyle made a settlement with the CAB in 1998, didn't he?'

'Bobby Doyle approached CAB to make a voluntary settlement. Bobby Doyle was an important conduit between Sinn Féin and Irish-American money on the one hand and between Sinn Féin and the business community in Dublin on the other. When the Good Friday Agreement was signed, and peace and harmony erupted throughout the land, Bobby Doyle was the subject of . . . well, you'd call it a whispering campaign, except no one was doing very much whispering. Where did he come from, how did he rise so far so fast, what did he get up to during the Troubles?'

'I understood the settlement was for undeclared rental income on the properties. Back taxes?'

'That's right. But the suspicions lingered. The whiff of cordite. Was he on the Army Council?'

'So what are you saying? That such a person?'

'That such a person, exactly. Not that there weren't a lot of them walking about, fully pardoned for slaughtering men, women and children. But they're all community workers or sociology postgraduates or no nonsense fuel smugglers and drug dealers, not developers lobbying for big government tenders in the South.'

'Not building flagship bridges to celebrate Irish independence.'

'That's right. So the Branch finally piled in to investigate. Two of them rolled up to my house on a Sunday morning, wouldn't give me the courtesy of letting me arrange a meeting on my own time. Pumped me for everything on the Fogarty case. No matter that it's not your fault, if you see your case collapse, it's your neck on the block, so I was on the back foot from the start. I was straight with them, no odds in not being, besides I had a mole in the SDU who was letting me know everything as it broke. The impression I got, and it was a true one, was that they wanted to know if I had uncovered any evidence to suggest that Bobby Doyle had had anything to do with the Fogarty killing. And the fact was, I hadn't: when the Owen conviction was overturned, before I was warned off, I did a bit of digging and I found nothing to connect Doyle with any kind of gun play or active paramilitarism. Not to say he couldn't have paid a hitman, but I didn't see any evidence of it. And I spoke to people in Jack Cullen's gang who were never going to go straight: none of them particularly liked Doyle, thought him a sell-out and so forth, but they laughed at the idea that he'd have someone killed, said that was the whole problem with Bobby Doyle and with Sinn Féin the way it was going, too many people wanting to build things, not enough happy to blow them up any more.'

'Doyle told me he was only involved peripherally in the North in the seventies: he might have held the odd coat, or bought the odd pint, but he was never on active service, never a volunteer. He was sympathetic for a time because he felt the Catholic, Nationalist community were under siege, but he was never in the IRA. That said, he seems to have been in the wider Republican movement a long time, raising cash and so on. The way he puts it, it was as if he was waiting around for them all to see sense and stop the killing. And finally they did.'

Sweeney's cold blue eyes narrowed with interest.

'You spoke to him? How'd you get to Bobby Doyle?'

'Through his assistant, Donna Nugent. She's a friend of

mine. He was having dinner for some Irish Americans in Shanahan's on Thursday night.'

Sweeney didn't exactly whistle, but his features creased as close to a smile as they'd come. I was smiling too, with embarrassment: every time I thought of Donna Nugent, I wanted to shout NO NO NO and I couldn't so I smiled instead, the kind of smile when you slip on ice in a crowded street and leap up immediately as if nothing has happened. And nothing had, Ed Loy: you just had a major dose of The Fear. Donna Nugent was your kind of girl, and you should just knuckle down and accept it. And read one of the seven texts she'd sent you since you left her bed. Sweeney was nodding his approval, as if his rookie colleague had acquitted himself well.

'That's pretty good access, Ed, well done. And how'd he strike you?'

'I guess, the way you're saying. A big beast, a player, used to being in charge, being listened to, a certain amount of charm. I wouldn't want to get the wrong side of him, but if I did, I wouldn't be worried about getting a bullet behind the ear.'

'I was sceptical, you know: I thought, this is what they *want*, for him to be clean. But there was nothing on him, certainly nothing in Dublin.'

'And what about earlier, in the North, did his version tie in with the facts?'

'I was never told officially. None of my business. Again, not even the courtesy. But my man in the SDU told me what they came up with.'

'Which was?'

'Nothing. There's no record of Bobby Doyle among Republican circles anywhere in the North. The house he said he grew up in was demolished, the neighbours don't remember the family, said that house was derelict for years before. No one who was on active service in that area recognized the photograph or the name. And they didn't just talk to Provos, they checked him out with dissidents: the Real IRA, the Continuity IRA, the INLA, it's not some kind of conspiracy to make out he's always been clean, like pretending Gerry Adams was never in the IRA. There are plenty of people out there, like with Cullen's boys, who'd love to smear Doyle any way they could: he's everything they despise. He has no police record under his own name, his photo doesn't match any mug shots the RUC had. It's as if he was never there at all, as if he emerged out of the ether in San Francisco in the eighties.'

'That's weird. He didn't strike me as American, if that's what you're suggesting. And he referred to his past as if it was an open secret.'

'Well, it's a secret anyway. So there you have it. Not ruled out, but not likely. I have to say I don't like those murderous fuckers he consorts with, I don't like to see them in power in the North, and I'd do anything I could to stop them here. But I don't think Bobby Doyle is our man.'

'A source I have thinks it was Jack Cullen, or more particularly, Lamp Comerford.'

I took Sweeney through what Tommy had told me about Lamp, Cullen and Ray Moran, the scuffles over drug territory, the rivalry within the Cullen gang, the possible involvement of the INLA, the way in which Ray Moran was Jack Cullen's creature. I didn't mention my visit to Moran's office with Tommy and Leo Halligan. I was still trying to pretend it hadn't actually happened.

'It's worth keeping Jack Cullen personally in the frame,' Sweeney said. 'It's always been a bit of a joke to me that Lamp Comerford was Jack's enforcer. Jack needed a bagman like Moran, and he found himself a good one, but Lamp's just a common or garden hard man: Jack was always vicious enough to do his own enforcing.'

'I assume Jack Cullen had a more visible career in the IRA then.'

'You could say that, yeah. He ran a gang across the border for specific operations. He was known particularly for his scorched earth policy: if there were innocent bystanders, family members, wives, children, that was nothing to Jack Cullen. He killed anything that moved, and he liked to do it himself. A prayer meeting in an old timber-frame church hall, twelve people, most of them in their sixties and seventies: Jack broke in on top of them with a Kalashnikov and shot them to pieces. In retaliation for some piece of Loyalist butchery, as if that's what retaliation meant: why not kill the Loyalists? Because it's too hard, and blood must be spilt right now, tonight. So kill a crowd of old Protestant ladies, that's what Irish freedom is all about. He tortured one of his own gang, Gerry Toal, grew up on Richmond Road there, father of two, not a bad lad, tortured him as an informer, broke his little fingers and pulled out four of his teeth, then fed him whiskey, a lad who was in the room told me this, Toal drinking whiskey and looking at pictures of his kids and crying, 23 years old, crying like a child himself until Cullen put a gun to his head and killed him. The lad that told me that also told me Cullen interrogated a mentally handicapped sixteen-year-old who claimed to have killed someone everyone knew the UVF killed, a grocer's boy on his way home from the chipper. And despite it being obvious the poor unfortunate was raving, Cullen ordered his death, his execution, they called it, as if they were an actual country, which in their own heads they were, of course, had a sixteen-year-old shot and buried in sand dunes on the Antrim coast. And do you know what Toal supposedly informed on? An arms dump that had been abandoned before the Troubles ever began, it was well known as having been used during the IRA's border campaign of the late nineteen fifties. A disused IRA arms dump that every kid in the area knew about. That's what Gerry Toal's kids had to lose their daddy over. And there's a dozen more stories like that. "Jack Cullen was a staunch and devoted physical force Republican who has always supported the Peace Process," was Sinn Féin's line when they were challenged about Cullen's alleged involvement in organized crime. And when you hear those words in future – staunch, devoted, peace – you can think of Gerry Toal, crying over pictures of the children he'd never see again.'

Sweeney finished his pint and looked at me, his face set, his blue eyes blazing. The passion was in the content of his words; his tone was even and cold.

'In a way, I don't care whether Cullen is guilty of Brian Fogarty's murder or not, unless it's a way we can get him. He's guilty of so much wickedness it's obscene that he's still walking about.'

'I have some contact with Lamp Comerford at the moment, for reasons I'd rather not go into. Anyway, I don't think he and Lamp are exactly happy together. And if Lamp thinks Jack is trying lay the blame for the Fogarty murder at his door, who knows what he might do?'

Sweeney looked at me with affected disapproval.

'And you'll stir it up with no evidence other than hearsay? What your source said?'

'I'm a private detective. Stirring it up is what we do. I don't work with evidence, I work with he said she said, with versions of the truth. When I get one I think fits best, if we're lucky, there'll be some evidence the cops, and better still, a prosecutor, can use. If there isn't that, we hope for a witness or three, if someone's left alive, that is. In the meantime, it's he said she said until the sky cracks open and the truth comes falling.'

'Just like it does.'

'Just like it does. But it's unbroken cloud for now, and the only thing falling is the rain.'

I looked at my watch. It was time I was leaving. I exchanged cards with Noel Sweeney, and told him I'd check in as soon as I had anything for him, and he suggested I get a taxi to wherever I was going since I had evaded my SDU tail for once, and by the time I made it to the door of the pub whose name I never discovered and which I looked for but never found again, there was a cab waiting.

I had wanted to ask Sweeney more about Aisling and Margaret, the Fogarty sisters I hadn't met, but I was on my way to see a Fogarty sister, after all, and if Anne didn't tell me what I needed to hear, I reasoned that I would always be able to ask Sweeney again. I was mistaken in this, and although I make many mistakes, this one has stayed with me like flesh badly snagged on barbed wire, a wound you think will never heal.

16

Anne Fogarty was waiting for me outside St Thomas's church across from the Grand Canal near Adelaide Road. She wore a black dress with a red rose pattern and a tiny denim jacket and black cross-buckled boots that came to her knees; her honey blonde hair was tied up and her lips were the darkest red and from across the road I could see her work her braces against them so that I couldn't think of anything except her mouth and completely failed to notice the small people who were waiting with her. Anne Fogarty kissed me on the cheek and presented two little dark haired, dark eyed girls to me. One looked about nine and the other about seven, but I couldn't have sworn to it. They were both exceptionally pretty.

'This is Aoife and this is Ciara,' she said. 'This is Ed Loy.'

'You have a black suit and a white shirt but no tie. Why?' Ciara, the younger girl, said.

'*Ciara*,' hissed Aoife, and clapped a hand to her brow in pantomimed embarrassment.

'I don't wear one.'

'Daddy doesn't wear one either,' Ciara said.

'That's 'cause Daddy doesn't wear suits, duh,' Aoife said.

'Actually, men don't have to wear a tie any more,' Ciara said.

'Thank you,' I said.

'Ciara you are so *embarrassing*,' Aoife said.

That seemed to exhaust the immediate conversational possibilities, and the girls went back to whatever it was they had been doing before I arrived, poring over comic books by the looks of things. Anne smiled at me and I smiled back and we all went into church together and I had a strange sensation of familiarity, as if it wasn't the first time I had done this, and it wouldn't be the last. And then I flashed on Donna Nugent clawing my back and screaming in my ear and the sweat spiked my scalp and I wondered just who the fuck I thought I was kidding. It was enough to drive a man to prayer.

There were prayers at St Thomas's, but it wasn't a conventional church service. There were Catholic and Anglican priests and Methodist and Presbyterian ministers on the altar, but the first speaker, a bearded man in a tweed jacket who looked like an academic and spoke like a poet, said that people of all faiths and of none were very welcome here today. He went on to say that Holy Saturday was a dark day in the calendar, perhaps darker even than Good Friday, in the same way the day after a funeral is more desolate because at least on the day of the funeral there is a certain kind of release, even in grief and in pain, an active participation in the intense process of loss, a catharsis, indeed, whereas the day after, when the mourners have departed and we are left alone, it is like the morning after the storm, and we are laid as low as we have ever been: there is nothing but silence and loss, and we have forgotten how to hope. But as for Christians, the desolation is followed by the joy of the resurrection on Easter Sunday, so grief, in time, abates, and hope, at last, returns. That process takes longer – indeed, it may not occur at all – when the death mourned is an unnatural one. And that is why, on this lost day, this day that falls through the crack in time, the only day in the calendar a Catholic Mass cannot be said, we are gathered to remember the deaths of some of those who lost their lives in the Troubles.

I heard Anne's breath catch, and turned to see her eyes wet with tears. The girls were deep in their comics – the *Teen*

Titans, kind of a junior *Justice League of America* – and paid their mother no attention. Anne made her mouth smile at me, and I offered my hand, and she clutched it as the bearded man outlined what shape the service would take. There was a book called *Lost Lives*, which consisted of factual accounts of every single person – British soldier, IRA volunteer, Loyalist paramilitary, civilian – who had been killed during the Troubles. It was a huge book, and two copies of it were on the two lecterns at either side of the altar. Readers would come from the floor and read selections from the book for an hour. This would not bring the dead back, or console the living, but it would, amidst the clamour of voices rushing to describe the Troubles as history, as politics, as conflict, be a still reminder of what was lost. It would serve as a bridge between the living and the dead. It would, for a short hour, give a voice to the dead.

Afterwards, shaken, wrung out, but relieved to have found our way back across the bridge, we stood in the churchyard and on the street and by the canal, talking and smoking and embracing, the living. Anne's ex-husband, Kevin, who had longish, very well cut hair and rumpled, brightly coloured, very expensive clothes, showed up to collect Aoife and Ciara. He had been at the service too, Anne told me, and a college friend of his, Gerry Coyle, was actually included in the book; he shook my hand and took off with his daughters, who made a point of saying goodbye to me and asking if I had a gun (Ciara) and apologizing for her sister (Aoife). When they left, and anyway after the service, I wanted a drink, a whiskey in fact, but Anne said there was something she needed in her car, which was in a car park on or just off Mespil Road, so we walked down along the canal and in to the car park and up to the third floor and Anne found her car, a navy Saab convertible, and there was no one around and she opened the back door and looked at me and I said, beginning to guess now from the way she looked at me, and wondering would I be able after last night, what was it you needed? and she said, you, I need you, Ed, I need you to fuck me, and once she'd said that I didn't wonder any more and she took me in her mouth and her braces felt weird but good and she said I tasted like beer with salt in it and kissed me so I could taste myself and she pulled me down on her and pushed her underwear aside and she tasted pretty good too only not like beer and then she guided me in and we fucked on the back seat with the door open, fucked like it was the last time either of us would ever have, and anyone could have heard us but I don't think anyone did.

'I wanted to do that from the first moment I saw you as well,' Anne Fogarty said afterwards, as we walked hand in hand down the canal towards Smyth's pub on Haddington Road, 'but I thought it might seem a bit forward on Thursday morning. Seeing as how we'd only just met. And it wasn't even lunchtime.'

'But now we've been to church together. And I've met your family.'

'Call me old-fashioned, but that's the kind of girl I am.'

A couple of drinks later, I started forcing myself to frown as a kind of prelude to getting my mind back on the case, and being the kind of girl she was, Anne picked up on this and did a bit of frowning herself, and finally spoke.

'So look, the other thing I didn't tell you . . . and I don't want you to think I'm being underhand or less than candid, I just didn't, for reasons I'll explain, okay, the house is for sale, the family home. Farney Park.'

'I know,' I said. 'I was there this morning. Noel Sweeney told me about it.'

Anne Fogarty's frown looked completely unforced at the mention of Sweeney's name, until I explained that he had come to very different conclusions about who might have killed her father. This had been occupying my thoughts throughout the Lost Lives service, as I'm sure it had Anne's, the idea that if Jack Cullen had killed Brian Fogarty in 1991, then he would have to be included in the next edition of the book, a victim of the IRA and yet another dead voice to be reclaimed.

'Well then, if he's going to cooperate with you, that's progress isn't it?' she said, and I agreed, and waited for her to say something more about the house. When she didn't, I had to.

'The house looked like it hadn't really altered since. Is it still in the family? Why wasn't it sold? It didn't look like anyone had lived there.'

Anne shook her head.

'After Mammy died, we . . . Aisling moved out when she went to college, earlier, she was the first to go. She got a flat, she worked in restaurants and . . . that's what she ended up doing eventually, she runs Le Bistro on Harcourt Street. She did a commerce degree and . . . where was I? Sorry, I'm fucking . . . gabbling, Jesus.'

Anne Fogarty picked up her glass of wine and had to put it down again, her hand was shaking so much.

'What's the matter? You don't have to—'

'I fucking *do* have to, though, don't I? I have to tell you everything, because maybe if I don't, if I leave out some minor detail, that could be it, that detail could lead you to the killer. Couldn't it? So don't say I don't have to, don't try and be nice, Ed Loy. That's not why we like you.'

Anne smiled at this last crack and tried to make the smile stick; she picked her wine up and sank the half glass she had left in one and gestured for two more drinks and drank half her fresh glass before she resumed.

'Sorry. When a murder . . . oh, I don't know enough to generalize, start again, when my father was murdered, it wasn't just his life, it was all our lives, it was the family that was murdered. And I wanted, I thought it was right that we should stick together, I don't know, middle child perhaps, that if we weren't crushed by it, then we could, what, recover. Not that I consciously thought that, or anything, but I think that was the shape I was following, the emotional shape, do you know what I mean? But first of all, Mammy was just in no condition, she couldn't bear it, she was worse than she had been beforehand, when she had found out about Daddy, just tranquillized to oblivion. And then, none of us had known about Ma and Steve Owen. So the whole thing of the trial, the whole way that unfolded, was just such a shock to us all. And none of us felt very warm towards Mammy. But you know, Daddy had started it, and . . . maybe you had to dig deep to stand by her, but that's what you're supposed to do, you're a family, you stand together.'

'And Aisling and Margaret didn't see it like that?'

'Aisling didn't give Mammy the time of day. Aisling didn't speak to Mammy from the day she found out about her affair until the day she died. If I hadn't gone around to Aisling's flat the night before the removal and begged her, I don't think Aisling would have come to Mammy's funeral.'

'What about Margaret?'

'Midge was younger. She cried a lot, and . . . then I suppose she kind of withdrew. And she wasn't let go to the trial. She made a lot of new friends around that time, and . . . I don't know. After Mammy died . . . I was at college, but I stayed at home, to . . . because I was afraid of what might happen if I left.'

'How did your mother die?'

'Heart failure. She'd been smoking and drinking like it was her life's work. Her heart couldn't take it. Died in her sleep, fifty-five years old. And then there were three. And Aisling moved out. And that was it. I saw Midge at Steve Owen's appeal. Aisling too. And I haven't seen either of them since.

I met Kevin, I was with Kevin then, and we got married, and . . . life began. I had a family of my own. And every so often, after house prices went mental, I tried to get them to agree to sell the house, but Aisling kept saying to hold on because prices were still climbing and Midge claimed she wanted to move back in, and I told her it wasn't her house to move back in to. Then Aisling called the top of the market, based on some stock analyst she was going out with, but by then, Midge had stopped returning my calls, and then I lost contact with her altogether. We're all executors of the estate, which means if one of us disagrees, we can't do anything. So we were paralysed. Meanwhile the house has just been sitting there. I said, we could at least do it up and rent it out, but Aisling said, what would happen if Midge just walked in there one day, you know, on top of the tenants. It's almost funny, actually, the . . . inertia, you know? And Aisling was really desperate for a while, and then she ended up marrying the stock analyst, he works for one of the brokerages, can't remember which, anyway, none of them pay peanuts so it kind of slipped off her urgent to-do list. Until now.'

'Until when?'

'Until about a month ago. Midge called me up out of the blue. Five years? God, more like eight. And I was all, how've you been, what've you been doing? Nothing from sister dear. Just, if you want to sell the house, go ahead, you have my per-mission. If you don't mind handling it all, lodge my third to my account when it's sold. This distant voice, like she was reading from a prepared script to someone she'd never met. And before I could tell her, for example, that I was divorced, or that my babies were girls now, or anything really, she hung up.'

'Did you get her number?'

'It was withheld. She said she'd call me, to advertise the house in the *Times*. I have her bank details, if they're any use.'

'They should be.'

'Don't go to any trouble on my behalf. I mean, if she doesn't want to see me, fine. It's not as if my weird sister has any bearing on which of Jack Cullen, Bobby Doyle or George Halligan killed my father, is it?'

'I don't suppose so. Just, I like to get the full picture, you know? I want to talk to Aisling as well. You never know what people remember, what people knew all along and they don't even realize.'

'Well don't expect me to set you up with Aisling, when I told her I was going to hire a private detective she went mental. She doesn't want to go back there, she doesn't want to remember.'

'Was it Margaret's phone call that gave you the idea?'

'I'd had the idea for a while. Midge's call spurred me into action, is what it was. I guess the fact the house had been hanging unresolved for so long had stood for everything to do with Daddy's murder, the sense of unfinished business. And when I went down there – originally I was going to give the place a complete makeover, that's what I do, new kitchen, bathroom, the whole bit, but the estate agent said there was no point, house like that, people want to put their own stamp on it anyway, just make sure it's clean and full of light – but walking around the house, I just felt it so vividly, like it had happened yesterday, you know? And if I didn't try one last time to get at the truth, it would be too late. The house would be gone, and so would all that goes with it, our family, our . . . my . . . Daddy.'

Anne Fogarty's face creased with misery and tears filled her eyes. She apologized, but couldn't stop, and finally, weeping, went out to the bathroom. I was treated to the kind of glares befitting a man who breaks up with his girlfriend and doesn't even have the decency to buy her dinner first, does it over a bar stool. I was glad of the reminder though: Brian Fogarty may have been eighteen years dead, but there were still people who wept for him. Like each lost life, it still mattered. It always would.

Anne came back with fresh eye make-up and a fierce smile; I smothered her apologies in an embrace, attracting even more glares as I did so, and told her I had to go.

Outside the pub, she pulled me close and we kissed, and I muttered something about not necessarily being the kind of man who could be trusted, and she said she wasn't made of china and no promises could be broken unless they'd been made first and neither of us had made any, and I said that sounded pretty tough and what if I wanted to make a promise or two, and she said that I didn't have time, that I had to go to work, and she kissed me again, and we left it at that, each knowing, or at least hoping, that there'd be more, a lot more.

17

Dessie Delaney knew there was something up the moment he stepped off the plane. Not from what he saw at the airport, not from anything in the Arrivals Hall, not from anyone at the concession desks or at the exit doors or in the taxi queue; Dessie had a keen enough eye for the kind of rubbish that might be sent out to clock them to be reasonably confident no one was watching their flight, and little wonder, on one level, weren't they going to show up at the church in anyway, that was an appointment they couldn't exactly reschedule, so if anyone wanted to keep a tail on them why not start then? No, Dessie knew there was something up with Liam. From having been a drunken shambles, he'd suddenly pulled himself together, gotten all efficient and business-like and serious and . . . sober, that's what it was, Liam was sober, not technically, he'd been drunk five hours ago, but he looked sober, maybe that's all it was, it had been so long. He wasn't shooting his mouth off like a blowhard, he wasn't weeping, he was quiet, reserved, like the Liam Dessie had vague memories of, his big brother, before he'd turned into Paddy Irishman, the professional fucking eejit.

But there was something else. He was sure of it. A look in the eye that said Liam was holding something back. They'd got to the hotel about eight, and cleaned up and changed and eaten breakfast and they were at the funeral home in Fairview around half ten, eleven. Fuck, that wasn't easy. Dessie was the one in tears now. Paul didn't look like himself for a start, whatever way they'd done his lips he looked like a fucking Presbyterian, although in fairness if Dessie had taken two behind the ear he'd be looking a bit miserable too. They'd done a good job of hiding all that, and he hadn't been shot in the face, so all in all, it wasn't as bad as it could have been. Still, it was Dessie's brother and he was lying there dead so it wasn't exactly good either. Almost the worst thing was, Dessie had made the mistake of kissing Paul's forehead, and of course it was full of chemicals and stuffed with whatever the fuck, it felt like he'd kissed a department store mannequin or something and he couldn't get the feeling – it was like a bad taste, it clung to his lips, the sensation of it, of thinking he was going to kiss his brother's brow and it not being his at all, not being him. Not easy at all, fuck.

And there was Liam all solemn-eyed and respectable, like grief had dignified the cunt. It made Dessie uncomfortable, not that that was necessarily a bad thing, kept you on your toes, watching for the next mistake you or some other cunt might make and let it be him not you, but he just wasn't used to it with fucking Liam. Still, it meant when Dessie suggested they walk down into town that Liam didn't once look longingly at let alone mention the few scoops to settle the nerves even though Dessie wouldn't've minded himself to be honest. On the way, Dessie laid it out for Liam: that there was a fair chance they might get hit, that on top of that, they were there to avenge their brother's death, that the same people – Jack Cullen, Lamp Comerford, the Halligans – were the likely lads in each circumstance, that they had to play it cool but they had to be ready, which was why they were going to take a taxi up to Larry Knight's place where Larry had some guns they might need for protection.

And Liam, no shouting or crying or grandstanding, said simply:

For protection, or to plug the cunt or cunts who done Paul.

Fair play, big bro, that's the correct fucking temperature.

Larry Knight's place was up in the Dublin Mountains. It didn't look like much from the front: hard against the road, electric gates opened and there was this sprawling concrete bungalow, like a bunker, Dessie thought, and he'd heard so much about it over the years, Larry's place, like it was a real fucking palace. More knackerology, more skin-pop hole talk, Dessie thought to himself.

And then they got inside, and wasn't the entire back wall of Larry's place made of glass, and didn't it drop down a floor and all, and wasn't there nothing beneath it but sloping fields and houses and then out beyond this fucking view, this panorama, Dublin Bay the whole way around, unbelievable even today, all slate grey and overcast; at night, Dessie thought, it must look like the world on fire.

And here's Larry, snow white ponytail, immaculate white sportswear, the gold chains, the shark's tooth earrings, the whole fucking deal: Larry Knight, the original and still the best, living like a king high above the city he turned on to smack and coke and dope. Many came after, but someone has to be the first, and Larry was that for so many: there were kids down there that Larry turned their fucking grandparents on, three generations of dealers who owed it all to Mr K. Dessie Delaney knew well it was fucking horrible, he'd seen the kids being taken off parents who were incapable, and worse, he'd seen the kids who weren't but should have been, he'd escaped a fate like that by the skin of his teeth. Still, he couldn't help admire Larry: there was something old school about him. He had class, Mr K, everyone was agreed on that. Must be nice up here, looking down on it all. And in a game where no one lasted very long, Larry had seen most of them off, and was hoping to see the rest before long.

Larry greeted them and said he was sorry for their trouble and led them downstairs and into a room with a full size snooker table and a darts board and a roulette wheel and a bar with taps and optics and all, like a club it was, all red velvet curtains and dark green leather walls with pictures of the seven rebels executed after the 1916 rising and the Proclamation of Independence they'd read from the steps of the GPO in O'Connell Street mounted on the wall. Mr K had class, of that there was no doubt. On the bar were three shot glasses of whiskey and they each knocked one back: For Paul. Which was a nice touch, Dessie thought. Dessie didn't really drink but he didn't Not Drink either, even though they warned him after rehab to steer clear of booze, it's the classic . . . transference mechanism, they called it, meaning you douse your craving for smack in booze and pretty soon you're just as hooked on alcohol as you ever were on heroin. Dessie had kept clear of booze anyway, mainly because he'd never really liked the taste. There were some times though – and seeing the embalmed corpse of your little brother was one of those times – when a cup of tea just wasn't going to do it.

The guns were on a dark wood table, wrapped in off-white tarpaulin. There were Steyr machine pistols and Glock semi-automatic handguns and an AK 47 and magazines and clips of ammunition. Dessie wasn't an expert but these were simple pieces that didn't really need much expertise. Larry was talking in that Dublin with an American burr accent of his about what a terrible thing the death of a blood relation was, and how, sadly, the only way to atone for this sin against the Great Spirit (along with the bling, Larry wore necklaces and wristbands of coloured beads and was known to have a Native American thing going on) was in certain circumstances to spill blood in return: eye for eye, tooth for tooth, stripe for stripe, blood for blood, said Larry, ramping up the preacher vibe a stretch. Dessie didn't disagree, but despite the grandeur of his surroundings, he couldn't help giving Larry a look; fair play, Larry cracked a grin and conceded that if Jack Cullen had to take a fall, it wouldn't just be the Great Spirit that'd be in greater harmony with the cosmos: the cunt has been asking for it for years, Larry said.

They had another drink, and then Larry loaded up the guns into the back of a black Range Rover. Larry had a house across on Griffith Avenue and Dessie and Liam'd be safe there, and more to the point, so would the ordnance. The driver had a shaved head and a black leather jacket and wore wraparound shades and didn't say a word the entire journey which suited Dessie, who was busy watching Liam for a sign, he wasn't entirely sure what of but something, and he backed the car into the driveway and got out to open the garage door and reversed inside and shut the doors again and then they loaded the guns into the house through the door that led from the garage into the kitchen.

Before the driver left, he finally spoke. Pizza on its way, he said in a surprisingly high-pitched voice. After he'd gone, and they'd heard the sound of the garage doors slam and the Range Rover driving away, Dessie and Liam cracked up laughing, and kept repeating to each other in the squeakiest voices they could manage, Pizza on its way, Pizza on its way, hysterical, Dessie knew, but fuck it, laughing was better than most of the alternatives, and they kept it up until the doorbell rang to herald the arrival of the pizza.

Dessie told Liam it would be best not to go armed to the removal – see how the land lies and take it from there. Then when Liam went to the jacks, Dessie loaded a Glock 17 with a ten round clip and stuck it in his coat. You never know, thought Dessie, you never fucking know.

At four they were outside the funeral home and what did they see passing by but a horse-drawn hearse, one of the elaborate black metal and glass jobs with the six black horses with plumes of feathers and a rider in a top hat. Dessie looked at Liam and Liam raised his eyebrows and shook his head. They waited and the hearse, which was empty, went on down the road. Not much doubt Paul was connected if he ended up being taken to the church in something like that, either a gangster or a knacker. It dawned on Dessie that he hadn't been clear about the arrangements: Sharon said she'd deal with things, and then she said – had she actually said Liam had made the calls? Fuck sake. Before he had a chance to ask him, Dessie saw Lamp Comerford on his way, all in black with his flat top gelled up, the suave fucker, and Dessie had his hand on the Glock and Lamp held his hands up, all friends here, big slap on the back hugs all round and in they went. Lamp went over and looked at Paul and bowed his head and made like he was saying a prayer, then he blessed himself and turned around and this is what he said:

Sorry for your trouble lads. He was a good boy. Now, I know you probably heard a lot of talk, but this is what it is: the INLA.

Dessie had heard a bit of this from Ollie and Dave, how the INLA were getting stuck into the drugs trade, how they saw the IRA as easy pickings, how they were ruthless and didn't give a fuck about anyone, well that part wasn't exactly news. And Lamp said, you seen that hearse roll past, out on the street? That's for the two INLA lads we done over in Beresford Lane, Dean Cummins and Simon Devlin, they're going to the church today as well.

Dessie asked were they the same lads who done Paul, and Lamp Comerford said he didn't know: he wasn't sure what time Paul had been killed and had they been to the Guards yet?

No they hadn't been to the fucking Guards, Dessie said, realizing as he said it, as Lamp Comerford flashed him a look, that that was the first thing he should have fucking done, that's what ordinary people would have done, innocent people, people who didn't know where Larry Knight lived and even if they had, wouldn't't've gone up to his house to get a big bag of guns and ammunition. Fuck sake. Dessie rolled his eyes. And Lamp said, maybe you didn't have time. And Dessie nodded. And Lamp said, chances are they'll be at the church anyway.

Of course they fucking would. Because you'll be there, Lamp, and look who else has just walked in.

Jack Cullen.

Dessie recognized him immediately, even though he'd never seen him before. Jack Cullen was a small man, about five four in height, and slightly built, and he'd worn his hair in a Number One cut long before it became fashionable. Jack Cullen wasn't much for fashion. Even today, going to someone's removal, he was wearing what he always wore: blue jeans and a blue naval sweater, the ribbed sort with the shoulder patches, round neck with no shirt beneath, and soft black shoes. No jacket or coat. He looked like he could have been standing outside a betting shop, or smoking in the pub doorway. He didn't look like the notorious fucker he was, like the major IRA gang boss who'd lost count of the people he'd killed and had killed. But then again, maybe he did, Dessie thought: look at the way we're all looking at him, and what he's doing, look at how we're afraid to talk among ourselves or pull any attention away from him. If a stranger walked in here, he'd know by the way we were standing just who was in charge.

Jack Cullen went over to Paul's open coffin, and Dessie'd never seen anything like it: Cullen put a hand on Paul's hands, which were folded across his chest, and burst out crying. Tears were rolling down his cheeks, and you could hear the quiet sobbing in the room, and everyone else still and silent. Dessie didn't know whether he shouldn't have looked at the ground, but he couldn't take his eyes off Cullen. GANG BOSS SOBS AT FOOTBALLER'S REMOVAL was the headline Dessie thought of. Not a lot that could be done about it now, he supposed: they could hardly tell Jack Cullen not to come to the funeral.

Finally, Cullen stopped crying. He blessed himself, wiped his eyes with the back of his hands and then came over to Dessie and held Dessie's cheeks with the palms of his hands and looked Dessie in the eye and said:

'I loved him like a son. Such a beautiful footballer.'

Dessie nodded, caught up in the emotion himself. Out of the corner of his eye he noticed that a priest had come in to the room. Lamp held a hand up to the priest, who nodded respectfully. Jack Cullen looked around at Lamp, then back to Dessie and said:

'He never done anything for me. Even tickets, I paid for my own. Do you understand?'

Dessie nodded. Cullen's eyes were like burning coals.

Everything that can be done, will be done, if it hasn't been done already, Cullen said, and kissed Dessie on the forehead. Then he went across and reached up and hugged Liam, and whispered in his ear.

The room started to fill up then: Paul's girlfriend and his ex-girlfriend and the Shelbourne players and other people Dessie didn't recognize. The priest kicked into a decade of the rosary, and then the men from the funeral home put the lid on the coffin and they assembled in the yard, ready to walk behind the hearse to the church. There was a squad of lads in white shirts and dark trousers in their late teens and early twenties, some bouncer size, some heroin build, all with mobile phones in their hands, who took it up on themselves to flank the cortège; Lamp had given them their instructions before they set off. And all the while, Dessie was wondering one thing: not about the INLA, or whether he could believe anything

Jack Cullen or Lamp Comerford said, or if a Halligan brother was going to walk off the pavement and plug him or Liam or both of them. What Dessie was wondering was, what had Jack Cullen taken so long to whisper in Liam's ear?

18

The Removal of the Remains is a kind of Catholic spin on the old Irish tradition of the wake, two or three days during which the body is laid out in the home and friends and relations gather to commemorate the dead person in a variety of ways, most of them involving getting drunk. That doesn't happen very much any more; instead the body – the remains – is taken from the funeral home to the church, arriving around five o'clock or so. Prayers are said and then people file past the family to pay their respects. And then people go to the pub, or to the house, or both, and get drunk, in part so that the funeral the next morning will unfold in something of an alcoholic mist, and in part because when you stand in the same room as a coffin, particularly the coffin of someone you knew, the natural human response is to get drunk. In this instance, because of Easter, the coffin would stay in the church for two nights, until the funeral on Easter Monday, so the opportunities for continuous, purgative drunkenness were much extended.

If you weren't walking behind the hearse, the thing to do was to wait outside in the churchyard until the coffin had arrived and the family were seated. This way you got a good look at the chief mourners, which might seem intrusive but was actually the entire point of the exercise, otherwise funeral would be conducted in private. You needed to see them, and they needed to see you, and that's the way it was. Of course, Paul Delaney's funeral had the added dimension of taking place virtually under the patronage of Jack Cullen, so the streets boasted a not very discreet Garda presence: there were uniforms and plainclothes detectives and bulky men in overcoats and anoraks who looked like the men who were trailing me. Noel Sweeney was in the churchyard but there was quite a crowd between us, and I thought I saw Dave Donnelly, but when I tried to reach him he had vanished. There were press photographers and TV cameramen outside the churchyard. The *Evening Herald* was full of the alleged feud between the INLA and the Cullen gang, with photographs on the cover of Jack Cullen and Shay Rollins who, at a swollen twenty stone or so, with a goatee and a curly black mullet and aviator shades, sitting on a balcony in immense floral swimming trunks, looked for all the world like a hood from a lurid comic book. The atmosphere in the churchyard was uneasy, and when Tommy Owens, with a baseball hat pulled down over his eyes, pushed his way through the crowd and took me aside, I discovered why.

'They bombed Ray Moran's house, Ed. About an hour ago. Charlie Newbanks called me. They used grenades and two pipe bombs, the first floor ceiling collapsed.'

'Is he dead?'

'Well, he was in there. And he hasn't come out. His minder was there too. Charlie had just sent someone over to relieve him. He said he didn't know whether Moran had told anyone about our visit this morning. Said he doubted it, that none of them trusted each other at the moment: Lamp thinks someone's touting them over the drug shipments, Jack thinks someone's leaking to the INLA, everyone's looking over his shoulder. Very tense, very fragile. On the plus side, Charlie doesn't have to tell anyone we were there, since the only other witness was the minder. And he's dead too.'

'Every cloud,' I said.

'Still and all, I don't think this is the wisest location for you, Ed.'

I looked at Tommy, the cap hiding his eyes, talking into his hand like a hood, the pair of us counting our blessings because two men were dead. What was happening to us? I could see the cortège now, edging slowly through the church gates. Shelbourne FC scarves were dotted throughout: red and white striped, they brimmed above the crowd like bloodstained standards, harbingers of worse, much worse to come.

'Where's Leo?' I said.

'He said he'd stick around.'

'Did he say anything to you about Dessie Delaney?'

'No. What would he have said?'

'Oh, I don't know. Maybe how Podge would like him taken out. How even Leo, your new best friend, wouldn't think it's right for someone who was ready to testify against the Halligans to walk around as if nothing had happened. Bad example that. And of course, we know Leo's gone straight now, we saw this morning how he's left his old life behind.'

'I didn't like what happened any more than you did Ed, but don't make out it was down to me. I didn't hear you object—'

'You brought him in. You can't trust the Halligans.'

'Is that why you were drinking with George out in St Bonaventure's on Holy Thursday? Get down and fucking walk, Ed, if it wasn't for me you'd still be in the jigs, mooning over that skank Donna Nugent.'

'All right, all right, I'm sorry. Tommy? Truce?'

'Truce. You self-righteous bollocks you.'

'Seriously. What's your best guess on Leo? Did he look like something was brewing?'

'The cunt always looks like something's brewing, he's relaxed like a fucking hawk. At Any Moment, know I mean: he'd gut you. I wouldn't put it past him, Ed, to take Dessie out tonight. Just cause we know the Halligans doesn't make them any more acceptable as human beings. It just means we know them.'

'I wonder what it makes us.'

'And there's been a lot of talk, how Podge's manslaughter sentence is going to be reduced on appeal, the judge gave him longer than he was entitled to. In fact, I'm not even sure if he needs an appeal, it's just some legal technicality. In either case, the cunt will be out on account of time served. Not looking forward to that.'

'I doubt George and Leo are either.'

I attempted a laugh, but Tommy didn't see the funny side, and I didn't blame him: Podge had only beaten me to a bloody mess; he had raped Tommy. We might have need of the INLA ourselves if Podge Halligan hit the streets again.

The hearse had stopped near the church doors. I saw Dessie Delaney and his beery looking brother Liam in discussions with the undertakers about carrying the coffin into the church. I saw the tiny, sinewy figure of Jack Cullen, whom I'd only ever seen photographed, take Liam to one side and point him towards Barry Jordan, the Shelbourne captain, who was surrounded by teammates. Liam went down and spoke to Jordan, who I then saw shaking his head emphatically; four of the other players pushed forward, one of them having first taken Jordan aside and waved an angry finger in his face. The footballers joined Liam and Dessie and they hoisted the coffin on their shoulders and set off through the church doors. Jack and Lamp looked set to join them when Charlie Newbanks appeared at Jack Cullen's side. For a big man, he could move with surprising grace. He spoke into Jack Cullen's ear, and then Jack Cullen seemed to lose the use of his spine: he swayed from the waist and his head fell back and his mouth opened and out came the most astonishing howl of pain, like the cry of a mortally wounded animal. Lamp Comerford and Newbanks crowded around Jack Cullen and moved him to one side of the church door and out of my view, but it was clear that Jack had just been given the news of Ray

Moran's death. Ray Moran said Paul Delaney was like a son to Jack Cullen, but of course, that was a role Moran himself knew well: to lose one son the night before you bury another couldn't be easy. The crowds streamed into the church and I followed. Tommy had vanished, whether inside the church or elsewhere, I couldn't see. I pushed as close to the front as I could get, and when Dessie, who stood in the aisle by the front pew watching the congregation, spotted me, he hailed me and we embraced and I was genuinely moved to see him, Dessie Delaney, the one who got away, genuinely moved and then genuinely shocked when his coat pocket scuffed against my hand and I felt the sickening heft of gun metal. I looked him straight in the eye, and he looked straight back.

'Self-defence, Ed. Until I know what happened. That's fair enough, isn't it? Do I know what happened? Do you?'

I quickly told Dessie as much as I knew: that Paul hadn't been dealing, that he had been favoured by Jack Cullen for footballing reasons, that he was most probably the victim of the INLA. Dessie nodded as if none of that was unfamiliar to him, and when I said I wasn't certain of any of it, and that there was a long way to go yet, the reckless look in his glittering eyes made my blood run cold. Dessie had been many things when I knew him, but he'd never been what he looked like now: a killer.

Dessie tucked me in the vacant pew behind him; across the aisle sat two rows of footballers in flash suits. Barry Jordan scowled at me, and I wondered whether Paul Delaney had been dealing after all, or whether Jordan was simply very clear-cut about the ethics surrounding associating with gangsters. I had a lot of sympathy with clear-cut ethics along those lines; unfortunately my chosen line of work meant I couldn't hang that sympathy out on display. I wondered also why the pew I was in was vacant when every other seat in the church was taken; my answer came when, preceded by a hush that was almost audible, Jack Cullen walked up the aisle and sat in beside me. Of Lamp and Charlie there was no sign, but still. This was going to do wonders for my reputation.

The priest was sixty, dark haired, and apparently not unused to the sudden, violent deaths of young men. The service lasted maybe twenty minutes: a few scripture readings, a few prayers, some hard talk about how another two men were being brought to a nearby church today, how all these young men were children of God, how drugs were the scourge of this community, how violence solved nothing. He was staring at Jack Cullen as he spoke, and Jack, whose head had been bowed until then, now looked up and stared right back at the priest. The priest broke gaze first, and looked down the church and appealed for calm, and for peace.

After the blessing, Jack Cullen was first to file past Dessie and Liam: Dessie moved him on quickly, but Cullen lingered with Liam, the pair embracing and talking quietly, intensely, and I could see Dessie staring at them as he shook hands with other mourners. When I stepped around, Dessie told me to call him in maybe an hour, and I said I would. I was shaking hands with Liam Delaney, who looked like Colm Meany in a fat suit, when I heard the sound: bigger than gunfire, not quite a bomb. I could hear glass breaking and masonry falling. There was screaming in the church, and people near the bottom spilled forward up the aisles; I moved quickly to the side altar and out a door at the top of the church. To one side was a garden that looked like it led to the presbytery; as I ran towards the front of the church, two youths in black hoods passed me, their faces further concealed by balaclavas. The first thing that struck me was the silence: not just in the aftermath of the explosion, but because the yard was almost deserted: the heavy Garda presence had totally dispersed, as had the TV crews and press photographers. There was broken glass and masonry dust strewn across the steps and smoke billowing out of the front porch of the church: a hand grenade, I guessed. Down the yard, I saw the slight figure of Jack Cullen, presumably the intended target, running, head down, ducking out the gates and vanishing from sight. Instinctively, I followed. When I got onto the street, all I could see were a couple of uniformed Guards across the street, stopping people from approaching the church, and the wail of sirens in the distance. I turned back and walked straight into Lamp Comerford.

'Ed Loy. You need to come with us,' Lamp said, and indicated a black Mercedes estate that had just pulled up alongside us.

'I don't think that's what I need, no thank you,' I said, and took a step back, and felt like I'd walked into a door. It was in fact a man the size and consistency of a door; he pinned my arms and lifted my feet off the ground and marched me to the Merc and Lamp opened the back door and I was flung inside. I sat upright and tried to punch my way out, but something meaty and hard connected with the middle of my face, and the back of my head slapped against the car window. I felt panic and pain, and then numb, and then nothing.

19

The first thing I was aware of was the contrast between two distinct sounds: one of them was a high-pitched gurgling pleading, a shrill supplication. The other was lower, jagged, a staccato voice with a lisp. The low voice chuckled every so often, whether sardonically or with true pleasure it was hard to say. I seemed to be lying on a two seater leather sofa. I was cold, and soaked in what I hoped was sweat, and the pain in my head was like the clenching and unclenching of a massive fist inside my skull: the closed fist was a tight, insistent throbbing in my brain, the open fist sent bolts of barbed wire dipped in acid shooting all over my body. That was where the sweat was coming from. I tried to sit up. It took a while. In the meantime, I opened my eyes. I could see Lamp Comerford's back. He was standing over someone who was seated, presumably the someone with the shrill voice. As the scene came into focus a little more clearly, Lamp did something sudden and jerky with one of his arms, and shouted something like, What do you think now? and the someone who was seated screamed, and then began to sob quietly.

My first reaction to this was to shut my eyes again in the hope, not that it would go away, but that it wasn't there in the first place: it was simply an illusion, some kind of macabre hallucination brought on through overwork, perhaps, or a side-effect of the ecstasy tablets which, among other things, Donna Nugent had encouraged me to take. I was unsuccessful in this, however, not least because when I closed my eyes the entire room began to spin, and when I opened them again the spinning didn't stop, and the sweating got worse, and before I knew it I had hoisted my head up over the side of the sofa and was vomiting onto the tiled floor beneath me.

'You scuttery fuck,' Lamp Comerford said, approaching me. I could hear his heels on the boards, hear his breath close by, but I couldn't turn my head around to look at him.

'You'll mop that up or you'll fucking eat it, you scuttery little fuck you,' Lamp said.

'Lamp,' said a quiet, authoritative voice.

There was silence, and then I could hear Lamp's heels on the boards. The quiet voice spoke again, and Lamp grunted. Then there was a loud cracking sound, and then renewed sobbing. I wiped my face with the back of my hand and sat up on the sofa and opened my eyes and looked around me. I was in some kind of farmhouse style kitchen, with an old fireplace and a range and exposed beams. There was a big table and chairs in a dining area to my rear; ahead of me were several sofas that matched the one I was sitting on. Jack Cullen was sitting on one of them in the centre of the room. In front of him, Charlie Newbanks was tied to a kitchen chair. Charlie's face was a bruised and swollen mess, and his mouth was leaking blood, and he was crying. Lamp was standing between Charlie and the fireplace, bending over the hearth. When he righted himself, he had a small poker in his hand whose tip was glowing red. He brought the poker close to Charlie Newbanks' right eye, and then around to his left eye. Newbanks whimpered. I got to my feet.

'Jesus Christ, stop,' I said. 'Put the poker down. For God's sake.'

Lamp looked at Jack Cullen, who nodded. Lamp put the poker back in the fire.

'Now, sit down,' Cullen said to me.

I shook my head, and immediately felt so nauseous I sat

down involuntarily. I gripped my knees with my hands and breathed deeply.

'Get him some water, Seán,' Cullen said towards the kitchen. There was the sound of a running tap, and then the gigantic man who had thrown me into the car appeared at my side and handed me a glass of water and retreated into the kitchen. Cullen came and sat down beside me. He spoke in a very low voice.

'We don't want any nonsense now, do you understand? We just need the answers to some questions, and we think Charlie should be able to answer them, and we think you will be able to help. But if you start trying to play the hero, first off, Seán will have to put a few more manners on you. Then we might have to tie you up and after that, well, Lamp might need to get to work. Do you understand?'

I nodded.

'Now, I know you were taking an interest in young Paul Delaney, looking out for him, and I appreciate that, even if you were worried that I might be what he needed to be protected from, fair enough, you weren't to know. I also know that you were looking into the killing of a tax collector, and you think I might be involved. I suppose that's a debit entry in the ledger, but since I had nothing to do with that death, I can't get too excited about it. And of course, Lamp has told me about the knife that killed Cummins and Devlin. We still have that, and we'll use it against you if we need to. So behave yourself. Charlie's a big boy here, and he knew what he was getting himself into.'

Lamp was staring at me, his eyebrows raised, his eyes flashing, as if he was trying to send me a message. I looked at him and, unseen by Jack or Charlie, he gave me a thumbs up sign. In the context, the gesture was so grotesque I thought I might throw up again.

'Now, here's what happened today, before the INLA threw

a grenade at me. In my own neighbourhood. A *grenade*. And before that, they attacked Ray Moran's house with pipe bombs. It's not as if they're worried about anonymity, everyone knows they're the only ones who use grenades and bombs. So. So they kill Raymond, and they badly injure his minder, Johnny Gara. They badly injure him, but they don't kill him. Contrary to what Charlie has told us. Lamp gets a call from the hospital while I'm at the removal, and he boots up there and has five minutes with Gara. And Gara tells him Charlie gives him a break this morning, and when he gets back, Raymond's taken a beating. He's acting as if nothing's wrong, but Gara can see his face has been badly bruised, his nose is swollen and out of shape, it's not pretty. What's more, Gara saw who did it. You see, when Charlie comes over and gives Gara the morning off, Gara doesn't like it. Now you've heard, and everyone's heard, that we've had a little tension in the organization. A little strain. And everyone's tense. Everyone's watching his back. So Charlie, who's only ever on the door of the Viscount or Lamp's drinking buddy, Charlie is not the one to be giving Gara time off. And Gara thinks, maybe Charlie's up to no good. Maybe Charlie is the wrong 'un. Maybe Charlie set up Paul Delaney. And of course, there's advancement in it for Johnny Gara, but self-interest is the great motivator. So Gara takes off for the pub like he's told, and then doubles back and makes a short film with his mobile phone. And in the film, we can identify you, and Leo Halligan, and a scruffy looking chap with a ruined foot that Lamp tells me is an old friend of yours by the name of Tommy Owens.

'Now, I have people out searching for Owens, and for Leo Halligan. But what I want to know is, first of all, what was said in the room, and what was done.'

Cullen walked quietly back to his ringside seat. There was no indication in his face that he found the sight of Charlie Newbanks upsetting.

'Charlie here says he wasn't actually present. But we find that hard to believe,' he said.

'He wasn't,' I said.

'Why did he call off Johnny Gara? Why did he set up this meeting with yous all?'

'Because Charlie and Tommy Owens are old friends. Tommy was dealing drugs for Leo Halligan in Trinity College way back in '90, '91, before Ray Moran and his INLA friends moved in. That's how you hooked up with Ray in the first place, remember? Tommy and Charlie were worried that someone was going to take me out, on account of my poking my nose into your affairs. We've all heard the rumours about you and Lamp there not seeing eye to eye. And people said Lamp and Raymond weren't the best of pals either. Coming on top of Cummins and Devlin laying into me that night – and they had a knife, and they were going to use it – well, they felt Ray Moran might be able to answer a few questions about exactly what kind of danger I was in, who to expect it from, that type of thing.'

'Provided Leo Halligan gave him the once-over first. I assume that was Leo's work? What exactly was Leo doing there?'

'Tommy and Leo go back. I think Leo acts as muscle for Tommy if he thinks the situation warrants it. And he knew Moran from before.'

'You don't think Leo had an ulterior motive?'

'I think Leo always has an ulterior motive. I just don't know what, in this situation, it might have been. Unless it's to do with Brian Fogarty's murder.'

Jack Cullen looked puzzled.

'Who's Brian Fogarty?'

'The tax collector. There are three suspects who had motives to kill him. You're one, and George Halligan is another. Maybe Leo is staying close enough to me to see if there's any threat to George.'

Cullen nodded.

'So what did Moran tell you?' Lamp Comerford said, his patience appearing to snap. Cullen looked annoyed, but Lamp didn't seem to care; with his goatee and his dark colouring and his grey flat top glowing red in the firelight, he looked like a low rent Satan taking a break from his infernal toil. There were brass fire tools in a coal scuttle by the hearth: pokers and shovels and so forth; I didn't know whether any of them would be enough if and when the time came; I'd probably need the scuttle itself when it came to big Seán. In the meantime, keep them talking and wait for an opening.

'Moran said Dean Cummins and Simon Devlin were in the INLA, and that the most likely thing was, they were laying in wait for him, but because we're about the same height and we both wear dark suits, they went after me by mistake.'

Lamp nodded at this as if it had already been established. Jack Cullen watched Lamp nodding.

'Only thing I wondered about that was, usually in the press they can identify fairly quickly who belongs to which gang or faction. They always identify INLA members straight away. There's been no mention of that with Cummins and Devlin.'

Lamp Comerford made a puzzled face, and Jack Cullen watched him make it.

'And Moran thought Paul Delaney was most likely murdered by the INLA, and Leo and Tommy seemed to think that was spot on.'

Lamp Comerford shrugged as if this was not exactly news, and Jack Cullen watched him shrug.

'So for a start, I don't see why poor Charlie here has to take all this flak, apart from it being par for the course in his chosen line of work. If he achieved anything, it was to reassure me that neither of you is trying to have me killed. Which is very nice to know.'

I smiled, and Lamp Comerford smiled back, and Jack Cullen watched him smile.

And Charlie Newbanks coughed, and a gob of blood shot out of his mouth and landed on Lamp Comerford's hand.

Lamp's face, already dark and hot from the fire, seemed to turn as red as the blood on his hand, and his mouth opened in a roar, and he turned to the fire and wrenched the poker out and brought the red hot tip around and brandished it in front of Charlie Newbanks' face and said:

'I'll burn your fucking eyes out and then I'll stick this poker up your fat fucking hole.'

And I did the only thing I can think of in circumstances like this: I made something up, and hoped it might be close enough to the truth to work.

I said, 'Lamp told me you had Brian Fogarty killed, Jack. He said you got those INLA lads from Belfast who strayed across the river into your territory to do it, and you made sure Ray Moran took part, and that's what tied him to you. He said he'd give me chapter and verse if I came up with evidence that you're a tout, Jack. He paid me five grand, with five more to come, to rout the tout. That's what he thinks you are. He thinks you've been giving up your own coke shipments. He thinks you've got some kind of deal with the drug squad that's going to get you off, and send him down.'

Lamp looked like he had been bewitched: the smoking poker held above Newbanks' head, the face like molten metal, the mouth struggling to get the words out.

'Fucking lying fucking—'

Jack Cullen held a tiny hand up, his face a mask.

'Shut up, Lamp. Go on, you.'

I needed more detail and I needed some facts. No matter what I got wrong, I needed to get more right. Like in love, like in life, what I needed was a little luck. Because for all that he was a gangster, if they did what they looked like they were going to do to Charlie Newbanks, I wasn't sure I could come back from it.

'Ray Moran said the INLA was one possibility. But he said there was an alternative.'

Jack Cullen stood up.

'Put the poker down, Lamp,' he said.

Lamp swung the poker in the air as if it was a sabre. A blue grey hunk of metal appeared in Jack Cullen's hand, and he waved the barrel towards Lamp.

'Put the poker back in the fire.'

The red seeped from Lamp's cheeks as if someone had chilled his blood. The huge hulking mass that answered to the name Seán materialized at Jack Cullen's side. Lamp slowly turned to the fire and put the poker back among the flames. Jack Cullen waved the gun at me.

'Go on.'

I remembered Dessie Delaney watching in dismayed fascination as Jack Cullen lingered on his brother Liam's shoulder at the removal. I remembered Cullen's operatic grief at the news of Moran's death, and the generally held view that Paul Delaney had been like a son to him. I remembered Tommy's tales of how jealous Lamp had been of Moran's fast-track induction into the inner circle. I rolled it all up into a ball and flung it as hard as I could.

'Ray Moran said there was an alternative explanation that was equally consistent with the facts. An explanation he in fact thought was far likelier. And that was, to take it in order, that Lamp had killed Brian Fogarty himself in order to curry favour with you, because he was jealous of how close you had become to Ray Moran. (And that squares with what the original investigating detective, retired Garda Inspector Noel Sweeney, now believes.) That Dean Cummins and Simon Devlin were Lamp's boys, hired from outside, nothing to do with the INLA, just regular guttersnipes, and that Lamp had set them on Moran because he'd had enough: he wanted to take you down, Jack, and that meant hitting you where it hurts most. But of course they fucked up; they got me instead of Moran, they got a beating instead of an easy kill, and then Lamp had to finish the job, and turn it to his advantage. Moran told me he never called Lamp that night, so how did he get to Beresford Lane so quickly? Because he had masterminded the whole operation. And we can assume that the earlier display at Tolka Park was down to Lamp as well, all part of his attempt to make it look as if the INLA were leading the charge. When it wasn't the INLA at all, it was Lamp himself, Lamp who blew up Moran's house on Pembroke Road and killed Moran because he was afraid he was the tout, Lamp who had two lads toss a grenade at you in the churchyard, Lamp Comerford all the way down to Paul Delaney.'

'This is just fucking lies, Jack—'

'No it isn't,' Charlie Newbanks said.

'Shut up the pair of yous,' Jack Cullen said. 'Go on you,' he said again.

'Lamp started seeing conspiracies everywhere. Ollie and Dave won't let him in the Viscount. He shoots the door up, and they take off on the lam. Where do they end up? In Delaney's Bar on a Greek island. Ollie and Dave and Paul Delaney, all on one side and Lamp on the other, everyone touting except Lamp. That can't be right, can it?'

'Did Raymond say Lamp killed Paul?' Jack Cullen said.

'Ray Moran thought Lamp killed Paul. Or had him killed. He thought Lamp's plan was to rub out everyone who was close to you who might be touting, and then if information was still being leaked then it would be obvious that you were to blame. But of course, he couldn't say for sure. He wasn't there. And neither was I.'

'I was,' Charlie Newbanks said. 'I rode the motorbike. I dropped Lamp off at the Viscount after, then took the bike up and burnt it out in St Anne's park after. I had no choice, Jack. But I didn't pull the trigger. Lamp did.'

'You lying *fucker*,' Lamp said.

Lamp had the red hot poker out of his hand and tracing a burning spiral through the air towards Charlie Newbanks' head, and Jack Cullen swung the gun up like it was part of his hand and squeezed it five times, briskly, methodically, like he was wringing out a cloth, and Lamp Comerford crashed to the ground and the poker fell against his shoulder and his neck and began to burn his leather coat and sear his flesh and Jack Cullen signalled to Seán to detach the poker from the lifeless body of his feared enforcer Lamp Comerford, now dead.

Jack Cullen looked at his gun and sighed and shook his head, then he shot Charlie Newbanks twice in the head. Then he turned the gun on me and nodded to Seán and before I had time to move Seán had picked me off the couch like I was a small child, trapping my arms in his, and the barrel of the gun came closer and closer and I could see Jack Cullen's eyes behind the gun, the darkness in his eyes and the darkness down the barrel of the gun and I didn't hear the shot, and all I saw was darkness.

20

Big Seán watched over me at gunpoint as I dug the graves. Strictly speaking it was one grave, but it had to be deep enough for two bodies, and Charlie Newbanks wasn't small. Seán had marked out the edges and turned the first sod and I was to do the rest. The thought occurred to me that I was favourite to join Charlie Newbanks and Lamp Comerford in their unmarked grave, but it didn't seem to me that there was a lot I could do about that. The ground was soft enough to turn, flat agricultural land that surrounded the farmhouse; we were in among a copse of pines but in the open, you could see for miles: Kildare, I thought, or the midlands, but that might be too far from Dublin for Jack Cullen, if the house was actually his and not one of a thousand 'safe houses' the IRA had at its disposal throughout the Troubles and still have now they've supposedly directed their attentions elsewhere. A thin sliver of moon leaked scant light though the cloud. Seán had a car flashlight by his feet; he sat on a kitchen chair among the pines; he cradled an Uzi in his lap. I tried to think of some heroic manoeuvre involving knocking the light off and blasting Seán out of it, but I didn't have anything to blast with except the odd stone, and while I was usually game in most situations, particularly those in which there was a strong chance of my being buried alive, or indeed dead, being buried at all, my strike rate against Seán hadn't been very impressive so far, and I wasn't convinced in a David and Goliath throwdown that he'd suddenly and miraculously evince a hitherto undetected weakness.

I went on digging.

My head was hot with fresh blood from where Jack Cullen had brained me, and I had to avoid patting it to see whether it had stopped oozing now that my hands were dirty with clay. I had been sick again, and it felt like it wouldn't be the last time; sweat had soaked through my shirt and dripped from my brow, at least I hoped it was sweat, and all the while the rain fell cold and steady; I tried to work harder to guard against the cold, until I wasn't sure whether my muscles were weakening or I was shivering. Two men were dead because I had told lies about them. Maybe if Charlie had denied driving Lamp to murder Paul Delaney he might have lived. But Lamp himself would have killed Charlie. Charlie had signed his own death warrant when he pulled Ray Moran's security. And that, at least, although Leo and Tommy's idea, was for my benefit, and hence my fault. I didn't really care about Lamp's death, except I'd rather not have been around to see it. Anyone who did what he had done and what he was about to do to Charlie deserved anything that he got. But Charlie Newbanks's death was going to haunt me for a long time. Provided I didn't join him prematurely, of course. Either alternative seemed equally bleak. I tried to empty my mind, but the faces of the dead kept looming before my eyes, leering at me: Paul Delaney, then Dean Cummins and Simon Devlin, Ray Moran, Lamp Comerford and Charlie Newbanks, and then Jack Cullen's face, those opaque eyes, as if killing was always and everywhere to be regretted but nonetheless had to be done. In the churchyard he had wept, but in repose he looked like a man to whom intense emotion was a stranger, a man used to living in the dark, a man well-acquainted with the void. He was in the house now, talking to the burly, straw-haired, red-faced barman from the Parting Glass, who was there when I had come to, and had maybe been there all along. He had looked like an ex-cop then, and he looked even more like one now, as he and Cullen looked down on me, their mouths moving sparingly, their faces devoid of expression. If they were a jury, I hadn't a prayer.

I went on digging.

Finally, I was down about four or five feet, up to my shoulders in the earth, when Jack Cullen came out of the house and spoke to Seán. I climbed out of the grave, and Seán gestured me towards the house with the barrel of the Uzi, and when I got there, the barman was waiting to help me lift the corpses out.

We took Lamp first. I had his feet and the barmen took his arms. We carried him through the rain in silence. By the grave, the barman stopped.

'On three,' he said.

We swung him twice and threw him in, and the barman hawked up a gob of phlegm and spat it down on top of him.

I felt so weak I could barely stand up, weak of body, weak of spirit. There wasn't a sound but the breathing of four men, and the falling of the rain.

Charlie was harder to carry. We had to hold him closer, at the arms beneath the shoulders, and at the legs beneath the knees, and we went sideways like crabs, and Charlie's bulk carried us faster than we wanted to go, and it was all we could do to halt at the graveside, and we didn't swing him so much as let him drop. He hit the side of the grave with a thud, and earth spilled in on top of Lamp, and the barman pushed at Charlie's side with his grey shoe, and Charlie Newbanks rolled onto his massive belly as he sank face first below onto Lamp Comerford. The barman hawked up another mouthful of phlegm on top of Charlie. For some reason, this obscene desecration upset me as much as anything I had witnessed tonight, torture and murder included, and if someone had suddenly given me a weapon, the first member of our company I'd have taken out would have been this revolting pig.

But of course, no one was going to give me a weapon. There was still between three and four feet depth in the grave. Room for one more. I waited, thinking that if this was how it had to end, out here among savages, it would at least have the macabre distinction of being as bad as it could possibly be.

Jack Cullen looked at the barman and nodded. And the barman turned to me and spoke.

'Well, I don't see any other cunt with a spade. Are you going to pile the earth back, or do you want to want to get in there yourself?'

I piled the earth back. The momentary relief I felt at not joining the dead didn't last. I had seen Jack Cullen murder two men. He knew I would take that information to the Guards. So it wasn't a question of if, but when, I would die. I looked at him now, as he walked back into the house with the barman and they resumed their perch above me, and wondered how often Cullen had stood witness to such scenes, how many bodies had he seen buried on lonely hillsides, among sand dunes, in lush pastures and deserted forests. I wanted to feel anger, and somehow to convert that anger into action, to slay Seán with a belt of the spade and then turn the Uzi on my two overseers, but that wouldn't be enough to bring the dead back to life, and all I ended up feeling was pity for the dead men, and fear, that I would surely soon be joining them, and the most profound, despairing sadness, that I lived in a world where such things not only happened but, to those like Jack Cullen, who had fought a long war supposedly for his country's freedom, were commonplace.

I patted down the mound of earth on top of the grave as best I could, and then Seán directed me to pull a few fallen pines across the bulging clay. He indicated that I should lay down the spade, which I did. The last thing I remember was Jack Cullen asking me questions I couldn't answer, asking them over and over again, and someone punching me in the face each time I failed to answer, until Jack Cullen was shouting, and then there was a flash of red just outside my eyeline and the force of Seán's boot as it connected with my temple, and then my head exploded in a ball of flame.

V

Easter Sunday

21

There are times in your life when you awaken and if not quite shocked to find yourself alive, you are certainly overwhelmed by the scale of the events you've experienced, and find it difficult to respond in the way you would prefer, or even to determine just what that preference might be. Maybe you've slept with your brother's wife, and worse, you don't know whether you regret it or not. Maybe that's her hair spilling over onto your pillow right now. Maybe your husband died, and this morning is the first time you don't think of it immediately, don't think of it for minutes on end. Maybe you wanted to die without him, and now, for better or worse, you want to live. Maybe you've been so sick for so long that when you wake up and suddenly feel marginally, but quantifiably, better, your immediate instinct is distrust, despair, even, because you had gotten used to giving up, and now you simply doubt you have the fire to rejoin the struggle for life.

When I awoke on Easter Sunday morning in Noel Sweeney's house in the quiet cul de sac off the N11, I was so elated still to be alive, in spite of the pain I felt, the excruciating headache that seemed to scour the inside of my skull like bleach, the eye that had completely closed and made me cry out when I touched it, the seeping wounds at my brow and my temple, the ear that leaked, the nose that was certainly broken and through which I was unable to breathe, the jagged fragments that were all that remained of two or three teeth, I hadn't the spirit to count, so elated to be alive and not in a cold grave among the pines on a farm somewhere no one would ever find me that it was a good fifteen minutes, or maybe five, or maybe an hour, it's hard to be sure, duration is elastic in these situations, let's just say that it felt like a very long time between the point at which I recognized Noel Sweeney and understood I was in his house and the point at which I realized that Noel Sweeney was dead, had in fact been stabbed to death, and that the knife, which I could see all bloody by his chest, was without any doubt the knife with my prints and DNA on it, the same knife Lamp Comerford had rescued from the murders of Dean Cummins and Simon Devlin. I was similarly certain, looking at my bloodstained hands, that at least some of that blood would be Sweeney's, that a fresh set of my prints would be found on the knife, and that, since the police sirens I had been vaguely aware of were getting closer and louder, all of these things would come to pass without delay this Easter Sunday morning. And part of me, knowing the worst had happened, was relieved. Afterwards, Tommy said to me, 'You could have run.' But that wasn't true. I couldn't have run. I couldn't move a muscle.

Dublin – M1 to Belfast, 9 November 1980
The Coyle Family

Gerry Coyle

The first thing I'd say, although I can't actually think of the circumstances in which I'd be asked, but if anyone actually asked me what you run through your mind to stop yourself from coming, the first thing I'd say is Jaguar Mark 2 specs, but then I'd say: but actually, I don't. I mean, I try not to run things like that through my mind during sex, the Lisbon Lions or Man United '68 or Brazil 1970, not because it's disrespectful or anything, although it probably is, but because they're really interesting, and when you're pounding away there working towards a big finale, the last thing you need on your mind is something interesting. Shit, that's not quite the way to put it. Good thing Claire can't read my mind. Although sometimes she can all but.

What I mean is, when I've tried it – say, okay, engine first: six cylinder XK engine, twin overhead camshafts, twin carburettors, 87 mm bore x 106 mm stroke, capacity 3,781 cc, 220 bhp at 5,500 rpm; compression ratios 8 to 1 or optional 7 to 1 – I kind of get caught up in it, feel the need to go through everything, from transmission and suspension to body and dimensions, and there I am, thinking about the four-speed all synchromesh gearbox on the manual, with the addition of the Laycock de Normanville overdrive controlled by steering column lever on the overdrive, and then the Borg Warner automatic transmission with driver controlled intermediate gear hold and steering column selector lever on the automatic, and there's Claire, looking up at me or down at me or over her shoulder going, what happened to you? And that's the problem: I find it so interesting, so absorbing, every physical attribute and contour of this unbelievably fucking beautiful machine that if I try and count the ways in which it's just the best car ever, I get so distracted I forget, in an embarrassingly physical way, exactly what it is I'm supposed to be doing.

Have an extra drink or two, is my final, or at least current, answer, maybe three but probably no more, sometimes you can still get away with it, though probably not like you used to. And keep football and cars out of the bedroom, where a man needs to concentrate on the job in hand.

Claire Coyle

It's nice though, to walk around without a care in the world, not worrying if you're in the wrong part of town or if you've used the wrong expression or if it's a Protestant pub or a Catholic pub, and even if Robbie did say Liverpool was the Protestant team and Everton was the Catholic team, Alison didn't actually know. More to the point, she didn't care, and clearly thought anyone who did was an idiot. That's the way it should be.

But when Robbie and Gerry got on to moving back to Dublin, I was reminded of all the reasons I wouldn't want to live down there. The Church, for one thing, with contraception still illegal, or only for married couples or some such, bloody ridiculous in this day and age, and teenage girls having babies in fields as a result, they go on about the Dark Ages in the North, but it's not as if it's a shiny new enlightenment down there. That's the other thing, the worst thing probably, the 'aren't we great' mentality, the way they all think they're so fucking wonderful, they're not exactly shy about diagnosing what's wrong with us but suggest they could do with drinking less and poking their heads out from underneath their mammy's skirts and telling their bishops and priests to keep their noses out of people's affairs and they get all po-faced and humour-less, with lots of 'At least we don't go round blowing the shit out of each other.'

Fair point.

Christ, catch yourself on, Claire. No sense in getting defensive, you could feel your spine stiffen at the border checkpoint and you're a Northern Prod, you don't have to put up with the kind of grief they give Gerry, and God knows how that compares to how they treat a Catholic who isn't a university lecturer.

Gerry's gone very quiet.

Probably thinking about his blessed car, we passed one twenty minutes ago, just before we crossed the border, an old couple on the hard shoulder, looked like they'd had a breakdown. Same model, or looked like it, same Burgundy colour at least. Don't think Gerry noticed, or he'd've been out on the road to help a fellow Jaguar driver.

I love that about him, that he loves his Jag like a wee boy. God, when he starts talking about it it's exactly the way Luke gets with his Thunderbirds. There's something incredibly attractive about a man with a passion for something, even if it is something as ridiculous as a fifteen-year-old car. And he really tries to interest Luke in it, and Yvonne too, I especially like that he never tries to leave her out. Not that I wouldn't expect it of him, but I notice it as well. Surrounded by knuckle-dragging Belfast men who think women should only leave the kitchen with their knickers round their ankles, it'd be hard not to.

God forgive me, it's a smug thought for a Sunday afternoon, but I do love my husband.

Yvonne Coyle

I know Mum and Dad think they're being so cool and trendy and advanced for sending me and Luke to state schools but raising us as Catholics, but frankly it's a complete and total pain. You feel like you're on display all the time, you're every middle-class Prod's token Catholic friend, and then when they start making their jokes about nuns being mickey dodgers and how Catholic girls have cobwebs down there you're supposed to be scandalized when all it does is make you embarrassed for them in their ignorance. I personally wouldn't care which we were, even if Mum is a Prod, except she is but she doesn't go to any church, a plague on both your houses, she says, churches, Dad says, you started it, she says, no we didn't, you did, back with Henry the Eighth, when Mum and Dad think they're hilarious that's when they're at their most nauseating, total boak, but because we're Catholics, I think we should just go to a Catholic school. But then you wouldn't see both sides of the argument, Dad says. But that implies all Catholics who go to Catholic schools are bigots, and they're not, I say. All I want is a quiet life, I say.

Well, we better move down south, Dad says, we won't see it up here. And Mum makes a face and says when another job in a Southern university comes up, in about fifteen years time, Dad can apply for it, which is to say they have no money down there and Dad gets all defensive and Mum says joke joke God leave them to it.

All I want is a quiet life. It's not too much to ask for.

Luke Coyle

One of the main differences between chipper chips and Mum's chips is that Mum never uses vinegar BUT when you put vinegar on Mum's chips they still don't taste the same as chipper chips also chipper chips are hot all the way through and soaky but Mum's chips are dry and crispy which is good sometimes to dip in a fried egg BUT the chips in the café were a cross between Mum's chips and chipper chips but not as good as either even though you could *get tomato ketchup AND brown sauce which they never have in the chipper and you're only allowed one at home never both and the tea tasted like piss with milk in it that's what Dad said to Mum when he thought we weren't listening but we always are.*

Mum got Yvonne a bra and I saw her in it. She's my sister though, so it just looked stupid. What's it supposed to look like?

I can't wait to tell everyone about the match.

I wonder what beer tastes like if you have more than a sip.

I wish we had real aunts and uncles not just Mum and Dad's friends, because real aunts and uncles send you presents and let you maybe stay up late if you go to their house, and watch the boxing from America at two in the morning like John Burley's uncle. Also Grannies and Granddads, who spoil you all year round and especially at Christmas, but all of ours are dead.

I wonder what's for dinner.

South Armagh, 9 November 1980

Ice felt a lot of what was wrong with the IRA was embodied in Red, and what that amounted to was hypocrisy. The Irish Republican ARMY, not lobby group or political party, ARMY. And what did any army since time began run on? The harnessed energy and unbridled aggressiveness, not to say ferocity, of young men. They were the foundations war was built on. Red made out that Ice was some kind of inhuman creature, one without real feeling, but that was a necessary part of the armour: Ice's job (and Red's too if he'd get down and do it) was to be a leader, not in the abstract, but a real leader of men prepared to kill at close quarters, in a war where civilians were present, not a romanticized battlefield where the men had been sent overseas and the women kept the home fires burning. Their job was to shoot a man in his front garden, with his family close by. How was that worse than shooting a man on a battlefield with his family safe two hundred miles away? Ice would like that explained to him. And how were you to do that, to shoot and kill a man in front of his wife and weans, if you hadn't hardened your heart first? Otherwise you'd be actively irresponsible, you'd hobble a boy psychologically, for life, if you didn't groom him for it. If you didn't make it clear it was an act of war to kill that man, just like the acts of war he, as a policeman or a prison officer, was carrying out every day against our comrades in arms, against our army.

No one was arguing for unnecessary cruelty or brutality. But there was a place for civilian deaths, just as there was in Germany towards the end of World War II, to undermine the morale of enemy combatants and strike terror into the hearts of the population that supported them. Ice regretted the deaths of innocent people, that went without saying, but no one could tell him that the killing of civilians, particularly on English soil, didn't have an effect – the effect of sickening the hearts of the British, and pushing them in the direction of inevitable withdrawal. And if the loyalists hit back at our own people, well, in a war, it was a case not only of who can inflict most, but who can endure most.

In a war – that seemed to Ice to be the point folk like Red glossed over. If the cause was just – the entitlement of the Irish people, as represented by the Irish Republican Army under the authority of the first Dáil, to wage just war on the British to liberate themselves from the yoke of imperialist oppression – and if Red and his Marxist friends thought there was something wrong with any of that, let them speak up and then get out – say it again, if the cause was just, then the war had to be fought by every means possible. The Brits didn't stint on carpet bombing German cities full of women and children; the Yanks didn't baulk at dropping the big one on the Japs; why? In a word, victory. Sometimes, with folk like Red, you felt victory was the last thing they wanted; they'd prefer to be sitting around tables having talks like politicians. Well, the botched talks that led to the treaty of 1922 that partitioned Ireland were the reason Ice and Red were hiding out among the hawthorns halfway up a hill on a November Sunday in South Armagh waiting to blow a British judge and his wife straight to hell. Ice didn't want his son to be doing this in twenty years' time. Talking to the enemy would never secure peace. Waging war against them would.

It wouldn't be long now. They had pictures of the car – a Jaguar Mark 2 3.8 litre, a big saloon with curved roof and boot and long bonnet, not as long as the E-type, dark red in colour. Shame it had to be such a class car, but still. Red watched the road, barely moving, the cold no longer an issue. At a certain stage, you moved beyond cold; anxiety and adrenalin played their parts; it was only later, only afterwards, thawing out, teeth chattering and hands shaking, that you realized how cold you had actually been. Or maybe that was fear.

~

It was one thing Red envied in Ice, the seeming lack of fear, or rather, because he must have had it, Ice was only human after all even though he went to great lengths to cover it up, how he had mastered his fear. Red might have had disgust for what he saw as Ice's ruthlessness, worse, his relish for the mayhem he inflicted, but deep down, he understood that this reflected as much on Red as it did on Ice: it encapsulated the divide within the movement between the military and the political wings. Just like any liberation struggle, just like war of any kind: the natural tendency of a significant sector in the army is to fight on, and to fight harder, and to murder and maim and destroy: there was no reason to despise them for that. It was their mission and their profession, they weren't blood crazed savages, and if at times they were prone to appearing that way, well, that was what war did: the entire point of it was that it didn't take place around a table. And Ice was a possessed and gifted commander, no doubt about that: his men were the most highly motivated, disciplined active service unit in the Army, and if Red found Ice's methods – particularly his insistence, contrary to recent advice, that civilian deaths were a necessary evil in wartime – excessively brutal, there was no question but that they were employed to further the cause of a united Ireland. Ice was staunch about the justness of the war in ways that Red, privately, simply was not.

Republican strategists invoked South Africa as an analogous situation, with the ANC as brothers in arms. Red found the comparison, not just inaccurate, but frankly embarrassing. In South Africa, a white minority imposed their will on an electorally disenfranchised majority by brutal force of arms; it was racist, fascist rule on a scale that demanded bloody and violent revolution.

In Northern Ireland, the Unionist majority got the bulk of the social housing and the industrial jobs, and there was discrimination in education and in the civil service. And the police were a bunch of violent, bigoted bastards and if Red had shed a tear or

234

given it a second thought when he heard that one of them had got his, he couldn't remember it, unless he'd been done in front of his kids. There was plenty wrong with the place – it had been rigged, after all, to ensure the Unionists had the whip hand, and boy had they cracked the whip – but the idea that it was like South Africa, or Chile, or El Salvador, simply didn't add up. Worse, Red was coming to believe that the struggle was starting to prove counter-productive, that ordinary, decent Unionists and Protestants who just wanted a quiet life and to raise their children in peace and didn't think Nationalists or Catholics should be discriminated against were so alienated by the IRA campaign that their attitudes were hardening. Soon there would be so much bitterness and division and grief that Red feared the wounds would never heal. The idea that the Unionists, having been bombed and shot at every day for years, would one day miraculously come to their senses and demand a united Ireland – a core belief in Republican thought – was positively demented. You couldn't bomb and shoot your way to peace, not when the peace you sought was to be shared with the neighbours you'd been bombing and shooting. The British weren't just the British Army, they were the people who lived here who called themselves British.

That was the challenge in the years ahead. It wasn't a challenge men like Ice were interested in meeting, or even in acknowledging. And that was understandable, Red thought, as he kept his eyes fixed on the motorway, waiting for the judge's red Jaguar to appear. When the time came, as with any war, the soldiers would be thanked for their service and sent back to their homes. Everyone knew what kind of society you got when the soldiers refused to go home. It wouldn't be easy. But when that time came, men like Ice would see that men like Red had a cause too, a cause they didn't just believe, they knew to be just, and in pursuit of that cause, they were capable of exhibiting a ruthlessness of their own. If the soldiers refused to go home, they would have to be removed by other means. When the day came, Red believed he would be ready.

22

My doctor didn't want anyone to come near me until they had the results of the MRI scan on my brain. Apparently I had lost consciousness again shortly after the Guards had arrived at Noel Sweeney's house. Whether they had attacked me or I had passed out because of the injuries I had received earlier wasn't clear. But it was late on Easter Sunday, and Jack Cullen was walking free, and I was in no mood to lie in a hospital bed. I had to get out, and in order to get out, I had to let the Guards question me. More to the point, once they had done that, I had to get them to let me go. It was up to me, so I demanded to be seen by the Guards. It took a couple of hours for them to arrive. There were two uniforms outside my room, but they were just there to ensure I didn't make a break for it. I spent the time working out a statement in my head, running it over and over so that I could stick to it without faltering.

The interview would be conducted by Detective Inspector Kevin Hayes of Donnybrook Station and Detective Superintendent Derek Conway of the Serious Crime Review Team, Dave Donnelly's current boss, incidentally, and neither Hayes, a squat, balding man with a salt-and-pepper moustache, or Conway, a bulky man with a chubby face and dark wavy hair that looked like a wig but wasn't, looked like they wanted to spend more time on me than they needed to. Short of a confession, they had everything they needed; indeed, they had enough forensic evidence to solve three murders, and while I could say what I liked, I was going nowhere for twenty years as far as they were concerned. The crucial thing for me was to seize control of the interview and not let go until they had heard what I needed to say. I saw immediately that my best hope was Conway; Hayes was the drunk cop who had pushed into my apartment and threatened me. Apparently sober now, he was still belligerent and stupid and I had a flash of his having been at the crime scene and screaming something at me, cop killer, perhaps, and very possibly knocking me down, probably out.

Once they had set up audio and video recording, and they had stated their names and ranks for the record, the first thing I said was that I thought there should be someone from the Special Detective Unit present, because I was certain there were individuals involved in this case who were in receipt of their protection. This got a derisive response from Hayes but Conway looked at the very least like he wanted to hear more. I then outlined a version of the case to date that wasn't far from the one that had resulted in the deaths of Charlie Newbanks and Lamp Comerford, taking care at every opportunity to emphasise the real or alleged IRA backgrounds of Jack Cullen and Bobby Doyle. The first time I mentioned Doyle's name was instructive; Hayes greeted it with the same snarl of loathing he had maintained throughout; Conway's eyebrows shot skywards, and, if he didn't quite grin, there was a look of recognition and of excitement in his eyes. I told them what had been taking place in Dublin was a feud within the Provisional IRA and that any talk of INLA involvement was a smokescreen. I took them through Lamp Comerford's role in the process: how he had targeted Ray Moran out of jealousy, but his boys had mistakenly attacked me; how I had left them breathing but Lamp had finished them off, and then tried to use the murder weapon to blackmail me into finding out who the tout was within Cullen's drug-smuggling operation (more eyebrow work from Conway); how Lamp Comerford had murdered Paul Delaney in the car park under Delaney's Parnell Street apartment block, a murder confirmed to me last night by Comerford's accomplice, Charlie Newbanks.

At this point, Conway stood up and turned the recording equipment off and, following a brisk muttered exchange with Hayes, left the room.

'Where is Newbanks now?' Hayes said to me.

'He's dead,' I said.

'Very fucking convenient,' Hayes said.

'Not for him,' I said. 'And not for me either.'

Hayes made a face, as if I'd been cracking wise. But all I'd been telling was the truth, in that at least. As for the rest, my brain hurt too much for me to know what might be true or false in the broadest sense; what I needed to hold onto was the truth that served me best. I could think about the rest of it when I got out of here. If I got out of here. I wasn't entirely sure where exactly I was, but given that there were uniformed Guards and not prison officers outside my room, I suspected I must be in a regular hospital. I flashed on Lamp Comerford in the red firelight last night, brandishing the smoking poker like a guttersnipe Satan, and then on tossing his dead body into a freshly dug grave and the barman from the Parting Glass gobbing on his corpse, and the horror and ugliness of it overwhelmed me; I brought the palms of my hands to my eyes and bowed my head, shaking at the enormity of it all.

'That's right, that's the yellow-arsed cop-killing fucker you are. Get used to snivelling, because when you go down, the lags'll use you as a shitbox and a fuckpuppet and you can snivel morning noon and night for all the good it'll do, you cuntsoaked holesucker.'

There was silence after this, and then the door clicked open. When I looked up, Conway had resumed his seat, and there was a third interrogator in the room, a grey-haired man of about sixty in a pale grey suit, medium build, round steel rimmed glasses, looked like a career civil servant.

'Please pick up where you left off, Mr Loy,' Conway said.

'Aren't you going to introduce your colleague?' I said. The man with the steel rimmed glasses looked at me through them without any expression in his cold eyes. They reminded me of Jack Cullen's eyes. Conway didn't even shake his head; he simply repeated his request for me to continue. I asked if I should recap what I had told them already and Conway said there was no need. I assumed Steel Rim was from the SDU or some branch of Garda Security; maybe even from the Department of Justice, why not? I decided to begin big, to see if I could get a rise out of him.

'Last night, I saw Jack Cullen, who I believe was touting his own drug operation to the National Drug Unit in return for Garda indulgence or Garda protection of some sort, murder two members of his gang that he believed had been disloyal to him, Lamp Comerford and Charlie Newbanks, in the kitchen of a farmhouse somewhere, I don't know exactly where. After they were killed, I was forced, at gunpoint, to dig a grave for them. Another man assisted me in burying the bodies, and filling in the grave. I had seen this man before when I first met Lamp Comerford at the Parting Glass pub on Talbot Street, where he was on duty as the barman.'

Still impassive, Steel Rim held up his hand and Conway switched the recording devices off again. Without a word, Steel Rim left the room, and after Conway had spoken in Hayes's ear, Hayes followed the bigger man out also and I was left alone, maybe for ten minutes, maybe for half an hour. I tried to think of something positive, a cold beer, or having sex with Anne Fogarty, but the images wouldn't stick; Anne's face kept morphing into Donna Nugent's, and Donna Nugent's face was far from friendly: she shook her head pitilessly, as if at my culpable stupidity, and said she could do nothing for me any more. Then I heard Jack Cullen's voice shouting at me before everything exploded, shouting about Bobby Doyle. But what, exactly? And why?

Steel Rim came back in, accompanied by Conway and a slim, tall man with close-cropped brown hair I recognized as John O'Sullivan. O'Sullivan had been a DI in the NBCI the first time I had encountered him; last I heard, he'd been promoted to Superintendent in SDU. He was a good cop, and had been straight with me when I'd sat in an interview room with him before. Whether being straight went with SDU territory was another matter entirely. No recording equipment was turned on this time.

'Well Ed, been in the wars, have we?' he said, a slight smile on his face. 'What is it about your face that makes people want to have a go at it, do you think?'

'I ask myself the same question every morning,' I said. 'But by afternoon, the pain has worn off and there I am again.'

O'Sullivan nodded, the smile already gone. Down to business.

'Tell me about Noel Sweeney.'

'I can't. I came to minutes before the Guards arrived on the scene. I have no memory of how I got there, or what I did. I'm pretty sure I didn't kill him, but I couldn't swear to it. But if the murder weapon is the same one that was used on Dean Cummins and Simon Devlin, then it's almost certainly a set-up; Lamp Comerford had the weapon, and once Jack Cullen murdered Lamp (I noticed Steel Rim wince slightly here) he must have gotten hold of the knife and killed Sweeney with it, and then set up the scene so I'd be caught red-handed.'

'And why should anyone believe that? It sounds absolutely incredible, especially when there's a common-sense explanation the jury will be happy to lap up.'

'The jury? We're in court already, are we? Why would I

kill Noel Sweeney? A retired cop, he did nothing but help me on the one occasion I met him. What possible motive could I have to want him dead?'

But as the night before flared up in my mind again, I realized that I had probably been the cause of Sweeney's death nonetheless. My face must have betrayed me; O'Sullivan looked at me with interest.

'I told Jack Cullen Noel Sweeney now believes that Lamp Comerford killed Brian Fogarty. Which wasn't what Sweeney told me, I just said it because I needed everything I could throw at Lamp Comerford. Cullen might have decided that he'd be better off without Sweeney hanging around poking his nose into his past. And he saw a way to use the knife and to get rid of me into the bargain.'

O'Sullivan looked at Steel Rim, then back at me.

'What did Sweeney tell you?'

'About the brutality of Cullen's IRA record, mostly. And about how nobody knows anything about Bobby Doyle's past, he seemed to rise without trace and appear as if from nowhere. Sweeney said Cullen was favourite, if not for Brian Fogarty's murder, for so many other vicious killings that pinning anything on him would represent justice for a lot of forgotten victims.'

'And is that your conclusion on the Fogarty case?' Conway said.

'What do you care?' I said. 'You instructed DI Donnelly to tell Anne Fogarty to forget about it. The IRA connection makes it too hot to handle.'

'So what *is* your conclusion on the Fogarty case?' O'Sullivan asked me.

I allowed myself a very hesitant smile. I found that it hurt my face to smile, but there was something about the air in the room that had changed for the better, so it was hard not to. They were protecting Cullen, or Doyle, or both, and the last thing they wanted was to charge me with a murder they knew I almost certainly didn't commit, not out of affection for me, but for fear at the very least of what I might say about Cullen in open court. For now, hold onto the truth that serves you best, Loy.

'The case hasn't concluded. I very much hope it will. But for what it's worth, I don't believe Jack Cullen murdered Brian Fogarty. And I doubt very much that Bobby Doyle was responsible either. And that's all I have to say at this stage.'

Steel Rim stood up and left the room. O'Sullivan and Conway followed him. After a relatively brief interval this time, O'Sullivan came back on his own and sat down.

'Why were you having me followed?' I said.

'What do you mean, were? We still are. For operational reasons, of course. And I think you're still bleary from all the beatings and concussion and medication: you don't ask the questions, we do. You have no idea where this farmhouse was?'

'No. Somewhere in flat country, the midlands I reckoned. I could see for miles around. But I couldn't see the road.'

'Did Jack Cullen say anything about Bobby Doyle?'

'No.'

O'Sullivan looked me in the eye.

'There's a man out there who thinks we should keep you in long enough to teach you a lesson. And depending on where you were kept, you might learn more than you were able to handle. But we're not sure we have enough for the DPP. And frankly, I think you're more useful outside than in.'

O'Sullivan looked at me again, this time as if he was inviting me to ask a question.

'Is Cullen being protected? Or is it Bobby Doyle?'

O'Sullivan nodded and stood up.

'I'm glad you asked me that question. And discovering the answer would be interesting for everyone, including those law enforcement officials who have conflicting opinions on the current policies being pursued. All right, Mr Loy, you're free to go. Although given the confused and wayward mental state you're exhibiting, I would advise you to stay in hospital as long as they let you.'

O'Sullivan didn't actually wink at me, but if he had, it would simply have completed the face he made as he was leaving. At the door, he turned, and presented quite a different face, the face that got him where he was, I suppose.

'And don't forget, this is all work in progress. We still have the knife in good chain-of-evidence order, we have DI Hayes more than ready to give a vivid account of the compromising situation you were in, we have interesting traces of several illegal drugs in your bloodstream, we have photographs of you in the Parting Glass, accepting a brown envelope from Lamp Comerford. You should have known we'd've had that dump watched. Altogether, we might not have enough for a case, but we'd have plenty to fuck you up in the eyes of every copper in the country.'

The last time I'd heard that threat it came from Lamp Comerford. I didn't have a lot of sympathy with the kind of mind that revelled in the occasional equivalence between law enforcement and organized crime, but I wished I could stop spotting the parallels.

By the time the nurse came in, I was dressed. She made a fuss, but I said it was nine o'clock on Easter Sunday night, and if there was a consultant to be found in the hospital right now, I'd do exactly as he or she told me, and by the way, which hospital was I in? There wasn't, of course, and I was in Vincent's.

I got a cab to Farney Park, where I'd left my car outside the Fogarty house, and I stood unsteadily in the rain outside the shabby old suburban semi-detached and marvelled at all the bloodshed it had been the occasion of.

On the short drive to my apartment, I noticed two things about myself, and remembered a third thing, and when I parked the car to the rear of my building, the first thing I did was switch on the light and study myself in the rear view mirror. Ignoring the bruised and rotting fruit texture my skin had, and setting aside the swollen and distended death's head aspect that made me look like a human fright mask, what I noticed of particular interest was that my eyebrows and eyelashes were singed at the tips, as was my hair. The second thing I did was identify the smell that had been clinging to my fingertips and lingering in my nostrils: it was smoke. And the thing I remembered before Jack Cullen and Big Seán and the barman had cast me into darkness for the last time was a flash of red flame. I didn't know where the farmhouse was, but I knew the farmhouse had burnt down.

VI

Easter Monday

23

In the morning, Detective Inspector Dave Donnelly said, 'Fuck's sake Ed, you're going to have to get a new head if you don't take better care of the one God gave you,' and I thought to myself, Dave Donnelly is a better class of dream than Jack Cullen and Lamp Comerford, but it's still not a patch on sex with Anne Fogarty. Then I thought, this seems amazingly real for a dream, and I can smell coffee and bacon. And then I realized that Dave Donnelly, in a navy blue anorak, with two cartons of coffee and two breakfast rolls, was actually in my bedroom at half eight in the morning, opening the blinds and rubbing his hands and asking me if I took sugar, he couldn't remember, would this rain ever end?

'I'm certain I didn't give you a key, Dave. Did you just break in? And if so, what kind of security do I need to stop it happening again? You're in my bedroom, Dave. You're the wrong shape and size and smell, never mind the wrong sex, to be in my bedroom, Dave, but here you are, in my bedroom, Dave, in my fucking *bedroom*.'

'Yeah, Tommy let me copy his key. Come on, eat your roll before it gets cold, the grease is not so clever when it solidifies.'

The breakfast roll is fried bacon, sausage and egg in a hunk of white bread, with, in Dave's case, brown sauce and mustard. It's a fearful wodge of carbs and fats much beloved of builders and white van drivers, and I liked to consider myself above such things. But on this particular morning, with shaking hands and five different pills to take and an eye that still hadn't opened and an awful feeling that everyone I had ever met, if not actually dead, was about to die, soon, and horribly, and an equally strong urge to burst into tears, it was in fact extremely comforting. And I was grateful for the company. Not that it would do any good to let Dave know that.

'Get off the fucking bed, you big shite. There's a chair there, and I didn't realize until now what it was for: unruly big heaps of Garda Inspectors when they come to visit.'

'Conway was on to me last night,' Dave said. 'The boss. Very interested in the Fogarty case all of a sudden. Ed, it was Conway who told me to shoot it down when Anne Fogarty approached me a few weeks ago. And now he's giving it "you and Ed are old mates, no harm the SCRT lending a hand there", calling me at home on a Sunday night to encourage me to share information with Ed Loy, Jesus Christ almighty.'

'What's the fucking world coming to?'

'Is my question to you.'

'I got the impression John O'Sullivan was giving me a nudge.'

'Well, some of this originates with the SDU, so I assume O'Sullivan has briefed Conway. Here's what I know: this is basically what you might call a turf war. Cullen was off limits because of his IRA background, never mind that he's always been a scumsucking drug dealer, Special Branch were under orders to look the other way. But now the IRA has stood itself down, things have changed: they went after Slab Murphy in South Armagh and they want to go after Jack Cullen in Dublin. At very least, the Criminal Assets Bureau want a major settlement; the National Bureau of Criminal Investigation would like to explore his current gangland activities, and we have a file the size of the phonebook dating back to the late seventies on the cunt, courtesy of the SDU. Not to mention what our colleagues in the North might have in store for him. So there's all that on one side, and on the other, there's the National Drug Unit in Dublin Castle.'

'What, Jack Cullen really is a tout? I don't believe it.'

'This is where it gets messy. Cullen is old school in his private life. He's been married for years, just the one kid, who died in a car crash, lives in a modest house, wife does the flowers for the local church and looks like Cullen's mammy, football, the few jars, very ordinary working class Dublin. And then word gets out that Jack has a lady on the side. And the lady turns out to be Rita Delaney, Dessie's brother Liam's wife.'

'Small world.'

'Don't be talking. Rita comes back here to visit her mother, or at least, that was the story to begin with. So Cullen's taking her to the kind of places he's not likely to bump into anyone who knows him, country house hotels type of thing. Quite by accident, a detective in the NDU spots him having Sunday lunch in some organic restaurant below in Kilpedder, all cosy with his lady friend, and then walking through the gardens afterwards, getting cosier still. And doesn't our man take a few snaps on his mobile, and his bosses think to themselves, well, it's worth a tumble, and they confront Jack Cullen with the incriminating evidence, not hoping for very much, because he has a fearsome reputation which, as you don't need me to tell you, is well earned. And Cullen goes to pieces. Seems the wife and the stable home life is crucial to him, he can't tolerate the idea of losing it, is willing to do anything to keep it in place. So first they ask him to give someone up: they suggest Lamp Comerford, because this is around the time Lamp starts getting wayward and shooting up the Viscount and so forth. And Jack point-blank refuses: no way will he inform on a friend, he says. Turns out he'll shoot them, but he won't inform on them. What he will do is, give up product. He says he's willing to tell the NDU details of the shipments he has coming in. He's undermining his own business, the very reason for his existence.'

'Where's that going to lead?'

'Well, you'd be surprised. This is early days, but already the NDU has seized drugs with a street value of one and a half million. Now, Cullen isn't giving them everything, but he's giving them enough to get them in the papers and to more than hit their targets so the Garda Commissioner can modestly announce that while the war against drugs won't be fought and won in a day, it's always encouraging to see a string of victories on the battlefield.'

'So it's like protection money. Cullen is paying off the NDU with enough action to make it look like they're tackling the drug menace. Meanwhile, he's got enough product coming through to keep the home fires burning. Everyone's happy.'

'Provided the shipment seizures don't get the troops down.'

'That was the problem Lamp had: he knew there was a tout. I don't know if he suspected Jack, but he had to have known it was someone near the top.'

'Well. I understand that's nothing Lamp has to worry about any longer.'

'And come here, is Rita Delaney caught up in this too? Because I noticed at Paul Delaney's removal on Saturday Jack Cullen shook Dessie's hand but he had the few quiet words for Liam. What was he, thanking him for the use of his wife?'

Dave Donnelly burst out laughing at that.

'As you do. Actually, I don't know what that's about.'

'Dessie noticed it as well, and didn't seem impressed to me about it.'

'Well, that's one for you and Dessie.'

Unfinished business. I had to get it out of the way today, because the way I felt, already, I didn't think I could take this case much longer: nine in the morning and my head alternately burned like my brain had been scalded and swirled in a fog of medication. Maybe Dessie could get along without me. On the other hand, Dessie had a gun. Maybe I couldn't get along without Dessie. Try to decide. No, pay attention to Dave, he's still talking. Mind you, he hasn't stopped talking since he came in. Look at the sauce he's got all over his tie, the state of the big eejit.

'So the NDU have been warning everyone off Jack Cullen, basically. But as of now, the gloves are off: after what you told them, they've decided they have to shut him down, basically. On top of which, there's no way he's going to take yesterday's INLA attacks lying down. There's going to be a major gang war if Cullen isn't stopped, is the reasoning.'

'Cullen murdered Lamp Comerford because he thought Lamp killed Paul Delaney and Raymond Moran, because I persuaded him that Lamp had simulated all the INLA attacks as a smokescreen behind which he could operate.'

Dave passed me a handful of newspapers.

'Well, these might persuade Jack otherwise,' he said.

The covers of the tabloids all had the same story: WE RULE GANGLAND, SAY INLA; TERROR IN THE CHURCHYARD; INLA MOUNT CITY DRUG TRADE TERROR TAKEOVER; INLA 2, IRA 2; INLA: DUBLIN FOR THE TAKING. There were grotesque photographs of Shay Rollins drinking champagne and posing in boxing gloves, and a statement admitting the 'execution' of Paul Delaney and Ray Moran for 'antisocial behaviour' was attributed to an INLA source.

'Jesus Christ,' I said. 'They're boasting about it now.'

'I think Jack Cullen will be coming after you once he finds out you're back on the streets. Which is an added incentive to help us take him down.'

'Jesus Christ,' I said again, the enormity of it looming above me again. 'I'm feeling a little out of my depth here Dave.

I mean, the IRA, the INLA, Special Branch or whatever they call themselves these days. This is not what I do. I'm a private detective, not a secret fucking agent. I mean, there was a guy at the hospital last night, wouldn't tell me his name, or who he worked for – the Department of Justice? The Army? The Guards? None of my business. Some kind of spook. Old boy with steel rimmed glasses, sinister looking fucker, just staring at me throughout. John O'Sullivan tells me he wanted them to put me away on any charge they could think of, for as long as they could get away with, and hopefully something would happen to me in jail to make my stay much longer, make it permanent. I mean, I'm used to the bad guys having a go, and I have the scars to prove it. But firstly, terrorists are off the scale when it comes to bad guys as far as I'm concerned, and maybe they all claim the war is over, but they're still fighting about something, aren't they? Once a terrorist, always a maniac, that's how it looks to me. And second, I assume Steel Rim is supposed to be one of the good guys, yet he wants me out of the picture in a major way. And sure, I've run up against cops before and had them come down hard on me. But in the round up, they've conceded, grudgingly but still, that I'm on the right side, that I'm doing the right thing.

'This doesn't look that way to me, Dave. Even if I come out in the end with a result, what difference is it going to make? I know Jack Cullen is a murderer, everyone knows he's a drug dealer, fuck's sake, the National Drug Unit are more or less sponsoring him to be one for the privilege of catching him occasionally. If he killed Brian Fogarty, the only difference it will make is to Brian's daughter Anne, who will at last know the truth. And that's one of two reasons I'm not still in hospital. The other is that I made a promise to Dessie Delaney to keep an eye on his brother Paul, and now Paul is dead, and I wanted a name to pin that death on: if it's Shay Rollins, then that job is done. I know that Dessie wanted revenge, but I don't think he's equipped to take on the INLA. I know I'm not.'

Dave Donnelly looked quickly at me and nodded and looked away.

'Very shifty, Dave, what are you not telling me? Is it about Bobby Doyle?'

Dave Donnelly's face flushed, and he glared at me.

'I can't talk about Bobby Doyle,' he said. 'Not yet. I mean, he's not connected to this.'

'Oh, but I think he is. He's been one of the Fogarty suspects all along, and you don't get to keep company with the likes of Jack Cullen and George Halligan by doing good works and giving your money away to the poor. But more than that, in the last while, Bobby Doyle is the name on everyone's lips. John O'Sullivan asked me if Jack Cullen had mentioned him, and then he made it fairly obvious that at the very least there's some kind of cover-up going on regarding Doyle. And the last thing I can remember at the farm is Jack Cullen firing questions about Doyle at me.'

Dave looked at the door like the SDU guys might be outside, then he flicked his chin up and rolled his huge head around on his neck.

'Fuck it,' he said, 'I think you've paid your dues on this one, just don't tell them it was me who told you. Noel Sweeney – what did he say about Bobby Doyle?'

'That nobody knows what he did before he popped up in San Francisco. That he had no record of involvement in terrorism, no IRA history, in fact, no history of any kind.'

'Yeah. I don't know who was running Noel Sweeney, the SDU or O'Sullivan at NBCI, but whichever, they were all on the same page over this one anyway, he was sent to you Ed, Conway told me to give you his details, he was intended to steer you towards Cullen and far away from Bobby Doyle and his activities back in the day.'

'Back in what day?'

'The seventies, the early eighties. He was an IRA volunteer, although it seems as if he never had the appetite for violence the likes of Jack Cullen had. He was always in the political camp, trying to get the politics moving, trying to build the Sinn Féin side of the operation at the expense of the IRA. He wasn't that well known. And then he fell off the radar entirely, around about 1980, '81, re-emerged in the States.'

'And look at him now. So what's the story? Surely he can't keep his past a secret.'

'Not at all. Sure the *Mail* ran a feature on it last year, short on all facts except the main one, that Doyle was in the IRA. They tried to blow it into a big deal, surely this is not the kind of man to be bankrolling such a major national building project, but nobody really seemed to care. I suppose when they're in government in the North, building a bridge pales into insignificance. I'd cheerfully see him hanged off the same bridge, I have no time for the fuckers, past present or future, but it's not up to me.'

'And so what . . . what's the deal? What are you saying?'

'Most of the government will be at the Independence Bridge opening ceremony today. The Taoiseach, the President, the Army, all the bankers and barristers and businessmen and the big rich, you know?'

'You sound as if you like them just as much as I do, Dave.'

'I'm paid a pittance not to take a view on that. And so the scrutiny's been tight on Bobby Doyle for weeks, months, really, has been pretty tight. Just in case something pops up unexpectedly from his, eh, colourful past.'

'And has it?'

'How well do you know Donna Nugent, Ed?'

I don't really do blushing, and I was in too much pain for embarrassment. 'Very well, as you're probably going to tell me,' I said.

'Sounded like a better Good Friday than I had anyway.'

'Did they bug the room and all?'

'I don't think they go that far. Anyway, serious question actually, how well do you know her?'

'Not very well, really. She'd do anything for Bobby Doyle, I know that much. Where "anything" begins and ends for her, I don't know. Where are you going with this?'

'Do you know what car she drives?'

'A red Mini-Cooper '08 reg.'

'Is there any reason you can think of for Donna to be driving around a corporation housing estate in Clondalkin in the middle of the night? Several times in the past two weeks?'

I was about as rough as Donna's sexual tastes tended, so I doubted she was cruising.

'Drugs? She does a lot of drugs.'

'She made one stop only, and though the house she stopped at is occupied by a drug dealer, he never keeps the product in the house.'

'Maybe she paid him and picked the drugs up later, or they were dropped off at her house.'

'Why couldn't she pay for them then?'

'All right, I give up. Whose house did she stop off at?'

Dave looked at me and smiled.

'The officer commanding of the Dublin INLA, Shay Rollins.'

~

I placed a call to Donna, but her phone went straight to message; I doubted, given the day that was in it, if I'd get hold of her at all today. I had a message on my phone from Anne Fogarty to ask if I wanted to meet her and her kids after the opening of Independence Bridge: there was a firework display on the quays and all manner of family friendly fun to be had on the streets of the city. I needed an antidote to the likes of Jack Cullen but I thought that might be pushing it a bit, although in fairness to Anne she did say she'd understand perfectly if I wasn't up for it: she wasn't a hundred per cent herself, but she couldn't let the girls down.

Before I got any further with my phone, my eye was drawn to a letter Dave had brought with him. I had assumed it was from him, an invitation from Carmel to yet another Donnelly party, or photographs from their canoeing holiday in Devon. But no: on the front of the cream, watermarked, lavender-scented envelope was printed Mr Edward Loy, and underneath that, By Hand. I opened the envelope and several faded newspaper clippings fell out. Each of the clippings had a photograph of a young family called the Coyles: Gerry and Claire and their children, Yvonne aged fourteen and Luke, eight. The Coyles had been driving home to Belfast from a weekend in Liverpool when they were blown to pieces by a roadside bomb outside Newry in South Armagh. The IRA had admitted responsibility, but regretted the incident, an error which they said 'was wrong', and 'shouldn't have happened'. The IRA didn't explain exactly why what shouldn't have happened happened, but one report speculated that the distinctive nature of the Coyle's vehicle – Gerry Coyle was a vintage motor enthusiast, and drove a red Jaguar Mark 2 3.6 litre – was responsible, although obviously the reports didn't allude to the identity of the likely target who also drove such a car.

There was a sombre footnote to the report: Gerry and Claire had each been only children without any other relatives, and so at one stroke, that was the end of the Coyle family history.

There were no personal details accompanying the news clippings, but I'd only met one person on this case who smelt of lavender, and that was Dee Dee Doyle. Dee Dee Doyle had given me her number and told me to call her because she got so lonely: I thought at the time she'd been making a rather broad merry-widow style pass; now it looked like she had something urgent to tell me. When I called, Dee Dee was somewhere between hair and make-up in a salon off Baggot Street; she agreed to meet me at the Merrion Hotel when she was done.

Dessie Delaney was next on my list, but I didn't have anything for him yet; I texted him to say that I'd be in touch soon, I was on the cusp of something big, and not to do anything until he heard from me; I hoped that would keep him from driving out to Clondalkin himself and blasting up Shay Rollins' windows.

I soaked my eye for half an hour in a solution the nurse had given me, and had a very careful shower, and by the end of all that, washed and dressed if not shaved, I had one eye open and one eye half, and a reset nose that was still swollen but substantially reduced from last night. I put fresh dressings on the wounds that needed them, and swallowed the painkillers but not the sedatives, washing them down with a double measure of ice cold Tanqueray and bitters for old times' sake. The gin played havoc with my broken teeth, but I felt the better of it, or thought I did until I looked in the mirror. Sweat beaded across my brow, which was the colour of sour milk. Short of a trip to the beauty salon myself, I couldn't do much about that. The eye still looked pretty grim though, so I put on a pair of sunglasses and decided that looking like a bozo who wore shades indoors was about as good as it was going to get and went down into the street.

24

Le Bistro on Harcourt Street opened for coffee at ten, so I sat and had a cup and then asked the server, who was Spanish, if I could see Ms Fogarty. She smiled and shook her head, and I said, 'Ms Fogarty? The manager? It's a business matter,' and she said she would find someone.

Aisling Fogarty, in a clipped accent, said she was Aisling D'Arcy, and asked me what I wanted. She looked like a streamlined version of her sister, Anne as a fashion designer would resculpt her: tall and slender, she wore skinny black jeans that displayed her narrow hips and thighs, tiny waist and long legs, and a black top that did the same for her skinny arms and torso. Her skin was taut but lush in an expensive looking way, and she wore her dyed blonde hair straight and long. Her eyes were smaller, darker, harder versions of her sister's: while not exactly hostile, the look she gave me through them made it plain I'd better come up with something worth her while. I couldn't think of anything off the cuff, so I took off my shades, and when dismay flashed in her face like a flare in a winter sky, lighting its austere features with something that bordered on sympathy, I said the first thing that came into my head.

'I've been trying to find out who murdered your father. But there are a lot of people out there who've been getting in my way. I wonder whether you'd like to help me.'

~

I don't know which brokerage Mr D'Arcy worked for, but it must have done well out of the boom years, because whether you judged the four-storey eighteenth-century house on Harcourt Terrace that Aisling and he lived in by the grand scale of the rooms or by the incredibly high spec of the design, the result was equally impressive. I was sitting in an easy chair in the ground floor sitting room, or it could have been the morning room, or even the drawing room, I'm not an expert when it comes to the eighteenth-century or to people called D'Arcy, but it was all a far cry from Farney Park, and unless Mr D'Arcy's brokerage was feeling the pinch in the new austerity, it didn't strike me that Aisling could be in a desperate rush to get her hands on the proceeds of any sale of the family home.

Aisling D'Arcy came back from putting her face on for a second time. The first time was after she'd burst into tears in the restaurant. She had apologized then, and said it was just the shock of it being brought into her own place; she knew Anne had hired someone, but over the phone it didn't have the same kind of reality. She suggested we take a walk around the corner to her house, having first called her sister to establish that I was who I said I was, and that I was adequately house-trained. The second time was when we walked into the house and there on a wall in the sitting room was a framed photograph of her father.

She sat opposite me now and gave a brisk smile that didn't reach her eyes, more of a grimace really. She was the kind of woman who usually kept a fierce grip on her emotions, and if you were present on the rare occasion when that grip slackened, her embarrassment at what she considered her display of weakness was converted into aggression.

'Apologies again, Mr Loy. The sort of thing . . . it's the sort of thing that you think has gone away for good, but then it surges to the surface again when you least expect or want it. Now, is there something in particular you want to ask me?'

Mrs D'Arcy didn't hang about. I felt like a tradesman being hurried through the house and out to see the rear guttering. My chippy feelings were my problem though, and I didn't see why I had to burden anyone else with them.

'Yes, for a start, do you think I might have a drink?' I said. From the expression on her face, I may as well have asked her for a ride, and as the silence continued and her expression got even more pinched, I began to wonder if I had. But my head was aching, and it was too early to take any more painkillers, and in any case, I wanted a drink.

'But it's eleven o'clock in the morning,' she said, and then, realizing even tradesmen merited a certain level of courtesy, stood and asked me what I wanted.

'Gin and tonic, Tanqueray if you have it.'

'Of course we have it,' she said, with a little Farney Park chippiness of her own, and clipped out the door. The drink she brought me was so strong I thought I mightn't be able for it, but a second sip reassured me on that score. Mrs D'Arcy had a small bottle of Evian which she took minute sips from, as if even water was a bit too much sometimes.

'I hope my sister is demanding receipts,' she said.

'I don't charge for booze,' I said. 'Were you aware of your mother's affair with Steve Owen before your father's murder?'

Aisling's face flinched three times during this brief question, and I felt sorry for her all over again.

'No, I wasn't.'

'I just wondered. You see, I went to the house on Saturday, and I stood for a while in the back bedroom, and looked out. You can see down Herbert Road from there, see all the way down to Marian College. When I interviewed Steve Owen, he said his affair with your mother had involved a certain amount of running around and climbing over walls and hiding on garage roofs, risk-taking, that kind of thing.'

Aisling D'Arcy's face was a study in disapproval and disgust; I suppose I couldn't blame her, but it looked like she was blaming herself.

'And I wondered, it's not exactly a huge house, it must have been difficult to carry on a relationship of that kind without being spotted, and so I wondered, since I understand you had the back bedroom, whether you had seen anything, even . . . I don't know, Owen on his way down the street?'

'What difference would it make if I had?' she said.

'I don't know, exactly.'

'Then why do you take it on yourself to ask me such . . . impertinent, actually disgusting questions, which you know must be painful to hear, if you don't have a concrete, logical reason for asking them?'

'Oh, I do have a logical reason for asking them. I just don't know how the answers will stack up until I hear them. And sometimes it's not the answers, it's what someone doesn't say, or the way they answer a question I didn't ask. I'm sorry if the questions are painful, but I don't believe they're impertinent: your sister hired me to investigate the case, and your mother's affair with the man who was convicted of your father's murder is a central part of that case.'

'Is it? I understood from Anne that it was completely irrelevant, that the suspects were three men Daddy was investigating for tax offences, that what Mammy . . . got up to had nothing to do with it.'

I nodded.

'That's certainly possible. It's still very difficult to rule anything in or out.'

Aisling D'Arcy raised her voice to a hard metallic pitch.

'Well, don't you think you have a responsibility to work out in advance where you are in the case before you subject me to this kind of . . . *ordeal*? I'm one of the victims, you know, and here you are, half drunk, covered in disgusting scars and bandages, looking like an escaped maniac, asking all sorts of . . . so incredibly *rude* . . . I'd like you to leave, actually.'

She stood up and went to the door.

'Not until you answer my question,' I said.

'I'll call the Guards,' she said. 'I'll have you arrested.'

'I was arrested last night for a lot worse. Covered in a murdered Garda detective's blood. They let me go. What do you think they'll do to me for sitting down and drinking gin and asking rude questions?'

Aisling D'Arcy's face set with something between rage and pique; her lip quivered, and I thought she might cry again, and for one heartbreaking moment I saw the teenage girl, the eldest daughter who had lost her father long before his murder, and with him her map of strength, and independence, and courage.

'I never saw Steve Owen in our house, or approaching it; I didn't even know who he was until the trial. Is that it? Will you go now?'

I nodded, and finished my drink and stood up.

'In any case, you haven't even got your facts right.'

'How so?' I said.

'You said I had the back bedroom.'

'That's what Noel Sweeney, the investigating officer, told me.'

'Well, you can tell him he got his facts wrong too,' she said.

'I would, but he was the detective who was murdered,' I said.

'Because of this case?' she said, her voice strained and wavering.

'It's all because of this case,' I said. 'His death, my scars, the gin, it's all because of this case. How did we get our facts wrong?'

'I moved out in 1990. I wasn't even living there when Daddy was . . . when Daddy died.'

'And who took your room?'

'My younger sister, Midge. Margaret.'

Before I left, I thought of another question.

'Was your hair always straight? It's just, in the house I found one of those . . . Afro combs, is that what they're called? With the long teeth and the handle? A dedicated comb for curly hair. And I wondered—'

'My mother had slightly wavy hair, a bit like Anne's. But Margaret's was the curliest, a total tangle. She used that kind of brush.'

'Would you have a photograph of her?'

'Did you not get one from Anne?'

'I don't think I asked her,' I said, and she shook her head in dismay, as if yet again I had shown myself up as clueless and incompetent. When she came back downstairs and handed me a photograph of Margaret Fogarty, taken when she was fourteen but looked twenty, I was inclined to agree with her assessment of my investigative abilities. For when I saw Margaret Fogarty's dark red head of corkscrew curls, I understood, if not exactly who had murdered Brian Fogarty, certainly who had not, and that, in a chastening rush of insight Aisling D'Arcy would have appreciated had I the voice to speak it aloud, almost everything I had thought about the Fogarty case up until that point had been absolutely wrong.

25

Working a case sometimes feels like the growth of a family. When you start out, it's very simple to keep it all straight in your head. But as it develops, there are all sorts of additions and complications, bringing with them new duties and responsibilities, and much and all as you'd sometimes like to get back to how it was before, because it seemed so simple then, you just can't. I wanted to leave far behind me the world of Jack Cullen and Bobby Doyle, of the IRA and the INLA, of secret policemen and security policies, leave it in the hands of the people who dealt in smoke and mirrors and thrived there, and do what I was meant to do. But I couldn't: not because Cullen and Doyle and George Halligan had a damn thing to do with Brian Fogarty's murder, but because I had made a promise to Dessie Delaney that I would keep an eye on his brother Paul. And that was why, instead of heading across to Fairview to Paul's funeral, I was meeting my second Southside millionaire's wife of the day in the Merrion Hotel.

Before I went in, I made a call to Larry Roe, a contact I had in the Allied Irish Bank. For a small cash consideration I would have couriered to his house, he was willing to give me certain kinds of information, on condition that they could never be traced to him. And since, if they were, I wouldn't be able to use him any more, and most probably my range of contacts in other banks and credit card companies would dry up also, I made sure they weren't. I gave Larry Margaret Fogarty's current account number and sort code and he had her address and telephone number for me within a few seconds.

The other call I made was to Tommy Owens, in reply to three missed calls of his. It was not a call I had been looking forward to. When Tommy heard what had happened to Charlie Newbanks, he took it hard, as I knew he would; moreover, he blamed himself for prevailing on Charlie to help us out. I reminded him that people like Lamp Comerford and Jack Cullen aren't our fault, and we couldn't be held accountable for their actions, but I don't think it did much to ease the sting. When I started to explain that, since the INLA had admitted responsibility for Ray Moran and Paul Delaney's deaths and claimed Simon Devlin and Dean Cummins as members, Jack Cullen would probably be on my tail, Tommy was ahead of me: Leo and he would get my back, he said. I told him where I was and where I thought I was going, and Tommy said I wouldn't necessarily see them, but they'd be there.

~

Dee Dee Doyle sat on a sofa in the lounge of the Merrion Hotel looking like she had her own personal lighting, such was the glow of opulent glamour radiating from her newly-set golden blonde hair and her freshly and impeccably applied mask of paint and cream. She patted the cushion beside her and I air kissed her and sat down. Stung by Aisling D'Arcy's scorn, I had already removed most of the bandages on my face; the effect was rough and raw, but I no longer looked like I had leapt from the back of a moving ambulance; I left the shades on; neither the Merrion Hotel nor Dee Dee Doyle was apt to think me a bozo for wearing them, or at any rate, neither would say so.

Dee Dee had other things on her mind. Her face was a picture of wifely martyrdom, of tremulous courage under domestic fire, but there was something about her eyes that looked vaguely unhinged. If marriage was for better or worse, Dee Dee looked like she couldn't remember which was which any more, and in any case, she'd had enough.

'Up in the house, at this very moment, supervising the preparations for the party that will take place after the opening ceremonies for Independence Bridge, *my* party, in *my* house, who do you think?'

'I don't know, Dee Dee.'

'Donna Nugent,' Dee Dee said, and paused significantly. I nodded, as if I understood the full implication of the pause (which I thought I did) and then Dee Dee resumed.

'I was willing to tolerate a certain . . . men are men, and Bobby couldn't manage without Donna, and if they were willing to keep it discreet and not embarrass me in my own town, among my own friends, for God's sake, then . . . well, as I say, men . . . I don't know any woman of my age whose husband hasn't . . . and it's a question of simply finding something to occupy oneself . . . Bobby and I are . . . I *thought* Bobby and I were too good a team to throw it all away. I'm not a prude, you understand. Don't you, Ed?'

'Of course I do, Dee Dee, of course I do,' I said, taking the hand that was offered me, and wondering idly if, by pressing it in a certain way, I could get her to speed the fuck up.

'Not one of those hopeless women, wailing and raging and making scenes, Lord God you want to say to them, if he wasn't having an affair before, he certainly will now, after witnessing all that. A deal more sophisticated, a deal more . . . *French* about it all. But there are limits. I am a hostess, Ed. I am known for my balls. Parties, dinners, receptions, black tie, full dress, balls. Known for them.'

'That's how I knew you, Dee Dee. Before I met you, that's what I knew you for.'

Dee Dee's eyes seemed to mist up at this tribute. She squeezed my hand and continued.

'How is it then that I am not considered sufficiently qualified to organize the Independence Bridge party? How can it be that I was told my skills were not appropriate for the particular kind of guests expected? I've given a reception for the Vietnamese Ambassador, Ed!'

'I know, I know.'

'And suddenly Little Miss Great Gas Altogether Cheeky Little Snip knows everything there is to know about the combination of dignitaries and politicos and cultural types and how they don't want anything too stiff and formal or too elaborate or showy, I was waiting for her to say vulgar, and I tell you, the smirk would have been on the other side of her face if she had. Cocky little wagon.'

Dee suddenly turned her head and stared into the full-length mirror by the fireplace.

'Ed, do you think they dyed this a shade too pale?'

I made a show of considering this.

'No, it's just so, Dee Dee.'

Dee Dee checked herself again in the mirror, all business, nodded, and turned back.

'I know what they're saying, I heard Bobby trying to explain it, they think I'm fine when it comes to a whole bunch of TV celebrities and businessmen's wives and nouveau riche builders and footballers and models, but this has to be a bit more . . . *cultural* . . . you know? Sprung on me, the Saturday morning. I had the Corrs booked, Ed. *The Corrs*. Told to cancel them.'

'And so . . .'

'And so I've just had it with the bullshit. I mean, poets and painters and the fucking Chieftains, it's far from that Bobby fucking Doyle was reared.'

Dee Dee swearing was so unexpected and yet so absolutely *right* I burst out laughing, and in fairness to her, she was in on the joke, and laughed a little herself.

'I mean, come on, you know? I don't see Jack Cullen on the invite list and we all know he may as fucking well be.'

'Do we? How do we all know that, Dee Dee?'

'Ah come on,' she said. But I wasn't laughing any more.

I removed my hand from hers and took the lavender scented envelope I had received that morning out of my coat pocket.

'You sent me this, didn't you?'

'What if I did? You can't prove it, can you?' Dee Dee said.

'I don't need to prove it, I . . . what has it to do with Bobby? Was he responsible? Was he in the IRA when the Coyle family were killed? Did he give the order? Did Jack Cullen carry it out?'

Dee Dee looked around her and leant in close to me.

'Bobby and Jack were the active service unit. They did the operation together. The pair of them. And of course, not a bother off Jack Cullen. But that was it for Bobby, when he found out what they'd done. Some judge had the same car and that's who they were targeting. Bobby took a long time to get over it. And after that, he did everything he could to push the movement towards peace.'

'And you're saying, if people found out about this . . .'

'They'd have a different opinion of Bobby Doyle, all the high and mighty, the great and the good. They'd think twice about lining up to celebrate his fucking bridge. Wouldn't they?'

I shook my head.

'I don't think so, Dee Dee. I mean, there's Sinn Féin people in power, in government in the North, and I'm pretty certain there's stuff like this you could dig up about them. But nobody does, or if they do, nobody publishes it in the press, and it doesn't deter anyone from lining up to shake their hands and have their photographs taken with them.'

'But Bobby Doyle and Jack Cullen . . . I mean, it's priceless, isn't it?'

'I agree, it is. But I don't think it will make any difference.'

Dee Dee looked at herself in the mirror again and sighed.

'I suppose you're right. I suppose when it comes down to it, it's in everyone's interest to pretend Bobby Doyle is completely respectable . . .'

Dee Dee Doyle fingered her white gold charm bracelet, and then completed her thought.

'Including mine,' she said.

~

I had told Dave Donnelly that, while I didn't know where the farmhouse in whose grounds the bodies of Lamp Comerford and Charlie Newbanks were buried was, I was pretty sure it had been set fire to, so if it burned to the ground, there shouldn't be too much difficulty about locating it. And so it proved: as I drove to Bobby Doyle's house, it was the first item on the midday news: two bodies had been found in a freshly dug grave at a burnt-out farmhouse near the Kildare/Offaly border.

I didn't know whether my SDU detail was still on the case, and I decided I wouldn't keep checking. Tommy Owens had texted me after I had left the Merrion Hotel to say:

Glad to see you with a mature woman for a change, instead of running after young ones.

It's all fun and games until someone loses an eye.

26

Donna Nugent was pacing the ballroom of Bobby Doyle's Clyde Road home, a huge detached Victorian stone pile set among mature oaks and elms in a garden the size of a park. She was shouting something about amps and arc lights into a phone and getting nowhere fast, when a dumpy bloke with a beard dressed entirely in black who was tidying loudspeaker cable took the phone off her and sent her across to me.

'Not my phone, not my call, you'd think I had enough to do, but no, Donna must be busy! Here you are, Laminate City, access-all-areas pass that ensures you're right in among the VIPs, and up close to the man himself, in fact this pass has you seated right beside my very-horny-to-see-you self the closer you get the better you look. Or in fact not, God Almighty Ed, what have you been doing, arguing with a horse? You should be in hospital, I'm serious sweetie, those wounds are weeping, Jesus. Here, let me call you an ambulance.'

I pocketed the laminate and put my hand on Donna's phone to stop her using it.

'I was in hospital. I came out, because there's some unfinished business I need to attend to.'

My hand was shaking, and so was my voice. Donna looked at me curiously, as if human weakness was something she was entirely tolerant of in the abstract, but found distasteful when confronted with it in person.

'What happened to you? Or should I not ask?' she said,

trying to keep the tone as Donna as possible, but not entirely succeeding.

'Jack Cullen and his thugs happened to me. They were very upset about the attacks on his gang by the INLA.'

Donna nodded, her expression simultaneously serious and slightly puzzled, as if no one should expect her, a girl, to have an opinion on the INLA or on gangland crime.

'And I thought it was interesting that Bobby Doyle and Jack Cullen used to be such close colleagues. They don't see each other any more, do they? Or do they? I don't imagine so.'

Donna looked across at the bearded technician, who was taping a hank of cable behind a long drape, and scowled.

'Let's go somewhere we can sit down, Ed. We don't want you to get delirious.'

I followed her out into an atrium off which there were half a dozen corridors; she led me down one and through a heavy oak door into a small Victorian chapel, complete with a full stained-glass representation of the Last Supper on high behind the altar. We sat in pews across the aisle from each other, and Donna's serious, possessed face gave an inkling of why Bobby Doyle put so much faith in her.

'Okay, first of all, where did you get this? Has that silly cow—'

'Where did I get it? I'm a detective, it's what I do. Bobby Doyle and Jack Cullen, the Coyle family, roadside bomb. Four innocent people, an entire family wiped out.'

'And Bobby Doyle has paid for it ever since. I've seen him cry his eyes out, last year, last week, and say that no amount of tears could ever be enough. He's had Mass said at dawn in this chapel every day for years. What he's done with his life, to atone insofar as he could, was devote himself to making sure such atrocities would become part of history.'

'History, it's always fucking history with the IRA, isn't it, never just murder, senseless fucking bloodshed. And in making their precious history, they managed to destroy the Coyle family's history entirely, didn't they? You know the parents were only children? Gone, forever, like a black hole, no descendants, no one to commemorate them in flesh. And that's what everyone will be celebrating today, won't they, with their fucking bridge? 1916? History? Bloodshed and glory and death.'

'Nice speech. Shame not to deliver it directly to its intended target,' Bobby Doyle said. He stood at the back of the chapel. Donna, who had been crying, leapt to her feet.

'I'm sorry, Bobby, I didn't know he was going to—'

'How could you? God might move in mysterious ways, but he'd still pick up a few tips from the boy Loy here. Not impressed by my . . . what would you call it, my hypocrisy? Or do you not think, having made a mistake, a man's not allowed a second chance?'

'I guess that's one way to look at it. But there's second chances and building monuments to yourself, and that's what this bridge is, don't you think? A means to glorify the gunmen, from 1916 right down to the IRA of the Troubles, a cathedral in their honour, a vindication of every informer buried in a shallow grave, and every child blown to pieces in the noblest of causes: Ireland's fucking freedom.'

'You know that's not the way it's playing at all. The Irish government have taken it on, it's official Ireland all the way, and it's reclaimed 1916 to keep it out of the hands of the IRA.'

'But there'll be plenty of people there today with blood on their hands, sitting pretty and looking respectable. Yes, it's the hypocrisy, it makes me sick.'

Bobby Doyle shrugged.

'By that token, it'd almost be a sign of greater integrity to be Jack Cullen, and continue to shoot and kill for no higher motive than profit,' he said.

'Maybe it would. Isn't that what remains when history winds itself up? After politics, profit? You're not building the Independence Bridge for nothing, are you? Here in Clyde Road with your own fucking chapel, Jesus. But maybe you aren't as different from Jack Cullen as you think, Bobby. Maybe you weren't then, and maybe you're not now.'

'I don't understand.'

'I'm sure Donna could explain it to you. Refresh your memory, that is to say. About her '08 reg red Mini parking outside Shay Rollins house half a dozen times over the past week. Coinciding mysteriously with the great INLA onslaught against Cullen's gang. I'm trying to get it straight in my head. Because I genuinely believe you've been a force for good, you've helped to steer the Republican movement away from violence. You've worked very hard for a very long time. And then, to jeopardize that work for . . . for what?'

'You haven't told this to anyone else, have you Ed?' Donna was always quick to cry, but the squall had passed as if it had never been there; her voice was a reed now, taut and shrill and urgent.

'I wasn't the one who spotted your car outside Rollins' house. Maybe they haven't pieced it together like I have. Almost certainly they don't want to. As far as I can see, the SDU want you to be respectable and above board, open and transparent, Bobby. And if they want that, so you shall be.'

Bobby Doyle looked at the floor, and raised a hand to his brow. It was hardly the most extravagant gesture, but coming from him, it was like another man's cry of abjection. When he lifted his face his eyes were filled with despair. Before he had a chance to speak, Donna cut him off and went to stand by his side.

'Bobby, listen: say nothing, this is Ed Loy, he's a person of no standing, of no consequence in the world, no one will believe his word alone, and we know there is no evidence, there can't be any evidence. It's slur and innuendo, carping and begrudging, bitterness and spite from a, from a failed person with a failed life.'

Donna's eyes glittered with a fair degree of spite of her own as she said this. I wondered whether the contempt she spat was a tribute to the loyalty and esteem she held for her boss, the love, perhaps, or if she had truly despised me from the off. I tried to rally, but found her words had cut deep: it was true that I was a nobody, at best a kind of puppet the Guards used to buffer themselves from actions they preferred not to be associated with. I had no friends that weren't either cops or criminals, I had no family, I had, in the popular expression, not so much a failed life as no life at all out with what I did for my very modest living.

And yet. Maybe it was all true – although it made me wonder, since Donna had been so persistent about pestering me to fuck her, and so seemingly ardent when I did, whether some portion of the contempt she expressed could as justly be directed at herself – maybe it was all true, and I was a failure, a worthless, embittered nobody. And yet. I was right and they were wrong. I wasn't doing it from spite, or begrudgery, or because I wanted to be on the viewing platform or the top table or the back page of the *Sunday Independent*, I wasn't even doing it for myself any more, except insofar as I had to get it done; no, at this point I was doing it for Brian Fogarty and Paul Delaney and Charlie Newbanks, and Gerry and Claire and Yvonne and Luke Coyle; I could hear the dead voices in my head, and I needed to bring it to a close so that we all could get some rest.

At some point, Bobby Doyle had begun to speak, and Donna had tried to make him stop, and now Bobby seemed to be talking her down.

'I'm not remotely worried about what Loy can do, or what kind of case the Guards might try and piece together. I don't have any doubts about Rollins on that score, and he's the only one in that organization who knows. I just . . . the man has suffered here, look at him. It demands respect. And I'm not exactly proud of what I've done. But it had to be done nonetheless.'

'What had to be done? Using the INLA as a proxy force to take Jack Cullen out?' I said.

In order to speak freely, Doyle evidently felt the need to put some physical distance between himself and Donna Nugent. He walked up the aisle and sat in the front pew, turning around to face me. Thus excluded, Donna turned on her heel and stormed out of the chapel. Doyle made a comedy grimace, as if he'd been a very naughty boy.

'Very protective of me. Doesn't like to see me come to any harm.'

'Lucky you. Whose idea was it to kill Paul Delaney?'

'I said I wanted Cullen and Comerford taken out, and after that, they had to be active dealers.'

'Paul Delaney wasn't dealing.'

'Who told you that? Jack Cullen?'

'Ray Moran.'

'My source says he was. Heroin. It was some kind of deal Jack Cullen had done which wasn't coming through the gang's regular channels, I think, which was making Lamp Comerford suspicious.'

'Who's your source?'

'Barry Jordan. He personally witnessed Delaney passing smack to young Shels players. Said he should have gone to the Guards straight away.'

'Why'd he go to you?'

'I went to him. Shay Rollins heard about it, told me to ask Jordan myself if I didn't believe it.'

'So chicken and egg . . . how the hell did you get into a situation where you're dealing with someone like Shay Rollins?'

Bobby Doyle looked up at the altar and sighed.

'Jack Cullen . . . is unfinished business. It's true that I was consistently an advocate for the peace process, and that I . . . after that day in South Armagh, I vowed never to get involved in violence again. But to see Jack Cullen down here, year after year, destroying his own community, feasting on it like this unholy pig, the sow that ate the farrow, and everything he did came to my ears, of course it did, and there were many times over the years when it was put to me that the least worst situation would be for Cullen to be taken out, and there were several operators who offered to do the deed in a manner that would look like just another gangland killing. And I said no. I'd made a promise. I'd taken a vow. And the old code dies hard, you know, one Republican to another, you don't inform, you remain loyal, however much you despise the man. And I don't know what made me change my mind, to be honest, maybe this bridge coming to fruition, maybe the threat that Cullen might one day compromise me. Mostly it was the sense that people know he's IRA, and they know he's a vicious, psychotic drug dealer, and they think those things are equivalent. Like you. And that's not so. And part of me thinks, if men like me hadn't been so principled and peace-worshipping and twenty-odd years ago we'd taken the twenty or thirty hardest cases in the Provos and shot them in the back of the head, there'd be a lot of innocent people walking abroad today, a lot of Coyle families watching their children grow up. And I think it was a failure of moral vision on my part not to see that, and a failure of moral courage not to do it. And maybe that . . . idealism, I think you'd have to call it, maybe I was full of it *because* of Independence Bridge, maybe it all blended together. And I didn't want it known . . . even in Republican circles . . . and I'd been told that, for all the mayhem that surrounds him, Shay Rollins could be trusted. As long as you made it worth his while.'

'So you approached him.'

'I approached him. I regret it's fallen out the way it has, particularly about young Delaney, that was wrong, he was just a kid. I regret in particular that they haven't done what they were supposed to do yet, which was to get rid of Jack Cullen.'

'You regret it. It was wrong. It shouldn't have happened. Up the IRA.'

'You're right, of course. But I was trying to do good. And if Jack Cullen is killed, I will have succeeded. The way of the gun is not the right way. But sometimes using a gun is the only right option.'

'I prefer it in the original Chinese. Kill them all and let God sort them out. You know Cullen suspects you.'

'I'd be amazed if he didn't. He's not stupid, and he's always been incredibly paranoid. And he hates me just as much as I hate him. I'll take my chances. I always have.'

I stood up.

'By the way, you're off the hook for Brian Fogarty's murder,' I said.

'That's a relief,' he said. 'Do you know who did it?'

'Yes,' I said. 'And I wish I didn't.'

As I walked down Bobby Doyle's tree-lined drive, I was aware that Donna Nugent was looking down at me from an upstairs window. I felt humiliated and wounded by what she had said, and a desperate urge to prove how far from being a failure I actually was. A woman's scorn. Maybe that was the first reason God invented gin.

27

Dessie Delaney couldn't fucking believe it. On a day as solemn as this, and fair enough, Dessie had his mind set on more than grieving, but the solemn duty of avenging his brother had a certain dignity to it, which would be compromised, quite frankly, by taking his other brother's head off with a bread knife and feeding the fat fuck to the dogs in Fairview Park.

Last night was bad enough, what with the INLA lobbing grenades and half the church getting hysterical and the other half repairing to the Parting Glass and getting locked and giving it hole talk about going out to Clondalkin and burning Shay Rollins' house down, real The-Revolution-Starts-When-This-Pub-Closes stuff if Dessie ever heard it. And with Jack Cullen and Lamp Comerford AWOL, Liam was back to his clownish worst, crying and singing and threatening the INLA with all sorts ('If they walked in now,' he said, and Dessie was that close to saying, 'We wouldn't see you for dust'), and nearly letting slip that they had all Larry Knight's guns stashed up in the house in Griffith Avenue. It was lacking more than a little dignity, it was like a fucking knackers' wedding so it was, with gobshites he didn't know who'd never even met Paul coming over to tell him how sorry they were, looking for free jar is all it was. When they started getting barred for being sloppy drunk Dessie warned Liam not to be making a cunt of himself or out the door with him, what it took to get you barred from a dump like the Parting Glass, for fuck's sake.

But last night was nothing compared to this morning. First, Dessie was woken at six by the sound of Liam sobbing. Couldn't get back to sleep, so up and down to the shops and bought some rashers and sausages, get a decent breakfast going, start the day off on a solid footing. Halfway through, Liam bursts out crying again, has 'a confession' to make. Jesus Mary and Joseph, Dessie thought Liam was tripping when he heard what unbelievable piss he was coming out with.

Apparently, Liam's wife Rita, the lazy-arsed one with the dying mother, had been having an affair with Jack Cullen, long distance, every time she went back to Dublin. As if that wasn't Technicolor enough, hadn't Liam got wind of it, and instead of beating the head off her or slinging her out on her ear, he encourages her to see if Jack needs any favours done, as if he hadn't been getting enough of Rita's hospitality as it was. Next thing, Liam has glommed onto a Greek smack dealer whose brother drinks in the bar, who runs the product from Turkey via Greece and on through the Balkans, and doesn't he order a regular package for himself, which Rita, working as Jack Cullen's fucking drug mule, God have mercy on us all, brings through customs, concealed about her person in ways Dessie didn't want to even think about. Dessie told Liam it was a fucking sin to have dropped acid the day of Paul's funeral, and Liam said he was straight as a die and that Dessie hadn't heard the worst of it yet, and then Liam burst into tears again.

The worst of it turned out to be that Paul Delaney *had* been dealing heroin, just on a small scale, to friends and teammates and so on, and that Liam had *known* about it. Dessie didn't know where to start. Liam said that, according to Rita, Paul had pestered Jack Cullen, who was fond of Paul in a fatherly way and didn't want him involved in anything to do with drugs, to let him do it, and Cullen, indulgent to the kid, gave in. Dessie asked Liam if he believed that, and Liam said he was so bewildered when he discovered Rita was having an affair that anything extra came as an anti-climax.

Dessie couldn't get his head around it. If Paul had brought it on himself – but Cullen was responsible for the heroin, always had been, brought it in and got people hooked – but this time, Paul's *brother* was the supplier. And Paul was considered a legitimate target by the INLA because he was dealing smack, he was a member of the Cullen gang in all but name. Liam said Cullen was to blame, that it all started with him, and that was true, but what was Liam doing conniving with the fucker? That's what all the whispered words between them were about last night, he supposed. Dessie needed to kill someone, that was the simple truth, and he couldn't kill Liam, it wouldn't have been right. It might have been justified, but it wouldn't have been right. Loy sent him a text message saying he'd have something for him later on today. Promises, promises.

Dessie had a cold shower, and then a hot one, and then another cold one. He shaved and dressed and loaded two Glocks and put them in his coat pockets. Then he loaded a third one and gave it to Liam, warning him first that he was very lucky not to have it shoved up his hole and fired. Liam, grateful for the reprieve, burst into tears again. Dessie waited for him to stop crying, and then he told him what they were going to do.

The only problem with what they were going to do was, you couldn't kill a man if you couldn't find him.

The funeral was quiet – compared to the removal, a football match would have been quiet – Dessie reckoned a lot of people had been scared off, or figured they'd paid their dues, or both – and afterwards, it was just the brothers at the graveside in Glasnevin. The barman from the Parting Glass had asked them to come back afterwards, and though Dessie wasn't keen for a reprise of last night, they didn't have anywhere else to go. Dessie thought it was a shame that Ed Loy hadn't made it to the grave at least, but he had to trust that Loy would come up with something.

By the time Dessie and Liam got back to the Parting Glass, it was like they'd arrived in a different country: there were lads in corners muttering and other lads shouting and there was just one topic on everyone's lips: the disappearance of Lamp Comerford and Charlie Newbanks, and the discovery of two bodies buried on a farm in Kildare. That farm was an IRA safe house, according to the talk, and had been used in recent years by several Cullen gang members. No way would the INLA have known about it, let along used it. People he didn't know kept coming up to Dessie, the same people who had come up to him last night, only last night they had wanted something from him, today they wanted to support him in some way. The message was the same: Jack Cullen had lost it, he had let the INLA in, whether deliberately or through a lack of vigilance, he had killed his own comrades to secure his position. Worse, he was a tout. Lamp had said he was, and look what happened to him. Jack Cullen was done. It was being said openly in the Parting Glass. Paul Delaney would be alive were it not for Jack Cullen. So would Charlie, so would Lamp (no one in the Parting Glass seemed to care about Ray Moran). Dessie watched the barman with the straw-coloured hair and the red face, who looked like he was capable of dispensing barroom justice with a bat or a gun and dumping the result in the back lane. The barman was biding his time, Dessie reckoned. The talk grew wilder, the shouts swelled in volume. Last night it had all been pub talk, hole talk. Today, Dessie wasn't so sure.

When Jack Cullen walked in, he was greeted with absolute silence. He approached Liam first, but Liam affected not to have seen him, and turned away when Cullen was halfway across the floor. Dessie wasn't going to playact like that. When

Cullen turned to Dessie, Dessie acknowledged him with a nod. Dessie noticed out of the corner of his eye the barman reaching below the counter.

'I'm sorry I wasn't there this morning, Dessie,' Jack Cullen said, his voice low but steady. Dessie nodded. He couldn't think of anything to say, and neither could anyone else for an awfully long time. Then a voice broke the silence.

'Where were you then?' a voice from the crowd shouted. 'Down on the farm were you?'

Jack Cullen's head whipped around towards his accuser, and for a short while there was silence again. But it didn't hold.

'Are you sorry Lamp and Charlie weren't there either, are you?'

'Maybe he was up in Dublin Castle having a cosy little chat about when the next shipment was due.'

'Fucking tout! Rout the tout! Rout the tout!

Dessie had never seen it happen so quickly: it was like a jester had stolen the king's crown, and the crowd had immediately forgotten everything the king had done for them, or resented him for it all along, and either way wanted him gone; Jack Cullen could sense it too; Dessie saw an unaccustomed look in those cold blue eyes: fear.

'I've just avenged your brother,' he said, his voice cracking a little. 'I've just killed Shay Rollins. Done it myself, out of respect. Because Paul Delaney was like a son to me. And that should be an end to it.'

That should have been an end to it, but it wasn't. There was another silence, but not as long a silence as Dessie had been expecting. A noise had begun to ripple through the crowd, a kind of muted growl, a guttural throb, like the sound of wild beasts holding themselves back from the kill, but only just, which fell away briefly when Jack made his announcement, but resumed again almost immediately.

'How much respect did you show Lamp and Charlie?' someone shouted.

Did you bury them yourself, did you? Or did you get them to do your dirty work one last time?

'That's how he knows where all the bodies are buried, he put them there himself.'

'The filthy fucking tout.'

'Well now he can fucking join them.'

The animal drone of the crowd had built, not so much in volume as in intensity. Tables shifted and stools tumbled as men came to their feet and began to advance on their leader. The front door was slammed shut and the bolt run home and the rear exit secured. Dessie felt himself being elbowed firmly aside as bodies piled forward like they were all part of one living organism. Dessie saw the first glass smash into Jack Cullen's temple and Jack Cullen brandish a gun that was knocked from his hand before he could let off a shot. He saw the barman rise to his full height and lay his hands empty on the bar and listen impassively to the grunts and roars, the crowing, jeering laughter and the obscene taunts as the customers of the Parting Glass punched and kicked and stamped and glassed Jack Cullen to, bloody, painful death.

Liam couldn't watch.

Dessie wished he could have watched at closer quarters. His major regret would always be he wasn't able to do it himself, alone.

28

Larry Roe from AIB had given me Margaret Fogarty's mobile number as well as her address, and now I sat in my car across the street from her house in Howth and keyed in the number. I could have called on my way to make sure she'd be there, but I was afraid she'd bolt if I did. She said hello in a tone of utter disbelief.

'My name is Ed Loy. I'm a private detective—'

'You're a *what?* Jesus Christ. How did you get this number? No one has this number.'

'I'm sure someone does. Maybe Steve Owen?'

'Did Steve . . . ?'

There was a long silence before Margaret Fogarty spoke again.

'What do you want?'

'Your sister Anne hired me to reinvestigate your father's murder.'

'And how're you getting on with that?'

'I think I know who killed him. But there are just a few final questions I'd like to ask.'

'And I'm the lucky girl you'd like to ask them of.'

'That's right. I have your address. I should be at your house in about fifteen minutes.'

'Why, are you disabled? Are you gonna crawl across the street on stumps? That's you in the old Volvo, isn't it? You think I was gonna make a run for it?'

'Something like that. I'm sorry.'

'Oh, we're all *sorry*. Sorry is just being alive. No, you tracked me down. You're a private detective. Your name is Ed Loy. Come in and ask me some questions. It's been a long time.'

Margaret Fogarty opened her front door and turned and I followed her through the shabby, damp hall to the kitchen, where every tired stick of furniture and battered appliance was transformed by the great picture window that looked directly out over the sea. Margaret Fogarty at fourteen had looked beautiful beyond belief; in her thirties, she was a beautiful woman, but her looks hadn't weathered the years as well as they might have. She still had a magnificent head of red cork-screw curls, and her dark eyes were alert and alive, and even in jeans and a plaid shirt, her body looked supple and slender, but her face was prematurely lined, and gin blossoms scarred her forehead and cheeks; she was smoking and drinking on her own at lunchtime; judging by the overflowing ash trays and the empty gin bottles, this was not a special occasion. The room smelt of stale smoke and sickly sweet alcoholic decay; I could never make up my mind if I found that particular aroma comforting or unsettling; looking around the damp room at the piles of newspapers and second-hand and library books, the unwashed dishes and the baskets of laundry, I was tending towards the latter. Seated now at the grimy kitchen table, her back to the blue sea, a completed crossword by her side, Margaret Fogarty gave me a glass and a crooked, ironic smile and pushed the gin and tonic bottles towards me. I thought I didn't want a drink, but as tends to happen, when I'm put on the spot, it turns out I do.

'Private detective. Is that a joke?'

'I found you, didn't I?'

'We've already established that. Shouldn't you have a hat?'

'That's a very personal question. Shouldn't you?'

285

'I don't want to get ahead. As you can see. Loy. As in Myrna? Or in spade?'

'As in both, I guess.'

'Make up your mind.'

'You first.'

'I did,' she said. 'And look where it's got me.'

'There's not a lot wrong with the location,' I said.

'I know, I know, it's the decor that lets it down,' she said, gesturing to herself. She had a cynical drawl that was very attractive, and I got the impression she hadn't spoken to anyone for a while.

'Not from where I'm sitting.'

'Oh Mr Loy, how you talk. I bet you're a big hit with the girls. Let me guess: Anne thought you were *gorgeous*? I'm guessing you're quite gorgeous behind all those cuts and bruises. And Mrs D'Arcy thought you were something she'd stepped on.'

'I wouldn't say gorgeous. But that's about right.'

'Loy. Spade. Digging things up. Very good. And have you been digging things up, Ed Loy? Is that what has your head in such a state? Did people object to your digging?'

'Not all of them. Just enough to make a difference.'

'And now you're here to do some more. Well, I promise, at the very least, if I have to hit you a dig myself, I'll aim it lower than your head.'

'Thank you. Where was the telephone in your house in Farney Park?'

'Where was the telephone? In the hall. There was a table in the hall, called, if memory serves, the hall table. And that was where the phone was.'

'Was it always there? Or was it moved?'

'Was the telephone always there or was it moved? I've got to say, I don't quite feel I'm getting your best private eye stuff here today Ed. I was hoping for a bit of where were you on the night of, is this the dress you were wearing when, I put it to you that this is the murder weapon and so on and so forth. And your big question is, where did you use to keep the fucking telephone? Who gives a fuck?'

It was the hair. As soon as Aisling D'Arcy showed me the photograph, I knew. Janet Ames's hair was good, but it wasn't a patch on Margaret Fogarty's. I bet that thought occurred to Steve Owen every day of his life as he sat in his chair, looking out across Dublin Bay towards Howth. I wonder if he knew she was here. The Fogarty he fell in love with. The daughter, not the mother.

'You give a fuck. Because you know where the telephone used to be. Because your father ran to the telephone, and he had to be stopped. The telephone that used to hang on a wall bracket just outside the kitchen. Steve Owen had to stop him telling anyone what he'd just seen. Was it upstairs, or in the living room? You and Steve Owen, a teacher and a fourteen-year-old schoolgirl.'

There was a split-second of shock, when I thought she might close down on me. But that was soon overwhelmed by what felt to me very much like relief.

'I taught Steve more than he ever taught me,' Margaret Fogarty said, her eyes flashing with the recollection. 'He wasn't the first. But boys my age were idiots. You can be old enough at fourteen, and too young at forty. You met Mrs D'Arcy there, my big sister. She's someone who's always going to be too young for sex, who thinks it's horrid and nasty and filthy and messy and really not quite right.'

'Maybe that's because her father was murdered when she was a teenager.'

'And maybe it was because she didn't get a bow wow when she was a baby. Who knows, Ed? Who knows what makes us want what we want? Aisling wanted a big palace and no risks, and she got it. I wanted Steve, and I didn't get him.'

'He killed your father . . . don't you feel anything about that? Anne said when she got home from school, she found you weeping in the porch. And you never said anything, at the trial or at the appeal.'

Margaret Fogarty sat silent, a curious smile on her face; it looked like bravado, like she didn't care what I thought, but that couldn't be right. The disconnect between what I was saying and what she appeared to be feeling was giving me vertigo.

'You were an eye-witness, for God's sake: fourteen years old, to see your father get beaten to death in front of you, and then to remain silent all this time. Look at you, in this cave. Drinking and smoking yourself to death, it's like you're in hiding, all to protect a man who . . . you know he has a girl-friend, about your age, with hair like yours?'

'Janet Ames,' Margaret said, shaking her head sadly. 'Fat ankles. The poor girl. What can you do?'

'It's not just about you, you know, there's Aisling and Anne, they have a right to see justice done. Why are you protecting Steve Owen?'

Margaret looked out the window for a moment. When she turned back, her expression had altered; the flip cynicism had gone, and her eyes were full of tears, though she still tried to blink them away with a smile, and as she spoke, it seemed to me that I had heard the words already, that somewhere in the pit of my stomach, they were exactly what I was expecting, and dreading, to hear.

'I'm not protecting Steve Owen. Steve Owen is protecting me.'

I waited, poured another gin and lit another cigarette and waited, and finally, she told me what had happened.

⌒

'I was in love. We were in love. He didn't want to at first, because I was too young, I was a schoolgirl, de da de da, but

I persisted, and I prevailed. Christ, he was doing it with the mother and the daughter, how cool was that, why wouldn't he've? I'd seen him from my bedroom, hopping over the back wall to see Ma, I was the only one who knew what was going on. But with Ma, it was a fling, they were using each other, I don't care what the letters said in court about him wanting her to leave Daddy, that was all talk, Steve wasn't serious about her. It was me. I was the real thing. I mean, he doesn't have a girlfriend who looks like Ma, does he? Janet Ames looks like me.'

'You were fourteen, how serious could he be?'

'Oh fuck that. Toytown rules. Over eighteens only. What a fantasy world people live in now, scared of their own shadows, so panicked about fucking child abuse they've become terrified of giving children any freedom at all, they're twelve or thirteen before they're let out on their own, they may as well lock them up in the cellar, like in *Chitty Chitty Bang Bang*, you know what it's about? The parents' peace of mind. Because everyone is so fucking anxious all the time. So lock the kids up with computers and so on and you don't have to worry about them, at least. *That*'s the abuse. Anyway, fourteen isn't a child: end of story. We were in love. When you fall, you fall. And that's the way it was.'

'And that day . . .'

'And that day I ducked out of class after first period and met Steve in the house. We were going to do it in every room in the house, a different position in each room. The clock was ticking, because Anne would be home for lunch. And we'd done all the upstairs, and we were in the living room, and I was on top, and Daddy, who had this big meeting in town and was due to be out for the whole day, came home unexpectedly, and we were making so much noise we didn't hear, and Daddy walked into the living room and caught us. Caught us rapid, as we used to say.'

Margaret Fogarty attempted a laugh then, but she didn't get as far as a smile; her hands were shaking and her voice had receded to a dry crackle at the back of her throat.

'And the thing was, I was so fucking angry to see him. I wasn't scared, I wasn't upset, I was raging: how dare he come back when he's not supposed to, how dare he interrupt me mid-ride, how dare he see my tits? In my head, of course, I didn't say anything, but that's how I felt. And when Daddy saw it was Steve, he just said, I'm calling the Guards, you'd better get dressed, and went straight out of the room. I didn't even think, I just knew I had to stop him, I leapt up and I picked an ormolu clock off the mantelpiece and I went flying after him, and there he was at the phone, his back to me, and I just smashed him over the head I don't know how many times. Steve said I was screaming and swearing and ranting, hysterical. It was all over in twenty or thirty seconds. Daddy was probably dead on the first or second blow.'

'How did you clean it up?'

'Didn't really need to. Steve got my clothes, and I got dressed, and he said, Anne will be here soon, if you say you came home and found him like this. The hardest part . . . we thought if I had come home and found him, I would have run to him and held him. And that way, I could be all bloody and it would be natural. That was hard, because . . . I was pretending, and then it was real as well . . . and that's the way it's always been, grieving, and not feeling entitled to grieve . . . I never wanted to kill him. I've never felt like that again. I . . . I'm sorry, it's such an entirely inadequate cliché, but it's the only thing that fits: I don't know what came over me.'

'And Steve got rid of the murder weapon.'

'Steve got rid of the clock, and the towel. And that was that, really. Ma thought Steve might have killed Daddy, and Steve broke with her – and he point blank refused to see me before the trial, and then . . . and then he was in prison. He went to prison to protect me. If there are ways of knowing what love is, I think that might be one of them, don't you?'

'And you never thought to speak out on his behalf? To say, he's not guilty, I am, I did it, I killed my father.'

The tears flowed freely down Margaret Fogarty's cheeks now.

'Of course I did, every day I did. But I never said a word. I was too frightened of what it might do to me, to my sisters, to my mother. And even after she died, I said nothing. And after the appeal . . . we met after the appeal. Because I kept writing to him, trying to contact him. And he still wanted me. After all I'd put him through. And that's when I knew we couldn't be together, that it would be wrong. That I didn't deserve it. I let him help me though. This is his aunt's house, and he let me live in it for nothing. Only his aunt died, and left the house to him and his sister, and now he has to sell it.'

'And that's why you contacted Anne, to put Farney Park on the market.'

'That's right.'

'Why did you block a sale for so long?'

Margaret Fogarty shook her head, and her Titian curls swirled against the blue of the sea behind her.

'I don't know. I sometimes think, to punish myself. I didn't want the money. I don't really work, I live on benefits. I read, and I drink, and I don't do much else. I don't . . . "have a life". I don't really know that I deserve one. Imagine how much pain my sisters would go through if they knew I'd killed Daddy. Even though I don't care about Aisling, I care about Anne.'

'Why would they have had to know? You could have built a new life. You could have left the past behind.'

Margaret Fogarty stared at me as if I was insane.

'But the past is all I have. Maybe that's why I wanted Farney Park to remain as it was, to fix it in the past. Sometimes you can't just pick up and start again. Sometimes it would be wrong to.'

'Wrong?'

'I killed my father, Ed. And I wasn't properly punished for it. And that's why I live like this. Every morning, I look out across the bay, and know that Steve is over there, with a woman that looks a bit like me, only plainer, with fat ankles, poor thing, wishing it was me, and I'm here wishing it was me too, but knowing it's right that it isn't. You can call the Guards and have me arrested and I'll tell them what I told you, but I don't think I'll be the one to suffer if it all comes out and I have to go to prison. Anne will, and Aisling will, and Steve will.'

Margaret Fogarty lit another cigarette, and took a long belt of her gin, her third since I had arrived, and looked at me.

'I don't think I could suffer any more than I do each day, and will until I die, which please God won't take too much longer.'

29

It would have been natural to drive along the coast and cross the river to get to Steve Owen's place on the other side of the bay, but Docklands was closed to traffic from the Eastlink onwards on account of the Independence Bridge opening ceremonies, so I cut off up the other direction and headed south via Christchurch and the N11 to Blackrock. Steve Owen was reluctant to let me in, but when I told him where I'd been and what I'd been told, he buzzed me up.

'This will have to be quick,' he said. 'Janet will be back soon.' His face had the same mournful, hangdog expression; when we'd met before, I attributed it to weakness on his part; I knew better now. Without asking, he went to the kitchen and emerged with two drinks. We sat in the sunroom as before, and I looked out across the bay towards Howth.

'You can see the house, if that's what you're wondering. I suppose if I had a telescope, I could see her wave. But she wouldn't wave. And I'd know better than to hope.'

His voice was composed, and laced more with resignation than self-pity.

'You're a good man,' I said, and was pretty sure I meant it.

'You know, I used to think that. How noble I was, how I'd suffered. But it was me where I shouldn't have been that got me into trouble, involved with a fourteen-year-old girl. At best, I think I was just unlucky.'

'More than that. You went to prison, you never spoke out against her.'

'I think most men would have done that. I can't see many saying, it wasn't me, it was the kid. What I wonder is, would it have been better if I had told all? Better for Midge, I mean. Because what she's done to herself . . .'

He came to a halt and shook his head.

'How did she look?'

'She drinks and smokes a lot. And you can see that in her face. But she's still an amazing looking woman. That hair . . .' I said.

Two large tears appeared in Owen's eyes and rolled down his cheeks. He started to say something, but couldn't get it out before he broke down completely and just sat there, a grown man in the afternoon sun, crying his eyes out. It wasn't easy to watch, but I thought it was the least I could do.

'I'm sorry,' he said when he had got himself together. 'I just . . . can you make any sense of it? I mean . . . we could be together. We could still be together. We wouldn't have to tell anyone what happened. Anne might not like it, but God, she'd get over it. In this day and age.'

'I don't think Margaret can get over it. In this day and age or any other. I don't think she wants to. Maybe you're right when you say if she'd paid for it at the time. Because now, it's like she's serving a life sentence. One she's imposed on herself.'

'Is she . . . do you think she's happy?'

'I think she's waiting around to die. I understand she has to move, you need to sell the cottage.'

'Did she tell you that?' he said, his voice cracking.

He shook his head, closed his eyes and breathed deeply in.

'She's welcome to stay, I told her so, as long as she wants. She's moving out for her own reasons, whatever they are.'

'She said your sister has a half share, after your aunt died.'

Steve Owen shook his head and scowled.

'My sister. I don't have a sister. My aunt died twenty years ago, the cottage has been mine since then. Janet doesn't know about it though, so . . . if you don't mind . . .'

'How much does Janet know? Because it was the hair that did it for me. When I saw a photograph of Margaret, and clocked her likeness to Janet Ames, the whole thing made perfect sense to me. Of course, I thought, after seeing her, I'd be sending the cops here to arrest you.'

'Are they going to arrest her?'

'Not for anything I might tell them.'

'What will you tell Anne?'

'I don't know.'

'It might be better to tell the truth, at last, rather than cover it up again.'

'It might be,' I said. 'You didn't answer my question. How much does Janet know?'

'She knows I didn't kill Brian Fogarty. And she knows I love her hair. And if I like to drink a little too much and look out across the bay every now and again, well, a man can have worse vices.'

It was a nice speech, but the anguish in his expression made me feel for Janet Ames, a facsimile of his true love, an insubstantial shadow in his ongoing imitation of life.

I stood up and thanked him for the drink, and shook his hand, and left him to his days and nights.

As I crossed the street to the car park, I saw a flash of red outside Steve Owen's building, and for an instant, I thought it was Midge Fogarty come across the bay to make everything all right.

It wasn't, of course. I didn't even have to look at her ankles to know that.

Dublin – M1 to Belfast, 9 November 1980
The Coyle Family

Gerry Coyle

Sunday night, God, it's always a downer, isn't it? Must be a hangover from school, even in the summer, on holidays, no work Monday morning, doesn't make a difference, this total kind of pall descends, and that's it, game over. Don't know that I'll even bother with the few jars, feeling pretty wrecked to be honest. Maybe just crash on the sofa, see what's on the box, cup of tea and then hit the sack. How's that going to work in the polls, I wonder? Will I get it in the neck from the War Office? I think I might still rise to the occasion if called upon to serve. Especially if she wears that lacy gear she had on last night, goodness gracious me, that would get the hairs on the—

Claire Coyle

I hope we do all right by the kids, I really do. I know Gerry always says, relax, they'll be grand, don't worry so much, but I know if I didn't, he would, the only reason he can keep his totally laid back and ever-so-cool routine going is because he knows I'm on the case. But that's all right. What you might call teamwork. And fair enough, he says, our parents didn't worry about us the way we worry about ours. But so what, our parents had a toilet in the back yard and no central heating, that's no kind of argument. Clothes for the week, I'll need to put two washes on tonight, and Luke will

certainly want a cooked meal, and if Gerry thinks he's slipping out
for a pint at this stage he's got another—

Yvonne Coyle

Sometimes I wish I was in boarding school, where I had some time and
space of my own, but the one time I mentioned it to Mum she looked
so upset I had to spend ages backtracking saying I was just wonder-
ing whether it would be better for studies and she said Yvonne your
grades are all A plus what are you aiming for and I know we can't
afford it but that's not the point, actually, boarding school is not the
point, the point is Mum is my mum and not my best friend and every
time we go shopping that's how she wants it to be, I'm supposed to tell
her about boys and giggle and it's all SO EMBARRASSING and
I'm going to get a lock for my room so I can have a little privacy—

Luke Coyle

Thunderbird 2 *would be the only one that could take you to school,*
Thunderbird 5 *is a space station so that's out and* Thunderbird
3 *is a space rocket and so is* Thunderbird 1 *so* Thunderbird 2 *it's*
like a jump jet but we would need a longer garden, not necessarily all
those palm trees, that's because Tracy Island is in Hawaii, and you
wouldn't need Thunderbird 4 *because that's a submarine and you*
don't need to go underwater to get to school, so the pod would have
some extra space, you could probably fit your schoolbag and your
lunch in there, actually, you could fit all your lunches for the week if
Mum did them up in advance, that might suit her actually, thought-
ful, the kind of thing she's always saying we don't think of, and you
could probably park Thunderbird 2 *with the teachers' cars I wonder*
if I got a paper round could we afford to buy some of the neighbours'
garden so Thunderbird 2 *would have enough room—*

South Armagh, 9 November 1980

Of course, even though it was only afterwards that Red fully understood what had happened, he acknowledged that it had actually been his blunder. He had spotted the vehicle approaching, and alerted Ice, but cautioned him to wait until he had made sure the registration was correct. And Ice said, ah for fuck's sake, what are the chances of two Jags identical in colour and model happening along at the same time? But Ice waited for Red to give the word. And Red was anxious he'd wait too long, and they'd miss the target, so he went early; he gave the word before he saw the reg, and then it was too late ever to see the reg, but as it turned out, not too late to know it hadn't been the reg plate of the judge's car. After the fire and the smoke, and the debris and body parts scattered about the fields, amid the smell of sulphur and burning flesh, and the savage whooping and hollering of Ice, Red stared out across the fields, the heartbreakingly beautiful hills and fields of South Armagh. Was it then he understood that only great and lasting dishonour and shame would be gained if they won the land back by this kind of slaughter? Was it then, or seconds later, as the sirens howled their strident requiem, when a burgundy Jaguar Mark 2 3.8 litres approached the scene of the atrocity in slow motion, or so it seemed to Red, but of course it had slowed down out of caution, and shock, and human sympathy; Red seemed to view it through a gauze, as if it were a ghost car and the whole sorry spectacle a nightmare, which of course was what it had become, a nightmare from which Red would spend the rest of his life trying to awake.

Ooops! said Ice, laughing, and he had to pull a gun on Red to get his hands away from his neck. Fuck's sake. You had to let off steam every now and then. Hadn't Red ever heard of gallows humour? It was all very regrettable, innocent family and so on, but this was not Ice's fault. This was the fault of those who made it necessary for Ice and his comrades to wage war. Ice had a clear conscience, and he always would have.

30

I was sitting in my office with Tommy Owens and Leo Halligan, who were regaling me with tales of what they'd got up to once they were assured of my safety, that is to say, once they'd heard that Jack Cullen had been found beaten to death and dumped in Beresford Lane, right where at least some of this began. Mainly, it appeared they had been drinking, and they proposed to continue doing this in a variety of pubs all over town, and suggested I accompany them on their crawl. I said I'd like to do this very much, but I felt obliged to attend the Independence Bridge opening ceremony. I was welcome to it, they said, they were going to watch it on telly in whichever pub they happened to land in, and I knew how to find them when I was feeling thirsty, and off they went, although not before Leo had received a personal assurance that George was in the clear on the Brian Fogarty murder. I never much liked ruling George Halligan out of any shenanigans whatsoever, but I'd never get this one to stick; besides, he had lung cancer. I gave Leo my condolences, and he looked puzzled, and I explained, and he laughed for a long time, and then *he* explained. George has a mail-order bride from Russia, very high maintenance, with a populous entourage of friends and acquaintances who visit rarely, but when they do, stay for weeks on end. George found last year's visit extremely trying on the nerves, so this year he arranged to have terminal cancer in advance with the assistance of a compliant doctor he employs and a generous contribution to St Bonaventure's upkeep. Turned out George had bronchitis anyway, which he's prone to, on account of smoking sixty a day since he was twelve, so that helped the masquerade along nicely. A month on his deathbed has seen them all off, and reduced his wife to a nervous wreck, as she's not quite legal and not quite a beneficiary if George were ever to get, for example, terminal cancer. So now he's ready to stage a remarkable recovery, and dictate a few new terms in his domestic arrangements.

I walked them down to the street, and while they turned up towards Merrion Square, I headed down to the Quays, saluting the smoking mothers as I went, an exercise in futility mostly, as they were a miserable bunch of hard-faced whingers at the best of times, and surely having a baby was the best of times and you could have expected a little better, but no matter, that, too, was Dublin for you.

The quays were closed to traffic and thronged with people – old and young, families and gangs of youths, drunk and sober, friendly and menacing, surging about or waiting patiently, all high in anticipation of the official launch of the new beacon in the sky, Independence Bridge. There were seated areas back as far as the Talbot Memorial Bridge, with screens on the streets relaying RTE television pictures of the action. Past Sir John Rogerson's Quay, you needed a VIP pass, which I had, of course, and once the security man on duty saw that I had no bag, he let me through without a body search. That was worth remembering. Quite a heavy Garda presence, but no body search.

The crowd was a little smarter here, a little more upscale. I recognized celebrities, or pseudo-celebrities, people off the telly; I even nodded to a couple, to my embarrassment, thinking I knew them, but I'm sure they were used to that, taking the misplaced intimacy as no more than their due. There was traditional Irish music playing, and more seating along the quays as you got closer and closer to the bridge. My pass, however, was for the top grade of VIP. Mine put you on the bridge itself with all the very important people indeed.

The structure was built in the shape of an H, with two towers of glass and steel on the corner of Sir John Rogerson's and Britain Quays and on the corresponding pitch across the river on North Wall Quay. Two hundred metres tall, they dwarfed everything around. Halfway up, the bridge formed the central bar of the H. I had thought it looked impressive a week ago; now, probably because of what I knew about the man behind it, I wondered whether it was vainglorious and ugly, a vaulting symbol of everything that was wrong with our great little country. I couldn't decide, and I thought it was better if I didn't: the case had left me weary of soul as well as of body, and judgment was not my strongest suit; I'd've no doubt been better off taking to my bed tonight, but something told me I had to be here.

I showed my laminate for the last time at the entrance to the towers – again, no body search – and waited in a large, fully catered reception area overlooking the river with a group that included two government ministers, a prizewinning author and a humanitarian rock star. Everyone who was anyone was here, it seemed. And I was here too. The elevator came, but before I could get on it, I was tapped on the shoulder. Donna Nugent was beckoning me aside, her face glowing with excitement, and walking me around the corner to a private room that overlooked the river also, a private room with just one occupant.

Bobby Doyle was beaming at me, and Donna Nugent was beaming at me, and I began to worry that if I wasn't careful, I might break out beaming myself.

'Well, isn't this cosy? The last time we three met, we were in church, but that didn't go as well as expected, did it?' I said.

Donna made her face go grave and serious. It appeared she could do this whenever she felt the need, and whatever she was feeling, as long as it was to the greater good of Bobby Doyle.

'Ed, I'm sorry, I know I said some awful things to you today, and I . . . I want to apologise. I didn't mean them, I . . . what you go through, not everyone could do, and it's incredibly brave, it's . . . whatever it is, it's the opposite of failure.'

She came across and hugged me, and then stood back, and I almost felt as if she had been completely sincere, and maybe by her lights, she almost had been, and I was almost moved. Bobby nodded contentedly, as if that was a satisfactory prelude, and then he moved in for the opera's first act.

'Ed, I'll keep it simple. Jack Cullen came out to Tallaght today and personally took Shay Rollins out. I'm not sorry he did that: Rollins was as much of a cancer in his own community as Jack Cullen was in his. That's why there was something right and fitting about the way Jack Cullen was killed. Did you hear? His own people rose up against him.'

'Right and fitting? Rose up? He was stamped to death in a pub by a bunch of savages. Have you lost your compass entirely?' I said.

Bobby Doyle's eyes narrowed, and he exhaled audibly, as if to remind me that his patience was finite.

'His death brings it full circle, for me, for the movement, for the entire country. And the fact that it was his own people. That's what gives me renewed hope. It'll send a message out to the last of the hard men: the old days are done. The National Drug Unit have leaked that he was a tout as well, so that's his reputation tarnished for good. I wish it could have been a clean kill. I almost wish I could have done it myself. But I have too many people watching me. I particularly regret young Delaney's death. If you know the boy's people, maybe you might send them to me.'

I nodded. Sure. I could do that. I could send Paul's people to Bobby Doyle. Why not? They might have quite a message for him.

'Come on, let's go up to the bridge, you won't believe the view up there. And don't worry Ed, once the speeches are made, there'll be plenty of booze,' Donna said.

'That's great, Donna,' I said. 'I just, my head is pounding, just going to get five minutes fresh air.'

'All right. Don't forget your laminate! See you up there.'

'See you up there, Ed,' Bobby Doyle said.

The last I saw of him, ex-IRA killer Bobby Doyle was giving the Taoiseach of Ireland a fist bump as they waited for the elevator.

See you up there! Don't forget your laminate! Yes indeed.

I left the tower and called Dessie Delaney.

'Ed Loy? Where the fuck have you been?'

'I've been working. Where are you, Dessie?'

'I'm on the quays here, having a look at the bridge. Around the Custom House.'

'All right. Do you want a seat up in the bridge itself? I have a VIP pass.'

'I don't think they'll let me through, Ed, on account of what I'm carrying.'

'Don't worry about that. Meet me at the end of City Quay, as soon as you can.'

The crowds had gotten denser now, and dusk was slowly falling, and it took me a while to pick Dessie out of the crowd. He was respectably dressed, in collar and tie, and he wasn't drunk, but there was a wild, despairing, reckless glint in his eye. I greeted him, and we embraced, and I told him how sorry I was about Paul.

'You look well, Dessie,' I lied. 'How are you?'

'I'm not good, Ed,' he said. 'I feel like I've been denied my chance to make things right. Jack Cullen killed Rollins, the INLA leader who killed Paul, or who had him killed. And then all Jack's thugs turned on him. It's just chaos, like Paul's death was completely meaningless. And it turned out Paul was dealing for Jack all along, and that Liam was in on it, Ed. I mean, there's nowhere to turn. There's no pure act that can make his death right, that's what I wanted, to say, you're the one who done it, or, you're the one who ordered it: I will take you out. Even if I go down myself.'

I looked at the pain in Dessie's eyes. I looked back at Independence Bridge. I could hear *The Patriot Game* drifting across on the air. I thought of Bobby Doyle, and of the Coyle family, and I thought I knew how to make things right.

'I can give you who ordered it,' I said. 'Or at least, who was running Shay Rollins. But there's no way back from it, Dessie, you wouldn't walk away.'

Dessie's eyes flared in excitement, and he gripped my wrists.

'I don't want to walk away. I'm finished, Ed. I can't go back to Greece, can't work with Liam again, can't look at the cunt, running smack for Jack Cullen, he's lucky to be alive and I'm telling you, I had to walk out of the pub today, Paul's funeral and I had to walk out before I blew my other brother's head off.'

'What about Sharon? And the kids.'

'The stake in Delaney's is in her name. And she can look after herself. And . . .'

His eyes misted over for a second, and I knew at once what he was thinking of, the future his kids would have that he would never see, and in an instant I was at one with Doyle and Cullen and the rest of the brave Irish patriots and gangsters, sending men out on glorious missions from which they had no chance of return. I wanted Bobby Doyle to die, and he deserved to die, and what a great message *that* would send out, to the hard men and the others, to everyone who beat the Patriot Drum and played the Patriot Game. But I wasn't one of them, and I wasn't going to become one of them. I shook my head.

'I'm sorry, Dessie, I can't do it.'

Dessie's face fell.

'Ed, please. I'm *entitled*—'

'Fuck it, you're not. Your kids are entitled, Dessie, entitled to their Da. I'm not having you on my conscience. I'm sorry, I should never have called you. I was wrong. Just . . . just go out and get drunk. That's what I'm gonna do.'

'And what do I do in the morning?'

'Go back to your wife and kids. Go home, Dessie. Forget about all this. Leave the dead well enough alone.'

Dessie held on to my wrists, pleading with me to reconsider, but I wouldn't budge, and freed my hands, and walked away. He shouted after me, and then I couldn't hear him shouting. My thoughts were astray, and I wanted to fling them further. The 'Prelude' from *Parsifal* echoed around my head. Drunks were filling up the streets. I would soon be one of them. I walked down the quays as the lights began to flash, and the cheering began, and the fireworks started to explode overhead. I was nearly at Tara Street when I got a call from Anne Fogarty.

'Hey, we're on the quays, do you want to meet up? Only the girls are a bit bored, so I think we're going to duck out and have a pizza or something. We're just at . . . hey, I think I can see you, across from Tara Street station?'

'No, I . . . sorry Anne, you're breaking up,' I said, and ducked into the pub on the corner. A pizza. Children. Jesus fuck. I ordered a pint and a Jameson, and I stood in the crowded bar with a lot of men who all looked like they were hiding from something. That was the spirit. That was exactly the company I needed. On the television, the Taoiseach was making a speech, and the camera flashed on Bobby Doyle, who was looking modest, and there was a photo montage of the faces of the rebel leaders from the 1916 rising, and the Taoiseach was talking about pride in our history and traditions, and then I felt a tug at my sleeve that nearly made me spill my pint, and I swung around, and there was Ciara, Anne Fogarty's youngest daughter, and I guess the way I turned must have scared her, and the state of my face must have scared her even more, because the smile froze on her little face, and her eyes began to bubble, and then Anne Fogarty, who stood behind her, leant a hand down and cupped her cheek and brought her child to her, safe within her embrace. It was a gesture so eloquent of love and tender care, and I recalled the first person I had seen use it, way back when I was the child in need of it, and I had to turn away. They were singing the National Anthem now on TV, the Soldiers' Song, and the men in the pub were joining in, stamping their feet, and having quickly wiped my eyes and downed my whiskey, I was wondering whether I shouldn't join in too, and sing to the glory of war, and to Independence Bridge, which when it came down to it was almost certainly a wonderful thing and fuck the begrudgers, when I felt another tug on my sleeve. This time it was Aoife, Anne Fogarty's elder daughter.

'Hey, it's getting a bit too noisy in here. Would you like to go for a pizza with us or what?'

Would I like to go for a pizza? Of course I didn't want to go for a pizza. What I wanted was to stay in this pub until I was so drunk I couldn't speak, or meet Leo and Tommy and get speechless with them. I wanted to celebrate my Irishness by singing songs about killing people, and laughing as if I had no fear, and drinking until I felt closer to the dead than I did to the living, until I could hear all the dead voices speak to me, and I could speak right back to them.

I looked around at Ciara's tear-stained, frightened face, at Aoife's impatient, anxious face, and at Anne Fogarty's beautiful, kind, smiling face. What did they want from me? Didn't they know Donna Nugent was right, that I was a failed person with a failed life? Didn't Anne Fogarty understand that having me fall in love with her was the last thing she needed? What the fuck was the matter with them? Would I like to go for a pizza?

'Yes,' I heard myself say. 'Yes, I'd like that very much.'

Acknowledgements

The following books proved especially helpful during the writing of this novel: *A Secret History of the IRA* by Ed Moloney (Penguin, 2007); *Killing Rage* by Eamon Collins (with Mick McGovern) (Granta Books, 1997); *Armed Struggle: The History of the IRA* by Richard English (Macmillan, 2003); *'Bandit Country' – The IRA & South Armagh* by Toby Harnden (Hodder & Stoughton, 2000); *Lost Lives: The Stories of the Men, Women and Children Who Died Through the Northern Ireland Troubles* by David McKittrick, Seamus Kelters, Brian Feeney and Chris Thornton (Mainstream, 1999).

Thanks to Roland Philipps and everyone at John Murray, David Highfill and everyone at William Morrow, and to John Saddler and George Lucas. Above all, thanks to Kathy Strachan.

Declan Hughes
Dun Laoghaire, 2008

Available in hardback

City of Lost Girls

Declan Hughes

In LA there's a killer on the loose. He kills young and rootless girls and he always kills in threes. Back in Dublin, Ed Loy, happy in a new relationship, is reunited with Jack Donovan, a film director friend from LA with a turbulent personal history. When the third young female extra fails to show for work on Jack's movie, Loy begins to suspect Jack. And when the previous victims of the 'Three-in-One Killer' are discovered in LA at locations Jack used for his movies, Loy's suspicion hardens.

Loy flies to LA to liaise with the LAPD on their investigation. He must find something in his and Jack's shared past that can point to the killer, and hope against hope that whatever he finds will point away from his old friend.

And then, when he finally unearths the truth, it looks like it may be too late. Back in Dublin, the killer has broken his pattern, broken cover and struck at Ed Loy where he is most vulnerable. Time is not on Loy's side as he mounts a desperate fight to outwit a ruthless psychopath and save the last of the lost girls.

Now read on . . .

I

Jack Donovan, *the* Jack Donovan, in a darkened Dublin bar, great handsome bull's head tipped back, plume of still-dark hair coiled over broad black-shirted back, full pint of stout held aloft to the east, shot of whiskey to the west, and the feet all pounding in a ring around him as he sinks the dark pint to rising hoots and cries, and then a roar as he knocks the shot back and lifts the empty glasses up through the flickering light: to east, to west, to north and south, a bacchanalian benediction, and bows until his hair sweeps the floor. Josh Tyler steps forward in jeans and *Mastodon* rock band T-shirt, slight, unshaven, pint of Guinness in hand, wrists braided and bangled, just another skinny student on the lash if you didn't know about the Oscar nomination or the thing with Mischa Barton. He embraces Donovan, kisses him on the lips, lifts the pint and tips it slowly over their joined heads. Donovan lifts his face into the falling beer and Tyler steps aside and drains the glass over his director with a flourish.

'Ladies and gentlemen, a Jack Donovan picture,' he says, and Donovan bows to whoops and cheers, elevated, as is everyone watching, by the Hollywood anointing: showman Jack, braggart Jack, broth of a Paddy-Irish boy Jack, back shooting moving pictures on the streets of his hometown.

There's a voice in my ear: dry, amused, ironic.

'Only trouble is, it's always the *same* Jack Donovan picture.'

Mark Cassidy, Donovan's director of photography, elegant,

Anglo, almost camp, with him since the no-budget movie they made in Dublin nearly twenty years ago, the one that started them all off. If it was always the same picture, Mark Cassidy should know. So should producer Maurice Faye, Jack's representative on earth, diplomat, scammer, fixer extraordinaire, elfin, tweed waistcoat, hoop earrings, raven thatch now silvering at the edges, phone at his ear as he slides out of the pub to take another call from the West Coast. So should Conor Rowan, First AD, chubby, ruddy, strawberry-blonde crop, permanently furrowed brow, implacable sergeant major, charged with waging total war for the good of the group. The home team, the Gang of Four, Jack Donovan's men since they were hungry guttersnipes dreaming of celluloid glory over the gantry of this very pub with barely the price of a pint between them.

I smile at the crack, always the eye-rolling same from Mark, only happy when he's cringing. I assume Mark means that wherever they go, and for as long as they've been going, and no matter what kind of film they end up making, it will all come down at some stage to Jack Donovan, carouser extraordinaire, professional Irishman, the life and soul of the all-night party, Jack Donovan howling at the moon, raging once more against the dying of the light, surrounded by the fans and the fakes and the flakes, the casts and the crews and the camp followers, Jack Donovan, lightning rod, channelling the savage energies, tapping the occult information, transmuting the base energies of a Dublin pub through his own alchemical powers into something altogether *other*, something exalted, into some strange kind of . . . magic, yes, no less than the intangible quality that pervades all of his movies, even the misfires (perhaps especially the misfires), a roiling, kinetic sense that the veil between this world and the next is gossamer thin, in places a mere shadow, that the concrete, the ordered, the rational, *that* is the illusion: magic is immanent in the world, and Jack summons it up, like some ancient fire starter, some witch doctor, some shaman. Or so it seems to us, to all of us, even Mark Cassidy, all of a hush now as Jack holds his hand aloft, the vibrations in the room at a precarious pitch, nothing to hear but the clink of glasses and the breath of a hundred souls, and just as I realize what he's going to do, Mark turns to me and shakes his head, aiming maybe for jaded incredulity but stalling at wonder, and Jack opens his mouth and the first line sails out in that extraordinary voice, pure tenor, not as fine as it was, wood-smoked and whiskey-basted by one careless owner, but still mighty, and the expressions on the faces of those who'd heard rumours of this but never dared dream it might be true, let alone that they would witness it, as 'E lucevan le stelle' from *Tosca* fills them, fills us all with sad joy and desperate longing for a love we didn't know we'd lost, for a home we'd forgotten we missed.

Afterwards, as people are first too stunned to applaud, and then as they do, the noise they make like thunder, and as reality descends in murmurs and in muted shouts, the evening running down, Mark turns to me.

'Typical bloody Donovan,' he says, his voice an acrid buzz. 'If he'd sung 'Nessun dorma', the room would have erupted. But Jack always wants to leave the audience yearning.'

As he says this, it seems to me that there are tears in his eyes. But I can't be sure, because there are certainly tears in mine.

It may still be the same Jack Donovan picture, but Maurice and Conor are on their feet as well, still crazy, still in his thrall. Even Josh Tyler, whose last day of shooting was today, whose party this was, is happy to let Jack take centre stage.

What's the matter with these people?

It's simple, really.

Jack Donovan is the matter with them.

I should know. A long time ago, he was the matter with me.

I make a brief appearance in a Jack Donovan picture (don't reach for your popcorn or you'll miss me). In his adaptation of *The Dain Curse* (1997), the Dashiell Hammett novel, I am 'Irish man in bar'. I even have a line. I was working as a private detective in Los Angeles back then, and Jack and I had become friends. We were in Hal's Bar on Abbot Kinney Boulevard in Venice one night while he was casting.

'Hey Ed, say "whiskey".'

'Whiskey.'

'There you go. You could be Irish man in bar, right?'

'I could. I often have.'

The movie starred Nick Nolte and Drew Barrymore and Lisa Eichorn and Michael Madsen, and if it didn't really work, everyone agreed the book didn't entirely work either. Besides, Hammett's mix of Californian religious cults, sexual deviance and violent gunplay was hospitable enough to the elements people loved in Jack's films: sharp dialogue, quirky humour, a strange, poetic sense of yearning, a fraught exchange of status and power between a beautiful older and a beautiful younger woman and an uneasy sexual relationship between a young man and woman who may or may not be related. A couple of the performances won Golden Globes, and there was an Oscar nomination for best adapted screenplay. (Jack's movies, without exception, got best screenplay nominations. According to Jack, it was because he always buried a quotation from Yeats or Joyce or Heaney in there, to act as a watermark denoting Quality Irish Literature: This Is The Real Deal. That may sound cynical on his part, but I believe it was actually self-deprecating: those quotations were never out of context or, at least, they never seemed so to me. And the screenplays were better written than anyone else's, although that didn't always make them better movies. But what would I know? When it comes to Jack Donovan, I am far from being a reliable witness.)

So there I am, waiting for Jack Donovan, and because I'm not drinking, I don't feel much like extending him the usual indulgence. Apart from on a film set, where he is always on time and available, Waiting For Jack is what everyone who knows him gets used to doing. Maybe it started out because of a romantic life that to be kind you might describe as 'complicated'. Maybe it goes back to his childhood (more on both of those later). Maybe he reserves any sense of order, discipline or basic forward planning for his work, allowing himself to be completely unruly and chaotic in his life. Chaos. That's something else we'll come back to. Whatever the reason, I'm not interested. Madeline King, Jack's PA, is coming towards me, late twenties, dressed in black, legs to here, all dark curls and twinkling smiles and professionally casual Galway charm.

'I know you're waiting, Ed—'

'I'm not waiting. I'm leaving.'

'Stop. It's the usual fecking nightmare with Jack—'

'It's one from which I awoke a long time ago. Jack called me. And I didn't mind the concert, or watching Josh Tyler play John the Baptist, but I'm not hanging around like a supplicant here. It's late.'

Madeline does a slight, smiling double take at this, and checks the time on her phone.

'It's nine o'clock. That's not late, sure. From what Jack told me, it's certainly not late in Ed Loy's world.'

I say nothing. It's true, a few months ago, nine o'clock wouldn't have been late, would barely have been early. But that was before I'd met a woman who puts her kids to bed around nine, and who has to be caught within the following hour or so, otherwise she's asleep. A woman who doesn't drink on a school night. A woman who wouldn't have fitted into Ed Loy's world at all and in almost every respect still doesn't, apart from the minor detail of my having fallen in love with her.

Madeline rolls her eyes at a text message and says: 'The thing of it is, Jack has gone on. He wants you to follow. There's a car waiting outside.'

I don't know if I roll my eyes, but I feel like I should. *Jack has gone on.* How many times have I heard those words? I don't think I ever once arrived at the appointed meeting place without Jack having left word behind the bar or with the waitress that he had *gone on*, and that I should follow. He would always have a car waiting for me, but frequently he would have departed the second spot by the time I'd shown up. Usually it was just a schlep across town: from the Formosa to Bar Marmont, or Musso's to the Ivy. Once though, during the private plane years, or was it months, however long the big deal with Warner's that didn't work out lasted, Jack had *gone on* to LAX, and was waiting for me on the runway. We flew to New York 'for dinner at Patsy's on 56th Street, because Frank says it's the best', Jack said, suddenly, improbably on first name terms with Frank Sinatra. And I think there was a trip to Mexico 'to find the real Mezcal', but the details are very hazy. They didn't last long, but those were the days. But those were also the days when I didn't much mind who I woke up beside, or where. Those days are gone.

'Tell him he has my number, we were due to meet an hour ago, I have somewhere else to be.'

Madeline clutches my arm.

'Please,' she says. 'I can't tell you what this is about, but he won't go to the Guards. He said you were the best. He needs you.'

I look at her, at her pale cream skin, at her deep blue eyes, stricken with anguished concern and evident adoration for Jack. Poor Madeline. I can recall an Emma, a Susie, an Amanda, two Aprils and a Cindy. It ended in tears every time. I haven't seen Jack in a while, but from what I've been told, it looks like it always will.

Before I can reply, Conor Rowan is there, red brow furrowed, mouth in a mirthless smile, beaded with sweat, perma-hassled and revelling in it.

'Excuse me folks, Ed. Maddy, I know it's not your area, it's not mine either, but Geoff had to go and I said I'd catch you, one of the extras, she's a friend of yours, Nora Mannion . . .'

'She's a friend's sister, I put her in touch with the casting agent, I don't really know her. If she's happening—'

'No, she's great, Jack's really happy with her, herself and two other girls have a look he really loves, black hair, blue eyes, that whole Connemara thing you have yourself.'

'Grand so. Glad it worked out.'

Madeline's pale skin reddens as the compliment hits home. She nods to Conor, then inclines towards me to exclude and dismiss him and fixes me with a peremptory look, waiting for me to consent; when Conor speaks again, she flinches visibly.

'Except, Nora, could be she's done a runner.'

'What do you mean, a runner? You know what—'

'She wandered off late this afternoon. One of the trainee ADs lost track of her. Jack wants to cut away to her first thing tomorrow—'

'You know what these young ones are like,' Madeline snaps, impatient, side of the mouth, an improbable oul' one all of a sudden. 'She's probably on the tear.'

'Geoff followed it up. Her mobile goes straight to message. The girls she was staying with, they said she doesn't drink, this is not like her—'

'She's twenty-one, she's not old enough to be like anything yet. This is her, finding out what she's like. Now I have a thing here, Conor, for Jack, I need to do.'

Conor gives her his blank smile, as if he understands, and is personally disappointed by his own behaviour, but he isn't going to go away until he gets what he wants. Madeline responds with a young one's petulant sigh.

'*What?*'

'Ring the sister. Ask if there's anything, you know. Anything we should know, why she—'

'She's just an extra . . .'

Conor's smile intensifies and his face gets redder, and Madeline stops short without him having to interrupt her. When he speaks, it's as if to a stubborn child.

'Jack wants to cut away to her tomorrow, do you understand what I'm saying to you? He's using the three of them like Fates, or Furies, you know, the way he does. He's already shot on her, made her focal. So if we can't get hold of her it'll be a fucking disaster. We'd have to reshoot with a replacement, and we can't afford to do that. Or we'd have to tell Jack to cut the three of them altogether, and that would still entail major reshooting, which would be worse, because not only can we not afford the reshooting but Jack will be pissed off because he can't do what he wants to do. That will be, if you know anything about this business, and I don't know if you do since this is your first job, or about Jack Donovan, an apocalyptic fucking crisis. So he'll want to know everything is being done.'

Madeline has been torn a new one, and it seems she has to take it. Her tone is as even as she can make it.

'If it's so major, why didn't he tell me about it?'

'Because he relies on us to do these things without being asked so that he can devote himself entirely to being Jack Donovan, which is his job. And enabling that to take place is ours. You got me?'

'All right. I'll find out what I can, I'll call you with whatever I have. Five minutes. All right, Conor?'

'Always a pleasure,' Conor says, and wheels away, his mouth set in his trademark grim smile.

Madeline mutters 'asshole', bites her lip, pushes air through her nose like a thwarted pony, then tosses her hair and turns to me. But I'm not looking at her, I'm reading a text on my phone:

Girls to bed too late, me too sleepy and too sorry, raincheck, will you still xxxx me tomorrow?

So now I have all the time in the world.

'Where's the car?' I say, feeling not a little thwarted myself.

Madeline asks me if I need her to come with me. I tell her that since I don't work in the film business, I can probably survive travelling by car without an assistant with my ego unbruised, and that in any case, she evidently has better things to be doing than minding me. Like keeping her job, I think. As I leave, the slight figure of Josh Tyler is surrounded by a ring of adoring women, their faces aglow with the light of his celebrity. All the stars in heaven.

Read more . . .

Declan Hughes

THE WRONG KIND OF BLOOD

'Brilliantly atmospheric . . . this book is a winner' Douglas Kennedy

'The night of my mother's funeral, Linda Dawson cried on my shoulder, put her tongue in my mouth and asked me to find her husband. Now she was lying dead on her living-room floor.'

Ed Loy hasn't been back to Dublin for twenty years. But his mother has died, and he has returned home to bury her. When an old school friend asks him to investigate the disappearance of her husband, Loy reluctantly agrees.

And suddenly in this place where he grew up, Loy finds himself thrown into a world of organized crime, corruption and murder.

'Top class . . . Fast moving, and paced with acutely observed dialogue . . . Highly recommended' *Irish Independent*

'Distinctive, witty, violent and moving, *The Wrong Kind of Blood* is reminiscent of the best of classic American crime fiction, yet ultimately Hughes's voice is utterly his own . . . Irish crime fiction has come of age' John Connolly

Order your copy now by calling Bookpoint on 01235 827716 or visit your local bookshop quoting ISBN 978-0-7195-6746-9
www.johnmurray.co.uk

Read more . . .

Declan Hughes

THE COLOUR OF BLOOD

The second in the Dublin-based series by acclaimed crime writer, Declan Hughes

Emily Howard is nineteen years old, slim and petite with a pale complexion and a red rose tattoo – and she's missing. She has been gone for three days, and her wealthy father has just received photographs of her naked body.

So he calls Ed Loy, a private investigator who knows the dark streets of Dublin better than most. But locating Emily turns out to be only the beginning. Within hours, Emily's ex-boyfriend is found murdered, and Loy finds himself in a race against time to catch a killer.

'To call Declan Hughes "a natural" is to engage in understatement' Douglas Kennedy

'The story goes at a fast pace, with a cast of vivdly drawn characters, and, above all, a great sense of place' *Sunday Telegraph*

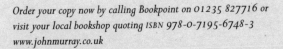

Order your copy now by calling Bookpoint on 01235 827716 or visit your local bookshop quoting ISBN 978-0-7195-6748-3 www.johnmurray.co.uk

Read more ...

Declan Hughes

THE DYING BREED

A missing persons case draws Ed Loy into the shady – and deadly – underworld of horse racing

Dubliner Ed Loy is no angel. He works hard, plays harder and knows how to turn on the charm. But right now, he's stuck for cash. Father Tyrrell, brother of dubious racehorse trainer F.X. Tyrrell, asks him to find a missing man, with a single name. Desperate for money, Loy takes the case and soon the clues – and the bodies – start to pile up.

On the eve of the Leopardstown Festival, Ireland's biggest horse-racing event, the intrepid investigator bets his life on a long shot, finding answers in a dangerous network of trading and dealing, gambling and breeding.

'Finally Ireland gets a hardboiled detective worthy of the name' *Ireland on Sunday*

'A very fine writer' *Sunday Telegraph*

Order your copy now by calling Bookpoint on 01235 827716 or visit your local bookshop quoting ISBN 978-0-7195-6750-6 www.johnmurray.co.uk